ROGUE JUSTICE

ALSO BY STACEY ABRAMS

While Justice Sleeps

Our Time Is Now

Lead from the Outside

ROGUE JUSTICE

A Thriller

STACEY ABRAMS

DOUBLEDAY · NEW YORK

All rights reserved. Published in the United States by Doubleday,
a division of Penguin Random House LLC, New York, and distributed in Canada
by Penguin Random House Canada Limited, Toronto.

www.doubleday.com

DOUBLEDAY and the portrayal of an anchor with a dolphin
are registered trademarks of Penguin Random House LLC.

Front-of-jacket photographs: © Westend61 / Getty Images; © pio3 / Shutterstock;
© Miramiska / Shutterstock; © Hugh Adams / Shutterstock; © Rob Crandall / Alamy
Jacket design by Emily Mahon
Book design by Maggie Hinders

Library of Congress Cataloging-in-Publication Data
Names: Abrams, Stacey, author.
Title: Rogue justice: a thriller / Stacey Abrams.
Description: First edition. | New York: Doubleday, [2023]
Identifiers: LCCN 2022059012 | ISBN 9780385548328 (hardcover) |
ISBN 9780385548335 (ebook)
Subjects: LCGFT: Legal fiction (Literature) | Thrillers (Fiction) | Novels.
Classification: LCC PS3601.B746 R64 2023 | DDC 813/.6—dc23/eng/20221220
LC record available at https://lccn.loc.gov/2022059012

MANUFACTURED IN THE UNITED STATES OF AMERICA

1 3 5 7 9 10 8 6 4 2

First Edition

To my parents, Carolyn and Robert Abrams,
who taught me to revere justice.
To Andrea, Leslie, Richard, Walter, and Jeanine,
who see what can be.
To Jorden, Faith, Cameron, Riyan, Ayren, and Devin,
who make it worth the effort.

Don't you plead me your case, don't bother to explain . . .
Take the sorrows you gave and all the stakes you claim
—From "Sleep to Dream" by Fiona Apple Maggart

ROGUE JUSTICE

PROLOGUE

The white walls of Mamiwata Incorporated's office space were painted with a clear coat to encourage scribblings and musings to be scrawled across the vast surfaces. Tall, tinted windows allowed the bright northern lights to bathe the space without blinding the inhabitants. Banks of computers and monitors occupied almost every flat surface, an array of standing desks, worktables, and a few traditional office desks scattered across the wide-open warehouse space.

Above the open floor for the engineers and programmers, a second level contained more formal offices. Here, an entrant gained access only via face ID or thumbprint. One person per space, and no visiting the second floor without invitation. Even the elevator required a code to be called.

Once upstairs, a visitor saw four rooms and more glass. The conference room occupied the largest area, complete with a high-gloss marble table and trendy, uncomfortable chairs. Only clients used the conference room. Two equally sized offices had been allocated to the CFO and the CTO. Their doors had the same frosted coating. Behind the final, opaque door was a slightly more generous room whose dark glass could transform to clear in seconds. In that last office sat the expat entrepreneur who controlled the workings of Mamiwata.

The glass accoutrements were her singular design, born after years of deployment on a submarine. Never again would she be hidden behind thick walls, barriers designed to be impenetrable by sound. By screams.

Her desk contained three oversize monitors, networked to one another and to a server that she alone could access. Halfway across the globe, the attorney she'd hired years before pinged her for a video chat. She accepted the call from Washington, D.C., to Johannesburg with the ease that so many of the younger generation took for granted. Few understood the mechanics of transatlantic calls, of pixelated discussions via fiber-optic cables and the power of the gods.

"The order is out?" She saw no need for preambles. All that could be said had been.

"Yes. The Supreme Court denied our petition. Sent us back to the Uniform Court of Military Justice. I told you, the Holy Nine don't mess around with the Feres Doctrine. Soldiers may protect them, but they don't believe in quid pro quo." The attorney awaited her explosion, but nothing came.

Instead, her reply was succinct. "Understood."

Thrown, he added, "I have asked the team to advise on a direct appeal to the president. It's an election year, and with all the scandals swirling around, he needs someone on his side. Standing up for a wronged, decorated veteran could be just the thing. We'll have a memo on your options by close of business."

The short, bitter laugh spoke volumes to anyone listening closely. "Ask Brandon Stokes for assistance? The man has been removed from office and is fighting patriotically for the only thing he cares about—himself. He won't help me."

"He might if we go public," came the limp advice. "Court of public opinion."

"No. It's been tried before. Whether we've been injured, maimed, or killed, the politicians with power do nothing. The courts with authority do nothing. And the public? Having perfect knowledge, they will do nothing." She processed the grief of rejection as she had the pain of betrayal. Swiftly compartmentalized to be reviewed and digested later. The ineluctable reality was that justice would not find her. Instead, she would manufacture a suitable alternative. Reluctantly. Resolutely. "Thank you for your service."

She terminated the call and swiveled to a different screen that was smaller and for her eyes alone. There, she tapped out instructions on a nearly invisible keyboard. Her personally designed VPN instantly disguised the source. A proprietary cipher app encrypted her message for the recipients, translated their unique lexicon into symbols only they understood, and displayed the communiqué once. But her team never needed more than one time. She'd chosen each of them carefully and diligently. Plotted each move assiduously.

Monitor the Myrina ISD/P results. Offer client incentive for ongoing screen for behavioral anomalies.

Report exfiltration status.

Deploy Myrina in RF/NP/WE.

After transmitting her latest instructions, she tipped her head in the massive chair made with the same deep brown leather that graced her lemon-yellow Maybach. Like her custom-designed car, the chair was handmade and ergonomically designed for her solid frame. She skimmed just below 6'1, complete with basketball player palms and sturdy yet agile legs. As a girl shooting hoops with her older brothers on the asphalt in St. Louis, she learned to hold her own and relish her explosive power. Both had come in handy until her body and her command failed her.

Once, but never again.

She keyed in one final edict to her chief lieutenant, exhaling as she released her vengeance onto the world.

She had offered them a chance to fix what had been done. She'd followed the letter of the law—both military courts and civilian courts. Both had denied her. Both had abandoned her. Both would regret it.

Initiate Takhar exploit T-10.

In Johannesburg, she had chosen to be reborn. To become a new scourge on those who had wronged her and so many others. To take down the mighty and those who loaned them the protection to go blameless.

Hayden Burgess leaned back in the tall chair. All who stood in her path had taken sides, whether they knew it or not.

ONE

Avery Keene took the assigned seat, her mass of black hair with its tight curls tamed into a sleek chignon at her nape. The hunter-green suit she'd chosen for today's inquisition complemented her caramel skin and clear green eyes. For jewelry, she wore department store pearls and a slim gold watch that had once belonged to her maternal grandmother—a woman she'd never met.

The circa-1920s piece kept excellent time, and the links were made of real gold. Her mother, Rita, had pawned it years ago. Fourteen-year-old Avery secretly bought it back with a sob story and $158 she had squirreled away from completing homework for overprivileged, lazy kids. She drew the line at cheat sheets and crib notes. Homework was for practice, and if they wanted to squander a chance at learning, that was on them. By then, she'd built a nest egg of $1,792, and only sentiment forced her to part with even a penny. Lucky for her, the pawn dealer hadn't realized Rita was telling the truth about the watch's value, which meant she got it back for a fraction of its worth.

After recovering the watch, Avery had stashed it with her emergency money and the precious few treasures she still had from her father, like the engraved knife she'd consciously left at home. On days like this, and nearly every day, she sincerely wished she still had him too. Arthur Keene had perished in a bus accident weeks after her ninth birthday, leaving her with a broken mother who'd crawled into alcohol, drugs, and destitution. Avery had decided that night at the pawn shop that she would never follow her mother's spiral down.

She hadn't gone down, but her life had certainly spun sideways.

Avery shifted in her seat, waiting for the proceedings to begin. She unfolded her copy of the *New York Times* and let her eyes scan down the front-page article that cataloged the current woes of the nation—and her own existence.

President Brandon Stokes, Removed from Office, Aims to Discredit Congressional Investigation; House Promises Impeachment Vote Within Days

By Linda Loewenthal

WASHINGTON—It has been four months to the day since the Stokes presidency was brought down by an explosive investigation begun by Supreme Court Associate Justice Howard Wynn, who currently lies in a coma at Bethesda Naval Hospital. In a controversial move, Justice Wynn's clerk, Avery Keene, 27, was designated to hold his power of attorney, and she followed an elaborate trail of intrigue left by Justice Wynn. After a tumultuous ten-day foray, Ms. Keene uncovered shocking evidence that has derailed the Stokes presidency—including accusations of genocide, treason and murder.

Several congressional committees have convened hearings based on Keene's revelations, and House Democrats are preparing articles of impeachment. For her part, the enigmatic Ms. Keene has become a legal pawn on Capitol Hill and political symbol around the world, from India to America. She has been interrogated in closed-door legislative sessions, lauded by a narrow majority of Americans and vilified by myriad conservative allies of the displaced president.

One beneficiary of the current political tumult is Vice President Samantha Slosberg. In the wake of the scandal, she and a majority of President Stokes's cabinet members invoked the never-before-used 25th Amendment, removing him from office. Slosberg has been silent about the impeachment proceedings. As the week begins, Congress is expected to hear additional evidence and move forward a vote on removing President Stokes permanently from office, which could come as early as next week. Republicans loyal to Stokes continue to rail against the confidential hearings with Ms. Keene and others, while Democratic leaders invoke "national security interests" to justify the secret interviews.

With a sigh, Avery scanned the rest of the article, tucked the newspaper into her bag, and glanced up at the ceiling. The reporter's story was thorough, but not the end of the story. Weeks of private bickering and public snarling led to Avery being brought back to the Capitol and once again before a select array of U.S. representatives ready to prove or disprove the accusations being leveled against President Stokes.

As they had before, her attorneys sat behind her, a team led by a grizzled barrister, Patrick Guarasci—highly recommended to Avery by Chief Justice Teresa Roseborough. Guarasci was managing partner of Wargo, Maxwell, Cofrin, and Guarasci, having earned his place on the firm's letterhead twenty years before when he saved a U.S. senator's daughter and the president's trade representative from extradition to Australia on embezzlement charges. For Avery's purposes, he had also come cheap. He agreed to represent her pro bono for the duration of the proceedings: the impeachment of the president of the United States. He had two associates from his firm burning through what should have been billable hours, and one ringer—her friend Noah Fox, a trust and estates lawyer who was mainly on the team for moral support.

Guarasci leaned forward and tapped her shoulder. Avery tilted her head back. "Yes, sir?"

"You'll need to hold tight for a while. Apparently, the minority leader is trying to get a few more of his cronies in here," he said quietly. "The chairman is having none of it, and a press gaggle is forming."

"Good lord," Avery muttered. "I thought they sorted everything out after last time."

Noah chimed in. "Last time you were here and he got kicked out, Representative Boylen raised nearly a hundred thousand dollars in twenty-four hours. He's trying for a quarter million, I guess. The right wing has made you their number one target, and these hearings are the gift that keeps on giving." He patted her back comfortingly. "Like Mr. Guarasci said, just hang tight, Avery. A few more hours and you're done."

Avery closed her eyes and bit back a sigh. While she appreciated Noah's half-baked pep talk, her life had been in a holding pattern for more than three months. She'd been interrogated by the full might of the federal government—not just Congress, but a full array of federal agencies now under the direction of the vice president. When that failed to unearth prosecutable offenses against her or the fallen commander in chief, the Defense Department honed in on her partner in uncovering crime, Jared Wynn, a retired Navy analyst. And estranged son of Justice Wynn.

Jared had been cleared, but the interrogations had not stopped. Avery doubted they ever would.

"I demand to be admitted!"

Avery's head snapped up, and others in the room also came to attention.

"He won't give up," Noah murmured. "Guess he thinks he can top two hundred and fifty thousand today with a good tweet and gotcha video."

The man in question, GOP rising star Congressman Luke Boylen of Indiana, loomed aggressively over a Capitol Hill security officer at the wooden double doors leading into CVC 1100. The stern-faced young woman with a Glock on her hip blocked his access to the rostrum where other members of Congress were seating themselves. Busy staffers adjusted nameplates and set important-looking papers on the slick wooden surfaces and tried not to gawk.

"Mr. Chairman!" Representative Boylen spat out the title. "Mr. Chairman, I demand to be seated! I am a member of Congress and a member of the Judiciary Committee. As such, I have a right to be in this hearing. To listen firsthand to the lies of this traitor."

From his perch in the center seat, Chairman Max Finberg refused to react to the shouts for his attention. Instead, he leaned over to a twentysomething who squatted next to his seat. With one hand, he covered the microphone, and he tapped a closed file with the other. The gold seal of the U.S. House of Representatives glinted dully in the fluorescent lights of the committee room.

"I want him removed from the room, Richman," Finberg hissed. "I will be damned if he's going to cause another delay in these proceedings."

Richman purposely looked down as he asked, "Do you want Capitol Police to remove him?"

"Fuck, no!" Max Finberg barely managed not to clap his aide on his ear like his North Carolina grandfather used to do him. .

After twenty-nine years in the trenches, the chairman had reached this post by knowing how to navigate both the politics and the perceptions of Washington. Politics required that Finberg deny Boylen a seat at the table that he hadn't earned yet. Being a rump member of Judiciary after a scant one term in office got him nothing.

But Chairman Finberg also realized Boylen commanded an army

of several hundred thousand on his Twitter feed and twice that on his Facebook page. Despite the prohibitions on filming, he had to assume someone would capture the brouhaha. The public images could not include the cherubic demon child Boylen being hauled out of the People's House.

"But get a few more bodies in here. I don't trust him."

Luke Boylen couldn't hear Chairman Finberg, but he realized that without the klieg lights of cameras to back him up, he would not be joining the dais today. However, he could milk the moment for as much as possible. Beginning by undermining one of the hated RINOs that still called his party home. This dying breed of moderate, well-intentioned pragmatists had shrunk over the years. True believers like him had jettisoned their like from party leadership, except in the halls of Congress. In the House, they had burrowed their way into near-permanence, and the return of earmarks had secured fealty at home.

Nevertheless, he figured now was a perfectly good time to start the end of another RINO's career.

"Madam Ranking Member!" Boylen took a step back and dodged right, trying to catch his colleague's attention. More importantly, he surreptitiously angled his phone's camera to capture her. "Representative Fairchild! Daphne!"

Congresswoman Daphne Fairchild of Arizona, ranking member of the Permanent Select Committee on Intelligence, focused intently on her matching impeachment folder.

Boylen and his antics made for great ratings and excellent right-wing fodder, but he rarely helped anyone but himself. She knew for a fact that he despised her. Decried her politics as soft and her leadership as weak. He was an arrogant son of a bitch.

She'd been in politics since before he was potty-trained. She'd clawed her way up and served her constituents with integrity. Regardless of who they voted for, her office helped every caller. Given that her first election had been decided by thirty-two votes, she took none of them for granted.

Luke Boylen and his ilk weren't going to jeopardize a single one, either. She typed a number and put her phone to her ear as though making an important call. On the other end, kindergartners wished her a lovely day. She'd heard about the recording from her granddaughter, and their cute little voices calmed her nerves and drowned out the noise.

Unable to get a rise out of her, Luke shoved his phone back into his pocket.

"Damn it, Daphne! I'll remember this," Boylen threatened as he spun around and stormed out of the room.

She believed him.

Glad of the exit, Chairman Finberg adjusted the table mike to perfectly capture and amplify his sonorous voice. Although the proceedings were not to be broadcast immediately, one day, they would air. A decade as a radio disc jockey had taught him how to command an audience and keep it entertained. *Showtime.*

"The committee will now come to order." He tapped his gavel, a gift from his staff once he ascended to the throne. "Ms. Keene, good morning. Welcome again to the House Permanent Select Committee on Intelligence, which, along with the House Oversight Committee, is responsible for holding this investigation. Our inquiry is simple. Should the president of the United States be subject to the gravest consequence we can offer for crimes against the state? His impeachment. Today's deposition is a vital part of that inquiry."

The chairman laid out the plan for the day, and he looked sternly at the small group of legislators gathered in the chamber. "The White House has repeatedly attempted to delay and interfere with these proceedings, and the administration has exerted its authority to direct witnesses not to cooperate with our inquiry."

Furrowing his brow for effect, the chairman continued. "Other key witnesses, such as Major William Vance, have absconded or placed themselves beyond the reach of this committee. But no one is beyond the reach of the law."

Chairman Finberg inclined his head toward Avery. "Before I recognize committee counsel to begin the deposition, I invite Ranking Member Fairchild to make an opening statement."

Representative Fairchild offered a polite nod to the chair. "Thank you, Mr. Chairman. We have before us an urgent and difficult question of propriety and power. A question that deserves the full transparency of this entire body, not the shadowy confines of this convening. While the Speaker may have sanctioned such an ignoble process, I urge the chairman and the witness to leave our politics by the water's edge."

Before running for office, Daphne Fairchild served as an assistant district attorney for Maricopa County. She'd faced down drug kingpins and coyotes turned cartel leaders. And yet, no one had scared her as much as the young woman seated before them. What Avery Keene knew and how she knew it had roiled Capitol Hill for months.

But rule one was never show fear. Instead, she promised, "Ms. Keene, while this body is here to understand what transpired regarding the so-called Tigris Project and the role President Brandon Stokes may have played, your conduct will also be subject to examination. Every second of it. So help me, God."

TWO

By hour five, Avery felt like calling on the Lord herself. For the umpteenth time, she was asked to recount the events of the past June, from the moment the chief justice revealed Avery's appointment as Justice Howard Wynn's guardian. The majority counsel for the committee peppered her with questions about what she knew and when she knew it. Finally, the chairman suspended the hearing for lunch.

Avery and her legal team quickly scarfed down chicken salad sandwiches from the cafeteria. After another hour of questions from the attorney, the chairman recognized a backbench congressman identified by nameplate as Representative Joe Hibner. Avery dutifully turned her attention to the gentleman from Illinois.

"Ms. Keene, have you ever traveled to India?"

"No, sir."

He gave her a genial smile. "To Asia or Europe or South America?"

"No, sir."

"Do you have a passport?" he asked, consulting his notes. He underlined something with a heavy pen that bore the congressional seal. As though he didn't want anyone forgetting where he worked.

Avery nodded. "Yes, sir."

"When did you secure the document?"

Her brow furrowed as she wondered about his point. Her one and only international trip had been a weekend hop to Jamaica, where she'd netted $28,000 at the blackjack table. "May 28, 2018."

"That's the exact date," he said with surprise.

"Yes, sir." Avery waited for the next query rather than explaining her uncanny ability to recall nearly everything she read or saw. Guarasci and her Evidence professor at Yale had drilled into her head—only answer the question. Don't volunteer information.

"Do you recall your dates of travel?"

"Yes, sir."

With growing irritation, Congressman Hibner prodded, "And they were? Also, please tell us where you traveled to and where you stayed."

"July twelfth through the fifteenth, and I went to Negril, Jamaica. I stayed at the Morant Resort."

"On vacation?"

"Yes, sir."

The genial grin turned sharp. "On that trip, did you gamble?"

Avery imperceptibly braced herself. Her proclivity for gambling and the resulting windfalls had been duly reported on her taxes, but Guarasci's warning put her on alert. "Yes." No "sir" this time.

"And did you happen to meet a gentleman by the name of Karriem Shabazz?"

"Not to my recollection." She was certain she hadn't, but the congressman was approaching a point. Based on his tightened grip on his pen, it was a point he was eager to make.

"Karriem Shabazz worked at the Morant Resort and Casino during your stay. To my understanding, he was a pit boss at the Morant Casino."

When the congressman fell silent, Avery asked politely, "Is that a question?"

"Yes, Ms. Keene. Did you have occasion to meet Mr. Shabazz during your gambling junket at the Morant Resort in 2018?"

"Not to my recollection." But now she understood where he was headed. "If I met Mr. Shabazz, we were not formally introduced."

"Not formally introduced? It is my understanding that Mr. Shabazz forced you to leave the casino when the dealer realized you were counting cards."

Responding carefully, she said, "The dealer took exception to my winning streak, and yes, I was encouraged to take my skills elsewhere. However, I did not ask the name of the person who suggested I not play any longer."

"You got kicked out of a casino where you were on a hot streak, but you don't recall who made you leave." Congressman Hibner checked his notes. "My research shows that Mr. Shabazz personally escorted you from the casino."

"That's possible. I explained to the staff that I was a guest at the hotel. I agreed not to frequent the casino again."

"Were you aware of Mr. Shabazz's other employment as a videographer?"

"Given that I do not know him, no."

"Did you later have an assignation with Mr. Shabazz?"

Avery bristled. "No, I did not. Because I do not know him."

"What happened after he asked you to leave the casino?"

"I cashed out my winnings, and I returned to my hotel room. I remained there until my flight."

"Two days later?"

"Give or take."

"You've been so precise with your other responses, Ms. Keene. But you don't recall how long you remained at the resort."

"I cashed out my winnings at 11:48 p.m. My flight departed thirty-eight hours later. Not quite two days, sir."

"Fine. Ms. Keene, I have here an affidavit from Mr. Shabazz that states he visited you in your room. That you two struck up a romantic relationship. That you have remained in contact for the past several years."

"Your information is incorrect," Avery retorted flatly. "I don't know him."

"Interesting."

"Not really," Avery muttered. When Guarasci poked her, she said, "I did not have a relationship with this gentleman or any person at the resort or in Negril."

"I would like to believe you, Ms. Keene. But I can't." Hibner barreled on. "Karriem Shabazz also attests that based on your relationship, you recently hired him to produce a series of videos that you used to blackmail Indira Srinivasan and Nigel Cooper. Fake videos that Nigel Cooper paid you to destroy. The same man who also produced the doctored images of Vice President Stokes and President Cadres."

"Mr. Hibner, please suspend," ordered the chairman.

Ranking Member Fairchild jabbed her microphone's button. "For what reason, Mr. Chairman? If Representative Hibner has information pertinent to this panel's inquiry, he should be allowed to continue his line of questions."

Chairman Finberg glowered at the congresswoman, the better to hide the stupefaction coursing through him. Jamaican lovers and fake videos? Blackmail and extortion? No one would say another word until he knew exactly what the other side had.

Motioning imperiously to his aide, he intoned, "To the gentlelady from Arizona, the chair is exercising his prerogative. The gentleman will suspend." He slapped the gavel with extra force and shoved his chair.

He hissed at his frantic aide, "Get Ms. Keene and her attorneys into my office right now. And find out what the hell the minority has that we don't!"

"Mr. Chairman—"

"If this whole goddamned scandal is a hoax, I will not allow these pricks to be the good guys. Find out what they've got. And have Marian contact the Speaker's office. I know he's got a leadership meeting and then some bullshit with the minority leader, but let them know I need to see him in an hour. Before we all go down in fucking flames."

Chairman Finberg paced his House office, the walls festooned with competing images of Tarheels and Blue Devils. With three kids, he dutifully sent one to each of the top two rival schools, allowing his youngest to scamper off to Vermont for his matriculation. Avery Keene occupied one of the two chairs in his office. Patrick Guarasci took the other. The committee's majority counsel leaned against the door, as much for support as for a quick getaway.

"Who the hell is Karriem Shabazz?" Finberg demanded. "We've gone over your testimony for months, Ms. Keene, and his name never came up."

"I don't know him," Avery bit out. "I have no idea what they're talking about."

The middle-aged attorney who spoke for the committee prodded, "And the money?"

With a quick glance at Mr. Guarasci, she admitted, "I did receive a sizable sum from Nigel Cooper—he transmitted it to me in June. He intended it to help me uncover what was happening with Tigris, and I did so. Money, I might add, that the FBI tracked since the day it arrived. If I had any nefarious intentions, I would have hidden it better, wouldn't I?"

"Perhaps," the lawyer conceded. "Did you have a relationship with anyone in Jamaica?"

With a stony look, she responded quietly, "No."

Chairman Finberg, ever the prosecutor, sensed a weakness. "And now?"

Avery checked with her attorney, who gave a light shrug of indifference. "I guess I'm dating Jared Wynn."

"Justice Wynn's son?" the attorney clarified, barely hiding his salacious interest. "Really?"

"Move on!" Guarasci barked. "Don't you dolts realize what the minority leader is doing here? He's trying to kick up enough muck and smut to discredit your star witness. Stringing together a manufactured vacation hookup from 2018 to craft some grand conspiracy to take down the president."

"That's ridiculous."

"Did you verify the videos that Avery provided?"

"The NSA did the analysis themselves," the attorney responded haughtily. "We have multiple AI experts willing to testify to authenticity."

Guarasci grunted. "Then their point is to stir up enough doubt to make you look like a fool."

Chairman Finberg prickled at the insult. "I know what they're doing, Patrick." He pinned Avery with a look. "But I've been in a sufficient number of courtrooms and on Capitol Hill for plenty of years to boot. They didn't drop that bomb without thinking they could sustain the charge."

"Why would they have to prove a damned thing?" Guarasci asked contemptuously. "With all your cloak-and-dagger bullshit, having closed-door depositions and denying access to members, you've made the process look like a kangaroo court."

"We've been following the letter of the law," countered the staff attorney. "Best practices say—"

"As someone who was already a big-boy attorney the last time this body tried to impeach a president, let me tell you, there is no best practice. Every day of delay is a day of doubt in the court of public opinion. And in the middle of a fucking election, when the leader of the free world has been accused of crimes against humanity, every day is a chance for Americans to let him off the hook."

Avery turned toward her lawyer. "Why?"

Chairman Finberg responded first, his voice somber and tired. "Because no one wants it to be true. We can handle regular scandals like extramarital affairs or botched break-ins, even a failed rescue mission in a third-world country or misappropriated funds for political payback. But murder and genocide?"

Guarasci added, "Half of this country loves Brandon Stokes, and the other half agreed to just bitch about him. What you've accused him of doing means that everyone got it wrong. The ones who trusted him have been duped. The ones who were suspicious let him get away with it."

"Which makes a story about a tryst and a fake video seem like a viable alternative. Better I'm wrong than they were," Avery summarized.

"Exactly."

Chairman Finberg stopped pacing in front of his desk and watched her carefully. The silence stretched, but Avery remained still.

At a poker table or a chess table, she knew absolute stillness unnerved your opponent and typically forced a reaction. If the player was lucky, she'd spot a tell that would predict the quality of the cards or whether the other player had found a way out of a trap.

"I'll ask you one last time, Ms. Keene. Is there anything about Jamaica or anything else about you and the accusations against President Stokes that we should know?"

She'd answered questions for months. Endured invective and innuendo and now, apparently, flat-out conspiracy theories. Her story hadn't changed because the truth, as convoluted as it was, remained constant. She counted on very few things in life, but truth held top billing. Everything else was window dressing and dreams.

She answered calmly, "No, sir. I have nothing more to add."

The chairman waited a beat, then slapped the desk. "So be it."

Avery entered her apartment with a weary exhale. Barely through the door, she kicked off the black heels that added three inches to her willowy frame. En route to the kitchen, she indiscriminately dropped her bag on the cluttered coffee table and draped her jacket on the arm of the sofa.

"You have a whole closet," Ling reminded her from the kitchen. "With hangers and everything. It's hungry to have more of your clothes inside."

Avery poked her tongue out at her best friend as she dutifully picked up the offending coat. "I thought you were on rotation. Cardiac intensive care."

"I start tomorrow. Traded off with another resident. Thought I'd catch up on some rest."

"Translation: Jared asked you to keep an eye on me because I had to testify today."

Ling frowned unconvincingly. "What? You had another hearing? Completely slipped my mind." She crossed to Avery and gently nudged her to sit. "Noah said it got ugly today."

"Noah is sworn to secrecy," Avery chided. "It's a closed congressional hearing."

"Who am I going to tell?" snorted Ling. "Everyone I talk to was either there or is sleeping with you. Plus, I've kept bigger secrets than your alleged affair with a mysterious island Lothario. Sounds like a bad romance novel."

"They're grasping at straws," Avery agreed as she slumped against the cushions. "But hopefully it'll be over soon. Then I can get back to ruining my own life."

As if on cue, her phone started to beep imperiously. Avery gave a small smile. If Noah had already alerted Ling, Jared was no doubt the one texting her.

She reached for her bag and fished out her phone. The text messages were pithy and direct and from an untraceable source. Definitely not Jared. The string of numbers identifying the sender revealed nothing of origin except the caller did not want to be recognized.

Take my call.

ETA 22:35.

Imperative.

With a quick look at the time, she realized her mystery contact would ring in eleven minutes. Enough time to decide if she would answer. The caller was likely Dr. Ani Ramji, who had disappeared months ago after revealing an international crime. Either that or it was the international criminal he'd exposed. She had little interest in speaking to either man, but she'd learned not to ignore their summons.

Ling had already been drawn into one of her dramas tonight. Avery decided there was no reason to make it two.

"Any chance you feel like running around the corner to the pizza place? I'm starving, and I'm nearly certain we have nothing here."

Ling gave her a flat look. "Lucky for you, I'm famished. Tell whoever is calling you that I said hello. And that I'm putting green olives on your half."

Wincing at the threat, Avery nodded. "Thanks, Ling." Alone, she slumped down and watched her phone. At precisely 10:35 p.m., it rang.

"Yes?"

"Ms. Keene."

The deep, stern voice immediately revealed itself. Major William Vance, once President Stokes's right-hand man, had vanished into thin air as soon as Stokes had been engulfed by their misdeeds and removed from power.

Avery's tone was terse. "What do you want?"

"To offer a warning."

"Call Homeland Security. Or the NSA. Or the White House," she retorted. "You and I are not friends."

"No, but you're one of the few honest people I know in D.C."

"That's your choice."

"True. But for now, just listen. I've heard chatter that a major action is occurring inside the courts, and the outcome could be costly."

"Ah, an incredibly vague and meaningless warning. Sounds about right. The Supreme Court is heading into session next week. There's always *major action* when they convene."

"Stop being a smart ass and listen," he barked.

"Screw you, Vance."

"Someone has infiltrated the federal court system," he persisted. "I'm not clear on motive or method, but the assault is scheduled to be carried out prior to the elections."

Avery thought for a moment. "How?"

"I don't know yet. But a cyberattack makes the most sense."

One of Avery's many make-work assignments over the past months included attending various seminars on technology threats, and it didn't hurt that her significant other was a military-trained security expert. She'd become the Court's de facto representative at several conferences designed to warn federal employees of vulnerabilities in the nation's infrastructure. The SolarWinds hack by the Russians in 2020 had been followed by similar attempts from the North Koreans, the Iranians, and any number of nonstate actors. Because SolarWinds had successfully breached federal agencies, the high alert hadn't waned over the years.

Curious despite herself, Avery asked, "What do they want? Information? Money? Chaos?"

"Unknown. Chatter indicates that the attack will likely be technological, and the threat actors are highly sophisticated and well financed. I've attempted to send up flares to the powers that be, but to no avail."

"How strange that they'd ignore a traitor."

Vance ignored the barb. "I trust my instincts, Ms. Keene; they've saved my life more than once. My gut told me you were a threat to the president, and I wasn't wrong."

"So you have a sixth sense. How am I supposed to use this aura of doom prediction about a potential risk to the judiciary?"

"You're clever and still gainfully employed by the Court. Keep your eyes open. Ask questions."

"Of whom? About what?" Her frustration with his ambiguous warnings seethed across the line. "You've told me less than nothing."

"I've told you what I know. But the fact that the danger is so nebulous also explains why I can't get anyone to listen."

"Perhaps the fact that you are a fugitive from justice also disqualifies your intelligence value," she suggested coolly.

"Indeed," Vance agreed without heat. "I'm a son of a bitch, I know. And eventually, I will present myself to be held accountable. But I'm also a patriot, Ms. Keene, and this chatter is the real deal. America is at risk, and I need a contact in the U.S. I've chosen you."

"No."

"So you'll risk a terrorist attack on your beloved Court because you don't trust me?"

"Despite our brief acquaintance, you've got me all wrong. It isn't my responsibility to trust shaky intelligence from someone who has already betrayed his country. I did my job, and I'm still trying to escape the fallout. You know people in the military. In the CIA. Tell one of them and leave me out of this."

"I'm sending you a link to an encrypted messaging app. Download it. I'll ping you as soon as I know more. Stay alert."

"Go to hell."

"Eventually," he allowed. "Have a good night, Avery."

THREE

President Brandon Stokes listened impassively to the reports from his army of attorneys. The number of lawyers currently under his employ exceeded fifteen at last count, but only four of them crowded into his study in Great Falls, Virginia. Their specialties included international crimes, extradition, murder and racketeering, and the pedestrian infractions of perjury and money laundering. For now, the Republican National Committee had agreed to foot the bill for his legal costs, a tab that had crossed into the millions back in August. But he was a formidable fundraiser and the party's best chance at holding the White House for another term.

"I understand the impeachment inquiry hit another snag today," he said to the room of pale men struggling to keep up with the charges arrayed against him.

One of the four Stooges offered, "The hearings are confidential, Mr. President."

A quick snort from Stooge Number Two turned the president's head. "My sources say that they laid into Avery Keene. Accused her of manufacturing evidence. The chairman shut down the hearings, so we will continue to monitor."

Two's partner added, "We've also been keeping up with some interesting chatter online. The acting president—"

"Call her that again, and you're fired," President Stokes said calmly.

"My apologies, sir," he stammered. "Slosberg is under pressure to reverse the letter invoking the Twenty-Fifth Amendment. We have calls in to a few cabinet members who are wavering."

"What the fuck is the holdup?" Stokes challenged his attorneys. "The election is already under way, and my name is still at the top of the ticket. If Slosberg thinks she's going to coast in on my coat-tails . . ." He whipped his head toward Stooge Number Three. "Where's the research on my ability to replace her when I win?"

"The law is murky, sir."

"Then clear it up. What the hell am I paying you for!" The room understood it wasn't a question.

Stooge Number Four wisely kept his thoughts to himself. His firm was still waiting for its first check from the RNC. Right now, no one was paying them. But at a net worth of $120 million and with campaign coffers tipping toward a billion dollars, his tony firm figured Brandon Stokes was good for it.

"By next week, I want a solid plan of attack. By Election Day, I want to be in the Oval Office and that usurper needs to be out on her bony ass. Understood?"

When the chorus of agreement faded, he waved a hand. "So get out and get me back to the goddamned White House where I belong."

As the most powerful legislator in the world, DuBose Porter held firmly to the old saw that he should walk softly and carry a big stick. To his mind, the Speaker of the House embodied the importance of this mantra by carefully navigating the roiling factions of his caucus. Jeers from the impatient progressives desperate to deliver nirvana within their first term. Assiduously immobile moderates who viewed their approach to lawmaking as the height of profundity. Grumbling conservatives who yearned to be understood as the cornerstones of stability rather than stumbling blocks to better things. In his twelve years occupying the big chair (four in his first go-round and eight on this second ride), he'd turned away uprisings, coups, and industrial espionage.

One of the former infidels he'd coopted was currently pacing across the plush blue and gold carpet of Porter's large Capitol office. Former U.S. attorney turned politico, Congressman Max Finberg joined the House of Representatives a decade before Porter was elected Speaker the first time. The upstart Finberg then proceeded to vote against him on every procedural motion, slowing the gears of democracy and pissing him off. Rather than going nuclear, Porter had sent him on a CODEL to Israel and another to Germany. In Israel, he made friends. In Germany, he made money for his district, delivering a $400 million manufacturing plant. Soon, Finberg had become Porter's staunchest ally and, not long after, chairman of the Permanent Select Committee on Intelligence. That's how relationships were expertly managed in Washington, Porter thought.

"Mr. Speaker, they've got something, but I don't know what it is. This bullshit about Keene going to Jamaica is a smoke screen."

"Are you sure?" Porter rocked back in an immense swivel chair, just stopping short of propping his boots on the shiny top.

"I had Keene and her lawyer in my office. No way did she pull off a hoax like this without anyone knowing. Wynn, maybe. But not her."

"Wynn is a canny son of a gun," the Speaker allowed. "Any chance this is part two of his plot against Stokes?"

Finberg paused as he paced the carpeted office. "I doubt it. Seems too labyrinthine even for him. But that old jagoff Guarasci made an excellent point. The Republicans have a better read on the American mood than we do most of the time. And they know no one in the country wants all this shit about Stokes to be true."

"Do you doubt any of it?" the Speaker asked.

"Not at all," Finberg responded with a sudden weariness. "DuBose, I've seen the evidence. Every shred of it." He shuddered. "What Stokes did was monstrous. Inhuman. And if we have to admit we allowed him to stay in charge? What the hell does that make us?"

"Rubes, if he gets away with it," the Speaker reminded him. "Which is why we can't fail." He rocked forward. "What do you need?"

"A hit squad to take out Boylen."

"Max."

"A man can dream." The wiry legislator began to tick off his list. "I need someone to find this Karriem Shabazz person. And we need to discredit this story before it gets legs. I have no doubt the minority leader plans to leak it to right-wing media this week and see who takes a bite."

"I've already got our friends on both items. What else?"

After Chairman Finberg finished his list, the Speaker leaned back, his fingers steepled on the glossy teak desk. "Keep in mind, we are peacefully overturning the results of an election less than six weeks before folks go to the polls. Hell, in half the states, voters have already cast their ballots."

"With all due respect, sir, this is not about winning an election."

"Bullshit." The curse had little heat, but more than a touch of exasperation. "Every action we take is about winning an election. Yours. Mine. Senator DeHart's if she becomes the president. Which she will if we stick to the game plan."

The Speaker rose and walked over to Finberg, who swayed like a metronome. He draped a heavy arm across the thinner man's shoulders. Like his idol, LBJ, DuBose leaned in close and tight. "Mr. Chairman, I want this impeachment inquiry wrapped up by Tuesday. Finish up with any witnesses you've got on deck, but do not bring Avery Keene back to Capitol Hill. No more evidence. We've got what we need. I intend to call the House to hear articles of impeachment by Friday. Vote on the following Monday. Four weeks before Election Day."

He shifted his hand to grip Finberg's shoulder, fingers digging deep. "Can you do that for me, Max?"

Finberg blanched at the schedule, but the python-like hold on his arm was its own answer. "Yes, Mr. Speaker. You'll have your October surprise."

FOUR

Thursday, October 3

On the computer screen, the excruciating video came to an end. A frozen image of Judge Francesca Whitner, in her signature pink power suit and perfectly styled blond bob, dominated the frame. The video appeared to be shot in a vaulted rococo living room, an audience of well-coiffed attendees standing in the foreground before the judge. For the gathered guests, Judge Whitner had just let loose a stream of invective that left no marginalized or disadvantaged group untouched. She'd matched colorful turns of phrase with clever suggestions about what those who disagreed could do about their own complaints. Chortles of laughter and questionable "amens" dotted the ugly monologue to its merciful conclusion.

"Should I play it again?" Preston Davies, Judge Whitner's career clerk, asked quietly.

"God, no," Whitner replied. "That's *not* me, Preston! You know that." She leaned to fill in the computer's camera, playing to an audience of one. "I am honored to sit on the bench here in Idaho, and under no circumstances would I say anything of the sort!"

"Judge, if there's something you need to tell me—"

She thought about her actions over the past year, how she had already compromised herself so much. Her stomach churned with guilt and fear. Last week, she'd tried to quit—to end the accursed partnership that had funded her personal bank account, the one she kept separate and sequestered in South Dakota. "This video isn't real, I swear to you!"

On his side of the screen, Preston raised his hands in defense. "But—"

"But nothing. Damn it, this video makes me look like I'm a drunken member of the KKK! I don't know who did this, or *how*, but it's a lie!"

"Of course, Judge, however—"

"This is a bald-faced lie. Fake news. I will not tolerate this defamation of my character." Her voice abruptly lowered to a throaty protest as righteous indignation crowded out contrition. "I don't care who you have to call or what law enforcement agency you need to bring into this, but I want this video confiscated and destroyed. Now!"

If that pissant assistant U.S. attorney Jason Johnson thought to blackmail her, he had another think coming. She might have made a mistake accepting a paltry $150,000 for greasing the skids for him, but destroying her reputation was beyond the pale. She wasn't due back in D.C. for several weeks, but he'd rue the day. Aloud, she railed against the video's authenticity and intention.

Davies pressed mute as the rant continued. He'd served Judge Francesca D'Grasse Whitner of the United States District Court of Idaho for eleven years. He understood her quirks, anticipated her needs. And having reviewed the offending video multiple times before he reluctantly shared the anonymous message with her, Preston knew three things for certain.

One, Francesca had indeed cast aspersions on Native Americans before. Plus Jews, African Americans, Latinos, immigrants, the whole of the LGBTQIA community, the lazy poor, the crazy liberals, and the crazy liberal poor.

Two, Judge Whitner refrained from drink but had no such qualms about weed. The judge hid her stash in a code-locked cabinet in her judicial chamber bathroom's closet along with a 9mm she'd gotten as a wedding present.

Three, the video depicted a perfectly believable rendition of one of her tirades. The slip of accent, which revealed her origins in West Texas, would be familiar to any of the court regulars or her siblings scraping out a living on their nearly defunct ranch in Irion County. He recognized the casual flip of box-dyed blond bangs, the absurdly plucked arch of a stubbornly brown eyebrow. Preston distinctly remembered the pink power suit with its oversize collar that softened the sharp-chinned face it framed. He could easily identify the trio of rings she habitually wore on her right hand.

He also knew, beyond a shadow of a doubt, the video was absolutely fake.

To authenticate the 2:54 diatribe, the fraudulent Francesca stood next to a fancy digital clock with the date and time in expensive yet tacky fashion. Yet he happened to know that on the night in question, Judge Whitner had been wrapping her car around a utility pole in Nevada. No way had she been recording a video guaranteed to put her under judicial review. Such a revelation would arrest her slow climb among conservative jurists positioned for the rare Ninth Circuit Court of Appeals opening rumored to be in the offing.

But to disprove the video, the judge would have to admit her DWI, and Preston had become very good at burying evidence of her mishaps behind the wheel. On that occasion, the local sheriff had agreed that a deer was to blame, even that close to the city; her husband had replaced her crumpled Buick Enclave from his dealership's inventory. No ticket. No report. No proof.

"Judge," he said carefully as she wound down, "I don't think you want to involve the marshals or the FBI or local law enforcement."

"Why the hell not?" No one else knew of her deal with AUSA Johnson. Sign a few warrants against shady businesses, pocket a bit of cash. She wasn't the first judge, and he would go down with her if he tried to expose her. But she could destroy him first. "I want an investigation."

"Judge, we can't ask for a probe, because we can't tell them where you were that night," he gently reminded her. "They'll have to conduct their own inquiries, including verifying timeline. That's a thread you don't want anyone tugging at, I don't think. We need to figure out another way."

"But this isn't me," she sighed, anger leeching into sincere puzzlement. "How'd they do this?"

"I don't know, ma'am," Preston admitted. "But before we blow up your career, let's find out what they want. In the DM, they said they'd be in touch soon. It may not be as bad as the alternative."

Francesca shook her head. *They.* She knew beyond a shadow of a doubt that this was the weaselly AUSA Johnson. He probably wanted some of his money back and thought this would be an opening salvo. However, Preston was unaware of her sideline or her slush fund. Pleading poverty, she whined, "I don't have the kind of money blackmailers usually want. And I can't go to Don. We just bought that cabin near White Cloud. Our funds are tight."

Preston thought about his two-bedroom condo that could fit inside the foyer of their White Cloud "cabin" and barely smothered a grimace. Her job was his job. "If we're lucky, they won't want more than you can afford to give."

The following morning, Judge Whitner slowly entered her courtroom.

"All rise."

Whitner took the bench and flicked a glance at the documents before her, thinking about the call she'd received last night on a phone delivered by courier. The instructions had been clear, and despite her arguments, she had no choice.

The defendant and his attorney sat quietly as she pretended to mull her next steps. The charges against him had presented like a dozen others before it: a materially false statement made to a federal agency. Open and shut—a guilty verdict—especially in her courtroom. She had a hard-earned reputation for being a prosecutor's judge. Strict adherence to the rules of evidence and an abiding fondness for the sentencing guidelines.

Court watchers had mocked the defense in this case for requesting a trial by judge rather than jury, especially from Judge Whitner. She too had been perplexed by the request when it had come. Thad Colgate had cycled through juvenile court by thirteen, state court by nineteen, and, at thirty-eight, faced his first federal charge. In the intervening years, he'd gone to college, gotten a job, and worked his way up. Then, out of the blue, he'd been on the receiving end of a call asking him to falsify submissions to the federal government. When he followed through, they had him on tape and he got his third strike.

Colgate had proclaimed his innocence loudly, denying the evidence of every listener's ears—including the expert in audiology that affirmed his voice patterns and intonation and the tech who traced the call to his phone. He had every reason to believe he was screwed. The smug look from the prosecutor signaled the same.

Judge Whitner waited for the court to settle before she rendered her decision. She read aloud the formalities required by law, and she pinned her attention to the oversize clock that hung in the back of the courtroom. She refused to look at the prosecution or the defense.

"The court finds the defendant *not guilty*," she intoned.

"Your Honor," the AUSA cried as he jumped to his feet. "I urge the court to reconsider."

She refused to look at him, the bile rising in her throat. "That's not a motion you can put before this court, Mr. Cortez. The defendant opted for a bench trial, and I have made my ruling."

Out of the corner of her eye, she saw his face redden, his fists clench. "You heard the tape, Judge! Saw the forms."

She had indeed. And her instructions dictated that she betray her own judgment. Wearily, she glanced at her courtroom deputy. "Court is adjourned."

With a short jerk, she rose from her padded chair and hurried from the bench. She brushed past Preston, returned to her office, and shut the door. Her pulse raced as she shoved into her private bathroom. Certain she was alone, Francesca punched in the code for the cabinet in the closet. When it popped open, she pulled out the burner phone.

Too late, she learned that AUSA Jason Johnson had been a tool, not the mastermind. Their demand last night had not been for money. As she waited for the phone to boot up, she carried it back into her chambers, unzipped her robe, and sank into a Henredon wingback with its tufted salmon upholstery. When the beep alerted her, she entered her password and then found the encrypted text messaging app, the sole application on the phone. No calls could be made. No videos recorded. No games played. Except with her. Robotically, she punched in the words as instructed: Alabaster sings.

A minute passed. Then the reply arrived. Await further instructions.

Knowing her next message would disappear in three minutes, she responded testily, I've done what you've asked. What else do you want?

Your continued cooperation.

The implicit reminder of the blackmail video they'd produced and the warrants she'd approved for AUSA Johnson slid greasily in her gut. They knew about both. Had orchestrated both. She'd violated her oath more than once already. To the court and to the country. Her once-righteous indignation had faded into compliance. She responded: Understood.

Good. Have a blessed day.

. . .

Nearly seventy-two hours later, Preston stood outside her chambers. He tentatively knocked at the door, half-afraid she'd respond. "Judge Whitner?"

"Enter," came the quiet summons.

The wall-mounted television played the gruesome images in graphic detail. Fourteen men and women gunned down in a workplace shooting. Seven children dead. Police had managed to take down the shooter, but not before the massacre.

"It was him." Judge Whitner sprawled on a paisley chaise, holding a blunt between her fingers, the acrid smoke rising to fill the air.

Preston stooped beside her, his eyes glued to the screen. "You couldn't have known."

"Doesn't matter. I released him. Knowing he was guilty of something. Knowing they wanted me to—I let him go."

Thad Colgate's mug shot lingered on the screen in the upper-right-hand corner as the news anchor described the scene. "Colgate was acquitted last week by federal judge Francesca Whitner. This morning, he returned to his former place of work and, using what police are calling a ghost gun, opened fire on his former colleagues. Tragically, parents had been encouraged to bring their children to the plant today as well."

"He killed babies, Preston."

"You didn't do this, Francesca."

"I did. When I betrayed my oath, I gave him permission to murder children. This is my fault."

Unable to argue, he asked instead, "What do you plan to do? Turn them in?"

She gave a short laugh of despair. "Turn *who* in? A fucking phone? You told me there was no way to find out who was on the other end."

"No, ma'am." Preston had tried surreptitiously to have the marshals trace the phone's origins, to no avail. "Well, at least you can stop now. Refuse to do anything else. They can't expect you to continue after this."

Francesca pushed herself up. "It wasn't a random act, Preston. They had him do this."

"Why would they kill all those people?"

"I don't know." She dropped her head. "But this isn't the only thing they've asked me to do."

"It's only been a couple of days. What else did they have you do?"

"I didn't know it was them. God forgive me." She leaned forward and kissed his cheek, her lips lingering as she reached behind her back. "You forgive me too, Preston. Please."

FIVE

Avery Keene sat in the last row of the drab hotel ballroom, her chair tipped back against the cream-colored walls. She had the whole row to herself, and not for the first time. It had been the same way all week. First thing in the morning, she dutifully arrived, steered herself to the back row, and, slowly but surely, each of the other occupants nearby eventually migrated away. A nearly instantaneous Fortress of Solitude. Avery understood their exodus. In such a cavernous space, no one had a reason to sit next to D.C.'s version of Typhoid Mary. She didn't blame them. She had a toxic reputation unlikely to improve anytime soon.

Just last Friday, the House had finally introduced articles of impeachment against the president of the United States, alleging among his high crimes and misdemeanors the charges of murder, conspiracy, and theft by taking. By Monday afternoon, with a solid majority at his disposal, the Speaker of the House had ushered Brandon Stokes into the exclusive club of impeached chief executives.

The Senate would take up the case as soon as the House selected its impeachment managers and delivered the articles for trial. Unlike the Speaker, Majority Leader Ken Neighbors had only a narrow edge over the loyal opposition, nowhere near the two-thirds necessary to sustain the articles. What would occur between delivery and trial was a monthlong campaign commercial, starring every member up for election and an embattled president.

All because of her.

Which explained the battery of reporters that waited outside for her to emerge from every building she entered. On more than one occasion, a hack managed to sneak inside with a camera and a dream of catching her unawares.

When Chief Justice Roseborough assigned Avery to attend the annual appellate judicial conference, she wanted to protest because she knew what would happen. All summer, the pattern had been the same. Endless conferences on a wide variety of legal minutiae to take up her time and distract her while paparazzi trailed her from location to location. Today, it had been from a brief stop at the Court to the Calvert Dupont Hotel. Several reporters loitered in the crowded lobby, looking for a fresh angle on an aging story. By day three, the conference organizers and the U.S. marshals had screened out most of the interlopers, but the damage was done. Her pariah status remained intact.

Avery reached for the day's agenda and idly flipped through the glossy pages. Cybersecurity threats, a new constant at these conferences. Her brief conversation with Vance a week and a half ago flashed through her mind. His warnings had told her next to nothing, and even with her "eyes open" she'd seen even less. At a podium near the front of the ballroom turned conference locale, the latest speaker droned on about the latest developments in cyberthreat interception, ransomware payments, and the role they played in liability for damages. Scintillating stuff.

When the next presenter took the podium, Avery gave up pretending interest. Instead, she pulled out her phone to scroll through her social media feed. Then, to pass the time, she crushed animated candy for another fifteen minutes with the flick of a thumb. The hypnotic array of colors was pleasantly distracting.

Her phone vibrated in her hand, startling her, and announced a new text message. Avery toggled to the screen.

94. 12. 13. All it takes to get to 1.

The message came from an unknown sender, and the garbled tag signaled use of a VPN—a virtual private network that masked sender information. Though she knew the answer instantly, recent history told her not to respond to unknown missives. Rolling her eyes, she flipped back to her game.

A second buzz sounded.

Too hard? I thought you'd get it right away. Overestimated you. You were faster last time you played in the park.

The reference to one of her pickup chess games in local parks gave her pause. Clearly, the user was trying to bait her. But, she reasoned, whoever it was obviously knew her. What was the harm in responding?

Chess is a game of strategy. Your "riddle" about the courts is child's play. 94 federal trial courts. 12 regional circuits. 13 appellate courts and 1 Supreme Court. Yawn.

A response arrived almost immediately.

18031819189619191966 meaning.

When the new query pinged, Avery looked at the string of numerals and snorted. The author had run together the years of several landmark Supreme Court cases. She had instantly filtered them into four-digit years. Disappointed, she swiftly typed her answers.

Try harder. Seriously. 1803—judicial review. 1819—implied powers. 1896—separate but equal. 1919—clear and present danger. 1966—Miranda warnings. The kids section in the app store has more difficult questions.

When no reply immediately came, she pinged, Who are you? A minute later, her screen remained blank. Shrugging off the silence, she listened with half an ear to the presenter continue his spiel. The brief distraction had seemed promising, if underwhelming. *Oh well.*

Okay, Einstein. 5018011885. 78117320.

Avery genuinely smiled at the latest series of numbers. Puzzles—be they words, numbers, or games of strategies—were her happy place. No one to disappoint but herself, and nothing to worry about except finding the right answer. This salvo from her mystery puzzle master was not the easiest sequence, but the opening digits contained the clue.

The masked texter eliminated letters and symbols, but any trial attorney or judicial clerk worth her salt recognized the first part of the pattern. It was a reference to the U.S. Code, Title 50. Which mostly dealt with defense, espionage, and foreign affairs. The rest of the sequence referred to the sections of the code from 1801 to 1885. She could look it up, but the test was her knowledge, not her ability to google. Which is why the last line of numbers stumped her. No court had 78 members or 781. Her quizzer might expect her to stray outside the courts for an answer, but that seemed counterintuitive. The sender knew she was a lawyer, one who recalled obscure details.

Foreign policy. Courts. Then the light dawned. The Foreign Intelligence Surveillance Court, created in 1978 to give a bypass for law enforcement seeking to monitor foreign powers or their domestic friends. 1978. Eleven judges. Seven-year maximum terms. With three judges drawn from within twenty miles of the D.C. area. Clever.

As she typed her reply, in the row in front of her, a man in his mid-twenties with a receding hairline and wire braces whispered to the woman sitting beside him, "My buddy on Capitol Hill says she made it all up. I'm surprised she's here. Shouldn't she be holding a séance with Wynn to find out what new lies to tell about the president?"

His companion laughed, piling on. "Someone should report her to the AARP for seducing senile old men. That Olivia Pope stunt at the Supreme Court undermined all of us. The Butler Society has filed an ethics complaint against her."

Good to know, Avery thought dismally. One more to add to the growing pile of hate mail in her office. Her summer confrontation with President Brandon Stokes split the Court, and, to her naïve surprise, America. For a brief instant, the nation had lauded her bravery until the fallout began. These days, depending on the commentator, she was alternately cast as an avenging patriot or hyperliberal wingnut.

She glanced up, and Receding Hairline caught her eye. He coughed into his hand. "Slut." The woman seated next to him giggled in agreement. Avery kept her expression blank. Ignoring the couple, she concentrated on her phone as her eyes burned for a second.

This too shall pass, she reminded herself for the thousandth time.

Until then, she would continue to trudge through the purgatory of her current existence, keenly aware that across town her fellow clerks were engrossed in the opening days of the new Supreme Court term, which began that same week in October. Avery knew the routine: reading briefs, listening to oral arguments, gossiping about who would take point on the thorniest questions of the day.

But she wouldn't participate this session. While all the other SCO-TUS clerks highlighted reams of case law and debated the finer points with their justices, she had been consigned to yet another mind-numbing seminar.

All because her boss, Associate Justice Howard Wynn, wouldn't wake up.

Four months after orchestrating an elaborate plan to take down the president of the United States, Justice Wynn remained suspended in a netherworld between consciousness and decay. Matt Brewer, Avery's arrogant counterpart, who had also clerked for Justice Wynn, had moved on to a lucrative position with McAllister, Steed, and Regan, complete with the $450,000 bonus that attended his prestigious internship.

She, on the other hand, hadn't moved an inch. Student loans continued to pile up, and she had no clear prospects after this year. No law firms came knocking. No life-changing bonuses from excited new employers filled her coffers. Like Justice Wynn, she was trapped in suspended animation.

"Good job with the last clue."

Startled, Avery quickly turned to look at the man who had appeared in her empty row. He stood by her shoulder and apparently had her cell number. "Do I know you?" she asked cautiously.

"Not exactly." He held up his hands in the universal gesture of harmlessness. Speaking quickly and quietly, he explained, "My ex-girlfriend works in the Administrative Office of the Courts. She gave me your cell. I told her it was for my judge."

"And you are?" she asked warily, committing him to memory. The process would take less than a second. Sandy brown hair, cropped military close. Soulful blue eyes. Mottled skin with an acne scar on his left cheek. Broad nose that had been broken at least once. Stocky build, roughly 5'6. A man she'd never seen before.

"Preston Davies." He offered his business card. As she accepted it gingerly, he continued, "I'm a career clerk for a federal judge." A camouflage backpack bumped against his hip, and he toyed with the strap. "Kind of like you."

I doubt that, Avery thought, giving the card a cursory glance. He probably actually did real work. "Where?"

"District Court of Idaho." He glanced over his shoulder and shifted uneasily. "Can I ask a huge favor?"

"You can try." Though he was standing and she was seated, he stood only a few inches taller. "What can I do for you?"

"I really need to speak with you, but I—" He broke off and looked around again. "I know this is gonna sound weird, but can you meet me in the bathroom?"

"Absolutely not." Avery sat up straighter in her seat and dropped the card onto her stack of conference materials. "I'm not sure who you think I am—or what—but I don't do random meetings in public bathrooms."

He held up his hands in apology. "Darn it, that came out wrong. I'm sorry, truly. I need to show you something, and I'm afraid to do it in here." Fumbling with his backpack, he unzipped the pocket and jerked out a folder. "It's really important but very secret. So I thought a bathroom might be more private."

Avery reared away from the outstretched document and got to her feet. Standing, she had him by several inches. "Sorry, man. I don't know you, and I will not be trailing you into a bathroom. Who's in there? TMZ? Newsmax?"

"No, no. God. Here." He shoved the folder at her, and reflexively, she clasped her hands behind her. "Please. Just read it."

Preston Davies was not a handsome man. His face had the look of a woebegone hound dog, but it was the sapphire-blue eyes that saved it from bland obscurity. Right now, they were glassy as though holding back tears. He wound the strap in tighter and tighter loops around his fingers.

With an exasperated sigh, Avery relented and plucked the folder from his trembling grasp. Flipping the cover open, she found a newspaper article clipped to one side with a few other pages beneath it. An obituary for Judge Francesca Whitner, late of the Idaho bench. On the other side, a note that had been crumpled up and smoothed out. She skimmed the documents quickly.

"So?"

"You read everything?" he asked incredulously.

"I read fast," she explained tersely. "So your judge released a man accused of lying to the Federal Energy Regulatory Commission. Thad Colgate. He then massacred his entire team at the local power plant. Twenty-one dead, including seven kids. When she found out, Judge Whitner shot herself."

A tear slipped down his ruddy cheek, and Avery softened her tone. The handwritten apology had clearly been touched multiple times. "The article says she didn't leave a note."

"Because I was there when she did . . . it. I found the note later but didn't want anyone else to see it. Didn't want to tarnish her memory."

Avery closed the folder. "This is tragic, Preston. But I don't know why you're showing this to me. I didn't know Judge Whitner or Thad Colgate."

His Adam's apple bobbed as he swallowed hard. "I know why she released Colgate."

"I assume it was insufficient evidence. The prosecution foolishly agreed to a bench trial. He rolled the dice and lost. It happens." She glanced around the room as the speaker finished his presentation. "Look, the session is over, and I actually do need to use the restroom."

"Wait, please."

Out of pity, she touched his arm. "It sounds like there's nothing you could have done. I'm truly sorry for your loss."

She went to move around him, but Preston blocked her path. "She was a complicated woman. Not politically correct at all. But she didn't mean for this to happen." Preston leaned toward her, his voice now afraid and barely audible. "I'm here because they killed her. I need you to help me take them down."

Avery recoiled. "You said you saw her commit suicide."

"Yes, but it wasn't her choice."

Summoning patience, she took a step back and sat down, then gestured for Preston to do the same. Losing your boss in a tragedy was something she uniquely understood.

"Okay. Help you take down who?"

Relieved to have her attention, Preston toyed with the strap on his backpack again. "Someone used a fake video to blackmail her into doing terrible things."

Avery edged away. Given her recent experience of being accused of manufacturing videos, his concern snagged her attention. Deepfakes were becoming a more and more regular tool for blackmail and disinformation. Still, conspiracy theorists had also taken to sending her their wildest imaginings. If his fake video had anything to do with hers, listening cost her nothing. Smothering her suspicions, she asked, "What do you mean?"

He fumbled in his bag and pulled out a phone as conference attendees began to stand and file out. "Look at it." He glanced around nervously and decreased the volume, handing the device to Avery. "Listen."

Judge Whitner filled the screen, and her invective poured out. A couple of times, Avery cringed. When the video ended, she fixed Preston with a look of disdain. "Your boss was a bigot who let a mass murderer go free. Not to be insensitive, but—"

He tapped the screen, then enlarged the image. "You see that clock. See the date?"

Avery peered down. "Yes. September seventh. Same as the date stamp on the message."

"Now look at this." Preston pulled up another video.

The image was grainier, but Avery clearly identified Judge Whitner as she leaned sloppily against the bent frame of a gray sedan. She could discern Preston's voice coaching her about what to say to the officer when he arrived.

Not long after his lecture, a uniformed man approached, and he asked her to identify herself. When she did so, he asked her the date. "I think it's the seventh, Sheriff, 'cause that's the day after Big Don got his naughty birthday present." Giggling, she rattled off the year and the time of day, slurring her words and clutching at the officer's arm coquettishly.

"And where are you?"

"Nevada, I think." Then she tittered, "Am I in Las Vegas, Pressie? Because what happens in Vegas doesn't get told to mean old Big Don."

The video continued as Preston convinced the local sheriff to let her go with a warning and not to report the incident. An envelope of cash went into the man's waiting pockets. Soon, a tow truck arrived to haul Francesca, Preston, and her totaled vehicle away.

"You filmed yourself bribing law enforcement?" Avery asked disbelievingly. "And your judge is clearly high." Annoyed with herself for getting sucked in, she turned toward her pile of materials and began to gather them up. "Have a nice day, Mr. Davies."

"Wait!" Preston clutched her arm.

Avery quickly reversed her grip to bend his thumb back. He yelped as she murmured, "Don't touch me again. Understood?"

"Yes! I'm sorry."

She released him, put the conference notebook into her satchel, and moved to stand. "I need to be on my way."

He held up his hands in entreaty. "I wouldn't have shown you these things if it wasn't important. They couldn't have both happened on the same day. The first video is a fake."

Torn between curiosity and irritation, Avery scooted her chair back. "You've got thirty seconds, then I'm out."

Anticipating Avery's interruption, he continued, "The people who sent that video blackmailed the judge. They forced her to release Thad Colgate. She was trapped."

"She was guilty."

"Yes." Preston hung his head. "Yes, she was guilty. But she didn't mean for anyone to die."

"Which brings me back to my original point. What do you want from me?"

He reached into his bag for another slim file and pressed it to his chest. "If I take this to the authorities, they'll ignore me or arrest me." Preston took a deep breath and continued. "You took down the president of the United States because he posed a threat to our nation. I know the impeachment is controversial, but I believe in what you did, Avery. You're a patriot. Someone willing to go to great lengths to protect us all."

Extending the files to her, he confessed, "I'm not brave enough to come forward, and I'm not smart enough to figure this out. You're the only person I could think of who can."

Avery reflexively accepted the bundle, hedging, "I'm not a detective, Preston. What happened with Justice Wynn was a fluke. Right now, I'm barely a law clerk. I don't think I can help you."

"Just read it. You'll understand. The passcode is 501801." With that, he hurried away.

Perplexed by the encounter, she sifted through what he'd left and opened the second folder.

A single sheet of paper rested inside. The chart included eleven names, arranged in alphabetical order. At quick glance, Avery recognized the names as federal district court judges, hailing from various parts of the country, appointed to staggered terms that required them to trek to D.C. several times a year. She knew for a fact that four of them lived close, within twenty miles of D.C.

As her eyes skimmed the list once more, Avery felt a sharp stab of alarm course through her. The innocuous list was anything but. The names of the judges weren't a secret. Anyone who knew where to look could find them—the dates of their appointments, the circuit courts where they sat, even an abbreviated history of their journey as judges. But the club to which they belonged was only slightly less exclusive than the court she served.

Avery glanced up haltingly, catching a glimpse of Preston as he headed for the exit.

The names on the list were the members of FISC, the Foreign Intelligence Surveillance Court—one of the most powerful judicial bodies in America. The eleven judges were appointed for seven-year terms and tasked with one job: to secretly review and approve of electronic surveillance, physical search, and other investigative actions for foreign intelligence purposes. These were the judges who decided spy warrants and authorized eavesdropping on terrorists— foreign and domestic. The judges' work involved top-secret intelligence and often affected the course of national security.

And Judge Francesca Whitner was one of them.

SIX

Avery shut the folder and surveyed the vast ballroom again for Preston. He had plowed into the crowd of lingering attendees that was logjammed at the exit. She scooped up her belongings and the phone he'd given her and raced to catch him.

Fixated on his movements, she bumped into someone and muttered an apology.

"Watch where you're going!"

"I'm sorry." She shifted to go around, but a woman blocked her path. The female half of the conversation about her she had overheard. Through gritted teeth, Avery said, "Excuse me."

The woman grabbed her shoulder with fake nails that dug in deep. "There's no excuse for someone like you. Going after a war hero, all on the word of a senile old man. He shouldn't be fighting for his job. You should be out of one."

Avery wrenched her arm free and perused the area near the door. No stocky guy with a camouflage backpack. Preston had slipped out. Frustrated, she snapped, "I bumped into you, and I apologized. Grab me again, and you'll be the one who's sorry."

"Are you threatening me?" The loud accusation caused heads to whip around.

Out of the corner of her eye, Avery saw at least two cell phone users activate their cameras. Beyond the doors, real reporters had much more expensive devices hungry for a story. She wrestled her outrage into place. A viral video would be catnip to the late-night comedians. Plastering on a look of contrition, she pitched her volume to match. "Like I said, I apologize for bumping into you. A guy left his phone, and I was trying to catch him."

Playing to the crowd, Avery waved the black case at the watching audience. "Does anyone know Preston Davies? He forgot his phone."

The attendees, robbed of an altercation, immediately lost interest. A few shook their heads in response, and her assailant sucked at absurdly white teeth. "No, I don't know him."

"Well, thank you anyway for your help," Avery intoned sweetly. She sped toward the door, careful to avoid another collision. Preston had a head start, but she'd be damned if he was going to drop a nuclear secret in her lap and disappear.

Pushing through the double doors, a couple of photogs lazily clicked their cameras in her direction. She ignored their perfunctory questions and glanced both ways. No sign of him on this lower level. She rabbited up the escalator that would bring her to the main lobby. Hopping off, she quickly checked out the people milling in the large space. Besides the judicial conference, the Calvert Dupont Hotel played host to a medical device convention, a training session for aspiring women in politics, a farewell event hosted by local law enforcement at the hotel's popular bar, and at least two weddings.

When she didn't spot Preston in their numbers, she made her way to the phalanx of glass doors that opened onto a motor lobby filled with Escalades, Yukons, and Navigators. A hopeful bank of taxis waited farther up, on the street level, cursing the Ubers and Lyfts that arrived in rapid succession to ferry their erstwhile passengers.

One of the yellow cabs idling fifty feet from the exit unexpectedly lurched to get around the taxi parked in front of it. Avery spotted Preston Davies watching her through the side window with his hangdog look firmly in place. He slouched low, as though hunching his shoulders would make him invisible, a three-year-old's trick. Trying to get to him, she squeezed through the knots of conference goers ready to head out to the airport or across town. From her vantage point, she could now see his impassioned plea for the driver to move. A wad of cash dropped through the plexiglass divider, and the cabbie was convinced. The taxi rammed forward, barely missing the bumper of the car in front, before Avery could reach the door.

"Damn!"

The cab surged up the driveway and merged onto Connecticut. Avery watched in frustration as the driver sped up. When another car slipped in front of it, forcing it to slow down, she saw her chance. She began to weave through the crowd, keeping her eye on the taxi as it inched forward down the block. As she reached the end of the hotel's portico, Preston's getaway car got into queue behind a Metro bus.

Avery weighed the importance of chasing him. Early rush hour meant that Preston's fast escape would be more of a crawl. She could probably catch up with him, but what would she say? She glanced at the phone still clutched in her hand. First, she could ask whose cell she was holding and why he gave it to her. Second, she'd welcome a bit more time to interrogate why he chose her to be his Nancy Drew.

She was still deciding her next move when a trim jogger in navy leggings and a matching fitted hoodie trotted along the sidewalk and headed directly for the cab. The jogger stopped, knelt, and reached for her shoe. When she stood, something caught Avery's eye. Maybe it was the sudden stillness of the jogger or the vain hope Preston would come to his senses.

Seconds later, the back passenger window shattered. *Pop. Pop. Pop.* Above the din of cars and buses, the sharp report of gunshots rose loud and clear. Soon, so did the screams from passers-by as the cabdriver tried to escape the assassin by swerving onto the sidewalk.

A moment later, another round of gunfire ended with the taxi rear-ending the Metro bus.

The jogger, now a sprinter, sped away from the scene as voices shouted for her to stop. She vanished down a nearby alleyway, but no one gave chase to the slender brunette. Avery's eyes whipped back to the cab, but no one stumbled forth from it. For an instant, Avery thought about running up to the crashed car that echoed with a steady honk.

Chills coursed through her. She didn't need to see inside to know both occupants were dead. Her stomach heaved, and her hand clenched spasmodically. She'd just witnessed an execution. Then she remembered the phone in her hand. A phone from a dead man.

A phone that was sending out geospatial data every second. Spinning, she tried to hurry inside the hotel, terrified someone had seen her pursuit of Preston. Perhaps the jogger had an accomplice. One looking for the same phone. Adrenaline gave her a jolt, and she forced her way back into the safety of the hotel, fumbling to turn off the device.

"Holy shit!" gasped a man as she shoved past. She vaguely recognized him from the conference. He'd asked generally intelligent questions about the role of stare decisis in privacy decisions. "What the hell happened?"

"Don't know," she lied and continued to burrow through the growing crowd. Every few seconds, she checked behind her. Others waiting outside belatedly began to run for cover. Some good Samaritans moved toward the accident. As Avery slipped in between a group of flight attendants in the hotel entryway, she looked again.

The disoriented bus driver exited his vehicle and had his hand clapped over his mouth, stricken. Preston's body had been pulled from the vehicle and moved to the sidewalk. More passengers got off the bus, some demanding to be on their way before they saw the blood on the ground.

Trying to control herself, Avery ducked her head even lower and finally slipped back inside the revolving doors. Across the lobby, reports of the gunshots and accident bounced back and forth, and the off-duty D.C. police in attendance streamed out of the hotel to the crime scene. For once, the news cameras ignored her, their attention fixed on the spectacle in front of the hotel.

Heart racing, Avery clutched the black phone like a talisman, while giving serious thought to chucking it into one of the receptacles that dotted the lobby. Instead, she finally managed to press the keys to cut off power. But the nagging thought taunted her. *Whose phone was it?* A louder thought tried to drown out her curiosity. The saga of Francesca Whitner and Preston Davies and Thad Colgate had nothing to do with her.

Nothing at all.

She repeated that mantra as she ducked into a small empty conference room. There was growing commotion in the lobby now as word of the shootings spread. Avery stood alone in the room, focusing on the task at hand. *Stay calm and get the hell out of the hotel.* Her mind clicked off a dozen scenarios as she methodically checked the items inside her bag, including the files from Preston. *Don't leave anything behind,* she cautioned herself silently. *Check everything.*

Avery glanced at the black phone. She desperately wanted to leave it behind, but it had her fingerprints. And Preston's. So the damn phone would come with her. From the bottom of her bag, she removed the special case Jared had given her. The Faraday cage would block anyone trying to track the phone's signal or hack its content. She shoved the judge's phone inside it, along with her personal one. She zipped the case with unnecessary force and returned it to her bag.

Deep breath. A stranger had given her a mystery file and a phone, accompanied by a wild tale that would be alarming if proven true. Then he'd promptly gotten himself gunned down. The smart play was to trash everything and run until whatever was happening had finished. Or hand the materials over to the Supreme Court Police to figure out what all this meant. Worst-case scenario, she could call Agent Robert Lee of the FBI, whom she trusted and had worked with before, to enlist his help.

That was the smart play. But as she slung the strap of her bag across her shoulder, Avery's mind raced over the details. She had been badly burned more than once when she had placed her trust in authority figures. She realized she wasn't ready to do the smart thing yet.

The jogger pressed her back against a damp brick wall. With efficient motions, she stripped off the dark brown wig with its high ponytail. Then she unclipped the body camera pinned to her lapel and set it on the dumpster lid. The hoodie and track pants followed. She shoveled the wig and outfit into a lined bag she'd stashed in the alley when she cased the area two hours before. Her kit included a solution of 80 percent acetone, which she poured onto the acetate fibers of her murder suit. While the material dissolved, she slipped into a shift dress that she'd brought along.

Certain her DNA was no longer detectable, she buried her detritus deep in the alleyway dumpster. Then she made her way out to the other side, where she merged into the pedestrian traffic of a Wednesday evening. Anyone who saw her would report a petite blonde with an oval face and cheery smile.

She turned on her phone as she walked along the sidewalk. Using the enterprise app their phones all used, she typed ID eliminated. Unlike previous jobs, she wasn't instructed to retrieve materials or take out her mark in private. The task assignment simply ordered her to surveil him upon arrival in D.C. and to stop him before he spoke to anyone of authority. Preston Davies made a call that afternoon requesting a meeting with a friend at the Department of Justice. That sufficed.

One loose detail bothered her, and it would bother her boss. The person she'd placed inside the judicial conference reported seeing Preston in a private conversation with Avery Keene. The famous law clerk who'd roiled a presidency had nothing to do with their project. According to intel, she and Preston had never met. Indeed, his last-minute trip to D.C. had scuttled their plans to handle him in Coeur d'Alene, where the lake and national forest would have made disposing of his body seamless. Instead, she'd had to track him to Washington.

Given her objectives, the boss would want to know about the conversation between clerks, but her partner had not been able to get close enough to listen. Six blocks later, she climbed the stairs to base, a modest redbrick brownstone she'd rented under one of the several passports she held. She conducted a thorough sweep, and then she connected the body cam device to the laptop and uploaded the footage of Preston's death.

Moments later, her device signaled that she should switch to video chat.

Hayden Burgess's face appeared on the screen in pixelated form. She could see her operative, but no one eavesdropping would be able to describe her.

"Status?" Burgess asked.

"Target eliminated. However, we had an unexpected complication. The young attorney at the center of the presidential scandal. She was spotted speaking to him."

"Do we know what they discussed?"

"No. It could have been innocuous. I could take preemptive action."

Hayden dismissed the suggestion. "Unwise. Every agency would be tasked with finding her killers, and someone could pull on the wrong thread. Keep her under surveillance instead and report any anomalies."

"If I discern a problem?"

"I trust you. If absolutely necessary, you have permission to take action."

"Understood."

SEVEN

Jared pulled his door open before she got her key in the lock. "Saw you on the monitor. Massaman Thai is in the dining room. I got your favorites—gaeng daeng and pad kee mao." He leaned in for a quick kiss. "Oh, and hi."

"Hi, you." Avery eagerly joined him inside. A few weeks ago, they'd exchanged keys. However, Jared lived alone in his spacious townhouse, and Avery shared a cramped apartment with her best friend.

"Good day?"

"Hmm." Stalling, she asked with false cheer, "What's the occasion?"

"I know you've got to see your mom tomorrow. Figured you deserved a treat."

With a tight smile, Avery followed him into the living room and gratefully accepted a glass of wine. Not quite sure how she would explain her afternoon, she latched on to the mention of her mother.

She perched on the arm of the sofa. "I'm trying not to be too optimistic, but she's done better here than anywhere we've tried before. With the new medication regimen to address the mood swings, plus exercise and meditation, I barely recognize her sometimes."

"And you said if she continues this progress, supervised excursions could be on the horizon." Standing behind her, Jared rubbed lightly at her shoulders, then squeezed gently. "So, if you're not worried about Rita tomorrow, what's wrong?"

"It can wait until later," Avery hedged. Her head told her to run as fast as she could in the opposite direction. But instinct and morbid curiosity nagged at her. To settle the tie, she would get Jared's advice. However, she knew exactly what he'd say. Not wanting to hear it yet, she instructed, "Tell me about your day first."

Jared cocked a brow. "While you decide how much you're going to share? No dice. I know that face by now. . . . What happened?"

Reluctantly, Avery sighed and leaned forward. "Don't get mad." She opened the news app on her phone and found the story. "Read this."

While he reviewed the link, she retrieved the documents Preston gave her. Shifting to a seat on the sofa in reach of the coffee table, she laid the two files out.

"Why am I reading about two men killed in a taxi near your hotel today?"

"Because I know the guy who got killed. He is—he was—a career clerk from Idaho." She took a deep breath. "He approached me at the conference and told me about his former boss. A federal district court judge in Idaho who committed suicide a few days ago."

Jared read the quick press summary again. No mention of the judge. "Guilty conscience. The man she released committed the workplace shooting and killed a bunch of kids."

"One and the same." Avery gestured to the pages splayed on the mahogany coffee table. "Preston Davies, her clerk, found me at the conference and handed me these papers. Tried to convince me that some conspiracy is afoot."

"To do what to whom?"

"He didn't say. Instead, he gives me her suicide note and a burner phone."

"That's all?" Jared asked sarcastically. "And how did he die?"

Avery braced herself for the explosion. "After he gave me these materials, he ran out of the conference room. I followed him outside, but I was too late. He'd gotten into a cab." She reached for her phone. "Then someone came up to the car and shot him. Then the cabdriver."

"What the hell?" He jerked upright, all sarcasm gone. "You witnessed this? Are you okay? What did the police say?"

Avery fiddled with her phone and refused to make eye contact. "Nothing. I didn't report it. Tons of people saw the shooting."

"Which means someone also saw you," Jared reminded her gravely. "With all the attention you're getting, there's no way your name stays out of this."

"I was one of hundreds at a judicial conference."

"And did Preston Davies specifically seek anyone else out?" He covered her hand to still its movements. Waited patiently until she looked at him. "Avery, don't do this. Don't get pulled into another person's drama. Between the impeachment inquiry, your mom. My dad. You've done your part."

"I'm tired, Jared. Tired and bored and worried—all the time."

"Then walk away."

"I would. I want to." Avery expelled a harsh breath. "But I'm not sure I can."

"Because?"

She reached for the second file with her free hand and flipped it open. "It's a roster of the members on the FISA court. Judge Whitner was on it."

"Whoa."

"Exactly. Now she's dead. And Davies is dead too. If I've learned anything, this isn't a coincidence."

Jared catalogued the array of items on his coffee table. "And you're sure you'd never met him before?" The question was more out of habit than inquiry. With an eidetic memory, Avery forgot very little. If she said the dead man was a stranger, he believed her. "Bringing this to you was bold. How'd he know you'd be at that conference?"

"That's one of a thousand questions I had for him. He said his ex-girlfriend worked with the court system. Maybe she saw my registration." Figuring out who his girlfriend was could be a trail worth pursuing, but she doubted he had told her why he was trying to connect. "I could find her, but it seems like a waste of time."

"I can check online. If he had a girlfriend, it will be on his social media feed."

"That's one of the reasons I came here first." She shrugged helplessly. "And I might have been compromised. I've been extremely careful, but you should run a check on my phone and computer." Jared's knowledge and expertise in tech had protected her before.

"I will." Jared squeezed the slim, cool hand resting in his. "Look, we'll get background on Davies and this phantom girlfriend, and make sure no one is hunting for you. But Avery, I'm worried about you. Like I said, between your mom, POTUS, and waiting on Dr. Srinivasan to authorize the tests on my father, you should be curled into the fetal position."

"Your bed is too small for that."

Jared grinned briefly. "If you didn't sprawl like a drunken octopus, there'd be plenty of space." Avery poked her tongue out at him, and he winked. "Promises, promises."

With a genuine smile, the first of the day, Avery teased, "Play your cards right." She relaxed against the deep cushion, the green eyes she'd inherited from her mother drifting shut.

Jared shifted to recline beside her, brought her hand to his heart. "You don't have to get involved with this, Avery. Give Preston Davies's suspicions and evidence—whatever they are—to the authorities. They'll be looking into his murder, and if national security is involved, you need to get ahead of this."

"You're right," she said, her eyes still closed. "I should just take all this to Agent Lee. Tell him what happened and let him follow up."

"That would be my vote."

"It's what I should do." She pried one eye open. "But—"

"I know . . . *but* you want to know more before you hand everything over." Without waiting for a response, Jared shifted to the edge of the leather sofa, scanning the documents. When he finished, he asked, "Where's the phone?"

"In my bag." She sat up, anticipating his next question. "I made sure it was off, then I put it in the Faraday case you bought me for my birthday."

"Not the most romantic gift," he confessed. "But it's all the rage for rogue law clerks involved in international intrigue."

"Ha-ha." Avery reached into her bag and removed the protective case he'd designed for her electronics. "Yes, I channeled you and your electronics paranoia."

"It's not paranoia if you sneak into other people's secrets for a living."

"Touché." While he examined the phone, Avery walked into the dining room that contained a hand-carved table made from reclaimed oak. The room also had a ring light in the corner and a couple of laptops open on the mahogany buffet he'd inherited from his mom. Opening a carton, the pungent aroma of pad kee mao nudged a growl of hunger. She piled the noodles and an egg roll on one of the plates he'd thoughtfully set out.

Moving back into the living room, Avery bit into an egg roll that tasted like sawdust. "What's wrong with me?"

"What do you mean?"

"I just saw a man get murdered. I'm sorry for him, but I'm not in shock." She waved the egg roll. "And I'm eating like nothing happened."

"Babe, there's nothing wrong with you." Jared shifted to her, forearms braced on his denim-covered legs. "In the Navy, during my tour in Afghanistan, I saw friends die. Enemies. Strangers. But I didn't cry every time."

"I didn't mean—"

"I know, it's okay. My point is, you're in shock, but you're not surprised. Not after what you've been through this year."

Avery thought about the body count from President Stokes and his lies. Friends. Enemies. Strangers.

Jared continued. "If Preston's death didn't matter, you wouldn't be here. But your brain has to keep processing, and you have to know why. That's who you are. It's how you survive."

"What if bringing this to you drags you down with me?"

"I'm a big boy, Avery."

"I know. I know." She'd had this debate with herself all the way to his house in Anacostia. Coming to Jared's place meant comfort and a gut check. "I realize this isn't my problem."

"But—"

"But I would like to know what's on this phone. And what had Preston Davies so rightfully terrified he came to find me. And died for his troubles. With everything that's gone on recently, my faith in the federal government to do the right thing isn't exactly robust."

Jared examined the Faraday case, a shield that protected the device inside from communicating or being tracked. But nothing was foolproof. Not strategies and not intentions.

Every day since he'd met Avery had proven that to be true. Jared weighed the phone and the risks and met her determined look. "Okay. Let's see what we've got."

Well aware of the vulnerability of the digital age, Jared had painstakingly outfitted his home to thwart hackers like him. The townhouse had a shared wall, but it had been reinforced—along with his floors and ceilings—to block piggybacking on his Wi-Fi or siphoning his data. Turning on the mystery phone would expose both of them to anyone hunting for its location.

Before he allowed a surge of electricity to restore the phone to life, he needed to limit who would know where it was. Step one meant a visit to an electronics panel constructed into a closet adjacent to his pantry and wired into the junction box. With the flick of a button, he activated a signal jammer that would block communication with all the devices in his home. His security system would also back-trace any attempts to locate him, depending on the device. A monitor built into his customized array would ping him if an infiltrator made it past his barriers.

Satisfied, he motioned Avery to join him at his work desk in the living room. He removed the phone from the cage—an aging iPhone. He pried the plastic case off and flipped it over. Older-model iPhones had few of the bells and none of the whistles of today's versions. A single camera lens. One SIM card slot. "Not the sexiest device on the market."

"I assumed it was a burner phone because of how old it is. Preston didn't explain it."

"Makes sense," he confirmed as he retrieved an ejector tool from the drawer. He pressed the slim rod into the SIM port. The slot popped open, and he removed the card. "Using an old iPhone as a burner is smart. Most I'll get from this is the phone number and the carrier."

"What about any contacts?"

"You can't back up or read data from an iPhone's SIM. Other phones store stuff like contacts or apps on the card. But that info is stored in the iPhone's main storage."

Avery crossed over to the desk and leaned over Jared's shoulder. "Meaning we'll definitely need to power the phone on to find out what's there."

"Or we can leave it off and turn everything over to your FBI friend." He tapped the phone. "Your decision."

Logic dictated that Avery give Agent Lee what she'd received. Though straitlaced, the FBI agent had proven himself when he saved Avery's mother. She trusted him. Yet instinct and curiosity urged her to learn more before she did so.

Four months of mind-numbing tedium and busy work, interrupted only by dozens of interviews with what felt like every lettered agency in the federal government, had two distinct yet complementary effects.

One, Avery was bored out of her mind. The law had never been terribly exciting before, but her weeks outwitting a coterie of bad guys had ignited a taste for adventure. She had no job prospects, no life outside her circle of friends—likely best described as a dot—and no ability to address either deficiency for the foreseeable future.

Two, knowing what she did about the Department of Homeland Security and the White House, her healthy distrust of government had become a claxon of doubt. Yes, she trusted Agent Robert Lee, but she couldn't vouch for his superiors or anyone else who might claim rights to explore what Preston Davies shared with her.

A blackmailed judge with access to the most secretive court in America. And she had her phone?

Avery nodded to Jared. "Like you said. Power it up."

"I suggest we go into the workshop. I might need to run some retrieval software." Avery followed Jared downstairs to the second floor of the townhouse. She waited as he double-checked the array of monitors in a workshop he'd crafted for such a purpose. The home he inherited from his aunt in Anacostia boasted a spacious master bedroom, a nicely appointed guestroom, a traditional office, and his specially designed, hard-walled office outfitted with modular RF/EMI shielding and a king's ransom in equipment.

Avery had teased him the first time he showed the fortified space to her, but their experiences in the past year had validated the paranoia sharpened by his time in Naval Intelligence and as a freelance cybersecurity consultant.

"Take a seat. I'll get set up."

While Jared tinkered with his toys, Avery sank into the overstuffed chair that camped out in the far corner of the room. The explanation for his precautions veered into the highly technical, but she got the gist. The minute he booted the judge's phone, an array of data would stream out, announcing its presence to anyone able to listen.

The IMEI, an identifier usually noticed only when calling customer service, provided a string of numbers that served as a beacon to hackers, trackers, and global positioning satellites. The unique sequence shrieked to nearby cell towers, and with its permanent place in any given phone, no user could escape.

In here, though, the screams would be muted, unless his examination revealed other issues. The average person kept their phone on and operational, rarely powering down unless forced to by a dead battery. Even the ritual of turning off a phone on a flight had been negated by the advent of "airplane mode." Instead of cutting off ties, most simply toggled off cellular access. But airplane Wi-Fi and Bluetooth kept chugging along, gossiping about locations and activities.

Jared settled into one of the task chairs in the small space, and he rolled closer to his keyboards. "Ready?"

Avery joined him. "Go for it."

The outdated smart phone flashed a familiar logo and winked back to black.

"Code?"

"501801."

He punched in the sequence. Soon, the phone lit up again. On the home screen, three applications were immediately visible. The green-and-white phone icon, a blue logo for a text-encryption program, and a third, purple application he did not immediately recognize.

Jared figured a search of the device would be useless, but he had to try. The phone history had no data. The text encryption software deleted messages within twenty-four hours. When he tapped on the third button, a video autoplayed.

"Look at this," he told Avery, turning the screen toward her.

A disheveled middle-aged man with black hair and a scruffy growth of beard stood in a nondescript office. With one hand, he held up a phone identical to the device Jared was studying. He brandished a Glock 45 with the other.

In rapid succession, the man fired on the office occupants. The staccato report of the gun vied with the screams of the dying. Less than two minutes later, the gunman turned the pistol on himself.

"That's Thad Colgate. The man Judge Whitner released."

"Why the hell is his rampage on this phone?"

Avery thought about Preston's entreaties. "If this phone belonged to Judge Whitner, it may be how the blackmailers stayed in touch. Receiving this would be a compelling motivator to do as they say."

Nodding in agreement, Jared returned to the text encryption program. "I want to take a look at the code for this app." He linked the phone to his equipment to decompile the code. Typically, reverse engineering iOS code proved harder than Android, but he and some friends built a tool that made it child's play.

However, what appeared on his monitor was anything but simple. Intrigued, Jared hunched over his computer and got to work. Avery recognized the silence. The jammer in his life-size Faraday cage meant no connection to the internet.

Avery felt the weight of the day slam into her. Leaden, she dragged herself to the only comfortable seat in the workspace. Weeks ago, she'd added a chenille throw to the decor because Jared kept the air set on arctic. She wrapped the fabric across her shoulders and curled into the chair.

"Shit!" Jared suddenly disconnected the burner phone and nearly threw it across the room.

Instantly awake, Avery jackknifed up. "What's wrong?"

"Whoever programmed this loaded malware into their source code. The fucking *source code.*"

"I don't understand."

"Whoever designed this built a virus into the program. A programmer can do it, but it's very rare." He tapped his monitor. "You'd have to parse your code from the program and try not to infect every device with the app. It's a time bomb."

"But you didn't get attacked, right?" Avery asked anxiously. Though she didn't speak computer programmer, she'd spent enough time around Jared to get the gist.

"Avery, I don't know who sent this phone to the judge, but this is serious software. If I'd logged on to a networked computer and compiled the code for my device, that code is the equivalent of Ebola. Everything it touched would be dead in minutes."

"Who can do that?"

His look of outrage morphed into sharp curiosity. And a hint of admiration. "I have no idea. But I've got a few buddies I can ask to sleuth it out."

"Discreetly?"

"Yes. There's not much for me to tell them, but I captured the basics. The phone had the ability to send and receive messages that were converted into a cipher text. I found the malware when I tried to reverse engineer the key."

"Could you read any messages?"

"No. Phone was wiped clean."

Avery crossed to him and lifted the device. "How long will it take you to hear back from your friends?"

"Not long. Programs like this are proliferating like crazy, but I saw a few anomalies in the code that I want to check out. I'll send screenshots and get their take. Should hear something this weekend."

She thought about the larger picture. A man was dead, and the D.C. police were already investigating. As of now, no one knew of her involvement. The minute she alerted Agent Lee, her information and her role would enter an FBI file. President Stokes had implanted cronies and toadies throughout his near decade in Washington. Any one of them could leak her name to gain favor.

"Be careful," Avery said. "Only send it to people you trust—with my life. Once you hear from your friends, I'll take everything to Agent Lee."

"You sure you want to wait that long?"

"Sure? Not at all."

EIGHT

The next morning, rather than listen to a diatribe on federal budget cuts to the courts, Avery skipped the final day of the judicial conference. Instead, she stretched out on Jared's couch and pretended to read the latest blockbuster, but her mind refused to focus. In a few hours, she would take the train up to Laurel, Maryland, where Rita was entering her fourth month of full sobriety. Avery believed her mother's sincere intentions this time, but too many false starts over the years gave cynicism the edge.

The leftover money she'd mentioned to Speaker Porter—and that the FBI grudgingly admitted she had every right to keep—had been put to good use. She gave $34,000 to Ling in repayment of a decade's worth of personal loans—for Rita's bail, her missed rent, and a variety of stolen items, courtesy of her mother's previous looting sprees at their home. The remainder had gone into a trust for Rita. Part of Avery felt somewhat guilty about saving for future treatment stints while her mom was in rehab. However, she had spent more than half her life waiting for Rita's eventual recovery. If it actually happened this time, Avery would celebrate and find other uses for the money. The trust was just in case.

. . .

At 5:55 p.m., her train arrived in Laurel. Avery grabbed a taxi, and less than ten minutes later she hurried into the welcome cool of the air-conditioned facility. The wide vestibule promised tranquility, a pledge echoed by soothing blue walls and faint notes of a cello piped through the speakers. Staff wore trendy scrubs in a shade of burgundy that matched the discreet signage separating patients from guests.

"Hi, Mom," Avery said when Rita met her at the front desk. Her mother wore a simple blue A-line dress with a modest neckline and ballet flats in the same hue. The outfit had been a birthday gift from Ling. Rita's trademark auburn locks had been plaited into a French braid that revealed the sharp green eyes she'd passed on to her daughter. A face that had been sallow and gaunt for so long now bloomed with the effects of a steady diet free of intravenous drugs. For a moment, Avery was nonplussed, seeing a woman who'd vanished years before she was old enough to let her go. Choking up, she swiftly gave her mother a hug and a quick peck on the cheek before the emotion escaped.

The uncharacteristically warm greeting made Rita give her a quizzical look. "Everything okay, baby?"

"I'm fine," Avery responded hoarsely, her face averted. She cleared her throat and smiled tightly. "What time does family group start?"

Rita looped her arm in Avery's and led her toward the reception area. "You're a little early. We won't start until six thirty p.m." She glanced at the residential area. "I'd invite you back to my room, but my roommate isn't feeling well."

"Linda, right?"

"That's right. She's got a stomach bug or something." Rita chose a small glass table that overlooked the community garden. With the late-summer heat still trapped in the area, the confused plants both shed and bloomed. "Want to tell me what happened, honey?"

Avery studied the garden, her hands on the tabletop. "I'm good, Mom. Really."

"I've got a black belt in lying, little girl. And a PhD in con arts." Rita reached for one of her lightly balled fists. "You've got no reason to trust me, Avery, God knows. But I want to be here for you, if I can."

The urge to share with Rita was novel and a bit unnerving. Since the age of ten, her mother had been addicted to drugs, misery, and, eventually, petty crime. The last time she recalled a sincere conversation with a sober Rita had been the morning of her father's funeral. At just nine years old, Avery had had no idea how much time would lapse before another heart-to-heart. A familiar bitterness rose up, and her fist tightened.

With effort, she didn't pull away. Rita was trying, and she'd promised herself that she'd meet her mother halfway. According to the facility's therapist, her mother had a long road ahead, and she had taken responsibility for doing the work. The clinical diagnosis that accompanied her drug use was cyclothymic disorder, a mood disorder that stopped short of bipolar but had been exacerbated by years of substance abuse.

Still, old habits, for both of them, died hard. Avery shook her head. "Trouble at work, that's all. The chief justice is allowing me to stay on through the end of term next June."

"Because of the impeachment?"

"Yes, and because getting a job would be nearly impossible right now." A new bitterness surged. "Matt Brewer—who was my co-clerk at the Court—is making more than six hundred thousand this year at a white-shoe law firm."

"Sweet Lord!" Rita covered her mouth, then asked, "For real?"

"Yes, ma'am. But I can't get an interview with an ambulance chaser." Avery moped. "None of the big firms will call me back, and smaller firms are afraid of alienating their clients. The Chief even reached out on my behalf. No one wants to risk hiring a whistle-blower who hasn't practiced a single day yet."

"This is temporary, Avery." With a gentle squeeze to the hand she held, Rita added, "You did the right thing by helping Justice Wynn. It was hard and dangerous and, if you'd asked my advice, foolhardy and likely stupid."

Avery arched a brow. "Don't hold back."

"But it was also brave and loyal." Rita reached across the table to tip Avery's chin up. Her daughter's green eyes were shades lighter than her own, and her light brown skin was compliments of Rita and her dearly departed husband, Arthur. A pairing that drew attention, and in the wrong areas, censure. "Your father would be so proud of you, honey."

"Thanks, Mom."

"We don't talk about him very much, do we?" Rita said wistfully. "I miss him."

"Me too."

"You lost him, and then you lost me." She took a shaky breath. "I will make amends, Avery. I swear to you. I'll get on my feet, and I'll be the parent you deserve."

The earnest vow tugged at Avery. This was as clear as she could remember her bright, curious mother being in years, but she tamped down the accompanying surge of hope. "You focus on your recovery, Mom. I'll focus on gainful employment. Not a sinecure from the Chief." Avery gave a wry smile. "Luckily, Nigel Cooper didn't want the rest of his money back. So I expect you to take full advantage of the Haven Recovery and Restoration Center."

Rita flushed, her naturally pale complexion no longer as sallow as it had been. "I'm still uncomfortable about you keeping his money and spending it on me."

With a shrug, Avery replied, "He refused to take it. You need rehab, and I'm stuck in limbo. My conscience is clear." Waving her free hand, she teased, "Isn't this better than that county facility in Dayton?"

"The one with the roaches the size of small house cats?" Rita chuckled ruefully. "I don't intend to do this again, but it's definitely an improvement." Around them, folks began to migrate out of the common room. Rita clasped her daughter's hand. "Family share time. You ready?"

Avery covered the narrow fingers with her own. "Lay on, Macduff."

Ninety minutes later, lamplight flickered in the waning dusk as Avery waited for her Uber driver. The parking lot slowly filled with other visitors heading home from group. She smiled kindly at a couple whose son had offered a poignant share in tonight's meeting. As they moved off, a gruff older man approached her. His partner of forty-four years had become addicted to oxy after hip replacement surgery.

"Where's your car?" He scanned the treatment center lot suspiciously. "If you need one, I can give you a lift."

"Thank you, Mr. Collard." Avery gently patted his arm. "I've got a car coming. App says it'll be here soon."

Her personal conveyance, an aging Honda Accord dubbed Mabel, was currently the guest of a friendly neighborhood mechanic valiantly trying to keep Mabel on the road. Dipping into the $10,000 she'd allotted herself from what she privately termed the Cooper Trust Fund, she decided to splurge and spring for a ride all the way back to D.C.

Though he understood why Avery refused to spend Cooper's money on a nicer apartment, Jared was perplexed by her refusal to buy a better car. Instead, she relied on her scarce use of rideshare services. Even before the events of yesterday, her face had become too recognizable for easy movement around D.C. So, out of an abundance of caution, when Mabel was incapacitated, she used the speedy private cars, but she only used the option for professional drivers. In addition to bonded drivers, doing so also meant no well-meaning chatter from side hustlers eager to make conversation and bump up their ratings and tips.

She checked her phone again. "He's eight minutes out. I'm good, Mr. Collard, I swear."

"No need to swear, young lady. And no use in trying to shoo me away. I was raised better than that." Her self-appointed sentinel railed about the latest loss by his beloved Orioles and recounted the oft-told story about how he wooed his Dennis at one of their games.

More and more cars exited the visitors lot until just a few cars remained. Avery recognized Mr. Collard's dark green Volvo and the alabaster Tesla driven by the twin sister of another resident—a cultural attaché stationed at the British Embassy. A third vehicle, a silver late-model Mercedes, was new, but not out of place given Haven's clientele.

Her driver arrived, and Mr. Collard gallantly helped her inside. "Take care of her," he instructed.

Endashaw, whom the app identified as her driver, spoke with a light accent she recognized as Ethiopian. "Yes, sir. Of course."

Mr. Collard shut the door, and Avery confirmed her destination, the apartment she shared with her best friend, Ling Yin. Endashaw inquired about the car's temperature and explained the accoutrements his car service provided by way of sanitizer, charging stations, and the like. Avery murmured her acknowledgment and settled in, lids heavy with fatigue.

The black Escalade made quick time to the interstate. Out of nowhere, a light rain began to patter against the roof and windows and lulled her into closing her eyes completely. In what felt like a blink, she felt the SUV slow to a stop.

"We've arrived, Ms. Keene." Endashaw moved to exit the car, but Avery waved him off.

"No need, thank you. I've got it." She pulled at the lever.

Ignoring her, he hopped out of the driver's side, calling back, "I insist!"

Avery chuckled to herself as he circled the bonnet. The rain had stopped, but droplets clung to the window. Soon, her solicitous driver opened the passenger door and held out his hand. She accepted the assistance, stepping onto the runner. Her foot slipped, and she tumbled forward.

"Gotcha," Endashaw announced as he righted her.

"Thank you," she said gratefully. "That could have been a disaster."

Muttering about the lost art of decent manners, Endashaw guided her safely to the damp sidewalk. Over his shoulder, Avery caught sight of a nearby vehicle parked halfway down the quiet street. A silver Mercedes S-Class that looked much like the one from Haven Center. Her area of D.C. rarely hosted luxury vehicles.

Torn between paranoia and caution, she asked him quietly, "What do you think of that Mercedes over there? I've been seeing them everywhere."

Endashaw bobbed his head in agreement. "I understand the feeling. However, this one was on the road with us tonight. D.C. is a small world, is it not?"

Paranoia for the win, Avery thought queasily. Nausea and adrenaline coursed through her as she mentally scrolled through her options. One, dive back inside the SUV and urge Endashaw to drive her to the closest precinct. Two, play it cool and hurry to her apartment door. Three, confront the Mercedes and die on the streets.

Avery quickly discarded one and three. The woman who murdered Preston Davies also killed the taxi driver with impunity. Endashaw could be a target too, if the driver had a reason to want her dead.

Which made getting Mr. Chivalrous away from her the priority. "Thank you again," she said as she pasted on a bright smile. "I've got it from here."

"No, miss. I can help you to your door." He held his grasp on her arm. "It is the least I can do for an American hero," he added sheepishly. "I recognized you from the television."

"I tried to do the right thing," she dismissed. Eager to get him to move away, she patted his hand. "But I appreciate the kind words."

"You earned them." He gestured to her front door. "The steps may also be slippery."

Avery shook her head vigorously. "No, thank you. I wasn't paying attention."

"This time, I insist."

The driver gave her a look of chagrin, but assented. "My family and I are very proud of you, Ms. Keene. Keep the faith." With a slight bow, he moved toward the SUV. Avery backed away, holding the Mercedes in her peripheral vision.

As soon as his door closed with a solid thud, Avery turned and fairly raced up the stairs. She jammed her key into the lock and yanked the front door open. Slipping inside, she tugged it closed and bumped it with her shoulder for good measure.

Avery eschewed the elevator, instead rushing up the stairs to her apartment. She heard nothing behind her as she jogged the three flights to her landing. Quickly, she let herself inside, reengaged the locks, and went straight to the video surveillance system Jared had installed on a side table near the door.

The system consisted of a standalone computer that monitored four cameras on its screen. One of the cameras, displayed in the bottom-right quadrant, faced the front of the building. In the shadows between two streetlights, Avery could make out the silver Mercedes. Another car passed by, then the silver Mercedes pulled out and drove away.

Enough was enough. Avery reached immediately for her phone and dialed a number from memory. The line rang twice.

"Agent Robert Lee."

"Sir, this is Avery Keene. Sorry to call so late, but I'd like to meet with you tomorrow morning if you're available."

Lee's voice filled instantly with concern. "Of course, Avery. Is everything all right?"

In the bottom-right box on the monitor, her mind overlaid an image of Preston Davies on the empty sidewalk. "No, sir. Not at all."

NINE

Friday, October 11

Friday morning, Avery opted to take the Metro to FBI head-quarters. Situated in a low-rise building of indiscriminate beige and age, the J. Edgar Hoover Building occupied a stretch of Pennsylvania Avenue between Ninth and Tenth Streets. Concrete planters festooned with red blooms and hanging green attempted to beautify the facade. American flags waved in the morning breeze, and tourists snapped photos in front of the iconic sign.

She made her way through the security checkpoint, relinquishing her bag and phone for a thorough search. Special Agent Robert Lee awaited on the other side.

"How's my favorite instigator?" Agent Lee teased as he escorted Avery to the elevators that would take them to the Criminal Investigative Division.

"I appreciate you seeing me on such short notice," she deflected. "It's been a while since I've seen you outside a congressional hearing room." On more than one occasion, they'd passed each other at the Capitol Visitor Center for endless rounds of testimony.

Agent Lee chuckled, "I might ask for reassignment to the Capitol Police." He pushed open his office door, where a desk, filing cabinet, and single guest chair jockeyed for space. His chair squeezed into the narrow space on the opposite side. But complaints were out of the question. He was one of the rare special agents with more than a cubicle for his work. So he sucked it up and sucked in his gut as he rounded the square corners of his cell.

"Sit, sit." Taking a moment, he sized up the law clerk he'd first met when she had found a former colleague murdered. Less than six months later, she had aged quite a bit. Not in any way noticeable to most, but he had been trained to look for markers. Microexpressions. And hers all signaled trouble. "What's going on, Avery?"

"Are you still with OLEC?"

The Office of Law Enforcement Coordination, or OLEC, as it was known, had the dubious responsibility of wrangling the egos and machinations of other law enforcement agencies at the local, state, federal, and international levels. Created after 9/11, their charter essentially gave OLEC the right to butt in when they saw fit.

"Yes. Why?"

"Because there was a murder yesterday, and I think you should look into it. One of the victims—"

"Was Preston Davies, originally of Boise, Idaho. Worked for a federal judge who killed herself. And Anatole Petska, the cabdriver, late of Prague, Czech Republic. Three shots to the head for each. No discernible connection except Davies got into Petska's taxi by chance."

Avery worked at not letting her jaw drop. "How'd you know?"

"D.C. police sent me the file yesterday."

"Voluntarily?"

"I've got a good friend over there. He caught the case and realized OLEC might be of assistance. Witnesses reported a woman who appears out of nowhere, kills two people, and vanishes. No attempted robbery. No road rage." He leaned forward. "What do you know about it, Avery?"

"I know this wasn't random."

"How?"

"I met Preston that afternoon at the judicial conference."

"He wasn't registered." With efficient motions, Agent Lee retrieved the printouts from the D.C. police. He turned the list around for her viewing. "I saw your name on it, though. Caught me by surprise."

"Why, because I don't technically have a job?" she mocked.

"That's right. And because I'd imagine you'd be laying low until Congress decides about impeachment."

"I thought I was. A judicial conference is about as low as you can lay." Avery handed him copies of the documents Preston had given to her. "Until a soon-to-be-murdered law clerk hands you these."

She recounted her discussion with Davies as Lee reviewed the items in question. Avery saw the moment he made the FISC connection. His brow furrowed.

"Exactly," Avery said. "FISA. There's also a burner phone in play."

"Where?"

She tried not to squirm. "I don't have it right now."

Lee muttered beneath his breath, and Avery knew the exasperation from Agent Lee was well deserved.

"You mean Jared Wynn has the device in question and is trying his hand at investigation. He's tampering with evidence. I want that phone, Avery—today."

"You'll get it as soon as possible," she promised. "But he's already dispatched it to wherever it's going, so the earliest we could get it back is Monday." Anticipating his outrage, she added quickly, "But there's also a thumb drive with a deepfake video that allegedly drove Judge Whitner to release Colgate. We sent that too. Jared's firm specializes in synthetic media and AI."

"So does the U.S. government," he reminded her stiffly. "As a former naval lieutenant should realize."

"Look, I asked him to do this. I can't come running to you with every weird story or conspiracy theory people bring my way. I'd never leave."

"I realize your recent notoriety has been troublesome," he agreed.

"I get requests to help unmask spies working at Panera Bread and to prove that Area 51 is hiding Biggie and Tupac. My plan was to make sure I'm not crazy, then bring everything to you on Monday, phone and all." She twisted her hands in her lap. "Last night, though, I went to visit Rita at her rehab. When I got home, I saw a car parked on my street that looked exactly like one that was at the center."

"Did you get a license plate?"

"No. And I can't prove it was the same Mercedes." She shrugged, but it came across as a shudder. "But twenty minutes after I met Preston Davies, he was dead. I can't take chances. Not with my mom."

"Or with yourself, Avery." The FBI agent came around to her side of the desk, looming over her. "I'm not telling you this, okay?"

Avery nodded. "What's wrong?"

"My friend from the D.C. police spent fifteen years with Interpol. That's why he sent me the file so quickly. Shell casings at the scene were from an IWI Jericho 941. It's not a common gun around here, but it's the favored pistol for an ex-Mossad assassin known as Nyx. The lady is renowned for clean hits, no trace evidence, and fast getaways."

"She could have been the jogger. Approximately five-six, a hundred and fifteen pounds, blue outfit with white piping. Hoodie, but her bangs were blond."

"You saw the hit?" he demanded incredulously. "Exactly where were you?"

Avery explained quickly, adding, "As soon as I realized what happened, I got my stuff and went straight to Jared's house."

"Yet you still think someone may have followed you to Laurel and back to your apartment." Agent Lee pinched the bridge of his nose. "I need to put you in protective custody."

"What? No!" Avery shook her head vehemently. "I'm probably

overreacting. Seeing shadows and tails where there are none. I've got Congress deposing me and strangers trying to drag me into their intrigues. Which is why I'm bringing all this to you."

After she'd called Agent Lee, Avery had practiced for this conversation. "OLEC can take the lead. Check in with the FISA court officers. Coordinate the murder investigation with D.C. police. Bring in NCIJTF to research the phone and the video."

At her mention of the National Cyber Investigative Joint Task Force, Agent Lee glowered. "We can handle the research without them."

"This involves the courts," she reminded him. "FISA warrants could be implicated. International terrorism."

"Because of a judge from Idaho?" He sounded skeptical, but Agent Lee knew Avery was right. His role at OLEC existed because isolated incidents before 9/11 had remained siloed until a tristate attack had reordered the world. If she was correct, OLEC, NCIJTF, and FISA were simply the beginning of an alphabetic clusterfuck that might have reverberations beyond the United States.

"I realize this isn't much to go on, Agent Lee."

He thought for a moment. "True, but the last time you happened across a murder, the president lost his job. I'll give you the benefit of the doubt." He scratched at the back of his neck where an itch had formed. The same itch he got when a case had layers he would need to peel. A combination of excitement and irritation—knowing he was already three steps behind but eager to catch up. "I want to assign a car to watch you this weekend."

Avery bristled for an instant, but the reaction was instinct. Years of living by her wits and mistrusting authority died hard. However, she'd come seeking help. "Can you ask Maryland State Police to keep an eye on the Haven Recovery and Restoration Center?"

"Absolutely," he answered without hesitation. "And I'll need the address of where you'll be and with whom."

As if anticipating his request, his phone pinged. "Already sent.

Ling comes off rotation on Sunday. If I'm not at my apartment, I'll likely be visiting Jared."

"I expect to see you on Monday morning. Bring Jared along too. And get me that damn phone."

The hacktivist collective called itself Bonsai—diminutive, elegant, carefully shaped. The individual hackers prided themselves on the precision of their strikes, the refinement of the code that invaded systems and sprouted chaos. Some of them did it for glory, and others were driven by a code of honor. A few were simply thrill-seekers who liked to make a mess. Strewn across the globe, Bonsai avoided the tendency of other groups to focus on distributed denial-of-service (DDoS) attacks as their primary weapon. Certainly, their members made their chops by disrupting websites, crashing servers, and doxxing targets. What they specialized in, though, was exfiltration. Sneaking into systems via cleverly disguised malware and coopting data from internal systems like network architecture, employee information, corporate secrets.

Then Bonsai had been hired by the most renowned hacker no one had ever met, charged with a straightforward mission that made no sense to anyone in the collective. Deliver a payload to chosen systems and execute upon command. After eighteen months of coding, debugging, and covering their tracks, Bonsai had successfully targeted more than 120 systems across the United States. The diversity of their quarry appealed to their quixotic notions of fair play—mega and minuscule, Fortune 100 behemoths with paper-thin security protocols that cost millions and pissant asshole entities that underpaid their workers and overcharged their customers.

The operational objectives, though, were fuzzy at best. Every target had a corporate mission that was reviled by at least one participant in Bonsai. Gas companies, banks, predatory lenders, power substations, chemical manufacturers, poultry processors, chip makers, and more. No one knew why the entities had been selected, and everyone was afraid to ask. Plus, the kind of money on offer softened even the hardest hesitation.

Over the months, Bonsai members mapped networks routinely scoured for cyber vulnerabilities. Their cleverest hackers had taken on the most complicated deployments, evading the tightening screens each time a new breach was reported or exploit discovered. They'd disabled network safety systems with a blasé dismissal of the idea that protection was a native good. Some of their work had been spotted and erased, patched, and defended against. But Bonsai moved on invisible slipstreams, and they'd effortlessly replaced one sucker with another.

Their most effective defense against discovery wasn't their brilliance, however. Bonsai relied primarily on the secretive nature of their victims. A lone desk jockey spotted a problem and solved it, never thinking to share her discovery with another. Their work, like that of Bonsai's members, was largely solitary. The technicians, isolated in their silos at each location, shared data only as required by law or circumstance. Nodes on a networked tree that relished their independence. Because they never told their counterparts of their discoveries or mistakes, they also never heard about hacking attempts that could have spared their employers. Bonsai counted on this quirk of human nature—the very people who could see them coming refused to tell anyone what they saw.

For Bonsai's fourteen members, $100 million in bitcoin had been equitably divvied up and transferred to cyberwallets from Kajang, Malaysia, to Montgomery, Alabama. As its final act, the collective's leaders vaporized the trails of their members, razing any message board, site, or dark web lair that could track them. Flush with cash and the promise of hacker glory, they dispersed with the vow never to contact one another again.

One of Bonsai's cyber prodigies was Leon Adams. Leon believed in very few things. Flats versus drums in the selection of chicken wings. Forces versus Jordans for superior footwear. Salt versus sugar when making grits. He paid tithes in church and attention in his computer engineering classes at Virginia State University.

Dismantling his Xbox at seven introduced him to the world of technology reengineering, although all he wanted was a way to defeat a level or two. He moved over to multiplayer online role-playing games that helped him escape the dull routine of life at home in Smiths Chapel, Virginia. In the vivid surrealism of online gaming, he found a community running from their own boring lives, escaping into distant lands. Better yet, he discovered a forum that taught him how to fight clean or cheat dirty, depending on his mood.

Leon could afford to buy Smiths Chapel, if he wanted to, all seventy-nine acres of it. His cut of the bitcoin bounty would net out at a little over $7 million, a fortune that he could double or triple if he played his cards right.

But he had no interest in gambling with his newfound wealth. Instead, Leon intended to set up a trust for his cousins and build his parents a beautiful new home right on the edge of town. He'd upgrade his equipment, prepare for graduate school, and walk away from his time as a hacker.

The alert he received directed him to a layer of the dark web he'd never seen before, and his eyes widened as he reread the incoming message several times. Leon was being offered additional money— truckloads of additional money. Ten million dollars. The payload: create another bit of code and direct his cousin Corey to upload it at his job next week.

Leon understood the source of the offer and his options. His answer was easy. Right next door to his parents' new house, he'd be able to build one for Corey's parents, too.

· · ·

The generous financier of the mission sat back from her computer screen and smiled, pleased that Leon had accepted the offer. Hayden Burgess felt the plan solidify, felt the burden of justice ease. She rose and walked across her spare office to pour a cup of tea. Now it was time to activate the next phase.

TEN

J udge Michael Oliver sat on the shaded front porch of his son's home in Georgetown and smiled wanly at his granddaughter as she chattered on about starting school in a few weeks. He intended his weekend visit to be a bit of a respite, to no avail. Instead, he listened as his most precious accomplishment reminded him of his greatest shame.

Nivea Oliver had dreamed of attending Blair College for as long as she could remember. After all, her parents met in their storied halls, as had her paternal and maternal grandparents. The tiny college nestled in the foothills of the Shenandoah Valley largely escaped public notice. With only 1,100 students matriculating each year, few outside its ambit had ever heard about the place. Yet the liberal arts college boasted two distinguishing features. The graduation rate had never dipped below 99 percent except during times of war. And not a single alumnus had ever fallen outside the top 5 percent of wage earners in America when stints in rehab were excluded.

Blair College did not accept applications for admission. The admissions committee identified its sought-after entrants and summoned them. Rarely did they refuse. Tuition did not exist. Its $7 billion endowment grew at a healthy clip, unhampered by student protests for divestment or public condemnation about whatever evil had become de rigueur. Upon graduation, graduate school beckoned a few, but most went right to work becoming millionaires who would send their progeny to Blair.

Judge Oliver had done his part. He'd met and married his sweetheart, Phyllis, at Blair. His son Mason Oliver met his daughter-in-law Eva Kirby Oliver there, and they had produced the apple of his eye, Nivea. At eighteen, Nivea could host a soiree, skipper a catamaran, and complete a triathlon with admirable speed. However, his darling Nivea was as dumb as a box of hair. Bolstered by tutors, private education, and discreet payments to susceptible instructors, Nivea would graduate from high school. Barely.

As a jurist, Michael Oliver prided himself on his unremarkable record. He had served on the federal bench in the Northern District of West Virginia for twenty-three years. During his tenure, he had ruled fairly, hewing as close to the middle of the road as possible without digging a trench. He eschewed bribes, favors, and even winks of preference.

Until a year ago. When he'd received a call from a classmate—one who sat on the admissions committee for Blair. Over scotch and soda, Quentin Forster revealed that Nivea's pedigree could not overcome her abysmal academic record and laughable interview. For the first time in three generations, an Oliver would be rejected.

Unless judge and celebrated alumnus Michael Oliver agreed to a small favor—to delay a ruling on discovery.

Quentin Forster descended from one of Blair College's original families. As a result, his vast fortune included railroad lines, energy concerns, tech start-ups, and bottled water. One of his railroads that snaked through the hills of Virginia and West Virginia had been the site of an accident that left an itinerant miner—a ne'er-do-well, in Forster's words—a paraplegic. A too-thorough review of the maintenance records would reveal some overlap between Forster's shady business practices and poor disposal practices. Well-greased palms had stymied state investigation by the West Virginia Rail Authority. But a federal lawsuit was harder to handle, unless a friend could help.

Tragically, Dawson Hawthorne, the miner injured in the crash, had no next of kin. His prognosis indicated that a stay of discovery might outlast his failing kidneys and struggling lungs.

Persuaded by the merits, with Quentin Forster's words in his head, Judge Oliver had issued the stay, and the case disappeared.

Then nine days ago, his year-old lapse of judgment came back to haunt him. Oliver was at home getting ready for bed when a detailed recording of his conversation with Quentin Forster arrived like magic on his cell phone. An app he'd never downloaded appeared on his home screen. Not the savviest of users, the judge assumed the new icon had come with a recent upgrade to his operating system.

The sound of his very private lunch with Quentin poured into his bedroom while his wife completed her ablutions.

"Michael, I'm jammed up pretty badly, my friend. This hobo managed to wreck one of my short lines, and now I'm on the hook for millions."

His light Southern drawl with its clipped consonants clearly identified Michael. "We're straying very close to ex parte, and I can't have that."

Quentin had snorted. "We've been friends for nearly forty years. You can't scooch close to the line for once?"

"What I can say is that if you were at fault, then, Quent, you might have to settle."

"I offered to settle," Quentin stormed in low, angry tones. "The little bastard wants his day in court. Some environmentalist bullshit group has taken on his case pro bono. They want to do discovery so they can have access to my maintenance records and traipse all over my property."

Michael could hear ice clinking against crystal. He recalled taking a bracing sip before he sent his old friend on his way. "I'm sorry about that, old man," he began.

"I know. Like I'm sorry that Nivea will not be getting an invitation to Blair College."

The silence that greeted his pronouncement felt as oppressive over the phone as it had in the private room at the golf club a year earlier. To his everlasting shame, Michael broke it. "She has to get in. It's all she's ever wanted. Eva and Mason will be devastated. And Phyllis. You know how dedicated she is to Blair's legacy. This will crush her."

Quentin cleared his throat. "I might be able to reverse the committee's decision, but not if I'm distracted by this lawsuit. I'm not asking you to rule in my favor, Michael. Just delay a bit. My lawyers say six to eight months should do the trick."

The app that played his conversation vanished the next day. Though he wanted to believe it was a weird fluke of technology, he'd known better. He'd upgraded to a newer phone of a different brand and vigilantly downloaded all the anti-hacking software he could find.

A few days later, a new app appeared, this one with video. He and Phyllis enjoying dinner at their favorite bistro. Banal conversation, nothing worth commenting about. Except that a text message followed.

Dawson Hawthorne died without justice because you played God. Now God is watching you. Make Him happy.

"PawPaw, you're not listening," Nivea whined as she flounced down next to him. The white oak swing gave an easy rock. "Gigi is coming down to visit me next weekend. Can you?"

"I'm sorry, sweetheart, I won't be able to make it. That's why I'm here now. I've got work in the city this week, then it's back home for a trial."

"I don't understand why you can't visit. Put off the trial or whatever."

At that moment Nivea's younger brother, Malcolm, appeared on the porch and hopped onto the other side of the porch swing. "He's the duty judge for FISA this week, Nivea." At fourteen, his entry into Blair was already guaranteed by his PSAT scores and multiple awards. "He serves on the FISA court, and that's why he's here."

Michael had explained this to Nivea before, but his patience with her lack of comprehension never wavered. "When the government has reason to believe that national security is at risk, it asks for the power to investigate quietly. Requests for electronic surveillance, phone records, or business records require warrants, and that's what I have to decide."

"All week?" Nivea whined with a perfectly lovely pout.

"Yes, ma'am." He patted her cheek, seeing his own mother in her vacant blue eyes. "I have to protect our country, missy."

Young Malcolm nodded sagely. "A patriot's duty."

When the phone buzzed, Michael jolted awake. *4:22 a.m.* He answered it hoarsely. "Who is this?"

"God."

The vocal distortion on the other end had Michael checking Phyllis's side of the bed. Her CPAP machine buzzed on, and she didn't stir.

"What do you want?" He swung his legs over and sat on the edge of the bed.

"You'll receive an email on Monday at seven a.m. from your bailiff. Open it on your system at the FISC."

He wasn't tech savvy, but the computer security protocols were clear. Due to recent attacks on their systems, no downloads on government equipment without prior authorization. "No. I can't."

"Really, Your Honor? This isn't a negotiation."

Michael thought of the pride his grandson Malcolm had displayed earlier on the porch. It steeled Michael's spine. "I will not do it. Release the recording. I'll face the music." He straightened his shoulders and felt a weight lift. "I shouldn't have betrayed my oath, and I will take my punishment."

"Check your texts, Judge, before you get too righteous."

Michael fumbled with the phone, trying to switch to the messaging app. He missed the ease of his other phone. This one tried too hard to be simple. Finally, he located the bubble and tapped. A new message had arrived without its normal ping.

"Press play."

A video quickly loaded and began to play. It looked like body camera footage. A slender hand raised a semiautomatic pistol in a steady grip, aiming it at a man sitting in the backseat of a car in daytime traffic. Quick reports of the weapon shattered the window and embedded bullets in a man's head. The hand then aimed at the driver, who died just as quickly. The high quality of the camera captured the eruption of blood and brain matter, the suddenness of death. Michael felt bile rise in his throat at the carnage. To his father's shame, he'd always been squeamish. He didn't even hunt. "Dear God."

"Let's not make this personal. Nivea and Malcolm matter to you, don't they? I'd hate to have to send my friend to visit them."

Michael choked out, "Don't you dare!"

"Open the email, Judge. Be a hero. It's a patriot's duty."

The call ended, and Michael collapsed back into the bed like a punctured balloon. He would do as instructed, as threatened. Turning over on his side, he sank into the dark. God forgive him.

Then his eyes snapped open wide. *A patriot's duty.* Malcolm's words. God's words.

They were listening.

ELEVEN

Sunday, October 13

A nd we're back with *PoliticsNOW Sunday.* I'm your host, Scott Curlee." He met the camera with the look of reasoned skepticism that had boosted his show to number one. His tousled black hair with disarming cowlick didn't hurt.

Scott thinned his lips and steepled his fingers to signal thoughtful assessment. Ratings told him that the impeachment had the opportunity to be his Walter Cronkite moment. In the modern war between Democrats and Republicans, his position was that of cage match referee. Time to ring the bell.

"Democrats continue to press forward with their case against President Stokes weeks before an election. Critics of the impeachment process are angry at the secrecy. Stalwart supporters of Vice President Slosberg fear that she has overstepped by maintaining the Twenty-Fifth Amendment letter that removed President Stokes from office. In the center of this storm is Supreme Court law clerk Avery Keene, who was central to the House agreement to put the president of the United States on trial in a matter of days.

"As lawmakers plot their next moves, Washington is waiting to see if President Stokes will return to the Oval Office before the Senate trial begins."

Curlee pivoted twenty degrees to his right to face a second camera. His cameraman heard the cue and tightened the lens in a portrait shot that evoked trust and authority. "This morning, *PoliticsNOW* brings you a stunning exclusive. Our next guest is the secretary of housing and urban development, Dr. Carlos Espinoza, one of the signatories of the Twenty-Fifth Amendment letter at issue. Secretary Espinoza, we have received information that suggests you intend to remove your name from the letter that has kept President Stokes from the Oval Office. Have you spoken with the president? Did he pressure you to rescind your support?"

Below Curlee, a blazing red graphic had already appeared: "EXCLUSIVE: 25th Amendment letter will be revoked, clearing way for Stokes to return to presidency."

Secretary Espinoza blinked owlishly at the camera, and Curlee settled in for his favorite pastime—making politicians squirm.

Hayden Burgess flicked the button that cut the American news broadcast. She rose from the low sofa and walked outside. Sunset hovered just beyond the railing of the rooftop garden. Pale pink clivia and wild yellow nemesia flourished in the well-tended space.

Leaning on the sun-warmed metal, she basked in the waning light of dusk. After years of living below deck, below the surface of the ocean, she craved the sunlight.

Activating her phone, she joined the international call that had been scrambled and routed through multiple locations. All participants silently awaited her voice.

"Where do we stand?" she asked without introduction.

"Ready for deployment."

"In every region?"

In geographic order from east to west, the team rattled off their targets and status. Joliet 29. Eagle Valley. Wabash River. Blenheim Gilboa. In total, ninety-seven locations were set for activation.

"Bonsai?"

"Disbanded."

"D.C.?"

The hesitation on the line was palpable. Finally, one voice answered, "The use of the Twenty-Fifth Amendment is unprecedented. President Stokes is likely to clear legal hurdles and be reinstated shortly. Our intel says the impeachment will proceed the following week."

"And Keene?" Hayden asked.

"We have no insights yet. Our surveillance confirms she had contact with Davies and likely is in possession of the devices. We have wiped all trace evidence. Davies had become too vocal, and he is no longer a vulnerability."

"Casualty of war," she replied. The terse dismissal was met with silence. Hayden continued stonily. "Keene is still a threat to Stokes, which makes her an ally for the moment. But she also has information that could be problematic." She tapped her fingertips on the warm metal railing. "Keep her in play. But be ready to move on her."

TWELVE

Monday, October 14

This is a question that begs for original jurisdiction, T." Associate Justice Mirtha Estrada dropped the formal titles that they used in polite company. She sat in the office of Chief Justice Teresa Roseborough, the plush carpet and easy familiarity allowing her to slip off the Louboutin heels that pinched her toes. At sixty-one, Justice Estrada held a string of firsts—first in her class at Harvard, first Latina judge in her state, first on her circuit. Like Chief Roseborough, she clawed her way through rank discrimination, subtle bigotry, and hostile misogyny. Though their paths had crossed several times over the years, it was their shared decade on the Court that had bonded them.

Their approach to jurisprudence set them apart. In her opinions, Justice Estrada hewed close to the line separating liberal and moderate and threaded them with conservative embroidery. Secretly, she yearned to dive headlong into the teeming waters of progressive policies, to author opinions that drew the invective of the right and the fawning admiration of the left. But she lacked Howard Wynn's brazen disregard for public opinion and envied Teresa Roseborough's deft handling of public disapproval. Instead, she carved her way straight up the middle and paved her legacy with concurrences and dissents that drew neither attention nor censure.

Estrada knew the Chief understood her tendencies toward private revolutionary thought, a safe space for the Mirtha she longed to be. That too brought them together. With her friend, T, she could dream. "The Twenty-Fifth Amendment is ripe for misuse, and someone should have brought the question before the Court. The fact that a cabinet secretary went on national television yesterday to rescind the letter invoking President Stokes's removal is deeply concerning. The law is silent as to process and how he gets restored to power. But no one asked us."

"We're not anyone's favorite babysitter, Mirtha."

"Hmph." Judge Estrada wasn't so easily soothed. "While the evidence for the VP's actions are clear in this case, what's to stop a real coup from occurring in the future? And how do we know if Secretary Espinoza was coerced into acting? Too much is left to the opacity of the political branch, Teresa."

"I agree," Chief Roseborough concurred. She sat on the opposite end of the taupe leather sofa that occupied her office as a welcome respite for her fellow jurists. At six thirty in the morning, she was on her third cup of tea since rising at a bit before dawn. By lunchtime, she would switch to decaf coffee. She curated a variety of nonalcoholic drinks to rival any beverage chain, and the rotation of visits from the other justices proved it. Mondays, Mirtha Estrada wandered into her office to spout off about the weaknesses of character she saw in the nation's leaders, but she would never see such vacillation in herself. Her drink of choice was an Indian gold tea that carried hints of chai and bergamot.

Late afternoon, Seth Bringman would find a reason to drop by and grouse about the overreach in the certs granted by his lenient colleagues. The Court of Last Resort, he believed, should weigh in only on issues of the highest order. The rights of the everyman be damned if the Framers hadn't considered them. Seth favored a Moroccan coffee blend she special-ordered for him alone.

Each of her colleagues had a brew and a mood she could predict with relative ease at this point in her tenure. Which is why she was prepared for Mirtha's dance.

Justice Estrada stirred in a packet of artificial sweetener and a splash of cream. "The vice president seems to be playing with fire on this one. With Secretary Espinoza switching his allegiance, hopefully she'll let the matter lie. Otherwise, we may have to weigh in."

"Congress seemed to have things well in hand with the Twenty-Fifth Amendment process," the Chief replied. "But no one has contended with a president accused of something as pedestrian and vile as murder. The vice president availed herself of a process that the Constitution allows."

"Like you said, the authors of the Twenty-Fifth never contemplated this exact scenario."

"No one did, I would wager." Teresa favored a traditional Darjeeling, which she flavored with orange peel and honey. As she prepared her drink, she waited for Mirtha's point to reveal itself.

"Especially when the president's accuser works for the Supreme Court." Mirtha took a bracing sip of tea before plunging in. As the Chief's oldest friend on the Court, their colleagues had drafted her to deliver the message.

"We all like Avery," she began. "Her intellect is undeniable, and her work product and output are exceptional."

"Which begs the question of why you're here to ask me to fire her," Teresa finished bluntly. "That's your task, is it not?"

Mirtha had the grace to squirm. "Giving her a hearing in June was unorthodox, but I backed your play. I even signed on to the majority opinion in GenWorks. You know where my loyalties lie, Teresa."

"Your point?"

"We have been thrust into the public eye ever since, and her presence is having ripple effects on the operations of the Court. Her fellow clerks are afraid to speak with her, just in case they get subpoenaed. Our colleagues are on tenterhooks themselves." She set the delicate porcelain cup on the marble coaster near her elbow. "The longer this debacle drags on, the more exposure it creates for the rest of us."

"We're lifetime appointees to the highest court in the land, which affords us the luxury of standing by our convictions unrelated to political winds," Teresa reminded her friend. "Exactly what exposure are you all afraid of?"

"The reputation of the Court could be damaged." Mirtha glanced down at her hands, refusing to meet the Chief's steady gaze. "Your reputation could be impugned."

When Teresa chuckled, Mirtha's head snapped up. "Do I amuse you?"

"You all do." The Chief stood and moved toward her desk. The gleaming surface contained the weekly order list the Court would release at 9:30 a.m., which would report on the Court's actions. In carefully tabbed folders rested a variety of clerks' memos regarding the oral arguments they would hear at 10:00 a.m., after she admitted new members to the Court Bar. Nowhere on the list was an allowance of time for the cowardice of her colleagues. Tamping down frustration, she allowed, "This conversation is ridiculous, Mirtha."

"How so?"

"We have the most secure jobs in America. Not subject to rules or conditions beyond remaining alive. Our ethical boundaries are ours to decide. Our decisions can only be overturned by an act of Congress or a constitutional amendment. Yet a few bad stories have you cowering."

"No one is cowering, Chief," came Mirtha's cold response. "We are simply trying to preserve the dignity of the Court. Which is your role. Howard is in a coma and unlikely to wake up. All on the whims of a law clerk who should have been dismissed back in June. We cannot understand why she remains on the Court's payroll or within our confines, when she simply invites chaos and threats."

Mirtha stood now, wounded and annoyed. She awkwardly kicked into her shoes as she protested, "I have gotten very ugly messages sent to me about her. The Supreme Court police are monitoring our phones and email due to the security risks she's caused. Use your influence to find her another post, but please do the right thing, Teresa. That's all we're asking."

Teresa let a small smile form as she inclined her head. "Please tell Seth and Lara and Roy and LJ that you delivered their grievances. I assume you all did not read Allegra or Dara into this intervention."

Mirtha blushed but said nothing.

"I'll see you in the courtroom in an hour, my friend." Her smile remained in place until Mirtha stormed out. Only then did she allow her face to settle into the lines of worry that had become a nearly daily expression lately.

Sitting down behind her desk, she reached for her phone and called out to her assistant, who shared her early tendencies. "Debi, I need to see Avery as soon as she arrives this morning."

"Well, she's actually sitting right here, Chief. Showed up after Justice Estrada went into your office." Dropping her tone to a whisper, Debi added, "She doesn't look too good."

Based on the briefing she'd received, Teresa imagined Avery felt much worse than she looked. "Send her in."

The Chief waited for the solid double knock that Avery preferred. "Enter," she instructed. Despite knowing the circumstances, she was shocked at Avery's appearance.

At twenty-eight, Avery Keene had lived several lives already. This morning, the Chief could see every one of them on her face. Her tawny skin carried a pallor, highlighted by the severe French braid that tugged her sharp cheekbones higher. Normally bright green eyes seemed tired and anxious, the wide mouth drawn. Scrupulously neat, the young attorney wore a spotless teal pantsuit, but one black shoe came to a pointed toe while the second rounded at the top.

Poor girl. "Sit down, Avery," the Chief told her kindly.

Avery took her customary seat on the edge of the Chief's sofa, and Roseborough joined her. In Avery's first term at the Court, she had entered the sanctum only once, when Justice Wynn brought both Avery and her fellow clerk by for a hurried introduction. The second term had swapped out Lisa Borders for Matt Brewer, and Justice Wynn hadn't bothered to bring her along. Her real visit happened five months ago, when the Chief upended her life with shocking news about Wynn.

Now it was Avery's turn. "Chief, thanks for seeing me."

"Of course. How was the judicial conference?"

"The conference is the reason I'm here." Avery had practiced her spiel on the way in, but recounting the events of the previous week got harder each time. Taking a deep breath, she plowed into the story. The chief justice preferred succinct to elaborate, the facts to observations.

"I'm supposed to go to the FBI at lunch today to turn over the phone and the thumb drive. Then I've been summoned to Capitol Hill to meet with the Senate majority leader about the impeachment trial. I don't know when that will finish."

"Take a breath, Avery." The Chief leaned forward and rested a hand on her shoulder. Avery did a quick inhale and a fast release. "Again."

Avery stiffened. "I'm fine, ma'am."

"I do believe that is the first time you've lied to me, Ms. Keene. Don't do it again."

"Ma'am—"

"You watched a man get gunned down moments after he roped

you into helping him with a conspiracy involving the federal courts, foreign operatives, and deepfakes. You're not fine."

"I only meant—"

"Hush." The terse command was followed by the Chief rising to fetch her preferred tonic for anxiety and death threats. As she prepared a cup of chamomile tea lightly sweetened with organic honey, she said, "Howard Wynn is a comatose jackass."

The politely offered critique startled a laugh from Avery. "I've thought the same thing, ma'am."

"As I said before, he asked too much of you. But you've borne up admirably under the strain." Steeping the bag, she continued, "However, this latest debacle seems less like circumstance and more like choice."

"I didn't seek him out," Avery countered.

"According to Agent Lee and by your own admission, you took these materials home with you rather than going straight to the FBI." The Chief returned to the sofa and pressed a sturdy mug into Avery's cool hands. "You are not responsible for saving everyone."

"I know." Avery took a sip of tea, marshaling her words. "Truth be told, Chief, I panicked. My instinct is not to turn to the authorities. When I have a problem, I solve it myself."

"You're no longer on your own, Avery." Teresa ignored the wince of pain that such a reminder was necessary. "Agent Lee recommends that you take a leave of absence. He'd prefer you to limit your travel, and he'd like to station an agent at your home."

"No."

"Avery—"

"Ma'am," Avery cut her off, "I will not be under surveillance again. I agreed to a car outside my building, and he's ordered one for Rita. But until there is more evidence that I'm in danger, I don't need a bodyguard."

"What evidence would you prefer? Bullet holes?" The question was offered without inflection.

"I've been under a great deal of pressure. I might have imagined that I was followed," she responded. "Jared and his team found nothing on the phone. And I haven't seen the car again."

"That's all?"

"Not exactly." Avery weighed how much to say, then conceded that the Chief would find out eventually. "There was no trackable data on the phone. The deepfake video is flawless. If Preston hadn't given us both clips, I would have no reason to doubt the one of the judge at her home."

"Is that all?"

"Judge Whitner's Instagram account has been deleted and the history scrubbed. Same for her Facebook account. No cached images or archived information that we can find. Nothing at all—which is crazy. Her entire social media presence has vanished."

The Chief weighed the implications. "So, at least a portion of Mr. Davies's story appears true. I'll need to alert the presiding judge for FISC. Given the public sentiment, Judge Newhouse may need to report this to Congress."

At the mention of congressional intervention, Avery broached the next subject. "I heard from one of the clerks that you've been asked to fire me."

Chief Roseborough gave her a steady look. The clerk grapevine served invaluable roles in mediating conflict between justices and obviating a number of personnel actions she'd otherwise be forced to take. The insular, tight-knit Court family relied on one another, which meant that tensions often ran high, information fast. The more polarized their ranks grew, the more vital the back channels of communication. Mirtha's opening salvo had been orchestrated for days, and now came part two.

"Until he resigns or otherwise leaves the Court, Howard Wynn is entitled to two law clerks. Mr. Brewer has found other employment. You have not. Unless I see a dereliction of your assigned duties, I intend to retain you as a law clerk. Is that understood?"

"Yes, Chief." The tea in her hand had cooled, but so had her worries. Avery ventured a soft smile. "Thank you, ma'am."

"Don't thank me yet."

For the sake of her already rocky future, Avery should not be involved in whatever transgressions were unfolding at FISA. And short of a court order, there was virtually no way she wouldn't try to insert herself in the investigation of Davies's murder. Chief Roseborough had a way to give both of them some plausible deniability. "I have an assignment for you. The extortion of Judge Whitner occurred via cyberspace. I would like for you to prepare a memo for me on the vulnerabilities of the judiciary, paying particular attention to the 2020 SolarWinds leak and ransomware cases. I'd like your initial draft on Friday."

Avery knew busywork when she heard it. Part of her chafed at the transparent ploy, but more of her was relieved. Agent Lee would investigate Preston Davies and Judge Whitner. Judge Newhouse would lead a review of FISA and vet its security. If she returned to her area of expertise, copious and obnoxiously thorough research, she could keep her job and feel like she'd done all she could for Preston.

Thank God.

"I'll have a draft to you by Thursday, Chief. I'll make it my priority."

THIRTEEN

J udge Michael Oliver parked his trusty Lincoln Continental
beneath the E. Barrett Prettyman Federal Courthouse and made
his way upstairs to the Foreign Intelligence Surveillance Court,
which shared the building with the clumsily named U.S. District
Court for the District of Columbia and U.S. Court of Appeals for
the District of Columbia. Renowned as an example of Stripped
Classicism, the courthouse occupied Third Street and Constitution
Avenue in Northwest D.C., a mere block from the United States
Capitol.

Oliver glanced at the illuminated hands of his vintage Rolex
chronograph, a gift from his wife decades earlier. The gold dial read
7:16 a.m. For the public, the courthouse would open at 9:00 a.m., as
it did Monday through Friday. Federal judges were not constrained
by the normal office hours, and his key card gave him access twenty-
four hours a day.

As the duty judge for the week, Judge Oliver already knew his
caseload. Requests for warrants from assistant U.S. attorneys—
known as AUSAs—from across the country seeking to convince
him of potential, though not imminent, harm to America. Invari-
ably, their pleas for assistance came with dense memos justifying a
most un-American pastime: permission from the court to spy on

someone. The targets for these warrants fell in three general buckets: American citizens who lived outside the United States and who were suspected of bad action; American citizens and permanent resident aliens inside the U.S.; and U.S. companies, regardless of where they operated as long as they originated here.

The surveillance telegraphed by the court's name could authorize wiretaps, business record requests, pen registers, or physical surveillance. Once granted, the government could listen to your calls, read your emails, surf your social media, and follow you at will. FISA warrants carried the special feature of bypassing notice to the suspected wrongdoer. No amount of begging or pleading would provide notice to the target. For the average law enforcement skell, eventually, the target would know they had been tapped. Not so with FISA. All FISA warrants were permanently ex parte, where only the government had a role in the proceedings. The warrants were impervious to discovery unless the government wanted it known.

He hurried through the lobby, past the early morning arrivals as the confab of attorneys, clerks, bailiffs, secretaries, and sundry staff made their appearance. When someone recognized him, he murmured his greetings, certain they could read his soul.

Each time he saw one of the officers patrolling the halls, their weapons at the ready, he imagined sharing with them what he knew. Warning them that their diligence had already been compromised by men like him. As one of the deputies tipped his head in greeting, Michael nearly rushed up to him to confess.

All that held his tongue was the image of two men and their brutal deaths at gunpoint. He hadn't needed to verify authenticity—like thousands in the D.C. metro area, he'd already viewed sanitized footage on the news. He shouldered his way onto the elevator, not waiting for its two passengers to exit. Recognizing his rudeness, he mumbled his apologies as he pressed the button for the court.

Too soon, he was in the chambers allotted to him, so different from the ones he had personally decorated in West Virginia. The shared space meant less room for personalization, and typically, this annoyed his sensibilities. Today, though, he appreciated the anonymity. The veil of distance.

Using his credentials, the judge logged into the system and scrolled through his emails. But no item appeared to compel him to violate protocols. Michael steepled his elbows on the desk, resting his forehead on his clasped hands. He forced himself to take deep, steadying breaths, the kind Phyllis's yoga instructor cajoled her into every Tuesday as he left the house. There might yet be time.

Nearly an hour passed, his watch now reading 8:09 a.m., and he'd shifted his attention to the current crop of requests. Pen registers for a Kazakhstani immigrant who sold after-market cell phones via the internet. Because his wife and business partner was an American citizen, the field agents needed a warrant to capture her conversations too. Based on the court staff's reading of the application, the nexus between the man's angry diatribes on Twitter and the likelihood he was trafficking information gaped too wide. He started typing up his rationale for denying the warrant, being careful to detail his reasons and what another judge might need to see. All denials were final, but he liked to give the government a way to earn a second bite at the apple with new evidence.

The judge skimmed the staff attorney's notes again. Rather than a denial, he decided to offer the government a hearing. He quickly scribbled notes for the staff attorney outlining what it would take to convince him.

A ping from his phone drew his attention. Michael glanced at the banner and his gut clenched. The notification had come from the evil app. With near-trembling fingers, he opened the phone and the message.

Turn on Bluetooth. Leave your office and your phone. Return in fifteen minutes.

Fear coursed through him, and he offered up a prayer for for-giveness. Episcopalian by culture and nature, he rarely publicly engaged his faith. If others saw him out in the hallways, chatting with other jurists, perhaps they would believe him if he claimed ignorance. He truly didn't know what was going to happen. Michael activated the Bluetooth feature and hurried to the door. While he made small talk with the secretaries who had never really spoken to him before, an indigo flashing dot indicated a successful upload. By the time he returned, the court's networked system had been compromised.

Pedestrians hurried along the wide corridors of Pennsylvania Avenue, taking full advantage of the autumn sunlight and the freedom of lunch hour. Tourists strolled casually between irritated government workers and harried attorneys. This close to the FBI, discerning which was which was a fool's errand.

Avery readjusted the oversize sunglasses as they threatened to slip down her nose. An old pair she borrowed from Jared, the attempt at a disguise left much to be desired. She'd covered her head with a ball cap emblazoned with their trademark *W*, again courtesy of Jared's closet. Her neat teal suit had morphed into slim-fitting black jeans and a black cable-knit sweater, paired with a black suede jacket. The embarrassingly mismatched shoes had been traded for low-heeled black boots.

She more closely resembled a curious tourist than a well-dressed attorney striding purposefully toward the Hoover Building. Care-fully, she rounded the corner and then made her way to the Tenth Street entrance. FBI police cars idled in yellow striped lanes, and fewer tourists crowded the sidewalks. As she neared the employee-only entrance, Agent Lee stepped outside. His furtive look around revealed no one out of the ordinary.

Avery entered ahead of him, and he jutted his chin at the guard on duty. An older gentleman with military posture waved them through. "One day, you're going to actually follow my directions," he admonished.

"You told me to meet you here at noon," she replied quietly.

"I told you I was sending a car," Agent Lee retorted. "Instead, I get a text from you saying en route before my guy could get to you. What if you'd been followed?" he questioned as he punched the elevator button.

"I wasn't. No one would recognize me, Agent."

"A professional would. You may have put on sunglasses, a cap, and dressed in black like a cat burglar, but a pro would recognize your gait, the way you angle your shoulders, the swing of your arms. Which Mr. Wynn would know. Where is he, by the way? Or does he too ignore my instructions?"

"Jared got called into the office on an emergency. I didn't tell him I was coming alone."

"Of course you didn't." They entered the elevator car alone, and Agent Lee continued his lecture. "I know you have an overdeveloped sense of responsibility and the generational arrogance to match, but my job is to keep you safe. I can't do that if you refuse to listen or follow simple directions."

"I'm listening now." Avery lifted her hands in a sign of surrender. He was right, and, at her core, she trusted him. Agent Lee, like the chief justice, had never let her down. "I'm really sorry. As a show of good faith, I brought everything." At his raised brow, she made a face. "Yes, everything."

"Good." The elevator dinged, and they exited onto a floor Avery hadn't seen before. Unlike the workaday environs of the Criminal Investigative Division, this floor seemed, well, shinier. Sleeker furniture, brighter lights. More clandestine than the average governmental offices.

Noting her quizzical look, Agent Lee explained, "We're meeting Dr. Sarah Beth Gehl, my liaison with NCIJTF."

He pinged Sarah Beth to let her know they'd arrived. Like Avery, he was impressed by the gloss and shine of NCIJTF, but he knew better than to slide into envy. To his mind, the National Cyber Investigative Joint Task Force was OLEC on steroids. His job required reaching across law enforcement agencies and convincing them to play nice and share information on crimes that everyone basically understood. The turf wars for the NCIJTF had nuclear armaments attached. Led by the FBI, the task force convened more than thirty domestic and international agencies to protect the digital infrastructure of America and its allies from hackers, coders, spies, and thieves who grew more sophisticated and bolder each day.

In addition to the expected soup of alphabet agencies, the reindeer games added the CIA, the NSA, the DNI, the DoD, DOE, DHS, and the State Department, and that was just a few of the interpolating groups that answered to the White House and had to cooperate with the FBI. Unlike the domestic OLEC, which preserved the illusion of independence, the lucky folks assigned to the task force had to colocate and work jointly to defend America's cybersecurity.

Avery craned her head to see inside. But no one could really get a good look at the living experiment in power and subterfuge, given the oversize insignia painted onto the bulletproof glass. A majestic eagle spread its wings across a field of blue.

It was a busy bird. One claw clutched an olive branch, the other held the traditional sheaf of arrows. A red-and-white-striped flag had been draped over its neck flanked with blue, but the scales of justice replaced the typical stars. Half of the *e pluribus unum* banner seemed to be snagged in its beak while the *unum* fluttered on the opposite side. Gold stars had been commandeered to ring a thin isosceles triangle that framed the eagle's escapades. The final embellishment was a ring of solid gold containing the unwieldy moniker of the NCIJTF and United States of America.

As Avery wondered whose fever dream conjured up the emblem of unity and efficiency, a woman in her late forties appeared. Dressed in the expected dark gray pants suit and modest white button-down blouse, she exited the sliding glass doors that snicked shut behind her.

Making a beeline for them, she caught Agent Lee's hand between her own. "Robert," she greeted warmly. "Long time no see."

"As you might imagine. I prefer bullets to bytes, my friend," he teased as he turned slightly to include Avery. "This is Special Agent in Charge Sarah Beth Gehl. 'Dr. Gehl' if you want to suck up."

Plucked from the FBI's Cyber Division, Sarah Beth had taken on the godawful task of wrangling some of the more obstinate members of the compulsory union. She and Robert had trained together at Quantico. With a less mobile smile, she extended a hand. "Pleasure to meet you, Avery. I've heard a great deal about you."

"Unfortunately, I can't seem to stay out of trouble," Avery quipped. "Hopefully, I can turn this stuff over and be on my way."

Agent Gehl nodded. "I secured a conference room for us down the hall. Based on Agent Lee's briefing, I thought a few of my colleagues should join us."

Avery followed the duo, half listening as they quietly chattered. When they reached the heavy wooden door, Agent Gehl keyed in a code in a discreet pad next to the lock. "Heightened vigilance," she explained wryly. "Come on in."

As they entered the room, Avery learned that "a few colleagues" turned out to be seven, not including Agent Gehl. The agent introduced the assembled quickly by name and agency. Two agencies stood out: Europol and the U.S. Secret Service.

Introductions over, Agent Gehl quickly shifted mood. "I understand you have some evidence that you'd like to surrender, Ms. Keene?"

Chafing at the language, Avery pulled out the RFID-lined bag she used for transport and corrected, "I have some information I would like to turn over. I have no proof that the devices are evidence of anything."

The agent from DOJ chimed in. "Who has handled the devices since you received them last week?"

"My friend Jared Wynn, who is a tech analyst, ran an initial scan. When he found malware in the source code, he asked other tech friends he trusted to see what they could determine."

Agent Gehl prompted, "And that would be?"

"Nothing. The device has been wiped clean, with the exception of the app. But they couldn't trace any transmission records or even determine how the app works." She shrugged. "Or, at least, not without risking an attack on their equipment."

"I understand there's a phone and a thumb drive." The nonquestion query came from the only other woman in the room. Agent Gehl had identified her as a representative from Europol, and the lightly accented English confirmed her identity. Avery speculated that she hailed from Belgium.

"Yes," Avery confirmed. She explained the paucity of data on the drive and the failed attempts to locate social media sites. "One of the guys, an AI expert, marveled at the quality of the deepfake. Both videos show nearly identical time stamps. He said he'd never seen video this sophisticated."

The Europol representative nodded. "May I ask about the shooting, Ms. Keene?"

Expecting the question, Avery still braced herself. "It's as I explained to Agent Lee. I tried to follow Mr. Davies outside, but I was delayed."

"Delayed by whom?" asked Agent Gehl.

"Some woman I accidentally bumped into."

"How long did the delay last?"

"Less than two minutes from the moment I saw Judge Whitner's name on the FISC list to me making it outside."

The Europol agent took over again. "That's when you saw the shooting."

"Soon thereafter." Avery looked around at the six silent men, each of their faces sporting identical expressions of impassivity. Including Agent Lee. "I saw a woman with brown hair in a ponytail stop by the taxi. I heard gunshots, silence, and then more pops. After she'd shot them, she took off."

"As did you," the DOJ representative said.

"Yes, sir. I did run from the scene of a double murder instead of attempting to apprehend the international assassin," Avery retorted.

"You are certain this person was not a U.S. national?" Agent Gehl challenged Agent Lee, whose expression didn't flicker.

Avery caught the look and covered for him. "Europol wouldn't be here unless there was an international implication. Since Preston was definitely from Idaho, and I doubt Europol is mourning a cabdriver expat, I assume the shooter is the international intrigue in this scenario."

"We have reason to believe the assassin known as Nyx has foreign ties," she concurred. "I assume I do not have to warn you about the need for confidentiality going forward. Now that we are involved, there can be no more sharing evidence or vital information with civilians."

"Jared Wynn has TS/SCI clearance," Avery explained, "but I will certainly follow your directions. I didn't know Preston long, but no one deserves to die like that. I want to be as helpful as possible."

Agent Gehl crossed to where Avery stood with Agent Lee. "We appreciate you bringing this information to us, Ms. Keene. However, given the highly sensitive nature of Judge Whitner's role as a duty judge issuing FISA warrants, we will need to terminate your involvement at this time. This is not the domain of a civilian."

Reading Avery's rising irritation, Agent Lee interjected, "While she is definitely a civilian, I can vouch for how useful Ms. Keene might be on this investigation. I suggest we engage her as necessary."

Agent Gehl lightly cleared her throat. "The assistant director is transferring the Davies case to NCIJTF and out of OLEC. The

Criminal Division will stand down and transfer the case files to our team."

The NSA's adjutant cleared his throat. "We would also ask Ms. Keene to consent to a search of her home and all personal property to ensure no information has been retained. We would also request that she secure Mr. Wynn's cooperation with the same."

"Absolutely not," Avery responded tightly. "I told you I have turned everything over. Trust me, don't trust me. That's on you. But no way am I giving the NSA access to my personal property. Assuming you aren't already there."

"I resent the implication," the agent retorted. "If you are innocent, you'll volunteer to help us clear this situation."

Avery gave a solitary chuckle and stood tall as she faced the group. "Your flawed logic works on foreign nationals without an understanding of the Bill of Rights, or terrified Americans who don't watch the more accurate legal dramas. Unfortunately for you, I'm neither. The answer is an unequivocal no. No, you cannot search my home and, no, I don't fall within your ambit for a warrant." She made eye contact with each agent in turn. "If anyone thinks they should try it anyway—I dare you."

The identical expressions of shock and outrage prompted Agent Gehl into action. "Ms. Keene, we were not implying that you were under investigation."

Avery jerked her thumb at the NSA guy. "He just said it. I speak legalese, Agent Gehl. And I am very fluent."

Beside her, Agent Lee's normally stoic expression settled into a frown. He tried to make eye contact with Agent Gehl, but she had locked onto Avery. "Ms. Keene, that's enough. The NSA made a reasonable request, and your attitude is not helping matters."

"Not helping—" Agent Lee began, but Agent Gehl cut him off.

"Agent Lee. Ms. Keene. I brought you in here as a courtesy. This is only going to work one way, and that's according to JTF protocols."

Agent Lee bristled. "Brought us in? I am the one who alerted you to Ms. Keene's involvement as a sign of good faith. Faith that I've apparently misplaced, Agent Gehl." He gave the room a stiff nod. "Good luck, gentlemen. Ladies."

"Avery, let's go," Agent Lee said without acknowledging Agent Gehl. Avery turned a baleful look to the assembled team, then reluctantly headed to the door.

Agent Gehl offered, "I'll need to walk you out, Agent Lee."

"Don't do me any favors," he grumbled.

"I'm not," Agent Gehl retorted. "It's my job."

FOURTEEN

Agent Lee exited the conference room with Avery, followed by Agent Gehl. The SAC pointed down the hall. "We need to talk in my office, Robert, and this isn't a request."

Holding his silence, the agent followed Agent Gehl into her domain. The wide, airy room was filled with expensive modern furniture that seemed more suited to television dramas than bureaucratic offices. Monitors adorned two walls, leaving the third for a whiteboard and the fourth for a broad window outfitted with blackout shades. She waved them toward a round metal table piled high with paper files.

"What game are you playing here? Ambushing Avery like that was low and unnecessary." Agent Lee fumed as he folded his arms across his chest. "I brought you into this, Sarah Beth."

"Perhaps Ms. Keene should wait outside," she cautioned icily. "This is agency business."

Avery stubbornly shifted her feet to show she had no plans of moving. Agent Lee's smile twitched in silent approval. "After that little show, she stays. Our conversation concerns her too."

"Robert, this is not a civilian matter." The stern warning carried a ton of meaning. "You know better."

"Do you?" He gestured toward a stone-faced Avery. "I can vouch for her. You're the one who's got me worried. What was that in there?"

"It was Distraction 101, Robert, and I thought you'd catch on since I learned it from you," Agent Gehl taunted. "Look, there's a lot more going on than you're aware of."

Agent Lee scowled. "Then don't play games, Sarah Beth. The truth."

"The truth is that all these agencies are pissed at being caught flat-footed and behind. Davies's murder is one more piece of a puzzle they weren't aware was even in play." She gave an apologetic smile to Avery. "The NSA is feeling a bit raw because the FBI had to read them in," she replied. "Europol has been after this shooter for years, and they had no idea she was on American soil."

"Then there's me—the political pariah who shows up in their secret clubhouse," Avery added. "I'm not the face they needed to see."

The agent allowed a mischievous grin to ghost her lips for an instant. "No, you are not exactly a harbinger of good tidings. But their requests were legitimate asks, Ms. Keene. And perhaps, a little bit of theater."

Agent Lee remained stern. "Turf battles aren't news. A murder in D.C. and a foreign assassin are unusual, but I saw a whole other level of paranoia in there."

"NCIJTF has got a thousand eyes on us, Robert. The past few years have been a shit show." Agent Gehl held up her hands and shook her head. "The SolarWinds hack a few years ago. Daily ransomware demands against nearly every single government agency in the world. The bastards at Pegasus and their willingness to sell software to any despot with a Swiss bank account. Add to it the potential reach of this Whitner case, and everyone is bracing for a major disaster."

"Covering their asses is only part of it," Agent Lee said flatly. "What's the rest?"

"Avery has no friends in law enforcement except for you. Almost every federal agency is in an upheaval because Daddy and Mommy are fighting, and we might be getting new guardians in a few weeks."

Agent Lee relaxed slightly. "Don't call POTUS and the VP 'Daddy and Mommy' again. Gives me the creeps. And all the girl has done is save our asses and do our jobs."

Avery reminded them mildly, "The girl is right here, and she can hear you both."

Agent Lee grunted, "You know what I mean." Facing a now-seated SAC, he probed, "What's your angle, Sarah Beth?"

"I meant it when I said this is a fraught time. The Joint Task Force is working well, but the possibility of a new threat that's targeting national security so directly has all the directors freaked out. This is beyond classified."

"I have clearance. So read me in." Agent Lee gave his old friend a somber look. "And I swear you can trust her. Avery is the only reason anyone knows there's trouble. She's not an agent, but she's damn smart and as reliable as my basset hound."

"Again, I can hear you," Avery muttered.

"My point is," he continued, "I made the mistake of trying to isolate her from a case when we first met. I learned two lessons. One, she's going to keep working on it, whether we like it or not." He held up a hand to stop Avery from responding. "Her family is possibly in danger here as well, Sarah Beth. She won't stop, and we can't cut her off. Two, she's got a once-in-a-generation mind—we'd be far better served to give her limited clearance and have her work with us, and not play catch-up later. Three, the FBI director can authorize the release of classified info to someone outside the agency, and your incredibly broad parameters should give you the room to explain it away if anyone takes exception. I'll take the hit otherwise."

"And the end of your career?" Agent Gehl demanded.

"That too."

Avery held her tongue. Already, her brain was processing the new information about the attack on the Departments of Energy and Commerce. Something tugged at her, but nothing coalesced.

"Trust me, Sarah Beth," urged Agent Lee.

"I do. But I am about to break a dozen rules that could end my career," Agent Gehl warned as she relented. "I appreciate you raising the alarm on this case, Robert. As soon as you flagged the likely extortion of a federal judge, I alerted my counterparts in CCIPS and the National Security Division."

Despite the unwieldy number of federal agencies in play, Avery recognized the most recent acronym. "CCIPS? Why would the Computer Crime and Intellectual Property Section care about a federal judge being blackmailed? All you knew was she had a phone that had been compromised. Surely that doesn't rise to the level of their attention."

Out of habit, Sarah Beth lowered her voice. "Proof of Judge Whitner being blackmailed is one of the reasons folks are on edge. Whitner was the duty judge on several recent requests for warrants, a number of which involved cases handled by CCIPS. A few months ago, she signed off on the final pieces they needed to shut down the largest international marketplace for hacked data."

"The CacheMoney Forum sting," Avery guessed. When Agent Gehl nodded, Avery explained to a confused Agent Lee, "Cache-Money Forum was a website where cybercriminals sold hacked data like passwords, credit card numbers, medical information. If a computer could record it, they tried to steal it. We're talking billions of dollars at risk. The feds got a big public win after the site shut down."

This time, it was Agent Gehl who watched her with suspicion. Quickly, Avery explained, "When you date a cybersecurity expert, shop talk is inevitable."

Mollified, Agent Gehl continued. "With that victory, we received more latitude to hunt for other threat actors. Agencies stepped up their output. In fact, multiple FISA warrants have recently come from agencies that sit on my task force because we're in the midst of a major operation. At the same time, there's been chatter about a massive hack that will reorder the world."

"You hear that every day on the dark web," Agent Lee reminded her. "Even over in Criminal Division, we know about the doomsday scenarios. Every hacktivist or nutjob claims to have the inside track to the new world order."

"Most of them don't have access to botnets that can take over the international finance system or shut down all information traffic out of Europe or Asia." Giving another harried sigh, she tapped a series of commands on her computer. The monitor opposite her desk flared to life. Avery and Agent Lee took her cue and sat at the overflowing table. "What do you know about the Coreflood Botnet attack?"

"Mercifully, nothing," confessed Agent Lee.

Avery furrowed her brow in recollection. "The cyberattack back in 2016. Millions of people affected around the world, and millions of dollars in damages. Jared told me about it. The botnets infected more than eight hundred thousand systems in the U.S. alone."

"This task force caught it and contained it. We netted ninety-five percent mitigation across seventy-two foreign governments."

Agent Lee didn't do computers, but he understood results. "Impressive. But what does that have to do with Judge Whitner or Preston Davies?"

"I'm getting to that. The rumor is that Coreflood was child's play compared to what is on the horizon. Our teams are trying to determine the likely target, the sector of attack, or, hell, the country of origin. So far, we have no leads."

"You think Judge Whitner is part of a redux of Coreflood?" Avery asked skeptically. "All you've got is an empty phone and a deepfake video of a corrupt judge. Seems like a stretch."

"Unless that's not all they've got," Agent Lee explained quietly. "That's what's wrong, isn't it?"

Agent Gehl nodded reluctantly. "There are no direct links to a potential attack yet, but Judge Whitner isn't the first person connected to FISA who has been compromised. Three weeks ago, we quietly detained an assistant U.S. attorney named Jason Johnson, assigned to our Financial Crimes division in the FBI."

She glanced around as though checking for surveillance. "He processed several FISA business record warrant requests related to companies headquartered in the U.S., each time claiming the surveillance was needed to track an international money-laundering scheme."

"But there wasn't one," Agent Lee anticipated. "Johnson was phonying up requests?"

"Johnson is in the midst of a nasty breakup. His wife's divorce lawyer found proof that he was hiding money—nearly two million dollars in cryptocurrency. The wife sent a scathing email to his section chief, and the section chief started looking into his cases. Johnson had been reporting out on this laundering scheme, but he had a good record, so no one questioned him about how he was building his case. Turns out, he was dummying up requests from various agencies, doctoring files himself, and never consulted anyone on the warrants or the investigations. He made it all up."

A knot formed in Avery's stomach. "So you have a corrupt judge and a compromised federal prosecutor who are using the nation's secret court for something nefarious," she summarized.

"Exactly. What I'm about to show you is classified. Not even Congress gets to see what FISA grants warrants for in real time."

Agent Lee scrunched his brow. "Sarah Beth, I believe we can help, but I don't want you to feel pressured. Maybe I have Avery step out and everything that happens thereafter falls on me."

Giving him a wink, Agent Gehl shook her head. "You're right about needing help. If there is an imminent threat, we're nowhere close to stopping it. We don't even know what we're looking at." She turned to Avery. "Rumor is you see patterns and connections that others miss?"

"Sometimes," she acknowledged. "I like puzzles."

"Then I'm putting my career in your hands. We mapped out Johnson's work and found this." Agent Gehl typed in another series of commands. The screen shifted to a graphic with an irregular series of spikes. She lifted her eyes to Avery. "Ms. Keene, is it also true you've got a photographic memory?"

"Eidetic, but generally speaking, yes."

"Then take a look at this." The screen changed to a list of entities, some incredibly familiar to anyone who had ever purchased an item in their lives. Banks, hedge funds, tech behemoths, entertainment companies. Others were obscure entity names that had no discernible pattern. Case files, requests, the requester, and the judge of record coded into a database. "Do you understand what you're looking at?"

"I think so." Fascinated, Avery murmured, "By my count, Johnson has asked for almost sixty FISA warrants in the last five years. Four his first year. Seven in the second. But he applied for warrants forty-eight times over the last sixteen months. And every application for a warrant was granted by the same judge. Francesca Whitner."

"Exactly. Warrants for business records. Pen registers, wiretaps. In a typical year, the FISC might receive less than fifteen hundred requests. Rarely more than a handful from any single assistant United States attorney unless they're working on a major operation. Johnson requested nearly fifty of them."

"Did all the info make it to him?"

"Yes."

"Has he given you anything?" Agent Lee asked. "Any hint of what he was doing?"

"No. He hasn't spoken to anyone since requesting his attorney. I've been able to keep it under wraps because it's a matter of national security since it went through FISA. But none of the agencies knew about his bogus case. From what we can tell, they each were told the request was from another agency, and everyone just complied."

"He played a shell game," Avery recognized with a hint of admiration. "Keeping that many organizations in the dark and doing his bidding is almost impressive." Remembering her audience and seeing their twin looks of disapproval, she clarified. "I said 'almost.'"

Agent Gehl turned back to the screen. "We've compiled all his moving parts, but we can't piece together a motive or even a use for all the data he's collected. Right now, a team is combing through what we think he found. He faked multiple agencies collecting information, using the FBI as his backstop. But without knowing what to look for, we can't tell what we're facing. We'll have to backtrack all the warrants, figure out which—if any—were legit and how he partitioned the data."

"Other than her signing off, are there any clear links to Judge Whitner?"

"Just one. We take AUSA Johnson into custody, then Judge Whitner dies and her clerk is murdered shortly thereafter, right here in D.C."

"Okay."

With a withering look at the monitor and its impenetrable data Agent Gehl shut off the screen. "Either Judge Whitner and Jason Johnson were working on a scheme together, or someone set them up as moles inside the FISC. I believe it's the latter, and I doubt they're the only ones. We've seen a spike in chatter, manufactured warrants, and now murder. Frankly, Avery, given all you have coming down on you, I truly don't want you anywhere near this case."

"And me?" queried Agent Lee.

Agent Gehl rose and circled her desk. Propping a hip on the edge, she bit her lip and wondered how much to tell him.

"All of it," Agent Lee prompted, recognizing the expression. "Just spit it out."

"I want your help, but the decision to pull you off the case came from upstairs," she admitted. "I'll keep you in the loop, but I can't have you in the middle of this. With all the turmoil at Sixteen Hundred, Director Alford is desperate to keep whatever this is from exploding before the election. You're too tied to Avery and to Stokes's fall. If he comes back, his wrath will be biblical."

She lifted her hands in the universal gesture of powerlessness. "Let's be honest: you're both political pariahs. Luckily, Robert, your record is spotless; OLEC would revolt if they fired you. But believe me, it's been discussed."

He couldn't argue. "The ADIC hates having his hands tied."

"Exactly. All the top brass at the agency want you a thousand miles away from this case. And they shit the bed when I told them Avery was involved."

With nearly thirty years on the job, Agent Lee had survived five administrations and six presidents. The best response was to keep his head down and keep doing the job. Today was all he could pretend to control. "Thanks for the honesty. But don't throw yourself on any grenades for me. You hear them coming, though, give me a warning, will you? If they focus on her, I need immediate notice."

"Of course," Agent Gehl promised emphatically. "I don't like this, but I've got to figure out what in the world is going on here." Her gaze widened to encompass Avery. "I can't have you in the middle of this, but if you see something, say something."

"Have you offered Jason Johnson a plea deal?" Agent Lee cocked his head. "Like you pointed out, since he got arrested, three people have died. He might be willing to talk in a way he wasn't before."

Agent Gehl gave him a thin smile. "Perhaps we do a reprise of that case out of Mississippi. Bad cop, borderline-corrupt cop? See what we can pry out of him. It's a national security case, but I can tell the ADIC I brought you in because of your interrogation expertise. Happens to be true."

Lee grinned. "It's been a while since I've been borderline-corrupt cop." He inclined his head at Avery. "We are both willing to follow your lead on this."

Taking her cue from Agent Lee, Avery agreed, "Yes, ma'am."

"Tell the higher powers, 'Message received.'" He motioned to Avery. "Let's get you back to work. Sarah Beth, text me with the details of our visit to Johnson."

He opened the office door, stepping back to allow Avery to exit first. In the wide hallway, an unfamiliar man stood waiting, his stiff stance screaming *parade rest*. Recognizing the military posture, Agent Lee shifted to put his body between Avery and their visitor.

"Can I help you?" Agent Lee asked politely. Behind him, he heard Sarah Beth joining them.

"Agent Eddy Morales of the Secret Service. I need to ask Ms. Keene to come with me." He took a step forward, and Agent Lee moved to wholly block his path.

"Why?"

"She is wanted for questioning regarding money laundering, wire fraud, and conspiracy."

Stunned by the accusations, Avery fought the urge to run. Quickly, though, the charges levied by Congressman Hibner came flooding back. She'd dismissed their line of questioning as political theater—she was simply a set piece. But the dark-suited Secret Service agent was no actor, and Agent Lee didn't seem to be taking it lightly.

Agent Gehl's warning about his status in the Bureau echoed ominously. Every time Avery got into trouble and Lee helped her, he risked his job. Heart pounding, she stepped from behind Agent Lee's protective bulk. "I—"

Before she could speak, Agent Lee blocked her gently with his forearm. He turned to Morales. "How did you know she was here?"

"I'm not at liberty to answer questions, sir."

Agent Gehl deliberately turned her head to the conference room. Agent Lee followed her line of sight. The Joint Task Force included representatives from more than thirty agencies and entities. Seven were in their little confab, including the Secret Service.

Relegated by most Americans to the role of protector for the highest-ranking political families, few knew the origin story of the Secret Service as a law enforcement arm commissioned by President Abraham Lincoln to root out counterfeit money. Their ambit expanded over time to include presidential protection, but their focus on financial crimes never ended.

And now they had Avery in their sights.

"It's okay," she said. All three agents turned to look at her—Lee with incredulity, Gehl with grudging respect, Morales with inscrutability. The latter worried Avery the most. "I appreciate the intervention, but I'll go with Agent Morales." She circled Agent Lee but gave him a wan half-smile. "I'd appreciate it if you'd let my boss know where I am. I probably will be late getting back from lunch."

FIFTEEN

The hulking black SUV left the asphalt highway for a stylish macadam road that tried unsuccessfully to blend into the surrounding landscape. Loblolly pines scraped low-hanging clouds that threatened rain with no real intent to deliver. In mid-October, the weather patterns of northern Virginia were fairly predictable: mild weather that allowed for a light jacket but didn't require much more.

Avery discreetly tugged at the black suede jacket she wore, wishing for a parka and a scarf. Cold streams of air blasted from an open vent, and her one request for a temperature adjustment had been met with stony silence. Likewise when she wanted to know where they were headed. The distance between the Hoover Building and the Secret Service HQ was a brisk ten-minute walk and a leisurely three-minute drive. Yet they'd been on the road for more than thirty minutes.

Only one person could summon the Secret Service to a private residence. A private residence he would be vacating soon to return to the Oval Office. Until then, the Secret Service agents assigned to him would follow his orders just the same, including instructions to take her cell phone and bag. Avery realized her sole record of the meeting with President Stokes would be her memory.

She agreed to come with them because picking a fight with another part of the federal government wasn't wise, and at her rate, she'd have to move to some backwater town in the middle of nowhere for gainful employment. An interview with the Secret Service would put the truth on the record, and she could move on. But this encounter owed nothing to accountability.

The crushed-stone road turned into a stretch of gravel that wound through old-growth oak trees, bordered by a carefully tended hedge of dappled willow. Avery had seen images of the stately mansion and its horse farm on documentaries that traced the JFK-like rise of Brandon Stokes. A bona fide military hero, a celebrated U.S. senator, vice president, and then the Oval Office itself, intoned numerous narrators, each extolling his virtue and pretending objectivity. The semi-meteoric rise came with a few caveats. One, it didn't hurt that his mother's family roots in Virginia stretched along the floor of the Atlantic to connect to a duke who'd funded an excursion to James-town. Raised in Arizona, he toggled between his father's military nobility and his mother's slightly more likely British royal lineage. Stokes inherited money and political chops from both sides of his family tree. Two, as tradition dictated, he married into even more by wedding Fontaine McDaniel of the oil baron wealth of Texas. Their bound fortunes and unwavering focus on power had united them more firmly than any fleeting notion of everlasting love.

During his exile from Pennsylvania Avenue, news vans had taken up posts along the state road that led out to the Tara-esque mansion. Avery watched as photographers took aim at their barreling truck, no doubt trying to suss out who might be inside. Stokes had man-aged to convince his errant cabinet to restore him to power, but the sword of impeachment still hung over his future.

The SUV churned up the gravel until it reached the wide expanse of a cobblestone driveway. Here, the best telephoto lens would cap-ture nothing of interest. The engine idled as the vehicle stopped and three agents jumped out in rapid succession. Agent Morales, who'd spent the entire ride ignoring her, was the last to exit. He checked over both shoulders.

"Ms. Keene, if you will." He extended a hand to assist her to the truck's running board, which she refused. Dismissing her petulance, he ordered, "Follow me."

Stubbornness and a sudden instinct for self-preservation kept Avery rooted to the spot. The last time she saw the president in person, she broke his nose. This occurred after ruining his legacy and accusing him of criminal conspiracies that would make Nixon blush. Now she had practically been abducted to his secluded ranch with armed guards and no witnesses.

Agent Morales spun on his heel and stalked back to where she stood. "Ms. Keene."

"You indicated that I was wanted for questioning by the Secret Service. Why am I here?" Avery demanded.

"They want to see you inside," was the flat response. "Please follow me."

She briefly thought about making a run for the news vans down the road, but Agent Morales would tackle her before her boots brought her down. *Better to play this one out, Keene,* she advised herself. "I intend to report this," she warned him.

"As do I, ma'am."

Warily, Avery fell into step beside the agent as they crossed the driveway and reached the ornate doors with their stained-glass panels. A variety of equines frolicked across swaths of green that seemed to mount to the sky. Morales radioed quietly, and the doors opened.

A neatly dressed older woman with graying hair and sturdy black shoes stood a few feet inside. Morales led the way, and after Avery entered, a hidden agent pushed the door closed.

"Thank you," Avery said out of habit.

"You're welcome," the agent replied. "This way."

The agent-slash-doorman walked them through a grand foyer and into a grander living room. Two fireplaces roared cheerfully despite the seventy-degree weather. Twin sofas upholstered in chintz stretched eight feet in parallel. Add a few pins and the long, narrow living room could have doubled as a bowling alley.

Beyond the living room, they passed through two additional spaces. Next, a more subdued den greeted the travelers, and Avery wondered whether to ask for bread crumbs so she could find her way out. Eventually, the on-site agent stopped before an imposing wood-paneled door and rapped briskly. "Sir?"

"Come on in," came the familiar voice with its golden baritone.

The agent escorted Avery and Agent Morales inside. President Stokes, phone to his ear, sat behind a smaller version of the Resolute desk, complete with the whorls and scrolls of the original. Two chairs flanked the guest side, and he motioned to them to sit. He continued his conversation, unconcerned about being overheard.

"Mick, you know where I'll be tomorrow?" He tipped back, hand stroking his chin thoughtfully, his tone even and polite. "In the White House, Mick. And you'll be in the shithouse for fucking me. Keep that in mind when you say your prayers tonight. And when you come hat in hand asking for a favor for those gas-guzzling monstrosities that California will find a way to ban, keep it in mind. For every day you have left running that failing company of yours, remember where you chose to stand when a friend called on you. Because I will remember, Mick. I absolutely will."

Brandon Stokes fervently missed the satisfying crack of a slammed phone, or even the tepid click that signaled the end of a discussion. Cellular phones removed the grandiosity and drama, leaving only dead air. Disappointed, he lightly tapped the button to end the call and lowered the phone to the desk. His call had two audiences— and both messages had been delivered.

"Ms. Keene, so kind of you to join us." He motioned again to the chairs. Avery remained stock still. The president shifted his attention to the agent waiting by her side. "Agent Morales, can you give us a minute, please?"

"Yes, sir."

Avery continued to watch President Stokes. "I didn't realize the Secret Service had become your personal goon squad."

"I simply asked them to escort you to see your president." He cocked his head at her, softened his smile to implore trust. "I believe you and I got off on the wrong foot early on."

"You kidnapped my mother," she reminded him baldly. "Threatened to kill her. Tried to kill me."

The smile tightened, then vanished. In its place was a perfect imitation of righteous indignation. "Major Vance kidnapped your mother. He hired thugs to kill you and your friends." He laid his hands flat against the desk. "I swear to God, I knew nothing of his treason. I fought for our nation, for our ideals. Why would I cast aside all the good I have done, could still do, for such a grotesque purpose?"

Avery knew she was hearing the opening arguments of the Stokes impeachment trial. Trouble was, although she intimately understood the utter bollocks he spewed, she easily believed others would take him at his word. Especially his colleagues in the U.S. Senate, a body where he distinguished himself as a warrior for accountability and integrity. Giving herself an internal shake, she let out a short chuckle.

"You've had weeks to practice, sir. That's the best you can do?"

For a nanosecond, rage flashed, then subsided. "I reached out to you, Avery, because we have a common mission here. To move forward and put the past behind us." He gestured to one of the two chairs again. "Won't you please have a seat?"

"No, I will not." She pointedly looked around the elegant study, its high ceilings and shelves of books with a librarian's ladder to reach the highest tomes. "Do you read, Mr. President?"

He swept his arms wide. "These aren't for decoration."

She wandered over to a section and plucked a random volume. Opening to the middle of the book, she skimmed random pages. Avery quickly returned to the president, who watched her actions with clear confusion. "Take it," she instructed, and he warily accepted the open hardback.

Avery clasped her hands behind her and began to recite. "'They are good husbands, or faithful wives, or something tedious. You know what I mean—middle-class virtue and all that kind of thing. How different Sibyl was! She lived her finest tragedy. She was always a heroine. The last night she played—the night you saw her—she acted badly because she had known the reality of love. When she knew its unreality, she died, as Juliet might have died. She passed again into the sphere of art.'" She gripped the chair she refused. "I remember everything I see, everything I read. I know the truth."

"Quite the circus feat," President Stokes offered in low tones, as he turned the spine toward him. "Did you choose *The Picture of Dorian Gray* on purpose? To teach me a deeper lesson about not underestimating you?"

She managed not to roll her eyes. Playing along, she replied, "Pure coincidence. Like the passage I picked."

"If you thought to impress me with your prodigious memory, Ms. Keene, I am not that taken by the interesting pattern of neurons that let you do what confidence men have done for generations."

"I'm the con artist?" she replied incredulously. "You managed to convince a nation that you had their best interests at heart."

"I did," he said haughtily. "I do. And your routine here or some performance on Capitol Hill will not divert me from my purpose."

"What? Genocide?"

His grip on the book tightened. "Protection. Opportunity.

Defense. Freedom. All things that I have pursued on behalf of my fellow citizens for longer than you've been alive."

"So you admit you authorized the Tigris Project?"

President Stokes gave her a thin smile. He stroked the book, and without looking down, he continued Avery's passage from memory. " 'There is something of the martyr about her. Her death has all the pathetic uselessness of martyrdom, all its wasted beauty.' "

He flipped the cover over, tapped the embossed name of the author from the priceless first edition. "Oscar Wilde reveled in the excesses of passion, didn't he? His Dorian Gray resolved to make his life count, to do what he could to wring out the last dregs of joy." His smile widened. "Perhaps, somewhere in the recesses of your astonishing memory, you learned that I wrote my undergraduate thesis on Mr. Wilde. He was quite the chameleon."

Avery held her silence, and he continued. "Writer. Philosopher. Classicist. A man ahead of his time but committed to his ideals. One whose moral turpitude was later placed into appropriate context. I committed my services to my nation, to each citizen having the ability to thrive."

"At whose expense?" Avery whispered. "You murdered people."

"Accusations like that will not end well for you, Avery. Our investigations have already uncovered your unsavory relationship with Karriem Shabazz."

"I had no such relationship," she ground out. "These lies won't stick."

"Information need not be permanent to be useful." He flashed his famous grin again, the one that charmed heads of state and diplomats. "Recant while you can, and I will not forget your bravery."

Pissed that she allowed them to keep her phone, Avery reminded herself of why she'd come. For the truth. And if she'd had the smallest glimmer of doubt, he'd quashed it. "I have nothing more to say to you, sir. I'd like to leave."

"Certainly. Once you finish the passage, Ms. Keene."

"What?"

"Your parlor trick has been helpful in setting the parameters of our engagement. So use that remarkable memory and tell me what Dorian says to Basil about suffering. I'll get you started. 'You must not think I have not suffered.'"

Fear washed through Avery, as cold as the blast from the SUV. Brandon Stokes was no cartoonish buffoon, no clumsy swindler who stumbled into power using invective and fool's gold. His patina of honor distracted attention, but a careful watcher would see what he showed her now. A rare, deadly combination of zealot and genius. A warning she'd do well to heed. Chilled, she murmured Dorian's complaint. "'I suffered immensely. Then it passed away. I cannot repeat an emotion. No one can, except sentimentalists.'"

He tapped a button on his phone. "Ms. Keene is ready to go."

Like a wraith, Agent Morales appeared in the doorway. Avery hurried out, ready to be as far away from Stokes as she could. Heading back the way they'd entered, she kept her head low, her mind racing.

"What the hell are you doing here?"

The exclamation brought her head up. Congressman Luke Boylen stood in the foyer, outfitted in a chambray shirt, jeans, and scuffed riding boots with a riding crop under his arm.

"Leaving," Avery replied shortly. "I'd ask the same of you, but why insult either of us?" She poked Agent Morales. "Please."

The agent shifted to allow her to precede him, and she gave the congressman a wide berth. Confidentiality of the deposition be damned. Although Avery had never been naïve enough to think secrecy applied, she hadn't expected the Republicans to be quite so brazen.

Gravel crunched beneath her feet as she made a beeline for the truck. Once inside, she stuck out her hand, the command wordless. The silent agent driving the vehicle returned her satchel and phone. Avery powered the device on and watched the cascade of text messages and voicemails with growing dismay. In the chaos of today's revelations, she'd forgotten her other appointment. "Shit."

Agent Morales slammed the heavy front-passenger door, and Avery scooted forward. "This puppy have lights and sirens? I'm late for a meeting on Capitol Hill, and it's all your fault."

The agent gave his colleague a brief nod. "Buckle up."

SIXTEEN

Speaker of the House DuBose Porter grew up on the edge of Alabama, where visiting the nicest grocery store meant a Sunday trip to Columbus, Georgia. A lifetime there yielded a few character traits. He tolerated ignorance with good humor, and he had a passing fondness for wicked sarcasm. But he hated being played for a fool. Intentional rudeness stoked ire, rarely forgiveness. Any combination earned you an enemy for life. He worked hard to be an unforgettable enemy.

Democracy teetered on the edge, but the precipitate cause—Avery Keene—was AWOL. Where the hell was she? He had no patience today. A good last week had turned into a shitty weekend, and Monday was off to an equally crappy start.

All because that weak-kneed Secretary Espinoza took his name off the impeachment letter, and now President Stokes was back in power. Instead of surging into the final weeks of the election with a moribund president held hostage by his unexpectedly cutthroat VP, Brandon Stokes had gotten a new chance to screw them over.

Majority leader and U.S. senator Ken Neighbors, who had taken up post on Porter's settee, swilled his third helping of Johnny Walker Blue. At 6'6, the lanky senator from Connecticut had the wingspan of a condor, not to mention a hollow leg. At the moment, he seemed determined to fill it with the most expensive whiskey he hadn't bought.

DuBose scooped up the bottle and twisted the top closed. "You already owe me a bottle of Michter's from Halloween. Don't think I've forgotten," he complained. "Where the devil is she?"

"Who the hell cares? Doesn't matter. The minority leader is waffling," Ken volunteered morosely. "Says his commonsense Republican members are starting to hear about a cover-up. Protesters are showing up on the campaign trail, at town halls. Son of a bitch promised me fourteen votes for this thing, but if he musters nine, I'll eat your hat."

Without Republican support for Stokes's impeachment, a doomsday scenario had started to take shape. Vice President Slosberg loses her grip on the cabinet, and President Stokes is reinstated. *Check.* The House votes for articles of impeachment, and the Senate holds a two-day trial. *Check and on its way.* The U.S. Senate, faced with the evidence of their eyes and the question of their valor, blink and acquit him a week before Election Day. *Likely.* Stokes coasts to victory, Democrats lose five seats in the Senate and dozens in the House. *Fuck.*

Neighbors mused about the prospects of returning to the mewling post of minority leader, which caused him to reach for another swallow of whiskey. As the liquid burn subsided, he asked, "Did your team call her again?"

"Called, texted. Hell, if we still had carrier pigeons, they'd be in flight." Speaker Porter stalked to the door that led to his outer office. "Lucinda!"

His chief of staff of nearly two decades appeared instantly. "Yeah, boss?"

"You find her yet?"

"I was just getting off the phone when you bellowed," Lucinda explained. "She is en route. Should be here in the next five minutes." Anticipating his response, she added quickly, "Capitol Police have instructions to wave her through, and I've sent Rocco down to escort her up."

He gave a brusque nod. "About damn time."

"Sir?" Lucinda used the soothing tone that had kept her twin boys from destroying her sanity during their formative years. "Congressman Boylen is scheduled to be on *PoliticsNOW* this evening. The booker called our office, asking if we wanted to slate anyone for rebuttal."

"Rebutting what?" he growled.

"Boylen claims to have proof that Ms. Keene manufactured the video evidence used to implicate the president. He also told the producers that you and Chairman Finberg illegally suppressed testimony that would exonerate Stokes. He's got witnesses."

"Get Representative Fairchild on the line. We read her in on the FBI's review of the videos, confirmed by NSA and CIA. She knows they're accurate. Hell, she met with Srinivasan and Cooper, who both confessed to the research Tigris was doing. Plus, she knew President Cadres well. That's why she voted for impeachment, for God's sake. Stokes is evil, and Daphne Fairchild's gotta be the one to say it."

"I already called her, boss."

"Good. She hates that little pissant."

"Yes, she does, but she's balking. Things are getting ugly everywhere—even in her race. Conspiracy theorists have been whipping up crowds across the country. State troopers have been posted outside her campaign headquarters since the vote. The latest polling shows impeachment up by only two points. If she publicly disputes Boylen, there's no telling what the nuts out there will do."

Porter moved through scenarios. If he and Minority Leader Kingston were on speaking terms, they could have coordinated a response to protect Fairchild and keep his decimation of Stokes on the move. Instead, the lily-livered sycophant would no doubt be encouraging the crazies to terrorize his members.

"Call Daphne back. Tell her that she should go on the show tonight to rebut Boylen. While she's at it, she can announce that we will be fast-tracking $2.5 million for the Tucson Innovation Center and $2.8 million for the Rural Revitalization Project. We'll get it into the reconciliation budget in December. That should be enough to push her over the top on election day."

Lucinda blinked twice. "Really? A carve-out for her? What about our guy? Gutierrez is within three points—we could take Daphne's seat."

"I don't need another Democrat out of Arizona if I lose the majority due to a late red wave. Fairchild is a Republican I can work with, and I've got to solve the problems in front of me. Let Gutierrez know that we'll have the governor appoint him to something big. He'll be able to take the seat in two years."

He calculated the fallout and deemed it acceptable. "And call Walt over at the DCCC. No last-minute heroics to salvage the race. Let Fairchild take it."

The intercom on Lucinda's desk squawked, "We have Ms. Keene."

"Go grab her and bring her into my office."

Moments later, Avery was unceremoniously ushered into the Speaker's inner sanctum. Majority Leader Neighbors rose to his full height, and his handshake seemed to swallow the lower third of her arm. He gestured to the settee and moved to a nearby armchair. Speaker Porter simply loomed.

"I apologize for my tardiness," she said as she sat across from the gentlemen who controlled the second branch of government. Rather than risk another summons by telling the truth, she hedged about her excuse. "I had another matter that's become rather urgent."

The vague explanation lifted the Speaker's brow. "More important than removing a would-be tyrant and confirmed murderer from office?"

"I'm not sure," she responded honestly. "But I don't know what else I can do to assist. Chairman Finberg and House counsel told me they wouldn't require any further testimony. To my understanding, the articles have been delivered to the Senate. My part is done."

Ken Neighbors, known for his courtly charm, took the lead. "This process is about more than simply securing the votes to remove President Stokes. You know better than anyone in America what he is capable of doing."

"Of course."

"And how you handled yourself this summer, you also comprehend the gravity of what could happen if he avoids impeachment and is reelected."

"I haven't allowed myself to imagine that could happen," Avery admitted. "Do you actually believe he'll get away with it? The news has been running the story here, and India's government is in shambles. Tigris has international implications. China has had to disavow their scientists, and other labs are suspending vital research. No international leader will do business with America as long as Stokes is in power."

"All true," the majority leader confirmed. "Have you checked your social media feed recently?"

Suddenly wary, Avery shook her head. "I've been advised to stay off the internet for the time being."

The Speaker took over. "The latest QAnon theory has taken up where your last deposition left off. You and some Jamaican heartthrob manufactured the evidence being used to attack Stokes, funded by Cooper's blood money."

"You know that's not true." Avery made the plaintive protest, but the twin videos of Judge Whitner proved how hollow the truth could be. "The NSA and the FBI have verified authenticity. And I put the money in trust for my mom."

"All of it?"

"Most of it. I had to pay off some debts."

"Like to your island Lothario."

"It didn't happen, Mr. Speaker!"

"I know it didn't. So do the Republicans. It's a right-wing cocktail of innuendo, coincidence, and false allegations. But they also know your protests of innocence aren't worth a damn in the court of public opinion. Stokes is a war hero and a whistleblower who protected our country as a civilian and a soldier." The Speaker got to his feet, preparing his pitch. "In a nation as polarized as we are, reality is fluid."

"No, it's not," Avery replied sardonically. "But I'm sure that's not your point."

"I'll correct myself. For a whole lot of folks, an unprecedented glut of information and a distrust of government have given them permission to create their own sense of reality." He paused for a second. "This impeachment, coming during an election year, has taken a nation already at a ten and shoved us to a fifteen."

Majority Leader Neighbors bent toward her. "I don't have the votes to impeach the president, Avery. Not sixty-seven out of one hundred."

Avery had spent too much time in D.C. to be surprised, but the clay feet of America's political leaders still hurt. In a defeated tone, she asked, "How many do you have?"

"Best guess is sixty-one, maybe sixty-two."

"So you're down several votes and afraid that Stokes will be acquitted." Avery folded her arms, her expression mulish. "Cut to the chase. How do you expect me to secure the first successful impeachment in presidential history?"

"I'll be blunt." Porter flanked her by settling on the arm of the sofa. "Americans need to be reminded how dire the situation is. This is a moment that requires patriotism—a symbol of what is at stake if we fail. No one represents our precarious state more than your judge, Avery. He risked his life and his reputation to reveal what President Stokes has done. He put himself on death's door to spare the nation the same."

Hearing his cue buried in the tortured metaphors, the majority leader made the ask. "You still hold his power of attorney, and we need Justice Howard Wynn to resign from the Supreme Court effective immediately. Let America grapple with the reality that the next president will appoint his replacement and possibly shift the balance of power on the Court. Will you do that for the future of America?"

"Absolutely not." Avery popped off the settee and waved her hands wide in rebuke. "I will not pretend to resign Justice Wynn for a second time. It barely worked the first time."

The Speaker got to his feet as well. "We're not asking you to pretend, Avery. We really want him off the Court."

Avery froze. "You want to give President Stokes an open Supreme Court seat two weeks before Election Day?"

"Hell, no," the majority leader retorted. "We want to spike turnout with the specter of Brandon Stokes filling that swing seat. Raise the stakes."

"You think Americans care so much about the workings of the Supreme Court that they will vote against Stokes just to keep him from having a choice?" She gave a voluble snort of derision. "Half of America hates Justice Wynn on any given day, and the composition of his detractors changes based on the issue. Every day, I read letters and emails from people who blame him for nearly everything. Inflation, the moon landing, the presence of racism, the weakened effectiveness of racism. No one will weep if Justice Wynn resigns."

"Our polling shows that Democrats are afraid of losing the Court," he protested. "This close to the election, it could be the issue that galvanizes turnout."

"I'm no political expert, gentlemen, but I do know the average person. She's worried about food, gas, rent, how bad her job is, and how desperately she wants to keep it. If she's got kids, then she's concerned about their schools, their teachers, and whether they'll make it home safely. For the past twenty years, the Supreme Court has been a feather on Osiris's scale of justice. A case here or there to tip the balance in our favor. Not in the favor of Democrats or

Republicans. In favor of the people. And the people don't give a damn about Justice Howard Wynn. They care about their lives."

The Speaker rubbed at his chin and motioned for silence.

Ignoring him, Ken argued, "We need a Hail Mary, DuBose." He implored Avery, "Because of you, Americans are more aware of the Court than ever. Fear of an open seat might make them act."

"Hush, Ken," the Speaker said quietly. "Ms. Keene is correct. We're thinking like the men in charge, not the men on the ground."

"Or women," Avery muttered.

"Or women," he added. "People don't move because of who is on the Court. They move because of what's before the Court. What issue will make their lives easier or infinitely worse? They don't give a good damn about an old man in a coma when he's one of the most powerful men in the country."

"So what is our play?"

"We'll have to give that some more thought." The Speaker extended a hand to Avery. "We appreciate your insights, Ms. Keene. Thank you for coming by."

"I'm free to go?"

The Speaker chuckled. "I don't intend to kidnap you. But I would ask that this conversation stay between us. You are not a political operative or at all beholden to Congress or any political party. I apologize if we overstepped."

Bemused, Avery shrugged. Of her experiences with the various branches of government, this one was certainly more benign. "I hope you all figure out a way to win the elections. I'll cast my ballot, but I can't pull Justice Wynn into political fisticuffs. I'm not even sure he is a Democrat."

"He's not." The major leader mirrored Avery's shrug. "I checked. He's never chosen a party. Never voted in a partisan primary."

"That's not hard to avoid in D.C.," noted the Speaker.

"It's probably why he lives here," Avery offered. "Absolute impartiality in all things." Snagging her bag, she headed for the exit. "Good luck."

The door shut with a quiet thud behind her. Speaker Porter waited for the second outer door to close. He motioned for Ken to sit. "Keene is right. We can't win this with an open seat as bait. We need something more tangible."

"How? The House is in recess, and I've only got the Senate until next week. No way will the minority leader let me bring up one of your bills to give every American a cow or outlaw fracking."

"Not what I have in mind, my friend." He thrummed the leather fabric, mind whirring. "Focus on rounding up your votes for impeachment. I'll get back to you."

SEVENTEEN

Nyx tagged Hayden and waited. Her device included a state-of-the-art private-label VPN that kept all her information scrambled, including the phone's IMEI. Her employer answered on the first hail.

"Target has been busy." Nyx ran through Avery's day. "Several hours spent at the FBI headquarters, and then at the U.S. Congressional building. I tracked her until she got whisked away by staff."

On the other end, Hayden knitted her brow. "No idea who she went to see?"

"I used facial rec to identify Agent Robert Lee of the Criminal Investigative Division. I assume she reported to him about Davies." Nyx hesitated, then continued. "Between her meetings, she departed in a Secret Service vehicle."

"Heading for where?"

"I tailed them to a house in Virginia. Had to drop back once the roads got isolated, but I confirmed my suspicion. She met with Stokes."

"They despise each other."

Nyx made a sound of assent. "POTUS had a second visitor too. Congressman Luke Boylen."

"Connected?"

"I doubt it. Their overlap was nominal. However, she was out of range for twenty-eight minutes. When they departed, the vehicle used its sirens to rush her back to D.C."

"Speculation?"

"I believe she knows something. But I can't break through her boyfriend's signal jammer. I'm contracting with local talent to get me a window. I need to hear what she's saying. Unless you wish to cut our losses and shut her down."

A moment's silence on the other end of the call. "Not until we have confirmation of a breach. Her profile is too high for mistakes."

"Copy."

Reams of pages spilled from the laser jet printer in the corner of Avery's small office. Like Justice Wynn, she preferred the tactile relevance of paper. Sure, she was contributing to the demise of the planet, but she was old-school. Highlighters, red pens, and close reads.

Per the Chief's request, she had pulled recent audits and reports on cyberthreats to the judiciary. Casting a wider net, she'd added related companies and hunted for additional leads. To do her job well, it was Avery's habit to immerse herself in a topic, sink as deep as she could until she felt as close to expert as possible. Thanks to Jared, she already had a head start on this one.

Her phone beeped with an unusual tone she hadn't heard before. Lifting the phone, she saw a notification from the app Vance had asked her to download. Reluctantly, she replied to the oblique query that asked her to connect. She waited impatiently for the call to connect. Nothing appeared on the screen other than a black box. Her image appeared in a second box. The anonymity confirmed her caller.

"What do you want, Major Vance?"

"Your communication skills suck, Ms. Keene." When she didn't take the bait, he said, "I have more information for you. If you're willing to listen."

Avery looked at the stacks of paper she'd printed based on Agent Gehl's leads. If Vance could give her a place to start, she'd take it. "I answered your cryptic call, didn't I? What do you have?"

"An Israeli assassin. An expatriated American with a grudge. And confirmation that a wide-scale attack is unfolding."

Avery kept her face blank. She too had an Israeli assassin on her list, and the plot had been Agent Gehl's guess. But an angry American was new information. "Who's the disgruntled American?"

"Unknown, but he is connected with the private defense industry overseas. Armies for hire. Have militia, will travel. The word is out that he intends to attack during the election, hoping to inflict maximum carnage when our country is at its most polarized. A brilliant plan—I've used similar techniques for regime change."

Avery felt a bit nauseated by his easy admission. "You shouldn't brag about overthrowing governments, Major."

"You're not a child, Ms. Keene. The world doesn't organize itself. Power players do. And like it or not, you are on the periphery of those decision-makers. With tutelage, you could become one yourself."

"I have a job."

"To the casual observer, it's not much of one."

Grinding her teeth, she bit out, "Other than these vague warnings and insults, do you have any actionable intelligence?"

"One of my informants intercepted a string of digits and a status update on a malware attack. I haven't tried to decrypt them, but you're as close to a human computer as I've seen, or your boyfriend might have a clue. See what you can do with them."

Avery heard a rustle of paper. "Are you texting?"

"No. Reciting. So listen closely. 434. 314. 982. 850."

"That's it? Random numbers?"

"It's what I've got. Apparently, a North Korean spy ring cribbed it from some communiqué, but they got booted out of the conversation before they could get any more."

"So you're consorting with North Korean hackers. Good to know." Nevertheless, she committed the sequence to memory. Out of good conscience, she warned him, "The last person to give me a string of digits to decipher got shot."

"As the recently deceased Mr. Davies learned, you are dangerous to be around, Ms. Keene."

"What do you know about him?"

Vance ignored the question. "Good evening, Avery. I'll be in touch when I have more."

The call terminated. Avery almost shifted gears to focus on his useless clue, but ego refused to let her dance to his tune. Instead, she turned her attention to a separate task. Avery opened a presentation document and began to type. Quickly, she built out an organizational tree identical to the one Agent Gehl had shown her. Calling on her memory of the screen she could never admit to seeing, she populated the chart in a mirror of the work she'd seen. Included in the branches were all the companies AUSA Johnson had identified and secured warrants against. Below the names, the JTF had filled in types of warrants, dates, and any subtargets.

Like before, she easily recognized several companies that Jason Johnson had gotten authorization to tap. Dozens, though, had names that gave no hint as to their relevance. Avery decided to compile a list of all available data on each company, hoping to see some sort of pattern emerge. Moving to a new screen, she created a spreadsheet where she repopulated the corporate names. The columns would contain identical information culled from LexisNexis and the great aggregator, Google. Place of incorporation. Chief officers. Any and all public information available.

In the U.S., even a private company was shockingly naked to a master of data collection. Once a person understood all the places data could be scraped, gathered, and reported, he could uncover a myriad of sins. So she would search EDGAR filings with the SEC to locate companies by the NAICS codes—the North American Industry Classification System. Her next haunt would be the websites of the relevant secretary of state, which would list date of incorporation and who was legally responsible for keeping records.

As Agent Gehl had warned, Jason Johnson tracked down forty-eight firms worthy of his attention. Judge Whitner signed off on warrants to violate the privacy of each of these companies doing business in America. The irony that Avery intended to duplicate their violations wasn't lost on her, but no alternative presented itself. If she wanted to understand what was going on, this was her way inside. Much safer, she told herself, than inserting herself directly into the investigation. Plus, she still owed the Chief a memo on cybersecurity by Thursday. After today's misadventures, research would be a welcome respite.

Cracking her knuckles, Avery slid closer to the computer. Diving into minutiae was her forte. Her specialty. And, after the past four months, her raison d'être. The printer continued to spit out warnings about cybercriminals and hacking scares. What she found in Agent Gehl's slideshow might expand the list.

She plowed through the list of companies, making careful notes about anomalies like common registered agents or geographic similarities. Something in the names snagged her attention, but she couldn't quite pin down what she saw. *Focus on the landscape first,* she chided herself. *Don't get caught in the details yet.*

A light knock startled her. It had been weeks since anyone had found a reason to venture near her office. She glanced at the clock, surprised by the late hour. 8:14 p.m. Hours since she started diving. Flexing her tight shoulders, she responded, "Come in?"

"You sure about that?" Carmen Patrick, a brilliant medical researcher turned star attorney, poked her head around the slightly open door. One of Justice Estrada's clerks, Carmen had been the one to warn her about the attempt to force her out.

"Since it's you, absolutely."

She pushed the door open and closed it behind her. "Avery, turn on some lights," she scolded, flipping on the switch. "Bad for your eyes."

"I have a lamp," Avery said, but silently admitted her eyes felt suddenly better. "What brings you to Boot Hill?"

Chuckling lightly, Carmen helped herself to the sole empty chair. "I didn't know you liked spaghetti Westerns. My grandmother loved them."

Pleased she'd gotten the reference, Avery smiled. "My dad spent every Saturday watching a strict regimen of *Gunsmoke, The Rifle-man, Wyatt Earp,* and *Big Valley.* Seems an appropriate moniker for a room where careers go to die."

"Avery—"

"Ignore my maudlin," she urged. "What brings you here?"

Carmen gave her a gentle smile. "Just checking on you. That must have been tough."

"What are you talking about?"

"You didn't see the president's presser?"

"No. When?"

"Twenty minutes ago. I'd have come sooner, but we've got oral arguments tomorrow and I had to prep Justice Estrada."

Avery shifted her full attention to her fellow clerk. "Give me the gist, Carmen."

"I think you'd better watch it." She circled behind the desk as Avery typed the search terms into the browser. "Brace yourself."

President Stokes struck a familiar pose that she'd seen before. Like the first time they'd met, he stood behind a podium in the Rose Garden. And, as the audio played, she was once again his chosen topic.

"Sadly, Ms. Keene and her Democratic allies have taken the actions of a traitor and tried to sully my name. My reputation. As commander in chief, I take full responsibility for my error in judg-ment, for putting Major Will Vance in a position that allowed him to betray our nation. I will take responsibility, but I will not lay claim to his heinous actions. I call upon Ms. Keene to retract her statements and for Congress to stop this illegitimate process before the damage to our nation is irreparable. We are a strong country, able to disagree without resorting to falsehoods, without besmirching character. If Democrats are so hungry for a victory, they can win on the playing fields of Election Day. Not in a kangaroo court."

Avery muted the sound. "He's an ass."

"Indeed." Carmen patted her shoulder. "I thought you should know."

"Thanks for checking on me." Avery turned back to the computer, when a second video caught her attention. Congressman Boylen had swapped out his riding gear for a tailored three-piece suit and a natty bow tie that hinted at fascism. The ruddy-faced anchor on the all-streaming news channel twisted toward him and rapped the desk.

She punched the volume up, and Carmen hovered behind her. "I didn't see this one."

"Looks like it's live," Avery said, pointing to the chyron. "Liberty News, your one-stop shop for propaganda."

On cue, the anchor intoned, "Congressman, the patriots here at Liberty News have appreciated your candor over the past few weeks. We've seen RINOs betray our president over and over again, including Vice President Samantha Slosberg and Representative Daphne Fairchild, who served on the secret panel that authorized the articles of impeachment. You voted against their treachery, but the sham has now moved to the U.S. Senate. Can you shed light on what is coming up next?"

"I have disagreed with President Brandon Stokes on issues ranging from tax policy to prayer in schools to our needless intervention in foreign wars. But I know him to be an honorable man who fought for this country like so many heroes before him. That is why I am willing to go to war to protect the office of the presidency from domestic enemies." He brandished his phone. "If your viewers will go to VerityVictory.org, I have uploaded recordings of the confidential depositions of Avery Keene, the nursemaid to senile old Howard Wynn. She has been credibly accused of manufacturing the evidence used to impeach President Stokes."

"What else will we find, Congressman?"

"Information on her co-conspirators. Dr. Ling Yin. Former Navy lieutenant Jared Wynn. Attorney Noah Fox. All the data is there, and I urge each of you patriots to review and understand what is at stake. We are fighting for our very souls, America."

"Oh, God," Avery exclaimed as she jumped up, barely avoiding a collision with Carmen. Her mind spun with the implications of what Boylen had just done, outing her friends, giving information about their lives, and putting them in grave danger. "He doxxed them."

"How can I help?"

"I don't know," Avery said, her throat tightening. "I just need to get home. Now."

EIGHTEEN

With efficient but terrified speed, Avery saved her research to a thumb drive, powered down her computer, and scooped up her bag. "Carmen, please tell the Chief what we saw and let her know I'll call when I get home."

Carmen raced to keep step with her. "Shouldn't you go see her yourself? Tell her what's happening."

When Avery ignored her, Carmen grabbed her arm to slow her down. Avery whipped around. "What?"

"Avery, take a breath."

"I can't," she exploded. "If you knew what I know—"

"I don't," Carmen interrupted. "But someone should. Starting with the Chief. Come on." Half leading, half dragging, she guided Avery to the chief justice's chambers. One look at their faces had the secretary waving them through. She buzzed the Chief in warning.

Chief Justice Roseborough opened her door before Avery could knock. She gave Carmen a warm smile. "Thank you, Dr. Patrick. I believe Ms. Keene and I can take it from here."

"Chief, I need to get home," Avery protested but allowed herself to be led into the office. Too keyed up, she refused to sit. "Boylen and his cronies have doxxed me and my friends. What if they find out where my mother is? A U.S. congressman just sent out a dog whistle for his rabid mob to come after us." Left unsaid was her fear of who else might be paying attention to her. The Mercedes that tracked her home was never far from her mind, and though she hadn't seen it again, she refused to take chances with her family. "I need to go. Now."

"I won't tell you to calm down, Avery, but I will ask you to listen." The Chief motioned to the television screen that juxtaposed the images of Congressman Boylen and Avery side by side. "The Supreme Court Police have standing orders from me to monitor stories about you. The moment this one surfaced, a D.C. police car was dispatched to your home. Our team also made contact with Agent Lee at the FBI. He, in turn, has reached out to your friends to ensure that they are escorted home tonight. Sadly, none of you work normal hours, so he has not been able to connect with everyone."

Before Avery could speak, the Chief lifted a hand. "The Boylen story broke only minutes ago, which is why I had not yet reached out to you. You were next on my list."

"And Rita?"

"According to Agent Lee, the Laurel PD continue to have a patrol near her facility. They will double their presence tonight, and they are in contact with the on-site security team." Teresa approached Avery, gently clasping her shoulder. "Everyone is okay, Avery. I'm so sorry this is happening."

"This is bad, Chief. Very bad."

"So I gathered from my brief conversation with Agent Lee. Would you care to expound?"

Aware of their pact with Agent Gehl, Avery temporized. "I turned over the devices to the FBI's task force. Then I was detained by the Secret Service."

"Excuse me?"

Given Boylen's breach of confidentiality, Avery felt more comfortable being completely transparent. "During my deposition in

September, a Republican congressman accused me of manufacturing the evidence I shared with the Court in June."

"They believe we were duped by a fake?"

"Chief, the videos they used to blackmail Judge Whitner were
exceptional. Deepfakes exist, but that's not what I got from Ani."

"Go on."

"Mr. Guarasci told me to ignore the allegations, as did Chairman Finberg. Then they never recalled me. All the members of the
committees that deposed me voted out the articles of impeachment,
except for three Republicans and that independent from Missouri."

"How is the Secret Service involved?"

"Agent Lee introduced me to Special Agent in Charge Sarah Beth
Gehl. She is leading the NCIJTF. They debriefed me on the materials from Preston Davies. Thirty minutes later, an agent from the
Secret Service comes to her office and tells me I'm under investigation for money laundering and conspiracy. The theory is that Nigel
Cooper paid me to have a stranger I never met create the video to
sink the president."

"That's absurd. And an imaginative stretch of their jurisdiction."
The Chief sank gracefully onto the sofa and patted the cushion beside
her. "Might I surmise that you did not spend so long out of the
office because you were being interrogated at their headquarters?"

"No, ma'am. They took me to see President Stokes." Chief Roseborough's eyebrow rose as Avery quickly recounted their meeting.
"For the trifecta, I went to Capitol Hill as well."

"Well . . . you've been a busy girl."

"A very long day." Shoulders slumping, Avery confessed, "I can't
put my family in danger again, Chief. It's not fair."

"Right now, the only person endangering anyone is Congressman
Boylen." She rose and circled behind her desk. "Debi, please connect me to the FBI director."

Avery took the opportunity to send an encrypted group text to

Ling, Noah, and Jared, apologizing for the latest security issue. Jared waved off her apology, and Noah joked about being flattered by the attention. As she waited for Ling's snarky response, the call with the director connected and the Chief engaged the speakerphone.

"Director, thank you for taking my call."

FBI Director LaTiesa Alford replied cordially, "Anytime, Chief. How can I help?"

"I assume you've been kept apprised of the situation surrounding Ms. Keene. She is here with me in my office, by the way."

"Yes, ma'am. We've got a team coordinating with law enforcement as we speak."

"Good, good. My deeper concern is with the source of the threat."

"Our threat response unit has had VerityVictory.org under watch for several months now. Their willingness to spew disinformation rivals QAnon."

"This is the first time they have involved part of our Court family," the Chief said. "What is of greater concern is the role that Congressman Boylen played in amplifying this breach of privacy. To have a sitting congressman doxxing a law clerk, a physician, and their friends is unprecedented and unwarranted."

Across town, Director Alford sat in her office listening to Teresa Roseborough on speakerphone. "Here's the operative question, Chief—is it illegal?" Alford looked across her desk at the two lawyers dispatched to her by the attorney general. In normal times, the chief justice of the Supreme Court would have placed her irritated call to the AG's office, but these were anything but ordinary times. As FBI director, Alford had built a career of careful agnosticism. Both of her Senate confirmations had been unanimous because her personal politics were ambiguous.

"I have some bright minds querying that very issue right now," Alford intoned. "If you'll give me until daybreak, I will have a plan of action for you. Until then, I encourage Ms. Keene to listen closely to her protective detail and to follow their directions. And unlike this summer, to not slip her leash."

The final warning carried a familiar note of exasperation, and Avery flushed guiltily sitting across from Roseborough. "She got your message, Director. I'll look forward to hearing from you in the morning. Good night."

"Thank you, Chief," Avery said. She leaned back into the soft couch cushion, and relief started to settle, but a moment later, her phone buzzed.

"Avery Keene."

"Ms. Keene, this is Agent Craig. I was asked by Agent Lee to notify you that we have secured Dr. Yin and are transporting her directly to the safe house."

"Safe house? What are you talking about?"

Avery heard Ling's voice in the background. "Give me the phone." A second later, she came on the line. "Avery, don't freak out. Some wack job called in a bomb threat to the hospital. The FBI is fairly certain it's a hoax, but the chief resident took me off rotation and sent me home."

"If I may," Agent Craig reappeared on the call. "We have instructions from Agent Lee to move Dr. Yin to a different site. We have reason to believe your apartment is no longer safe. There are demonstrators in front of your building. Our assessment is that they are largely nonthreatening, but we intend to avoid confrontation."

"Where are you taking her?"

"Agent Lee will explain. He's on his way to your location. I am to convey his apologies for a delay in contacting you. Per his instructions, he said to tell you, quote, you're damn complicated, unquote."

Avery thanked the agent for the message and disconnected. "Agent Lee is meeting me here," she said to the Chief, knowing plans had already been made.

"Carmen saved us the trouble. If she hadn't steered you here,

Court security would have herded you back." The chief justice gave her a troubled look. "Is there anything else you need to tell me, Avery? Perhaps about your meeting with the JTF?"

Torn, Avery hesitated. She'd promised Agent Gehl secrecy, but she owed the Chief more of the truth. "I saw something in the data I gathered when we spoke with them. I don't know what it is yet."

"Is it something the smartest minds in cybercrime can figure out on their own?" The question, though mildly sarcastic, held a true note of inquiry. The Chief had seen Avery at work. Her unique mind and absurd attention to detail were two of the qualities that boosted her up a deep pile of applicants for a Supreme Court clerk-ship. "Is it worth the risk?"

Avery chose her words carefully. "I don't know, Chief. Two men are dead, and so is a judge. I won't insert myself into their investiga-tion, but I can't wipe my mind clean."

Roseborough assessed her, letting the silence fill her office. "How do you plan to resolve that?"

Avery knew the question was coming. "All I can say is this impeachment battle is splitting the country in half, partisans are shooting first and asking questions later, and I'm not sure how the deaths of a federal judge and her clerk are related to the impeach-ment. But I've got a pit in my stomach after digesting reams of raw data—and I haven't figured out why." She decided not to mention her new line of inquiry from Major Vance. Taking clues from a fugi-tive would not reassure the Chief.

"You're putting yourself at risk, Avery—and those you love."

"President Stokes and his cronies are the reason my family is in harm's way. Nothing I'm researching has anything to do with it. I haven't seen a tail since I thought I was followed last week. Besides, I've got the FBI camping out with me, and apparently I'm on my way to a safe house."

"Glib doesn't suit you."

She stood and slowly moved around the Chief's office. "Glib may be all I have. The president of the United States intends to ruin my life. We both fully comprehend what that means."

"Yes." The simple response spoke volumes. "Agent Lee should be here shortly."

True to the Chief's word, Agent Lee arrived eight minutes later. "Thank you for your help on this, ma'am," he said as he walked through the door.

"Glad I could be of service," the Chief replied. "Perhaps you can update us on what is happening."

"Dr. Yin, Mr. Fox, and Mr. Wynn are at Mr. Wynn's home." His jaw clenched. "They all refused to go to a safe house despite my strident urging."

"If you look at the address on VerityVictory.org, it's a dummy address he uses to get his mail," Avery explained. "Jared has state-of-the-art security, and we discussed this as a contingency plan months ago. His name isn't on the property records because of the threats Justice Wynn used to receive. Instead, the property is listed in the name of a family trust. Not foolproof, but nowhere you put us will be better."

"I appreciate your faith in the Bureau," Agent Lee retorted sardonically.

"We have faith in you and your agents," she placated him. "But the summer taught us to be prepared to take care of ourselves. Keep a team on us, but his house is the safest place for me to be."

Unwilling to argue a point he wouldn't win, Agent Lee shifted gears. "We're working directly with the security team at Haven, but we can move your mother if you'd like."

"If you recommend it."

"We haven't received any credible threats against any of you, but these elections and the impeachment have ratcheted up the tensions across the spectrum. I advise that you let me lock you down for the night, and we will continue to monitor the situation." When Avery nodded, he added, "But I reserve the right to move you and the Scooby Gang at my discretion. No arguments."

"Agreed."

The Chief stood and returned to her desk. "Agent Lee, I expect a briefing in the morning and a report on any changes. I have also spoken with Director Alford about my concerns."

"Yes, ma'am. I've heard. We're on it."

"Good. Please take care of Ms. Keene, and yourself, Agent Lee."

He ushered Avery toward the door, and he felt the urge to bow as he left. "I'm all good. It's her you have to keep an eye on."

Avery made eye contact with the Chief and gave a grateful smile. "Thank you, Chief. Unless you disagree, I'll plan to work from home tomorrow."

NINETEEN

P ut the crystal globe from Prime Minister Dubrov in the corner. Have the NSA in here tomorrow at 6:00 a.m. to sweep
again for listening devices. Daily sweeps, in fact. And I
wanted Slosberg in my Oval Office five minutes ago." President
Stokes barked out the orders to a line of terrified staffers who had
been plucked from their regular assignments across a variety of
departments. A wave of termination emails had gone out at midnight Sunday, at his direction, disguised as reassignments. He craved
the blind panic of those scurrying to do his bidding. The hiatus that
bitch had forced on him would not be forgotten. Neither would
any of the underlings who helped her usurp his post who wondered
why they'd been cast out of the West Wing and over to the General
Services Administration.

In his exile, he nevertheless kept his command structure in place.
Eight years in the White House—between his tenure as vice president and president—meant that he had allies in unexpected places.
Secretaries willing to copy and share memos. Janitors who emptied
waste baskets into mailing envelopes instead of shredders. Among
the faithful, Brandon Stokes was the victim of hubris, but not his
own.

"Where the devil is the vice president?" he barked at the closest
trembling twentysomething aide. "I told you I want her here now."

Frightened, the hapless young man rabbited out of the office, ostensibly to fetch the VP, but he knew he wouldn't find her. Office gossip had her entrenched at the Second Family's residence, licking her wounds. Instead, the aide was getting his crap and heading to a bar. A fellow staffer who had worked for both presidents—the real one and the acting one—gave him two pieces of advice when he'd been called up that morning: keep your mouth shut and get the hell out as soon as you can. It was time to update his résumé.

Inside the Oval Office, President Stokes told the remaining staffers, "Go away and wait by your phones. Tonight will be a long one." He barely bit off a guffaw as they rushed to escape his domain. Amateurs.

Will Vance would have appreciated the abject fear and obeisance. The errant thought hit Stokes with a pang of real grief mixed with anger. He and Vance had shared a camaraderie he didn't have with other colleagues. Fucking absconder.

Stokes stomped around the actual Resolute desk and prepared for battle. The opening salvo had been launched by putting Avery Keene on notice. He planned to watch Luke's television interview later, but reports were already flooding in about protesters. Twitter was alight with speculation and invective. Better yet, the FBI had been dispatched to soothe the frayed tempers. Excellent opportunity to show his leadership and beg for reason from the outraged masses.

"Mr. President?" His longtime secretary poked her head inside. "Congressman Boylen is here to see you. Said you're expecting him."

"Show him in, Carla."

Bounding into the Oval Office, his first visit since a high school trip that let rising young conservatives peer inside, Luke tried not to be awestruck. An impossible task. He gawked at the iconic rug, the broad windows that framed the seat of power. "How'd I do, sir?"

President Stokes greeted him with a hearty handshake. "Splendid, Congressman. Perfect return to my volley."

"Word has it that demonstrations are being planned in front of the Supreme Court tomorrow. Also, I have some good folks who plan to demand the vice president's resignation. They'll be appearing on some shows tomorrow to start the call."

"Good, good." He pointed to one of the massive leather chairs that flanked his desk. Obediently, Luke sat down. "Yes, sir?"

"My understanding is that you face only token opposition in your seat, and you're likely to coast to victory in November."

The congressman drummed his fingers on his knee and grinned. "I have a very conservative district, sir. No Democrat has gotten more than twenty percent of the vote in decades. Indiana may have blue spots, but that's more like a rash than an actual problem."

President Stokes laughed appreciatively. "Well said. In fact, you have consistently impressed me with your communication skills. You seem to have mastered all the forms—speeches, social media, television."

"I'll take the compliment. But given the competition, the bar isn't exactly high."

"Your point?"

"Our side gets credit for being better at messaging. The other side likes to flout how smart they are at policy. But messaging isn't worth the paper it's written on if the delivery sucks. Or if our messengers aren't credible—like Slosberg or Fairchild or Larkey. RINOs undermine us, sir. When they corrupt our message by compromising with the enemy, we not only lose ground, we lose focus."

"I've been called a RINO by some of your allies. In fact, I believe you mentioned it in a commercial during your last campaign."

Luke squirmed for an instant. Somehow, this hadn't come up before during his visits with the president, and he should have expected it. "The media played up your willingness to work with the opposition, and for those of us in God's country, we got concerned."

Stokes cocked his head at the nervous acolyte before him. "And now?"

"Mr. President, I hope you understand my heart, sir. I stand with you. I am ready to fight for you. I believe you'd agree I already have," he responded testily.

"I'm not questioning your loyalty, Luke. But I have been burned by my closest friend. Surely you understand my caution."

Boylen settled back. "Yes, sir. Makes perfect sense."

"I have a reason for these queries, son." President Stokes came around to the front of his desk. Luke Boylen had the jawline of a Hollywood leading man and the instincts of a honey badger. His choice made complete sense. "How would you feel about a promotion? I'd like to make you my chief of staff."

"Starting when?"

The president's eyes narrowed. "Immediately. My former chief secured employment in the private sector during my absence, and I require an adjutant who can help me navigate the storms headed our way. Impeachment, the elections, and the rift growing in our party. You're the man for the job."

"Sir," he began, "I'm flattered. But you're asking me to give up my congressional seat before the election. Yours or mine."

"I'm asking you to take a leap of faith. I'm going to beat the Democrats with their bullshit show trial. On the first Tuesday after the first Monday in November, I'm going to crush them at the polls on Election Day like Ronald Reagan and Barack Obama's love child. Once I am inaugurated for the second time, I will reclaim our country and my honor." He reached out and gripped Luke by the shoulder. "I want you with me when I do."

President Stokes pinned him to the chair with a startlingly firm hand and a steady gaze that seemed to promise the world. Or dire retribution if he answered wrong. Two years into his time in the House, and he already had the minority leader by the short hairs. His stock at home was rising, and his coffers exploded every time he railed against the godless Left. Why give all that up to become lackey to a lame duck?

Before his ascendancy in the ranks of the conservative corps,

Luke Boylen excelled as a mechanical engineering student at Notre Dame. He burnished his credentials with a master's from MIT, and he had six patents to his name by twenty-three. One day, he'd be behind that desk under his own steam. One day.

"There are two types of chiefs, Mr. President. The glorified help-mates who carry your water and hope nothing splashes. Or the ones who carve a path and bulldoze the way to victory." He met the level regard with his own. "Which would I be?"

A sneer curled the president's upper lip. "Neither. I want a chief of staff who'll blow them all to hell."

The congressman rose to his full height, equal to that of Brandon Stokes. He extended his right hand. "It would be an honor to serve, Mr. President."

Bonsai had been dismantled, but Leon Adams still had one remaining task. For it, he bought his cousin Corey lunch at the local gas station, which boasted the best fried chicken in Smiths Chapel. Two clear plastic cups filled to the brim with sweet tea balanced precariously on the hood of his 1969 Dodge Charger. Leon reached for his drink and took a deep draught. In a few days, he would vanish. Where he was headed, no one had ever considered the epicurean delight of gas station chicken washed down by the heady brew of Southern legend. After thoughtful consideration, he had decided to live out the next phase of his life in Belize.

Like most Southerners, Leon reveled in the heat and had no use for snow. Like everyone he knew, he spoke only English, which made Belize as far south as he was willing to venture. The English-speaking nation featured affordable luxury homes for purchase, sandy beaches for lazing about, and faces that looked like his.

"Corey, can you do this?"

"No problem, cuz. Just plug it in, right?" He tucked into a rame-kin of coleslaw. "What does it do?"

"Makes us very rich." Leon admired Corey, the first of the Adams clan to go to college. Corey was the owner of the PlayStation that got Leon started. "You won't have trouble with security?"

"I'm good." Corey jutted his chin toward the badge clipped to his lapel. "I have access, and no one will question me. But you promise no one will get hurt?"

Leon hedged, "No one important, no."

"Wait—"

"Kidding!" Leon forced a laugh. The virus he was sending inside would trigger a specific set of events, and if he'd done his job, harm would come to some. He wasn't lying, though, when he said it was no one important. "I'm not a cartoon villain, C. Just trying to make a living."

"With your mind, you could be the next Bill Gates."

"He's good, but I'd rather be Tope Awotona."

"Who?"

"Black billionaire out of Atlanta by way of Nigeria." Leon wiped his mouth and his hands on a napkin. "Thank you, C. I owe you one."

"We're family." Corey embraced his cousin, who held on a touch longer than expected. Worried, Corey clapped his shoulder and eased him back. Best friends since childhood, he saw a shadow he'd never noticed before. Leon was the brightest of them, the steadiest. He might be older, but Leon was better. If Leon needed help, he'd do whatever was needed. "You okay, man? Seriously."

"I'm good, man. You take care of this, and our lives change forever." Leon stepped back and fist-bumped his cousin. "I'm better than good. Almost perfect."

TWENTY

What did you do this time?"

Noah lobbed the question the minute Avery was ushered into Jared's house, Agent Lee having preceded her through the door. Avery took her time, hanging her bag on its customary rack and dropping her jacket on one of the nearby hooks. Kicking off her boots, she reminded him, "They taught us not to blame the victim in law school, Noah. As my attorney, you should know that."

"That wasn't law school. It was *Law & Order*," he corrected, crossing over to envelop her in a hug. "I thought the impeachment hearings were exciting, but the fun continues. How are you?"

"Fine." She returned the embrace before craning her head to scan the empty room. "Where is everyone?"

"Jared is downstairs walking the FBI detail through his security setup. Ling is upstairs on a Zoom call with the hospital administrator and her chief resident. We thought you'd be here hours ago."

"At Ms. Keene's insistence," Agent Lee said flatly, "I took her to Laurel to visit her mother. She did not trust my team's evaluation."

Avery narrowed her eyes. "In D.C., the motto is trust but verify."

"How is Rita?" Noah asked quietly. "Did this, um, affect her?"

With a kind smile, Avery shook her head. "She's good. Worried, of course. But her counselor is keeping an eye on her, and she's got group tonight. I told her it was okay to share with her cohort anything she was feeling. Now isn't the time for her to be keeping secrets."

"A lesson her daughter would do well to internalize."

Avery spun around to see Ling descending the stairs. Disregarding their audience, she allowed her best friend to wrap her in a long hug. "Oops, I did it again," Avery quipped.

"Being clever won't stop me from kicking your overly intelligent, troublemaking ass," Ling warned, her arms tightening. "You okay?"

"I'm okay. Crazy day, though." Avery pressed their foreheads together briefly, and she felt a wash of calm comfort. Taking a step back, she said, "Let's wait for Jared. If y'all yell at me all at once, it will be much more efficient."

Noah stepped forward to join the knot of friends. Though he'd met them only a few months ago, they'd endured what seemed like a lifetime together. "Italian is in the kitchen. From my boyfriend's restaurant, so it's good even when it's cold. Grab a seat, and I'll make you a plate."

Grateful for the respite, Avery scooted up to the table and motioned for Ling to join her. "While we wait for the Grand Inquisition, tell me what's going on with the hospital. Do I need to get Agent Lee to write you a note?"

"The administrator is new. He's never had to deal with a bomb threat before." Ling turned and spoke to the FBI agent pretending not to listen. "I think your guy on-site has been more forthcoming with possibilities than is helpful. Dr. Wong is toggling between panic and hysteria."

The agent nodded. "I'll follow up. We don't expect the situation to escalate to an actionable scenario. We traced the call to a cell phone in Tennessee. The same IP address logged in to the Verity-

Victory site before making the threat. Our field agents should have the dunderhead in custody by morning, but we suspect it's an armchair warrior."

Ling laid a hand over Avery's. "And her safety? Is that at risk?"

Agent Lee glanced at the stairwell that led to the basement. "I agree with your friend. We should save that until you're all present."

"Gotcha." With that, Ling bounded out of her seat and jogged to the stairs, yanking open the heavy door with its RFID core. "Jared Wynn, stop showing off your toys! Your girl is home, and it's time to read her the riot act!"

Heavy boots thundered up the steps, and Ling barely had time to jump out of the way. Jared jerked Avery up from the table and swallowed her in a tight hold. "You okay?"

Wrapping her arms around him, she responded with a muffled, grateful "Yes. I promise." She allowed herself a moment to sink in, then gently pushed away. "Jared, I swear. I'm fine."

As they leaned into each other, the FBI detail came upstairs, crossed the living room, and, at a silent command from Agent Lee, exited. They would remain on duty until 8:00 a.m., when the next shift arrived.

"When you left the house this morning, the plan was to turn over all the devices to the FBI and get out of the way," Jared reminded her. His tone slid from welcoming to resigned by the end of the sentence. "How did we wind up under house arrest? Again."

Agent Lee stepped forward. "In Ms. Keene's defense, today's events appear unconnected to the Davies murder."

"The what?" Noah, who carried a tray laden with plates and serving dishes, set the platter down with a thud. "Who has been murdered?"

Avery and Jared exchanged looks, and Ling prompted with annoyance, "Unless you want the body count to go up, one of you needs to start talking."

At Jared's shrug, Avery began. "A few days ago, I met a law clerk whose judge committed suicide. He asked me to find out who was blackmailing her."

"Why you?" Noah asked, suspicious. "He just laid this on you?"

"Of course, he did. Because people now think she's Trixie Belden." At the blank looks from the men in the room, she mockingly translated, "A more mature version of Nancy Drew." Turning her attention back to Avery, Ling prompted, "Continue."

"There was a possibility it might be linked to the impeachment and the fake video they accused me of commissioning during the hearing."

Noah nodded. "The accusation was ludicrous, and no one seemed to believe it."

Avery shook her head. "I couldn't risk not knowing, so I agreed to listen. He gave me some information, and pretty quickly he ran off." She let the horror wash over her again. "I followed him out of the hotel, but before I could catch him, he and his taxi driver were murdered—probably by an ex-Mossad assassin named Nyx." On a roll, Avery plowed through the rest of the story, ending with the morning transfer to JTF.

Ling cleared her throat. "I'm sorry. What? You witnessed a murder and didn't call me?"

Expecting the reaction, Avery flipped her palm up to squeeze Ling's hand. "It was Wednesday. You were just starting a twenty-eight-hour shift on a four-day stretch," she explained hurriedly. "My plan was to tell you tonight. Over wine and a carrot cake from Delphine. Lots of wine."

"I'm not joking, Avery. Witnessing a death is traumatic. I know that firsthand." She turned to Jared. "Did she talk about it?"

Holding his hands up in the universal sign of innocence, he said, "I pressed her. But you know Avery. Compartments to spare."

"I can hear you both," Avery snapped as she pulled her hand free.

"None of today's fire drill had a thing to do with Davies. After I met with the FBI, I was detained by the Secret Service."

"Did you call Guarasci?" Noah asked quietly.

"No. I would have had they not confiscated my phone and driven me out to the home of one undeposed Brandon Stokes." Waving off their interruptions, she continued. "He basically warned me that if I didn't retract my testimony about Tigris, he'd come after me. I pushed back. He pushed harder. And as I was leaving, I saw his new pal, Congressman Boylen. They are the reason we're under house arrest, not me."

"No one is blaming you," Jared offered.

"I am." Ling crossed her arms in defiance. "President Stokes is an asshole, and you did save the nation from a genocidal tyrant. However, I'm willing to bet my entire savings account that you have research on the Davies case in your satchel. That the reason you were at work late was to somehow figure out what's going on because your hyperactive neurons and overdeveloped capacity for guilt and accountability don't know how to take a fucking hint from your exhausted body."

"You don't know—"

"Prove me wrong. Pull out your computer and show me what you were working on before this latest whirligig of fun."

"What you would see is a stack of research requested by the Chief—she asked me to look into cyber vulnerabilities after I told her about Whitner, the judge who was being blackmailed."

"And did you stick to that or go rogue?" Ling asked.

When Avery didn't respond, three pairs of accusatory eyes fixed on her.

Agent Lee cleared his throat. "I assume she is following up on data that she memorized when we visited with my colleagues at the FBI," he volunteered. "In truth, my counterpart is eager to understand what is happening, and Avery's reputation precedes her."

Agent Lee turned to Noah. "Mr. Fox, I advise you to accept a dollar from everyone in this room after I leave. Attorney-client privilege goes a long way."

At Noah's nod, Lee looked to Avery. "There is another matter to discuss." Together, they moved to a corner of the living room. "Agent Gehl and I met with AUSA Johnson, Whitner's co-conspirator. He and his lawyer are considering our offer. We will revisit the discussion in the morning."

"Understood. Did you get information I should consider?"

"Not yet, but do keep me apprised if you find anything worth asking him about." He walked her back toward her waiting friends. "I'll be in touch with the team in case any issues arise. Please be careful and, for heaven's sake, be circumspect as you disobey orders. I'll see you all in the morning to read in the morning detail. Enjoy your dinner."

As soon as the door clicked behind him, Jared followed to engage the locks and arm the security panel. He tested the mic system with the agents outside, who had been patched into an audio system. At their signal, he could lock down the entire house and move everyone to the basement. Satisfied the house was secured, he returned to the table and lightly rubbed at Avery's shoulders.

"I propose a truce," he said. "Noah brought dinner, and I am starving. Ling hasn't slept in days, which is doing nothing for her normally sunny disposition. And Avery has to formulate a reasonable explanation for why we might all be headed to federal prison after she shows us what's in the bag. So, in the words of the Romans, *Avē Imperātor, moritūrī tē salūtant!*"

Avery instantly translated the ancient Latin phrase. *For those about to die, we salute you!*

Nyx lifted the telephoto lens and took more images of the FBI detail stationed outside the home of Eleanor Felton, maternal aunt of Jared Wynn. Her instinct had paid off. After the botched tracking of

Avery Keene from her mother's rehabilitation center, she had taken over surveillance personally. Hayden had authorized additional support staff, and they'd staked out Judge Michael Oliver's home as well as their other targets.

Routine had Avery traveling from her apartment in Dupont Circle over the past few days until today's tour of the greater D.C. area. By the end of the day, with reports of the doxxing all over the internet and a blanket of feds shadowing her movements, Nyx had taken a page from her first trainer. Tracking prey is inefficient if you know where it will go to ground. Translation: it was easier to ambush a target at home than to try to trace its movements. Using Mamiwata's resources, Nyx had obtained Jared Wynn's address and had already secured a high-tech surveillance perch in a home across the street. A decade earlier, this would have required months of covert planning, shell companies, or decoys. Today, courtesy of the gig economy and Western culture's comfort with strangers touching their personal items, the best resource was Airbnb. For a few hundred dollars a day, she'd set up camera and sniper spots that had an excellent view of his home.

The five-person detail included two she identified as ex–Special Forces. From her days in Mossad, she recognized the gait and stance. The remainder were regular-issue agents, ones who had been pulled for the assignment. Only one showed familiarity with all the personnel present, the man flagged as Special Agent Robert Lee. His recurring presence raised questions that she had tasked the group with answering.

The speed with which Avery contacted the FBI after Preston Davies's death concerned her and Hayden. Although the young lawyer's troubles related primarily to a vendetta from the president of the United States, she had turned so quickly to the FBI based on whatever Davies had passed to her. Nyx granted that she was unlikely to learn any new intel tonight by conventional means. Jared Wynn armed his home as she had—impenetrable by conventional surveillance. RFID technology pinged off her sensors, and a drone overhead had been unable to intercept any stray signals.

Inside Wynn's home, Avery was unhackable, as were the others identified as her closest companions. But now that Nyx had a home base and all her targets were in a cluster, she had options.

TWENTY-ONE

Dinner was quickly demolished because no one felt like making small talk. Plus, prior experience with bugs and surveillance devices had bred a caution to wait to speak until Jared gave the all clear. One by one, they cleaned their plates and stacked them in the sink. Avery's mind whirled; and she ate the slowest, reluctant to reveal what she'd found so far. Because nothing looked like an answer.

Finally, she scraped at her empty plate and met the varying looks of irritation and impatience. She gathered up her things, and like lemmings, Jared, Ling, and Noah traipsed silently behind Avery as they descended into the basement. They waited as Jared engaged the privacy protocols. Ling took the ratty recliner Avery preferred, and Noah snagged one of the task chairs. Jared gave Avery his seat at the terminal and leaned against a column near the monitor array. They all looked at her expectantly.

Avery cleared her throat. "Okay, here are all the details. Davies somehow had my cell phone number and sent me a series of numeric puzzles that piqued my interest. I agreed to talk to him, out of curiosity. Once he told me what happened, I assumed his file of information, and the blackmailed judge, must have something to do with the impeachment case."

"Why?" asked Ling curiously.

"Like I said, it could have been a variety of things. Why else would a law clerk from Idaho track me down and give me a fake video and warnings about corruption in the courts?" She gestured ruefully. "I hear corruption, and I think President Stokes."

"As does the rest of the country, if we're lucky," Noah added.

"But based on what I've discovered since then," Avery continued, "I don't think the FISA connection relates to the impeachment. I think Davies came to me because he was afraid. I recognized that fear. He was in over his head, and unlike me, he had no one else to turn to for help."

"Nice way to butter us up," Ling said. "Now tell us what's going on."

"Give me a sec." Familiar with Jared's setup, Avery connected her device and called up her files. Starting with the slides on Jason Johnson, she led them through her research, which was based on what she'd seen on Gehl's screen. "These are the companies he said were being investigated for foreign intelligence violations. From what I can tell, the businesses are all over the map, literally. They're dotted across the country. The only clusters are the big industries like tech companies in Silicon Valley and financial companies in New York, Delaware, and South Dakota."

"South Dakota?" Ling asked. "Why in the world would people put money there?"

"It's the American version of the Cayman Islands," Noah explained. "Ever notice that your credit card payments go to an obscure lockbox in Sioux Falls every month? To make a complicated long story very short, in the 1980s, South Dakota and Citibank met and married in order to raise interest rates on credit cards. Since then, the Mount Rushmore state has become a financial services haven where you can shield your wealth and funnel funny money without needing a passport. More than a few international scoundrels have learned to love South Dakota's charms."

"Which an excellent trust and estate lawyer would know all

about," Avery deadpanned. "How many clients do you have parked in trusts there?"

"A sufficient number to guarantee partnership in a couple of years," he allowed. "Speaking of clients, before you go any further, that reminds me, I need a dollar from Ling and Jared."

"Bill me," Ling retorted.

Jared pulled a five from his wallet. "That should cover us both."

"Okay, you now have attorney-client privilege," Avery announced. "Though that's not exactly how this all works. Officially, Noah should have you—"

"Quit stalling, Avery," Jared said, staring somberly at the screen. "I recognize quite a few of these tech firms. A handful do cutting-edge work. Pen tests, exploits, you name it."

"Pen tests?" Noah furrowed his brow. "I don't speak tech."

"Penetration tests," Jared explained. "Companies hire them to find weaknesses in their security systems. To burrow in and find the bugs before a hacker can. I've done some work for these firms here." He tapped a handful of names on her list.

Avery scrolled down. "Each of these companies currently has a surveillance warrant giving the Department of Justice permission to spy on them. Which I am not supposed to know because all these warrants are classified."

"What does that mean for us?" Ling asked curiously.

"It means if we get caught, we could be rightfully accused of violating federal law," Noah explained.

Ling rolled her eyes. "Oh, that. Got it."

"The number of companies Johnson tagged is highly unusual," Avery continued. "But I can't find any link between them, other than Johnson and Judge Whitner. The one recurring factor is that eleven of these are energy companies or related to the industry. Varying sizes. But again, no direct connection that I could find. No overlapping board members or public contracts."

Avery tapped on the sheet she'd curated. "The next-largest grouping is tech companies, but their offerings differ. There's an IT consulting firm named Redhorse that came up in a federal lawsuit. Another entity does headhunting and recruitment for information security firms across the country. Several of their clients have contracts with the Defense Department and Homeland Security. Then there are financial services firms, a few telecom providers, and a maintenance company—they provide janitorial services in Norfolk, Virginia."

Ling raised her hand. With a laugh, Avery called on her. "Yes, Dr. Yin?"

"I thought you said the warrants had to prove that the companies were somehow a national security danger. I don't see how a cleaning service in Virginia or a business like, say, Foster Energy in Clovis, New Mexico, could pose a threat to the U.S. government."

Avery located the company and flipped to a screen that allowed her to plug its info into Google Maps. "I agree, it makes no sense. Foster Energy operates a power station in rural New Mexico. I thought there might be some connection between these various companies, but I can't see one. That's why I've been stuck."

She'd assessed the screen, studying the data multiple ways. "Take these energy companies. Look at where they're located. Western Wisconsin. South Mississippi. Oregon. Vermont. Beaumont, Texas. A maintenance firm, but this one specializes in power plants. An EMC that joint ventured with a traditional energy company out of Nebraska. The boards don't overlap, and neither do their service areas."

"What else is on the list?"

Avery shook her head. "Finance companies with no common deals. Tech companies with different products. I've gone down a few rabbit holes where a fintech works with another entity, but I can't find a sinister link. Like I said, no clear patterns."

Jared came over to the computer station and opened a new task. He plotted the companies that Avery had identified, color-coding based on industry. He then overlaid them with a different shape based on the size of the firm. With a flick, he sent the map to a freestanding clear board connected to his setup. "Let's look at it a different way. Whatever is going on with Johnson, you know he had to have a reason for surveilling these companies. What do you see on a map?"

"Other than pretty colors, not much." She absorbed the data, hunting for connections.

"What don't you see?" Ling asked. "What's missing?"

"Overlap. Motive. Rationale." Avery took a physical step back. "To solve a puzzle, always start with the basics. What are the knowns?"

Jared answered, "For starters, Jason Johnson was willing to commit treason for this."

"True." She cocked her head and frowned. "To secure surveillance warrants, Johnson had to create a theory that suggested foreign interference." Walking closer to the map, Avery confronted a jumble of colors. Money managers, finance firms, energy companies, data brokers, consultants, and janitors. Some of the pieces touched one another, but none formed a clear picture of what could be at stake.

Jason Johnson had broken his oath and risked spending the rest of his life in prison for millions of dollars. Who was paying him and what did they want? Convincing a Harvard-educated attorney to gamble with his nation's safety hopefully required more than money.

Avery thought about Vance's warnings. She needed to tell them, but she didn't relish the explosion to follow. Eager to delay the inevitable, she asked, "Jared, can you do a background check on Jason Johnson? As far back as you can go, as much as you can find."

"Sure. Why?"

"There might be a name or something that signals who hired him. Why he said yes."

"My question for you is, can you get your hands on the actual warrant applications?" Jared asked. "Maybe Agent Gehl will let you review. You'd be able to see what Johnson said he was looking to find."

"Absolutely not," Avery answered emphatically. "FISA applications are classified and rarely released. And with the Secret Service, the NSA, and the CIA warning her to keep me as far away from the JTF as possible, she'd be crucified if they knew I had this much information already."

Avery kept her eyes on the map, forcing her vision to relax, to blur. "Gehl suspects this is bigger than Whitner and Johnson. But I have only one vector of information, and a game of chess or poker has other players. Other sides making moves that reveal more about what you're seeing. I need to look at more than the warrant list. I need to understand the eleven judges on the FISA court."

"I thought it was Judge Whitner on all the warrants," Noah reminded her.

"Yes, she signed off on forty-eight of Johnson's warrants, which proves there's something going on. All FISA cases are secret, but every judge on that court is also a federal judge with a public docket, like Judge Whitner. Whoever is behind this, whoever forced her to release Thad Colgate, might be trying to get to other judges too."

Jared nodded in agreement. "So you have Johnson's warrants, Whitner's cases, and a bunch of other judges to study. I'll pull background checks on all of them, not just Johnson. What else would be helpful?"

Avery braced herself. "I have one other source that I should mention. Will Vance contacted me."

"What?" Jared came toward her. "When? Did he threaten you?"

"No," she replied quickly. "He says he's trying to help me. First time he called, he said there's a credible rumor about an imminent attack, and he has informants who implicate a private defense contractor. Likely run by an expatriated American with an ax to grind."

"The first time?" pressed Ling, her distaste clear.

"Tonight, he contacted me again."

"Since you got home? Or before a congressman tried to get us all mobbed?" she quizzed.

"No, while I was at the Court. He gave me a set of numbers. I haven't really given them much thought because I found out about Boylen's press conference a few minutes later." Avery typed the digits into the document. "434. 314. 982. 850."

Noah started at the numbers. "Didn't you say Davies made contact by giving you codes?"

She nodded. "His were easy—basic stuff for an attorney. Code sections. Number of judges on certain courts. This feels different—"

"Avery," Noah interrupted, "the last time you had interactions with Vance, people were murdered. I don't trust him. Given the cloud of the impeachment hearings, I think we need to report this contact to Mr. Guarasci. Assuming we're still your attorneys?"

"Let's put a pin in Vance and the impeachment," Jared said. "One problem at a time. Go back to the warrants."

Grateful for the reprieve, Avery summarized, "I'll start there, and I'll also comb through the FISA judges' federal district court cases. The warrant records are confidential, but some of the names on Johnson's warrants might pop up in other courts—in other venues. District court dockets are public. I can do that from the convenience of this basement."

Jared nodded in approval. "What will you tell Agent Lee?"

"I haven't decided yet. I trust him, but this idea doesn't have legs yet, and I don't want to put Agent Lee in a position where he has intel he can't use." Left unsaid was that the involvement of Vance—a fugitive—would be off-limits for Lee.

Ling stood and walked toward Avery. "Okay, miss, if you plan to uncover an international plot to attack American supremacy, you'll need to get some sleep first. Come on. Doctor's orders." Herding Avery to the stairs, she commanded, "Jared, save and shut down her equipment, and do not let her sneak back down here tonight. Noah, you have kitchen duty."

"Aye, aye," Noah mocked in response. "See you in the morning."

Water rushed in, endless waves of suffocating darkness pulling her under. She struggled against the pressure, but the weight bore her down. Down, down, down. Time stretched and looped around itself. Like the water, it had no end. No beginning. In the blackness of the water, in the emptiness of time, she ceased to exist. Again.

The scream woke her, tearing Hayden from her nightmare. She fumbled for the bottle she kept on the nightstand in anticipation. The cool liquid soothed her throat, calmed her nerves. She'd relived the terror of those weeks at sea for nearly seven years.

Therapy had failed to offer respite, and Hayden had devised a treatment of her own. She forced herself to remember why she had chosen this route. Rising from her bed, she wrapped a silk robe around her body and took the familiar path to her mirror. There, she would recount her journey and restate her purpose. As she murmured to herself, she let the images play in her mind, ready for their rending and tearing. Ready for the endgame.

Trapped in a metal tube of men, she had been one of the first women sailors commissioned for a submarine. The honor of her assignment buffeted her against complaints and muttered comments, against the disdain of crewmen who resented her stars and her skills.

She rose quickly, becoming a leader among those deployed. Her computer skills and savvy with electrical systems had impressed her commanding officers, and eventually won over the chauvinists who questioned whether women belonged in the depths of the sea. Lieutenant Hayden Burgess had proven herself.

In the life of the submariner, close contact yielded a camaraderie between the officers and crew. While fraternization was frowned upon, no one really paid attention. She'd made friends—Hank and Carolyn and Richard. They'd bonded over their love of the water, and they'd become their own subunit. Loyal and true. Hayden had been their leader, her natural gravitas providing a protective bubble within the confines of the hierarchy below the sea.

Until one man stripped her of a sense of security. One man denied her humanity and her autonomy. For days, he'd preyed upon her body and twisted her mind. Lied about her and her friends. Warped her mission, toyed with her memory. When she surfaced—when they surfaced—she found herself again. Reported his treachery.

And watched him walk away without consequence. Instead, she became the predator, a woman out of her depths trying to blame him for a failed relationship. Her witnesses were rejected, and they each paid a price for defending her. They'd believed him, not her— not the evidence. Instead, the Navy promoted him and drummed her out of her life's work.

Still, she fought back. Letter after letter sent to the president of the United States and his successor. Yet the commander in chief refused her a hearing.

So she returned to what she'd learned as a child. She asked the civilian court system that she protected as a naval officer to protect her as an American citizen. She followed the chain of command and then the labyrinthine ways of the civilian courts. Requested her day in front of a jury not of military men who dismissed her as a peer, but of twelve ordinary citizens who would recognize the perversion of rape for what it was. They would unravel a conspiracy that was not a singularity.

But more than seventy years ago, the military had found a way to avoid liability for its actions. The death of a young soldier in a fire on a base and two acts of medical malpractice had been bound together in a case before the nation's highest court, in the name of one of the dead, Feres. The U.S. military argued that they weren't responsible even though they were clearly at fault. The U.S. Supreme

Court agreed, using the fig leaf of sovereign immunity from the Federal Tort Claims Act. Instead of giving the grieving families and wounded servicemen relief from their country's negligence, the wisdom of the Court said that the military was more like King George and his ilk—immune from the obligation of taking care of its own.

Others had tried to defeat the absurdity of the Feres Doctrine, which essentially permitted blanket absolution for the U.S. military's carelessness, to no avail. But surely, the grotesque assault she'd faced would yield a different outcome. Surely, a court would hear her plea. A federal district court judge accepted her claim, but subsequent judges—en banc and empowered—refused her justice. Until her only hope remained at the U.S. Supreme Court. Only they could allow her to sue the U.S. Navy and the man who preyed on her body and stole her future.

Yet even there, in a court led by a woman of power, she had been denied.

She would be denied no longer.

TWENTY-TWO

Tuesday, October 15

After a morning phone check-in with Rita, Avery had sequestered herself in Jared's office. Ling occupied the guest bedroom and power-slept. Noah was working from the dining
room table, and Jared had gotten a ride from the FBI to a client
meeting in Baltimore.

By noon, Avery had filled a dozen pages of the legal pad at her
elbow, constructing a list of all eleven judges who had served on the
FISC during the past three years, as well as a thumbnail of all their
public caseloads. She spent several more hours churning through
the details—reviewing three years of court dockets for half of those
judges. She knew college majors, law school alma maters, and
hometowns. Jared would fill in the gorier details that might have
been missed during their confirmation hearings.

Her first deep dive began with Judge Whitner, the name that
represented the tip of the iceberg Avery hoped to reveal. The Idaho
judge had managed a routine calendar, spiced up occasionally by
cases of wire fraud, use of explosive materials, and complex trafficking cases. Thad Colgate's case served as the only anomaly she identified, but for the first time, she zeroed in on a detail she'd elided.
Colgate's rampage at work wasn't simply a horrific massacre in an

office building. He'd murdered his coworkers at their Idaho power plant.

The next few judges on Avery's list had deeply innocuous records and equally vanilla rulings. Nothing that struck her as odd or raised a concern. Judge Mandisa Supris of the Middle District of Florida. *Clean.* Judge Justin Kirnon sat in the Northern District of New York. *Squeaky clean.* Judge Jerel McLean, who had the shortest commute possible from the D.C. District Court to FISC by changing elevators, not only had no skeletons—she couldn't identify any closets.

"I have got to get a hobby," Avery muttered as she read through yet another case from her current target, Judge Ruth Hoyt of the Southern District of Texas. An alumna of Bryn Mawr, one of the Seven Sister colleges, Hoyt had made her way to UCLA for law school, where she distinguished herself in moot court with her sharp tongue and steely mind. By her third year, incoming students had learned the legend of the first-year law student who'd made her own partner weep. She eschewed the traditional path of clerking right out of law school, opting instead to join her uncle's practice defending oil-rigging outfits that were under constant assault by environmentalists and tree-hugging ecoterrorists.

Hoyt, whose trademark stilettos lifted her to 5'3 with a bun, did an about-face as she crested thirty. She quit working for her uncle and sought a clerkship with a fellow Bryn Mawr alumna, who put her on track to become a federal judge by forty-one. No one doubted that her uncle's ties and hefty campaign contributions that cycle also helped pave the way. At fifty-three, she was on her ninth year on the federal bench and her first turn on the FISC.

The case on Avery's screen seemed harmless enough, a subpoena request from a Mexican family seeking detailed information from a company that operated on both sides of the Rio Grande. She skimmed the record and stopped, squinting at the screen.

What caught and held Avery's attention was the subject matter. The trial order granted the plaintiffs the right to secure records that would detail the circumstances surrounding a series of power outages. The outages had cut power to a hospital, and a child died when backup power couldn't keep his ventilator going. The bereaved parents lived on the Mexican side of the Electric Reliability Council of Texas. Better known as ERCOT—the company responsible for the section of the nation's power grid managed by Texas. The subpoena sought permission to debrief and detail almost any entity that touched the process. Including a now-familiar company—Foster Energy of Waco, Texas.

Avery leaned toward her screen. This was the first time she'd seen a direct connection between a FISC judge's public case and an entity being surveilled through the FISA court. Foster Energy, a company under surveillance by Jason Johnson, care of Judge Whitner. And also ruled on by Judge Hoyt. Avery scowled. The subpoena had been granted a year ago, the surveillance warrant a few months ago. Whatever was happening inside Foster Energy had to be unusually exciting to invite such scrutiny.

She opened another tab and pulled up her research into Foster Energy. One of the smaller players in the vast Texas market, Foster Energy held no obvious role that could be tied to tampering with the power grid.

"One step at a time," she warned herself. "Know the players, then learn more about the moves."

Switching back to her judicial investigation, she plowed through the next set of targets.

Her quarry was Judge Michael Oliver of West Virginia. Graduate of Blair College, an obscure institution of higher learning that had no social media presence and only a cursory web page, Judge Oliver was possessed of a remarkably undistinguished pedigree. He had been appointed to the federal district court at fifty-six, after years of a long tenure on the county and then state court bench. All his rulings followed a pattern of moderation and complacency. Judge Oliver treated everyone equally. His orders split legal decisions like

Solomon—straight down the middle. If one side got an extension for a motion, the other side could count on reciprocity on a ruling.

More notable was the speed of his court docket. Nothing took too long, nothing dragged out. Speed and efficiency seemed to be his lodestars. The only deviation Avery found involved a railroad accident a few years before. A West Virginia mogul stalled discovery until the destitute victim, Dawson Hawthorne, died without heirs or anyone to plead his case. Despite repeated pleas from the young man's attorney, Oliver had turned a deaf ear.

Intrigued by the deviation, Avery began to hunt for other pleadings related to the tragic case of Mr. Hawthorne. His initial attorney had been a personal injury guy who placed flashing ads into the corners of the online West Virginia papers. On a whim, she punched his number into one of her new burner phones, from a batch courtesy of Jared.

"Vic Parker here," came the cheery smoker's voice. "We beat the insurance without you breaking the bank."

"Hello, Mr. Parker. I'm Tracy Floyd, a law student at WVU College of Law, and I'm doing research for a paper," Avery lied, selling the ruse with a soft drawl she mimicked from Rita. Though she'd never been to her mother's home state, she had the intonation down pat. "Do you mind if I ask you a few questions about a case you worked on?"

Ensconced in a threadbare office in a Charleston strip mall, Vic Parker rocked back in his chair and kicked his feet up on the desk. Business was slow, and his caller sounded like she was nubile and pretty. "Fire away, darlin'. Fair warning, though. I'm bound by attorney-client privilege, so I might not be able to tell you much."

"Of course, Mr. Parker."

"Call me Vic, honey. I'm not old enough to be Mr. Parker to you. Finished up at WVU myself just a few years ago."

The bar profile she had on screen listed his age at forty-nine. Middle-aged math and wishful thinking had Avery rolling her eyes, but she gave him a flirty laugh. "Um, thank you. I wanted to ask about the Dawson Hawthorne case. I see you were the first attorney of record."

Vic felt his easy smile slip into a bitter frown. "I could have made millions on that case. Dawson got hit by one of Goodwin's rail cars, and my boy was outside the right of way. Train derailed coming fast off a curve, tipped over, and clipped him. Made him a double amputee who pretty much never got out of the hospital. Clear case of negligence. Insurance company should have rushed to close the books."

"My goodness," Avery sympathized. "Who or what is Goodwin?"

"Quint Goodwin, one of the wealthiest sumbitches in all of West Virginia. His family comes from old money, like they were here when dinosaurs started decaying into coal, so they knew just where to look. Now they are the reason Karl Marx got so pissed off. They own the means of production here—from coal to trains to manu-facturing, they've got a finger in everybody's piehole."

She made a note to research Quint Goodwin and family and to forget Vic's colorful imagery. "So what happened to Dawson Hawthorne?"

"Fuck if I know. I get the case, start digging around, and then Dawson calls me up and says an environmental outfit wants to take over his case pro bono. Asks me how much he owes me."

"What did you say?"

Vic squirmed a bit in his chair, his back suddenly itching like bed bugs had him. "I told him fifty thousand. Kind of a finder's fee. I did the leg work for them, and they snatched the case. Motherfuckers. No offense."

"None taken. Did you relinquish the case?"

"Didn't really have a choice. Besides, they paid me immediately. Sent a wire and everything. Easiest fifty K I'll ever make, but that wire should have had a few more zeroes." Vic sighed. "But then the judge started slow-walking the case and that poor SOB Dawson died in the hospital. No heirs, no lawsuit, no judgment."

"Do you recall the name of the organization that paid you?"

"Absolutely. Called Pacifica Protection. Thought it was weird they'd care about a train wreck in the Appalachian Mountains. 'Cause of their name and all."

Avery was already pulling up their website. "Anything else you remember, Mr. Parker?"

"I told you to call me Vic, sweetie."

"Vic," she repeated dutifully. "Do you remember anything else?"

"I don't want to sound greedy, but this case had it all. A train accident. Double amputee. Moonshiners in the hills and a power plant sitting in the middle of fucking nowhere. I was already doing some research to see if I could make it a toxic tort. You'll learn about those later."

Avery sat up straight. "Did you say there was a power plant involved?"

"Not really involved, and not one of those massive ones. But when I got an aerial map of the place to figure out what could have caused the accident, there was a substation, I think it's called. Don't quote me on it."

"Of course not," she murmured. "What happened?"

"I filed a motion to expand discovery so I could take a look at the plant and surrounding areas. Judge denied my motion. Before I could take another run at getting information, that Pacifica group called me up and shoved me out."

"So you never got close to the plant?"

"Nope. Right after they took the case, I caught a mesothelioma client and had to focus on him."

"Do you still have your discovery files?"

"Sure."

"Would you mind sending them to me?"

"Why in the world would you care?" For the first time, Vic began to sound suspicious. "What type of paper are you working on exactly, Tracy?"

Avery scrambled for an excuse to keep him mollified. "Actually, Vic, I do know about the Goodwins. My paper is examining how they've manipulated the legal system in West Virginia. But I promise I only want the information for background. I won't mention the case or you."

On the other end of the line, there was only silence. Then, "Use my name if you want. I'm not afraid of Quint Goodwin or his goons. Give me your email address and my girl will send you the documents this afternoon."

"That's wonderful! I really appreciate your time, Mr. Parker. Vic." She quickly rattled off an email account she kept for spam and strangers.

"Anytime, sweetheart. Just give me a call if you need me again. For anything."

With that last bit of innuendo, Vic disconnected the line and Avery turned to the whiteboard. *Idaho. Texas. West Virginia.* A power station in Idaho where Thad Colgate committed mass murder. An energy company that lost power in Texas and Mexico. A substation in the middle of nowhere in West Virginia.

Mind whirring, Avery switched screens and pulled up a map of the national power grid. She shot the image to the big board and overlaid the two maps of the country. Crossing to it, she began ticking off the overlay with a marker. The nation's grid was divided into sections that interconnected to create one massive power system. With her markers, she tagged what she'd found.

One. Two. Three. Western. ERCOT. Eastern. A bright red circle in each segment of the power grid. And each one with a connection to a judge on the FISA court. It wasn't proof of anything, but something about the symmetry bothered her. She was still staring at the map, trying to ferret out its meaning, when she heard the doorway to the basement open.

"Time's up—we're coming down!" Ling yelled from the top of the landing.

"I'm on my way," Avery called back. "Just let me wrap this up."

"That's the same lie you told Noah two hours ago," replied Ling, her voice now just behind Avery. She examined the multiple open screens and the color-coded map with its marker stains. "You're obsessing."

"I'm researching." She pointed to the map. "Look. I'm on the verge of something. I can tell."

Ling stepped between Avery and the board. "What time is it, counselor?"

"Four o'clock, doctor," she retorted.

"Wrong. It's nearly seven p.m. You've been down here all day."

"What?" Avery blinked rapidly, eyes suddenly arid. "You said Noah called down for me a couple of hours ago."

"He tried to coax you to take a break right after I woke up. Then again two hours later."

Jared and Noah came down the stairs, and Avery gave a sheepish grin. "I lost track of time."

Looking around, Jared noted the progress she'd made. "Would you like to explain your work to the class? Dinner will be here soon."

Grateful for the sounding boards, Avery nodded. "Okay . . . in one of the endless seminars I attended this summer, there was a speaker who talked about attacks on the nation's power grid. He warned that doing so would be easier than people imagined. But his presentation focused on physical attacks on the substations, aimed at knocking out the grid in a targeted region."

She retrieved another dry-erase marker from Jared's desk. Drawing on the map, she said, "Look, there are three major power regions—East, West, and, not surprisingly, Texas is its own universe.

The energy supplied by all these power stations across the country surges across transmission lines, and the load is balanced by toggling up and down production and usage. But they don't deliver outside their domains."

"For those of us who don't live inside your beautiful mind, what point are you making?" Ling asked.

"That if Vance is right, and there is an attack planned, taking down the power grid is one hell of a statement. Based on Agent Gehl's information, Jason Johnson could have used his access to help a foreign entity infiltrate the power grid by granting them surveillance. There are more than ten companies with energy profiles in Johnson's docket, but they're hidden in plain sight among the other warrants."

"Like Russia or China, maybe?" Ling suggested.

"Perhaps." She pondered the color-coded map with its new lines, and a frightful reality dawned on her. "This is big. . . ."

"You believe Johnson is part of an international conspiracy to knock out electricity? One that required infiltrating a power company in Wisconsin?"

Avery began to circle the room, a theory taking shape. "You remember when Texas lost power in that winter storm a few years ago? More than two hundred people died. Or when New York had a blackout in 2003? What if you could orchestrate not just a regional event, but a *continental* blackout?"

She indicated the two companies in Vermont and Oregon from the warrant list. "Canada is part of the interconnection system. The American Eastern section goes into Quebec. The American Western section includes British Columbia and Saskatchewan. And the Texas grid extends down into Mexico. Shut down the three largest economies in the Western Hemisphere. American business operations would grind to a halt. The financial industry, tech, manufacturing, everything. Paralyzed."

"Hospitals would be in chaos," Ling added. "As would 911 operations and any emergency services."

Jared piled on. "All tech gets shut down. No grid, no cell tower transmissions, no security defenses."

"Banks are vulnerable too, especially the hundreds of millions of currency transactions that happen daily." Noah looked around the room with growing horror. "Exactly how many power plants would you need to collapse the national grid?"

"The seminar speaker didn't specify, but I recall her stating that the number was absurdly small. But why would you need the entire grid?" Avery mused as she returned to the board. "If you target key sectors of the economy and certain geographically vulnerable areas, all that's left is the looting. Unless your goal is a complete continental collapse."

Judge Michael Oliver trudged up the driveway of his son's home, eyes red from hours of reviewing a thorny Section 702 application. While he failed to meet the twenty-mile threshold for local judges mandated for the court, his home in West Virginia made him the fourth man for the presiding judge when he was in search of someone to handle more complex, longer-term filings. He longed for a warm snifter of brandy, his comfiest pajamas, and a back rub from his wife. What awaited him inside, he knew, was a tepid glass of red wine, leftover meatloaf, and the light snoring of his beloved.

He was about to insert the key into the lock when a cold object pressed against his neck. He'd never been held at gunpoint before, but the certainty that his luck had changed was borne out when his assailant spoke.

"You were told never to turn off your phone or leave it behind," the harsh voice reminded him.

Trembling, he explained, "I dropped it in the sink this morning. I swear! I was making breakfast for my grandkids."

"Ah, yes, Nivea and Malcolm. They're at such fragile, breakable ages."

His heart thumped loud in his chest, and his ears burned in a mix of rage and fear. "You leave them out of this!"

"You were warned, Judge." The lightly accented voice pressed closer. "But this is your one mistake. You've seen what we do to those who disobey."

"I understand," he promised. "My phone is destroyed. It was an accident, I swear, but I don't know how to fix it."

"I left a gift for you inside. Your gorgeous daughter-in-law signed for it. Have it on you at all times tomorrow and keep it next to your computer, fully powered. Follow the instructions when they arrive."

"Yes, yes," he babbled. "Yes, I will. I promise. It won't happen again."

Silence met his vow. Spinning around, he saw only the shadows cast by the streetlamps. No stranger with a gun. No death tonight. Without warning, his legs gave out, and he sank onto the stoop, dry sobs heaving through him. They'd kill his precious grandchildren over a silly mistake like a phone in a tub of dirty dishwater. What horrible monsters . . .

Yet he would serve as they commanded. What other choice did he have?

TWENTY-THREE

My plan is to finish up the rest of the judges list tonight, and then make some calls tomorrow to Idaho and Texas," Avery explained. "I want to explore this power grid theory. And I haven't found anything else that connects the judges or their histories to one another."

"Are you afraid this is confirmation bias?" Jared asked as he scanned the notes she'd taken. "Is it really so odd that three of your judge targets have some connection to the nation's power grid?"

"No, it's not, given the broad range of cases that a federal judge hears during a year. But there is a connection buried in here. The power grid concept is the best I've got for now, but I'm still spinning out theories. Financial services could be the target. Or a massive ransomware attack."

Jared pulled a flash drive from his pocket. "Based on what you told us yesterday, I reached out to friends. The chatter about a cyber-attack is getting louder, though no one else knows the target either." He handed the drive to Avery. "Here's what I dug up on Mr. Jason Johnson and your judges."

"Thank you," Avery said gratefully. "I'll switch gears and go through this later. I want to finish researching my list and then dig into Foster Energy, Thad Colgate's company, Goodwin, and Pacifica Protection—"

Ling interrupted. "Avery, you've been at this nonstop. Is there some avoidance going on here? You haven't asked anyone about the fallout from VerityVictory, and you still have an angry president on your back and a mean-spirited troll of a congressman looking to make a name for himself at your expense."

Avery glanced up with an expression forged from something between defiance and affection. "I'm safe, Ling." Puzzles were her forte, and she'd be damned if she wasn't going to figure this one out. "I promise I'll knock off early tonight and get back to it tomorrow."

Hearing the concession, Ling volunteered, "I'm not back on rotation for a few days. I'll take a look at Pacifica Protection for you. In the morning."

Avery squeezed her hand. "I appreciate it."

"Did a monthlong due diligence stretch in Beckley, West Virginia, during my first year at the firm. Great hiking," Noah offered. "No one expects to see me in the morning. I can dig up dirt on Quint Goodwin and clan."

"That's my cue to take Foster Energy." Jared crossed to Avery and wrapped his arms around her waist. "Note that all of us are planning to dive into this *tomorrow*, correct?"

Leaning her head back against him, she hedged, "Just one more hour tonight. I promise."

"I'm not trying to police your time—"

"I am," Ling corrected.

Jared ignored her. "But we do have that meeting with my father's doctors and Dr. Srinivasan tomorrow. Dr. Toca sounded hopeful when we spoke today."

"Jared, I'm so sorry! I completely forgot—I've lost track of what day it is."

"He's my dad, Avery. You're his guardian, and I'm his son. We tag team this. However, I'll need you to be really there when they explain his options."

"Of course," she pledged. "And I appreciate everyone taking on parts of this. I may be chasing shadows, but something about this doesn't feel right. It's like, I don't know, moonlight on water. You can see something moving, but there's no telling what's going on below the surface."

"We get it," Noah said quietly. "And you'll find it."

Avery expelled a quick breath. "Okay. We'll huddle up in the morning before the doctor's appointment. I also texted a friend of mine from law school who works at the Department of Energy. I need a crash course on how we keep the lights on."

Jared's phone buzzed. He glanced at the screen. "Before you dive back in, Agent Lee is at the door. He wants to speak with you."

Agent Lee was waiting for them in the living room. "Hope you don't mind, I had them let me in."

"Third night is free," Jared deadpanned.

"Did you have some news?" Avery asked. "Any updates on the VerityVictory website?"

"Chatter is still high, as I imagine Mr. Wynn knows. Your name is a top search across platforms. However, we have no credible threats against you, Dr. Yin, Mr. Fox, or Mr. Wynn. Still, we will continue to monitor the right-wing channels."

"But?" She recognized the careful tone Agent Lee used with her when bad news loomed.

"The Chief and I agree that you will need to maintain a protection detail at least through the impeachment trial. Congressman Boylen has declined to walk back his statements about your role, and we have an indication that he intends to ratchet up his attacks on the impeachment all week."

"The trial doesn't start until next week," Noah protested. "They'll let a member of Congress put her life in jeopardy for the next seven days?"

Agent Lee allowed his indignation to show for an instant. "The minority leader has declined to pursue disciplinary measures, citing the First Amendment. However, my boss reminded him of how bad it would look if a member of the legislative branch continued to endanger an employee of the United States government."

"Luke Boylen would love to be reprimanded by the FBI director," Avery argued. "I saw his face yesterday when we passed at Stokes's house. He and Stokes smell blood."

"Which is why it is best that you stay here for the time being. Dr. Yin as well. We'll keep a protective detail on your apartment." He looked at Avery and Ling in turn. "I recommend that Dr. Yin accompany a pair of agents to your home to collect what you might need for the next few days."

Ling nodded. "Is it safer if we go tonight or in the morning?"

"The team can transport you now, if you're ready."

"Sure. Noah, come and help me." Ling snagged his elbow and led him to the door. Agent Lee made his good-byes and followed them. Outside, he murmured to the agent on duty, then closed the door.

Jared turned to Avery with a serious expression. "The president is terrified of you, Avery. You know that if you pull on this thread for FISC, you might make new enemies."

"Only if they know I'm doing it." She sighed. "I keep seeing Preston Davies in that ballroom, begging me to help him. Ten minutes later, he was shot in the head, Jared. He trusted that I would see something in the data, and I did. Just not in time." When he started to speak, she held up a hand. "I also know I'm using this to distract me from Stokes and the impeachment debacle . . . and right now, it's working."

"Fair enough." He planted a kiss on her forehead. "Go find your white whale, Ahab."

Back in front of her terminal, Avery cued up the cases from the next judge on her list, Judge Alvin Lake of Wisconsin. On his second tour of duty on the FISC, Judge Lake had a conservative streak that fit well with the president who appointed him to the bench. No one got the benefit of any doubt; and when discretion was allowed on sentencing, he refused to take it if it meant reducing sentences.

Corporations sufficiently lucky to draw his court found their most peculiar whims satisfied beyond imagining. No class actions found their way beyond his pen, and no arbitration agreements dissolved under his watchful eye.

Which is why the case of *Redhorse v. Starhorse* stood out. Redhorse Tech, a security company based in Madison, Wisconsin, had been founded by a trio of computer science students on the campus of the University of Wisconsin fifteen years before. With careful tending, their campus excursion into on-call tech services for computers had become a national concern. Their kiosks in malls grew into storefronts and strip malls. By the time they were ready to take the company public, Redhorse offerings included next-generation firewalls, cloud security, endpoint security tests, threat detection, and more. Silicon Valley had come calling and valued the firm at $3 billion, a number beyond the wildest imaginings of its founders.

Days before their public sale, though, Redhorse's giddy founders were beset with horrible news. A brand-new firm had been horning in on its narrative and trademark. Starhorse, as the doppelgänger called itself, had applied for a slot in the industry's mega trade show, where companies shopped for their latest gladiator. If Starhorse proceeded, with its similar name and oddly identical logo, Redhorse stood to lose market share.

Soon, the Madison team sat in a courtroom as their highly trained, absurdly expensive counsel argued for a temporary restraining order to block Starhorse from ruining their lives and pending IPO. Based on the American tradition of claiming trademark infringement, the attorney pled their case, complete with renderings to show the conniving sneak-thief Starhorse to be a lying cheat. The lawyer assured his clients that the Delaware upstart proved no match for the hometown crowd in front of a pro-corporate, anti-guff judge like Alvin Lake.

Until he summarily dismissed the application for a TRO with the scantest explanation possible. Starhorse cheered and Redhorse reeled, their new rivals now able to sow brand confusion. When Redhorse exhorted their attorney to appeal, she explained that the judge had absolute discretion—even when the outcome was patently absurd. Starhorse proceeded to mimic every aspect of the Midwest entity, from the logo to the color scheme. Tensions escalated when both Redhorse and Starhorse set up booths at the security trade show, the rivals competing for every scrap of opportunity. In subsequent filings, Redhorse plied the court with spreadsheets and lost contracts, to no avail.

Avery found the case interesting, the picayune drama mildly diverting. Judge Lake had diverted from his traditional approach of siding with the big guys, but in a business-to-business battle, such a departure wasn't earthshaking. But Starhorse's client list was.

Buried in the list of customers that Redhorse alleged Starhorse had poached was a midsize firm based in Racine, Wisconsin. A client that, by regional rights, should have been theirs. A client whose affidavit attested to the aggressive marketing and misunderstanding that had them abandoning a hometown hero for an East Coast interloper. The contract had been signed and funds transferred before they knew better. By then, the subcontractor for several members of the Midcontinent Independent System Operators had already spent its hefty budget, and it couldn't justify legal fees when they were perfectly satisfied with their security provider.

Avery froze, drawn to the initials formed from the subcontractor's client base: MISO. It was an acronym she'd learned earlier as she memorized the contours of the national power grid. MISO served as one of a collection of entities responsible for the regional transmission and distribution of electricity that powered the vast middle section of the United States and crossed into the territory of Canada. The area encompassed fifteen U.S. states, one Canadian province, and forty-two million souls. Judge Lake had opined on a case involving the power grid—with a ruling that ran contrary to expectation—another piece in an increasingly worrisome puzzle.

She reached for her cell phone, then stopped. Jared and the FBI had strictly recommended against using her own phone to reach out to anyone without permission. So far, she'd obeyed, even using burners to contact the Chief and her mom. But what she needed next required that she contact a friend willing to take her call at 12:38 a.m. As her thumb began to press down, she hesitated. This was the kind of magical thinking that got people killed. Whispering her prayers, she reached for a burner phone and dialed.

"Hello?" The groggy voice did not sound pleased.

Talking fast, Avery plowed in, "Sorry, Baz. It's Avery. I wouldn't call so late unless it was important."

"What do you want?"

"To come and see you tomorrow. Early. I need to borrow your big, beautiful brain."

"Getting you into my section will be impossible on short notice," he griped. "We don't invite guests. Give me a few days."

"I'll need you to get me credentials tomorrow," Avery wheedled. "It's important that we meet on-site, and I'll be in a hurry."

"You always are. And right now, you're toxic. Can't this wait, Avery?"

"No, it can't. And before you whine, Baz, you do remember that jam I got you out of in Baltimore. I told you not to split sevens if the dealer is showing a nine. Saved you six grand and an explanation to Sadie for why you pawned her engagement ring."

The groggy profanity was surprisingly clear. Baz hissed, "Fine. Text me your info. Be there by eight."

"You're my favorite bureaucrat, Baz!"

"Go away."

Grinning, Avery disconnected. She could be at his office bright and early and then head out to Bethesda to join Jared and Justice Wynn's doctors.

"Who are you bothering at this hour on your forbidden phone?"

Avery twisted around to face Jared and his stern disapproval. She handed him the offending device. "I had a good reason to break protocol."

He didn't bother arguing or looking down. "Who?"

"Baz Okune. We were at Yale together. Now he's a staff attorney at FERC."

"The Federal Energy Regulatory Commission."

"One and the same." Avery quickly brought him up to speed. "Lake, Whitner, Oliver, and Hoyt. Four of eleven judges on FISC who had some connection with energy companies and nonconforming judicial behaviors."

"Nonconforming?" Jared asked with a raised eyebrow.

"Actually, just plain unexpected and bizarre," Avery clarified. "It's not an answer, but it is a start."

She stood and arched her back, joints popping in defiance. With a quick roll of her head, Avery let the bun she'd perched on her crown collapse in solidarity with her exhaustion.

"It's a thin reed to hang a conspiracy on," Jared warned, his gaze pinned on the map he'd thrown up on the whiteboard the night before. "But if you believe you see something—"

"I do," she insisted. "Now I need Baz to do me one favor."

"Which is?"

She returned to the color-coded map before them. "I need him to commit theoretical treason. I've got to convince a government attorney to tell me how I could use four companies, a mass murder, an intestate quadriplegic, power outages in Juarez, and a trademark case to cripple the entire power grid on the North American continent and get away with it."

TWENTY-FOUR

Wednesday, October 16

"T hanks for seeing me, Baz." Avery squeezed into the narrow office that seemed more like a cubicle with windows. "I could have worn sunglasses and a fedora, but I doubt they'd have let me through security."

Baz Okune sat behind his desk and refused to smile at the attempted joke. A framed photo of his wedding day from four years ago rested on the ledge behind him. Avery had read a scripture that day at the invitation of his bride, Sadie Daniels. The three of them had become close friends in law school, where being fellow students of color created lasting bonds. She hoped.

"How are you?"

He looked beyond her to the bullpen where a few watched his door with interest. "What do you need, Avery? I've got work to do."

The terse welcome did not bode well. She tried to warm him up. "How's Sadie? When is she due?"

Baz's scowl softened instantly. "In January. Neither of us wants to know what we're having, but our parents are wearing us down."

"Stick to your guns," she advised. "Sadie loves surprises."

The scowl quickly returned. "I don't. So what do you want? You're not doing my career any favors showing up like this." Again, he checked the audience her presence had drawn. "In about five minutes, my supervisor will be knocking on this door. He's not as nice as I am."

Avery quipped, "I know I'm persona non grata in the Stokes administration, but you're a civil servant. I'm not shoving you off a partnership track here."

"It's still a problem, Avery. I may not be an appointee, but my promotional opportunities will plummet when the political folks realize I'm friends with Mata Hari." He shot another quick look at the bullpen beyond his closed door. "I'm not a fan of this administration, but the work here is important. So let's hear it, why did we need to meet in person?"

She hesitated. Telling him she was afraid that her phone and emails were being traced would put an end to any cooperation, but she could give him part of the truth. "I need to show you something, and I didn't want to send it over email. With everything swirling around me, I figured in person was cleaner. I didn't mean to put you in a bad spot."

Suddenly sympathetic, Baz said, "It must be tough. You're the topic of nearly everyone's conversations. Not always in a good way."

"I was doing my job," she reminded him. "He sanctioned genocide, Baz."

"I know, man. I agree with you. You did the right thing. But Americans have a short memory. Brandon Stokes doesn't. His impeachment is already polarizing, and that speech about you was taken as a warning by everyone in the administration, even us civil servants. He wins reelection, and he's going to clean house. Firings, demotions, you name it." Baz nodded at his wedding photo. "Like you said, I've got a kid coming in a few months."

"Then help me fast, and I'll be out of your hair." Shaking off the wave of guilt, Avery pulled out her legal pad and the deck she'd compiled with her findings. "What can you tell me about the Office of

Energy Infrastructure Security? As one of the attorneys in the Office of General Counsel, you advise them sometimes, don't you?"

"How do you know—oh, right. I forgot I was talking to Mata Hari and the guy from *A Beautiful Mind*." Baz rocked back in his seat. "Yes, part of my bailiwick is legal advice to the OEIS. Why?"

"I've been looking into a few cases from around the country, and they all have the common thread of affecting power companies. Mostly small ones and from across the different interconnections."

"Did someone apply for cert?"

The lawyer shorthand referred to a request for the Supreme Court to take up a case. Avery chuckled ruefully and hedged, "I'm not part of the process anymore. This is busywork since my boss is in a coma. But I have to report back on my findings." She stopped short of invoking the chief justice, given that Roseborough had no idea what Avery was doing. "As I looked through the different pleadings and filings, I noticed that the major connections were the various roles the companies play in power generation. When I tried to dig deeper, things got very convoluted."

"Most folks have no idea how electricity gets inside their homes. Convoluted is a generous word to use."

"Which is why I called you." Avery checked her notes, feigning ignorance as she built up to her ask. Baz always liked showing off, and if she got him talking, she could simply sit back and listen. "The companies I've been looking at are mostly independent power producers. But when I tried to understand how they fit together, up popped electric utilities, qualifying facilities, and power exchanges. Which are not to be confused with power marketers who just buy and sell electricity, I think."

Baz cocked his head. "Avery, clearly you've read our website, and you're trying to pretend ignorance. You're way too smart for that, and you're bad at it."

"I'm not pretending ignorance," she countered, caught. "I probably don't need a primer on how all this works, but I do need help."

"Which you can get from a dozen videos on the web, including one on FERC's site. I still don't see how that brings you to OEIS."

Dropping the pretense, she admitted, "Look, Baz, I want to know if someone could organize a way to attack the power system without physically attacking a substation or a transmission hub?"

Baz peered at her intensely. "Absolutely. Is this a confession?"

"Ha-ha. It's information gathering."

He crossed his arms but said nothing.

"Look, I have a theory about some of the cases I'm reviewing, but given my recent issues with grand conspiracies, I don't want to get ahead of myself. I also don't want to have a search history peppered with queries about how to collapse the power grid." She gave him an ingratiating smile. "Ten minutes of tutelage and I'm out of your hair, I promise."

Baz recalled the night she'd rescued him at a seedy Baltimore casino and saved his impending nuptials. In addition to stopping him from losing his shirt, she'd also noticed his tendency to begin, continue, and end his days with more than a little alcohol. She'd gotten him to seek help and convinced him to tell Sadie. Not once had she rubbed his nose in it. He owed her more than one, FERC audience be damned.

He propped his elbows on the desk and reached for her folder. "Okay. What do you understand about the power grid?"

Holding back her relief, Avery said, "Most of the nation's electricity comes from independent power companies, divided up by regions. FERC is responsible for making sure that the bulk electric system—the power grid—actually works. But that means regulating private and public providers as well as protecting the whole infrastructure. I don't think I realized how much of our power grid is run on cooperation and alliances, not government services."

"Most people know their power company, maybe who supplies gas if they get it. But the whole system is a giant jigsaw puzzle run by one of the oldest monopolies in America. A small group of companies get to control how, where, and when electricity is delivered."

"I guess what I'm asking is exactly that—who moves the pieces? How could someone tamper with the entire system?"

"That's the big weakness in our energy model. Old, antiquated systems designed by Edison and Tesla, running on only slightly newer technology, mostly relying on goodwill and cooperation. Our goal is to make sure no one can take advantage of this by moving to a smart grid. Basically, all these various providers are now incorporating information technology systems into their operations so they can communicate better. They've got to talk to each other, they've got to talk to the regional commissions that are balancing loads. They have to connect with their substations and transmission operators. IT is the best way to do it, but by moving online, everything becomes more vulnerable."

"Which is why we have OEIS."

"Exactly. So show me what you're concerned about."

Flipping through the pages in the deck, she pointed to the story about the mass shooting in Idaho. She then laid out still images from the video Preston had given her. "Thad Colgate was employed by Ketchum Power, which is the main provider in the area. His résumé lists him as an engineer for the company. There's video before the massacre, where he's moving around the plant's office. For nearly three hours before he starts shooting, he sits at his computer. What could he have done during that time?"

"How do you know all this?" Baz asked suspiciously. "This video is an internal feed from the company."

"I didn't steal it," she deflected. "Tell me what he could have been doing."

"Any number of things. I can't tell from a grainy photo."

"Speculate. If Thad wanted to undermine the smart grid, what could he have done?"

"Weakened some of the security protocols. Uploaded a virus to the system. Let a hijacker into the system by opening a back door."

"Would anyone know?"

"If the company is running the protocols that we've asked for, yes. But probably not. I imagine they did a cursory review of his workstation and his system, but he'd just murdered his coworkers. I doubt anyone suspected he was aiming for anything more complicated than violent deaths."

"What about a substation in West Virginia? What could you do there?"

"Depends on the size. One transformer at a substation might hurt a few businesses, but if enough are taken out of service, the rest of them are crippled too. They can't transfer enough power to load centers, which could take down power to a town or a city or a major manufacturer."

"A power plant in Texas?"

Baz considered the question. "A power plant is the heart of the grid. It's how we generate power in the electrical system. Depends on whether it's hydro or wind or nuclear, but they house the turbines and generators that produce electricity."

"And Wisconsin?"

"Avery, what the hell is going on?"

"Honestly, Baz, I am not certain, and I cannot take my wild imaginings to the authorities without more information."

"Well, I'm fucking terrified, if it helps."

"Scared enough to help me?"

"Yes."

She gave a furtive peek over her shoulder, then reached into her bag. Quickly, she palmed an envelope and slid it across the desk. "It's a burner phone. I'm the only one with the number. Please keep it with you. I may have more questions."

"Why do I need a burner phone?"

"Because now I'm more convinced that someone has set up a plan to take down the entire power grid without anyone noticing. I won't put you or Sadie in danger. However, I might need your help." She stacked up her materials and returned them to her satchel. "If I'm right, OEIS may need to take over, and there's nothing like saving the world for job security."

"Be careful, Avery. I'm serious."

"So am I. Thanks, Baz." She stood and slung the strap over her shoulder. "Give Sadie my love."

"What are you doing next?"

"I have a few appointments this morning, then I'm going on a field trip."

"Where?" But he thought about the files and knew instantly. "To West Virginia?"

"I'll see you later, Baz. Take care."

"We have a problem," Nyx reported flatly. "She had a meeting this morning at the Department of Energy. Lasted for more than an hour."

"Do you know who her contact is?"

"Facial recognition identifies him as Basil Okune. He's an attorney with the Federal Energy Regulatory Commission. Profile says he's with the Office of General Counsel, and a social media scrub shows that before he became a lawyer, he studied computer science. He and Keene attended law school together."

"Computer science background means he likely works with their cybersecurity division. Let's get eyes on him."

"Already ordered. His wife is an attorney with the NAACP Legal Defense Fund. I have a watch on her as well, but she seems low priority."

"Use your discretion. But no detection."

Nyx stiffened at the reminder of the failed tracking of Avery Keene at the rehab center. "I brought in talent I trust. Five operatives on the ground, three more en route. I'm staying on Keene personally."

"Good." Hayden absorbed the information, speculating about what Avery could have discovered from public records. One of the first rules of intelligence was to never overreact to data, particularly findings that confirmed panic. Yet Avery Keene had managed to unravel an international conspiracy funded by the U.S. government. A second rule of intelligence warned never to underestimate the capacity of your target.

"What's Keene's status?"

"Target is on the move again. Heading toward Bethesda. Likely going to Bethesda Naval Hospital, where Justice Wynn is hospitalized."

"Another interesting person in Avery Keene's orbit. He may be of some utility as a point of leverage."

"Understood. Will keep you posted."

TWENTY-FIVE

As they left Dr. Toca's office, Avery reached for Jared's hand and squeezed. "I know it's not the progress we hoped for, but Dr. Srinivasan sounded optimistic."

He scoffed. "What progress?"

"It's only been a few months, Jared. She and Nigel warned us that until their merger is complete, the sharing of technology that might help treat your father would be limited."

Jared stopped in the wide hospital corridor and gently pulled Avery to the side. He leaned against the cold blue wall, the fluorescent lights washing the passage in a strident glow. "Just so it's said aloud, I know you shouldn't have to placate me. You know my father better than I do. You've done more to save his life."

"Don't start that again," Avery warned. "What matters is what we do right now. And right now, Dr. Toca advises keeping him in a therapeutic coma." She hesitated. "He also reminded us that Justice Wynn would benefit from more contact with us."

"Are you asking me if I'll come to see him more often?"

"I can do it, too. Or I can do it alone. No judgment."

"Bull. Of course you'll be judging me. I would. I'm the one who's barely had a relationship with him for all these years."

She offered a tentative smile. "Not sure if that's a yes or a no."

"It's an 'I'll try' and see how it goes. When do you want to start?" Jared gave a pointed look to the two gentlemen standing a few yards away. "And will our details take a turn?"

Avery's smile faded, and her voice dropped low. "That reminds me—I didn't have a chance to update you about my meeting with Baz. He agrees that I'm on to something, and he showed some significant alarm, but he's also skeptical about what it all means." She moved closer to him so their faces were nearly touching, speaking more softly. "I need to go out to West Virginia and take a look at the site Vic Parker mentioned."

"Are you telling me because you want me to help you lose your detail? If so, I can't do it, Avery. It's not worth the risk."

"I concur. I've already asked Agent Lee to meet us here—but I don't want anyone else to know. I'm going to get him to drive me out there."

"You're going today?"

She nodded. "It's almost a four-hour drive, so we may stay overnight. I don't know how much cell service I'll have, but can you check on Rita for me? Ling went out there today, but if you can call her tonight, I'd appreciate it."

"Parental oversight is my specialty, it seems," he said with a smile, dropping a light kiss on her mouth. "Take care of yourself, okay?"

"Absolutely."

Hours later, Agent Lee and Avery were bouncing along the rutted roads just outside Lewiston, West Virginia. Gravel spurted beneath the wheels of the SUV, which was followed by a second Suburban. The follow car was driven by a stocky, silent agent whose body language when they departed had signaled his dissatisfaction at the assignment. His compatriot in the front passenger seat had managed a polite greeting to Avery, but he had closed her vehicle door with unnecessary force, she thought. Apparently her protectors were not necessarily her fans.

Avery spent most of the drive typing into her laptop as Agent Lee guided the heavy truck through the Appalachian Mountain roads that snaked through the state. Most of her attention focused on synthesizing what she'd learned from Baz. Any conventional attack on the power grid would likely focus on the generators at the power plants. A frontal assault on the equipment required manpower and stealth, or overwhelming force. A cyberattack had the benefit of being stealthy but also scalable without simultaneous individual deployments.

"You ready to tell me more about why we're heading into the backwoods? And why you had a meeting with the DOE without checking in with me first?" Agent Lee's even tone would have fooled no one.

"I'm formulating a theory, and I required more information."

"Information about the U.S. bulk power system, I gather?"

Avery arched a brow. "How did you know?"

"While you might moonlight as a detective, I play one in real life, Ms. Keene." The even tone shifted into one of censure. "I thought we'd reached a point in our relationship where you'd trust me enough to tell me what's going on."

Chagrined, Avery said, "I planned to—it's why I called and asked you to come with me."

"No. You asked me to come with you because your detail would have refused, and I am the sole reason you're not currently on full lockdown."

"Both can be true," she argued. She shifted in her seat to face him. "Here's what I've been up to. I used SSA Gehl's list and plotted out the types of entities that Jason Johnson had under FISA surveillance with his avalanche of warrants. The companies he targeted run the gamut, which is probably why no one noticed any patterns."

"Actually, according to Sarah Beth, they do think there's a pattern. The most promising leads are the financial services firms and the tech companies. They suspect a massive malware attack or some type of ransom demand to undermine the financial system."

"Hmm."

"I take it from your tone you have another idea."

"I took financial systems into account, but I went in a different direction."

"Superior to the top intelligence agencies . . . in the world?"

"Not superior. Different. Yesterday, I reviewed the federal district court dockets and decisions for every FISC judge for the past three years."

"Why three years, and why look at their district court cases?"

"Three years is because AUSA Johnson has been assigned to the FISC for five years and the ramp-up in warrant requests started a year ago. Assuming he was compromised into betraying our country, I figured it would have happened over the past eighteen months or so. Most of the FISC cases are classified, and public filings tell very little."

"Cases? If Johnson is seeking warrants, no cases have been filed."

"Correct. But if someone could compromise Judge Whitner and AUSA Johnson, I presume they want more than one judge to hedge their bets. Whitner got the Thad Colgate case a year ago. What if our adversary has been working at this longer? Three years is arbitrary, but it covers a lot of bases."

"Proceed, Sherlock."

Warming up to her topic, Avery explained the aberrations she'd identified, including the Redhorse case. "I plan to call someone at Redhorse when we get back to D.C. to verify my facts on Judge Lake. My friend Baz basically verified the footage from Idaho."

"How? He should not be digging around on this."

"He's not," Avery conceded. "I showed him the video on my phone, and he confirmed—by look—that it seems to be a control room at a power plant. He said they'd shown the footage around FERC after the mass shooting. He recognized it. That's all."

"Texas? What did you find on Foster Energy?"

"Jared is doing a search on them tomorrow. Just financials and corporate records that I couldn't find with a traditional search."

"Which bring us to West Virginia," Agent Lee said.

"Judge Michael Oliver sits on the bench here, and because he's fairly close, the presiding judge seems to rely on him as much as the D.C.-Maryland-Virginia judges who live within the twenty-mile radius of D.C. required by statute." Avery leaned into the backrest. "On paper, he's a model judge. Straight shooter, no preferential treatment for anyone. Except in the case of Dawson Hawthorne. There, he bent over backward to protect a college classmate from a lawsuit."

"That sounds like favoritism, not corruption."

"Agreed. Until I spoke with Hawthorne's original attorney. He'd filed for extended discovery that would have allowed him to go onto property near the accident that Goodwin owns."

"A power plant?"

"Vic wasn't sure, and I don't think he pushed too hard beyond filing the motion. I read it. He listed the address and its proximity to the accident, but the rationale for giving him access was flimsy at best."

"So Judge Oliver may have simply followed the law."

"Yes, his ruling was legally sufficient. But the presence of a power plant in a recent decision by a FISC judge puts it on my list. A four-hour drive to dismiss a possible act of corruption strikes me as time well spent."

"You're not the one driving," Agent Lee reminded her drolly.

They drove in silence for a full minute. "Let's go to the heart of the matter," Lee said. "Do you believe someone is plotting an attack on the U.S. power grid?"

"It's a definite possibility."

"Every few years, someone warns that the nation's electrical system is at risk. Doesn't work."

"Because most of the terrorist plots—domestic and foreign—attempt to overpower the generators physically."

"That's true. In 2020, we stopped a plot by some white supremacists who thought they could hasten the apocalypse if they destroyed the power grid. They call it *accelerationism,* meaning they can use mass violence and chaos to destroy society. We've been scooping up offshoots of the movement for years."

"You don't think an attack on the grid is likely?"

"Possible, yes. Likely, no. The variables are too complex. I'm sure your friend Mr. Okune explained that the system has four parts: generation, transmission, distribution, and control. The most vulnerable, effective part to damage is generation. Go after the turbines and the machinery at the source."

"My research says you'd need to take out fifty generators to cripple the Eastern Seaboard."

"To coordinate that scale of physical offensive is the stuff of armies. Unless you have air cover, which means either an air force or the sudden collapse of the air traffic control system."

Avery nodded in agreement. "Unlikely, but that's why I went to see Baz. If the goal is massive system disruption, a cyberattack is more efficient."

"The NCIJTF has run the scenarios there too. The level of coordination necessary would require a state actor. A nation both so pissed that they're willing to risk the catastrophic response from the U.S. military and pockets so deep that our economic reprisals mean nothing. There isn't a nation on earth with both the cockiness and fiscal stability to pull it off."

She'd entertained and dismissed it too. "But—what if?"

"What if what?"

"What if someone had the resources, the know-how, and the

strategy to do it. The models say that an offensive that takes out ten percent of the control rooms and the systems they service could do the trick."

Agent Lee disagreed. "You'd have to gain access to the control rooms, take over the vulnerable generators, bypass any security protocols, and simultaneously conduct your raid across three independent—"

"Yet interdependent—"

"Systems," Agent Lee concluded. "The level of organization, information, funding, and rage it would take is unlike anything we've ever seen. This isn't hijacking airplanes. It's hijacking several dozen separate facilities and infecting them with a malware that can transfer control at precisely the right moment. Not even the most loathsome terrorist has been able to pull that off."

Processing his analysis, Avery sank into contemplative silence. Baz had cautioned her about the same limits, but from a technology standpoint. Logic and experience rejected her premise, and she had no effective counter. Except a gut feeling that the patterns she identified signaled an unparalleled threat level.

Agent Lee nudged up the volume on the jazz that poured through the SUV's speakers. He noted the slight slump to Avery's shoulders, the irritated tapping on her computer case. With a mind like hers, she rarely faced a puzzle she couldn't solve. And her recent track record was sufficient to endow even a seasoned field agent with outsize confidence.

Lee admired Avery—how she connected dots no one else noticed. She had a bravery he wished for his own kids. Too often, though, it was buoyed by a sense of invincibility. The combination, he knew, could be deadly. A four-hour trek to the foothills of the Appalachian Mountains seemed like a small price to pay to remind Avery that she was as fallible as the rest of them.

Following the directions of his GPS, he wrestled the truck along the uneven ground that ran parallel to the railroad tracks. Undergrowth battled with metal structures that attempted to hold back nature's expansion.

"Where exactly is this power station?" he asked dubiously. "Nothing around here that would suggest a power supply that significant."

"Vic said it was a quarter mile away from the accident site." She opened his email and called up the map from his motion for discovery. Tracking the location, she gave Agent Lee directions as the GPS fell quiet. They crested a low hill, and out of nowhere, a concrete structure popped into view. Transmission lines ran overhead, connecting to the ones that ran alongside the railroad tracks. A barbed-wire fence circled the building, and getting as close as he could, Agent Lee brought the SUV to a halt.

"Well," he admitted, "there is something out here in the middle of nowhere."

Avery scrambled out of the truck and began making her way to the fence. A quick scan revealed surveillance cameras from every direction. She walked around the perimeter, studying the wire fence that surrounded the equipment and a building the size of a Wendy's restaurant. Agent Lee trailed her as she completed her inspection.

"Other than the fence and camera, this site has pretty flimsy security," Avery noted. The fencing had seen better days, and despite the dangerous-looking equipment, the area showed signs of disrepair. Overgrown weeds strangled the base of the fence, and kudzu climbed a rear segment.

"Sign says it's private property, Avery. I don't have probable cause to go on-site."

"True," she responded as she removed her satchel, reached inside for a slim case, and handed the bag to Agent Lee. She shoved the case in her pocket. "But I'm not a state agent. At worst, I'm a trespasser."

With a quick dash toward the fence, she squeezed between a gap and popped out on the other side.

"Ms. Keene!" Agent Lee jogged toward the fence, but, aware of the cameras and his jurisdiction, could only seethe with frustration. "Avery, get back here, damn it!"

"I'll be right back," she promised as she made her way across the property.

TWENTY-SIX

Behind her, the second SUV lumbered to a stop. Avery could hear Agent Lee ordering them to stand down. The FBI had to follow strict rules of conduct. She didn't.

Cautiously, she approached the building, crunching through a gravel lot that had no cars and no recent evidence of visitors. The structure itself was dull concrete with a flat industrial roof, unremarkable and aged. As she got closer, she heard a low humming sound. She took out one of the burner phones and turned on the video. Quietly, she circled the building, noting the absence of windows except for narrow insets near the roofline. Too high to see inside. The structure had three doors. The front doors were heavy and bolted with a padlock looped through the door pulls. Same with the back. The side entrance had a simpler mechanism—a hasp secured by another large padlock.

On her second circuit, she stopped by the side door and removed her case. Out of sight of Agent Lee but in view of the cameras, she sidled up to the door and turned her body to block sight of her hands. In seconds, the lock opened. She replaced her tools and unlatched the shank.

No alarm blared at her entry. The only noise was the rising thrum coming from inside. Avery eased the door open farther and stepped inside, prepared for her eyes to adjust to the dark.

Instead, her eyes widened with surprise. Lights flashed in random order, their coded messages in blue, green, white, and red. Row after row ran the length of the building, the occupants sentinels to a million calculations and communications. She lifted her camera and began to film again. Vic Parker hadn't stumbled across a power station.

He'd identified a server farm.

Avery snaked her way through tall rows of towers of black computers, then silver columns of hardware, stripped of keyboards and monitors. Instead, sleek uniform devices whirred away as they processed information streaming in across invisible connections. She snapped still photos of the servers from various angles, trying to capture as much information as possible. Fans spun overhead, churning up cooler air in assistance to the thrum of powerful air-conditioning units. Nevertheless, the heat of the devices hit her in waves.

Once she was certain she'd captured every possible angle without climbing atop the machines, Avery exited the building. Across the lot, Agent Lee and his two minions waited with identical stances. Legs akimbo, arms folded, sunglasses emphasizing their stern visages. She took her time closing the distance and shimmying through the gate.

Without a word, she returned to the truck and climbed inside. Agent Lee spoke in low tones to the other agents before he joined her. The quiet thud of the door and the precise turn of the ignition key let Avery know he was livid. Eventually, the Suburban champed through the gravel and underbrush and returned to the county road leading to the highway. Nearly fifteen minutes had passed in absolute silence.

"I'm sorry—" she began.

"No, you're not," Agent Lee cut her off. "You aren't sorry or regretful or apologetic. Once again, you chose to do what you wanted without regard to the position you put yourself in, let alone me or my men. What if the gate was electrified?"

"I could tell it wasn't," Avery protested. "The wiring was wrong."

"You could tell no ground wires had been hooked up to the fence at an electric substation? When did you become a contractor?"

Avery squirmed but replied, "I read a book about them. I've seen schematics. I wasn't risking my life."

"And you also read a book on X-ray vision, so you knew what awaited you inside? Or who might have shown up to face us while you were isolated and unarmed?"

"No, sir." She twisted in her seat to face his profile. "I thought I'd considered all the risks. I hadn't. I am truly—um—remorseful."

"Avery! I could have put you in cuffs for breaking and entering state property." It was the first time she had heard him raise his voice beyond controlled modulation.

"I'm sorry, sir. I'm convinced an ominous danger is coming our way."

Agent Lee gave a terse nod and continued driving. "So?"

"Yes?"

"What did you see?"

"The building is not a substation. It's a computer server farm. Rows and rows. The entire building is full of them, and they are all fully engaged."

"Who would be running a server farm in the middle of nowhere?" Agent Lee cocked his head. "The gentleman who owns the railroad, he owns the server farm as well?"

"According to Vic Parker's filing, the Goodwin family owns all the land that the state or the federal government doesn't. My cursory research of public land use records shows that there was a substation on that property, leased out for use. But the land seems to have reverted to Goodwin."

"How does that fit with your theory about a rogue attack on the electrical grid?"

She had mulled over the question during the rugged trip back to the highway. "To attack the grid in a major way, one scenario says the attackers would need to take thirty substations offline. That assumes physical attacks like the snipers who shot up the PG&E substation in 2014. They took out seventeen transformers."

"Russia targeted Ukraine using hackers in 2016. They knocked out a major section of their grid. We responded by shoring up our security."

Avery reached for her computer. "From what I've read, the U.S. response to Ukraine did try to harden the system, but technology keeps changing. Those systems, like the one in Ukraine, used to be air-gapped—keeping them away from the internet. But more and more are using high-tech monitoring and diagnostic tools that link several systems together to increase efficiency. They're heavily encrypted, but they use the internet to communicate."

"So the more sophisticated the grid gets, the more vulnerable it becomes."

"Precisely. Plus, a cyberattack on industrial control systems can target multiple vulnerabilities at once. A physical attack relies on exposed equipment like generators or transformers. A hacker team can target local power distribution, power flow management systems, smart thermostats, you name it."

"And still also attack generators and transformers using malware. But how many systems are there?"

"More than three thousand electric utilities across the country." Avery contemplated the numbers. "A cyberattack would need cutting-edge reach, have multiple targets in case of detection, and be prepared for faster recovery to take down another target."

She let the statement hang in the air.

"Which would require a great deal of computer power," Lee added grimly.

"And coordination without risk of detection."

"Like a private server farm tucked away in the middle of nowhere that could be used to coordinate a massive attack or be the prime location for deploying whatever malware they might be using."

"Yes, sir. Exactly."

He pressed a button on his console. "Dial Special Agent in Charge Sarah Beth Gehl."

Her image appeared in the video screen. "This is Agent Gehl. Hello, Agent Lee."

"Sarah Beth, you've got Robert and Avery Keene. Are you alone?"

"I am, still, hold on." She vanished for a few seconds, and they heard a door close. "Now I won't be interrupted. Ms. Keene," she acknowledged, "to what do I owe this call?"

Avery quickly brought the agent up to speed. "I haven't quite figured out how Texas and Wisconsin fit into this, but I am confident there's a connection."

"I can convene the task force to review your theory, but I can't give you credit for it."

Avery imagined the feeding frenzy that would ensue. "You'll be doing me a huge favor. I'm all for anonymity."

"Good to know. You'll need to fully debrief me and show me your work. I'll present it to them. When will you be back, Robert?"

"Not before nine p.m. However, I can have her in your office at eight a.m. tomorrow morning. I would also consider it a personal favor if you reached out to the director tonight and updated her. If you find this as compelling as I do, I'll need a warrant to send a team back to the server farm."

"Actually, no, you won't. Remember, AUSA Johnson already secured a FISA warrant for that location. I'll review it tonight, but unless it was a pen register or trap and trace only, I think we have permission to go onto the premises for a search. Legally."

"Let me know when I can assemble the troops."

"I will. And here's another piece of good news: AUSA Johnson's attorneys responded to me this afternoon. It looks like the prospect of life in prison is a strong motivator. He's agreed to speak with us tomorrow. Could be a game changer."

. . .

Nyx reviewed the video footage again.

"They have the server farm—Avery Keene and the FBI agent she works with." Nyx noted how the FBI stayed out of range after the first circuit. "Keene is the one who made the connection."

"Impressive," Hayden replied admiringly.

"You're pleased?"

"No, just impressed. However, there's no need for precipitant action. The West Virginia location has been useful, but we have the backup location in Kentucky."

Nyx was agitated by the breach. "Avery Keene has proven to be more formidable than expected. How would you like to proceed?"

Hayden turned to look at the monitor on the right side of her wide desk. It displayed Avery's image and dossier.

"Nothing yet."

Hayden had already memorized Avery's history, learned about her parents' tragic love story and her mother's spiral into addiction. In another life, she imagined they might have become allies. "So far, Ms. Keene has shown herself to be a woman of great character and mild irritation."

"Who threatens to undermine nearly two years of work," Nyx reminded her. "She's too close. The mission has three prongs, and she's uncovering the first fairly quickly. What if she discovers what else you have planned?"

Hayden folded her hands beneath her chin and let her eyes drift shut. Nyx fell silent. In her two decades as an assassin, she had worked for a variety of clients whose motives ranged from megalomania to ideological zeal. To her, death was death—an inevitable outcome to every life.

"I appreciate your sense of concern, my friend," Hayden said thoughtfully. "The loss of the servers will be inconvenient. But if harm befalls Ms. Keene, such an event will activate multiple agencies and will likely delay our timeline. Instead, I've decided to launch Myrina ahead of schedule."

Nyx was stunned by the news. "How soon?"

"Imminently," Hayden conceded. "As to the other facets of my plan, Ms. Keene is no closer to understanding what is unfolding than any of my targets. If she becomes more than a nuisance, we will act."

Nyx disagreed with the hesitation regarding Keene, but she resisted the urge to quarrel with Hayden. So far, her plan had moved exactly as predicted. "I hope you're right."

"I don't believe in hope, Nyx. Only action. Send the team to retrieve the West Virginia servers now. Make sure they destroy the location. Burn it down."

TWENTY-SEVEN

Thursday, October 17

SAC Gehl ushered Avery and Agent Lee into her office. Sunlight streamed through the wide windows, casting a halo on random objects. "Coffee? Tea?"

"Coffee, please," Avery answered, smothering a yawn after a late return from West Virginia. By the time they'd returned to D.C., Noah had gone home, and Ling was fast asleep.

Jared had listened to her report of the day's activities, but he was clearly preoccupied with his dad. She'd tried to distract herself by completing her make-work assignment for Chief Roseborough. The end result was a wholly banal analysis on the proliferation of ransomware attacks on ill-equipped government sites, knowing as she typed it that the threats facing the judiciary went deeper than any law clerk would glean from conference papers and law review articles. Indeed, she'd come away from her research and her visit to West Virginia with more questions, fewer answers, and a hefty sense of unease. Now, though, she needed to clear the cobwebs from her brain.

"Robert?"

He appeared not to hear Sarah Beth and was staring at his phone.

She hovered near the coffeepot and a small array of condiments. The machine whirred through the packet and slowly dripped liquid caffeine into an FBI mug. "Do you take anything?"

"Cream and sugar, thank you."

Agent Lee suddenly snarled at his phone. "Son of a bitch."

"What happened?" Agent Gehl stopped mid-pour. In nearly twenty years, she could count the number of times Robert Lee had cursed in her presence. Twice, the expletives had come with a body count. "Robert?"

"The tactical unit is on-site in West Virginia. This is what they found." He turned his phone toward them, and Avery and Agent Gehl crowded in close.

"What am I looking at?" Agent Gehl asked. "The building is empty. Scorched."

Avery muttered the same curse Agent Lee had spit out. "Yesterday, it was full. Wall to wall with servers. Wires and cooling fans. The works."

"Are you sure it's the same location?"

Agent Lee glared at the question. "I doubt there are two cinderblock buildings situated in the middle of nowhere. They cleared it out. Every screw, every wire. Looks like they used thermite to torch any traces of evidence."

"Because they saw me go inside." Avery's shoulders sagged. "I'm sorry."

He dismissed her apology. "An outfit tight enough to move what you found—overnight and without any warning—this isn't on you."

Agent Gehl went behind her desk. Tapping in a series of commands, she brought up the footage Avery had shared last night. "I had our tech team review your images. The devices in that room are state-of-the-art. Most of it is next-gen tech, not available here commercially yet. Companies like NSO and Palantir use this level of equipment. The task force isn't even using its older cousins yet."

"Does that mean you believe me?" Avery asked quietly. "Someone is plotting to attack us."

"I'm not all the way there yet, but the evidence does support your theory that bad actors are operating in the U.S." Before she could continue, her desk phone rang. "Agent Gehl." She listened to the other end in silence before uttering, "Damn it. Get a full autopsy. I want it done this morning. Use the director's name if you need to."

She slammed the phone. "Jason Johnson is dead. Found in his cell twenty minutes ago. Looks like a massive heart attack."

"He's thirty-six years old. Was thirty-six." Agent Lee surged to his feet. "Who the hell is behind this? How are they in a federal prison—how do they know we're talking to him?"

Agent Gehl shook her head. "They are in the DOJ, in the FISA court. We can't know how broad their reach goes."

She closed the screen and motioned to the door. "Avery, you are now in imminent danger if anyone finds out you're helping us."

"I was in danger the minute Preston Davies found me. What do you need?"

"Until news of Johnson's death, I'd changed my mind about taking credit for your work. The task force needs your help, and I had to tell the director about your involvement. She agreed to allow you to keep collaborating."

"What if I object?" Agent Lee protested. "Avery barely survived her last attempt to help us. We don't know who we're facing. Any one on that task force could be compromised."

Agent Gehl disagreed. "I know these folks. If we're going to figure out what's going on, every idea and every bright mind needs to be at the table." She looked at Avery. "But if you're concerned, I can pass on what I find out. We can keep you out of it."

Avery gave both agents a look of confidence that belied how she really felt. "I'm already in the middle. Let's go find a terrorist."

The trio entered the conference room to be met by the same

baleful looks from Friday plus a few new faces that signaled mild disapproval. Agent Gehl strode to the front of the room near a microphone embedded in the futuristic table. She opened a panel that lifted a keyboard to the surface. With a few keystrokes, the lights dimmed, and the shades drew closed around the room. "What is said in here is code-word clearance only."

"Then why is a civilian in here with us?"

Even in the dim light, Avery recognized the jackass from the NSA. Before she could respond, Agent Gehl shot her a warning look. "She is present at my request. For the record, we have representatives from the NSA, DOJ, DOE, Secret Service, DOD, Homeland Security, State, and NGA."

"Where is Europol?" asked the State Department representative.

"For now, this is an inside-the-family discussion. I'd like to keep it that way for the time being."

Turf wars across agencies were as familiar and natural as breathing, but when an American asked to keep Europe in the dark, no one argued. Expecting as much, Sarah Beth called up another screen. The image of the continental U.S. interconnections and NERC regions for the bulk power system flew onto the screen. Another tap overlaid the map with the dots Avery had placed in her makeshift presentation. She tossed Avery a laser pointer for the wide screen where the images were displayed. "Ms. Keene, would you care to explain what we're looking at?"

Taking the laser pointer, she began, "As you know, I recently met with Preston Davies, who clerked for Judge Francesca Whitner."

"And as I recall, you were told to stand down." The DOJ liaison threw up his hands. "She has already wreaked havoc at the Supreme Court, Sarah Beth. Why are you dragging the rest of us into her maelstrom?"

"Shut up, Claude," Agent Gehl said mildly. "The fewer words you say now, the less you'll have to eat later."

The room fell silent. Gehl pointed to Avery. "Continue."

"I have not looked at Mr. Davies's murder; however, on my own time, I did conduct research on Judge Whitner. Her last decision, which freed Thad Colgate, resulted in his attack on the Idaho power plant where he was an electrical engineer. According to footage from the scene of the shooting, before Mr. Colgate murdered his colleagues, he spent a bit of time at his terminal."

"Perhaps working up the nerve to massacre children," muttered the Secret Service agent who'd ridden in the passenger seat on her trip to Great Falls. When heads swiveled in his direction, he added, "Sorry."

Avery continued grimly. "Based on a hunch, I started reviewing the recent decisions of all the FISC judges going back three years."

"How did you get your hands on FISC documents?" the Homeland Security representative demanded. He blustered at Sarah Beth, "We agreed she would not—"

"Like I told Claude, please shut up, Andrew. No one in this room has broken a law or violated our obligations." She glowered at each occupant. "If anyone else interrupts Ms. Keene, I will suspend this briefing and reach out to your supervisor to have you replaced. Not simply at this meeting but on this task force."

At the summoned silence, Avery plowed on. "Three other judges came to my attention based on their rulings at the federal district court level. Judge Ruth Hoyt of Texas, Judge Michael Oliver of West Virginia, and Judge Alvin Lake of Wisconsin.

"In her district court, Judge Hoyt granted a subpoena to give a plaintiff access to records related to the power outage in south Texas a few years ago. The records expose several companies that are part of ERCOT."

She tapped another part of the screen. "Judge Alvin Lake sits on the Wisconsin federal district court. He popped onto my radar because he denied a TRO for trademark infringement for a security company. The rivals have similar names and logos, but Redhorse— the plaintiff and a local company—came first and was on the verge of a big IPO. Starhorse swooped in, stole their branding and then some of their clients. Mostly midsize fish, but in an industry that stood out. Redhorse lost its contract to service several utility providers in the MISO operating region."

Avery used the red dot on the end of her pointer to emphasize the final area. "Yesterday, I went to check out a location that had come up as part of Judge Michael Oliver's tenure as a federal judge in West Virginia. The incident in question was a motion for discovery that Judge Oliver denied in a railroad accident."

Before anyone could interrupt, she continued. "I looked at this case only because Judge Oliver veered from his typical pattern on issues of discovery. I spoke to the attorney of record, and he told me that the discovery motion included a request to access a facility that the lawyer thought might be a substation or an electrical plant of some kind. Judge Oliver shut him down promptly. Several days later, the injured party with minimal financial resources was represented by a high-end law firm, and new attorneys took over the case. Agent Gehl, can you play the video, please?"

Sarah Beth clicked another device, and the cell phone footage of the server farm gave the room a clear depiction of what she'd seen yesterday. After the video ended, the SAC played the video Agent Lee had gotten from his team.

"Is that the same room?" The question came from the woman who spoke for the National Geospatial Intelligence Agency.

"Yes. Fifteen hours between the two recordings," Agent Lee spoke for the first time. "I was on-site yesterday when the first video was recorded at 4:57 p.m. My agents found the entire facility had been cleared out by 8:06 this morning when they arrived."

Darnell Strom, the representative from the Department of Energy, raised his hand. Sarah Beth nodded, and he asked, "Was that the substation Ms. Keene had heard about?"

Avery confirmed, "Same location, and the server farm required copious amounts of electricity. But it looked like some transmission lines had been dismantled or abandoned."

She returned to the map. "I'm not an expert on this, but based on what I have found, there have been possible intrusions of the bulk power system in the West, the East, and ERCOT. A security company, a rogue electrical engineer, a server farm, and detailed information about the Texas power grid." She laid the pointer on the table and turned to Agent Gehl. "I'm happy to answer questions."

The agent restored the light and shut down the map. DOE had his hand up again. "Mr. Strom?"

"With all due respect to Ms. Keene, I fail to see the point, Agent Gehl. She has old cases tied together by random occurrences and a theft ring. Why is this before an elite task force? I've heard scarier bedtime stories. From my four-year-old." A couple of chuckles signaled agreement.

"I don't know if it adds up to anything actionable, but based on the response last night in West Virginia, I found sufficient cause to brief you all." Agent Gehl pinned him with a quizzical look. "Do you not find it suspicious that an abandoned utility became a hub for computer data and vanished overnight?"

"No, I don't." He squared his shoulders. "FERC has protocols in place to detect suspicious activity and potential attacks on the grid. This task force has already run a threat simulation based on a power grid attack, and the findings were clear. No known threat actor has the ability to coordinate the scale of action necessary to effectuate a system-wide shutdown."

"What about an unknown threat actor?" Avery responded. "What if this is an operator none of you have on your radar?"

"But you managed to find it by reading a few unrelated cases?" He didn't bother to scoff. Instead, he turned to the rest of the room. "We know Ms. Keene came to see Mr. Okune yesterday, and that he provided her with a friendly overview of how electricity works in America." He threw her a condescending smile. "As I am certain Mr. Okune explained, FERC and NERC have developed a robust strategy to respond to cyber incidents. I can assure you we have well-trained personnel who constantly scan for anomalies."

Claude from DOJ posited, "It might be worth taking a look, Darnell. The legal pattern—"

"Is not actually a pattern," Darnell responded in exasperation. "For God's sake, we did this already. Six months ago. Now, because she's on television, we allow her in here to spin another story. She has four data points and a TikTok video to prove her conspiracy. Which is nothing."

He got to his feet. "The NCIJTF is designed to respond to relevant cyberthreats and share agency data. While I appreciate the interest from the FBI, on behalf of the Department of Energy, I encourage our task force head to focus on more actionable data. I have a meeting with the assistant secretary in less than an hour, and unless there is more I haven't seen, I'm going to take my leave."

Others looked around the room with varying degrees of agreement and incredulity as Darnell fairly stomped out. The NGA rep ventured, "The data is rather thin, however, we'd be happy to scan our records for any activity in and around the West Virginia site last night. If it might be useful."

Agent Gehl smiled gratefully. "Thank you. It would be helpful." She scanned the room. "Anyone else want to participate in some interagency cooperation?"

Claude offered, "I'd be interested to see what records the plaintiffs got out of Texas. If I can share it, I will."

DHS chimed in with an offer to look into Starhorse and its security contracts. "I agree with Darnell that this is weak gruel, but we won't lose any ground by poking around."

The Secret Service agent spoke up. "I feel obliged to remind everyone that Ms. Keene should not be made privy to any classified information or documents. Indeed, she shouldn't be in this room."

"Understood," Agent Gehl said coolly. "Please direct any and all findings to my attention. I'll compile what we get, and if it rises to the level of concern that we should reconvene, you'll hear from me."

The task force members filed out of the room, chatting quietly among themselves. One tight chuckle was audible. Once the room cleared, Avery dropped into one of the padded leather chairs. "Well, that was pleasant. But maybe this is all in my head," she admitted. "The asshole from DOE wasn't completely wrong."

"No," Agent Gehl said. "Darnell wasn't disbelieving. He was defensive. Because he sensed you had a point, but he doesn't know what to make of it."

"That's why the other agencies agreed to help." Agent Lee joined them at the table. "For the last twenty years, every group has been taught not to share data and not to ignore chatter on the web. If you're wrong, you've cost some bureaucrats a couple of hours of time."

"But if you're right," Gehl continued, "we still have no idea what someone is planning, or even who it might be. Any idea where we start looking?"

"The dark web," Avery suggested. "I know you're already on it, but how deep are your networks?"

"We can request that the NSA go fishing, but I doubt this will take priority." Agent Gehl shook her head. "I believe you are on to something, Avery, but I cannot justify compelling any of the interagency partners to prioritize this theory."

Avery felt a knot twist in her stomach, but she had an answer. "There's a guy I know who might have a place for us to start. He has connections with the very worst of the bad guys. He may be privy to chatter or able to point us in the right direction."

"Who might that be?" asked Agent Gehl with a raised brow. "Is this a colleague of Mr. Wynn's we can read in?"

"Not exactly." Avery dreaded the coming revelation. "I got to know him recently, and we've been in touch."

Agent Lee leaned forward in his seat. "Who do you know with that type of intelligence, Ms. Keene?"

She felt his condemnation even before she answered, "Major William Vance."

TWENTY-EIGHT

Herded back into the office of the Special Agent in Charge, Avery waited for the eruption from Agent Lee. Part of her regretted springing this information on him in front of the SAC, but she had precious little time to keep new secrets or hide old ones. Especially from the one person who consistently seemed to believe her.

"How long have you been in contact with an enemy of the state?" Agent Lee demanded icily. A vein throbbed at his temple, and his fists balled by his side. "And how long have you been hiding this fact from the authorities?"

Avery kept her eyes level, her tone the same. "Sir, Major Vance contacted me anonymously after I testified in September. Warned me that there was chatter about an attack on the U.S. I didn't give it much credence, considering the source. He reached out to me again the night Boylen doxxed us—he gave me a string of numbers he said one of his informants had provided. I haven't had time to decipher them—and I don't know that it's worth the effort. I haven't spoken to him otherwise."

Agent Gehl, taking on the role of good cop, inquired patiently, "Why did you not report contact with Major Vance?"

"Honestly?"

"A novel concept," Agent Lee groused beneath his breath.

Avery inhaled sharply. "I didn't lie to you, Agent Lee."

He grunted. "A lie of omission and a lie of commission both send you straight to hell, Ms. Keene."

The outraged expression couldn't mask the disappointment she read in his eyes. "The first call happened after I'd just been grilled by the House attorneys and accused of yet another crime. You were working on your own issues with the impeachment, and bringing up Major Vance would have muddied the waters. The second call came right before my mother's life was put in jeopardy."

Lee rejected her explanation. "You weren't too overwhelmed to tell me, Ms. Keene. You chose not to do so."

"I chose not to," she admitted, "because I didn't think it was relevant yet."

"That's not your call, Avery," Agent Lee snapped, taking a step closer to her. "I have always done right by you."

"Yes, sir." She bit at her lip and sighed. "But those around you haven't. I know too much about how all this works, Agent Lee. Plus, trust has never been my strong suit. I should have told you, but I didn't. And I will probably muck up something else. Still, you have to know that I did not intend any disrespect."

Agent Gehl stepped between the two of them and gently pushed them apart. "Robert, regardless of how she came to have contact information for a potential war criminal—" She paused on the descriptor before continuing, "If Ms. Keene can quickly secure intelligence that explains what is going on, we should leverage the asset."

Profoundly disappointed, he corrected, "Sarah Beth, no explanation or justification or legalese will make collaborating with the enemy okay. Ever. William Vance took an oath as a Marine, and he besmirched the uniform. He sanctioned atrocities on behalf of our nation. Real people lost their lives, and he would have continued if they hadn't been shut down. The commander in chief will face trial for his role. Yet Vance slunk off and is hiding in the shadows, calling you to chat about old times."

Avery bristled and corrected, "He called to warn me."

"About what?" Agent Gehl asked.

"He was vague the first time. Like I said, he told me he'd heard chatter about a major action in the U.S. Nothing specific or clear. I pressed him for details, including why he called me instead of a spy or an agent."

Agent Lee grunted, "Because we would have tracked his ass to whatever hole he's hiding in."

Agent Gehl gave him a quelling look and returned to Avery. "And the second call? What kind of numbers did he give you?"

"It was a random string of three-digit numbers," Avery explained with a shrug. "I did a cursory review, but I haven't been able to figure it out yet. I was going to focus on it today."

Agent Gehl grabbed a pen and pad from her desk. "What are the numbers?"

Avery quickly recited, "434. 314. 982. 850." She shrugged again, a bit defensive that she hadn't paid more attention to the information. But in the back of her mind, she had been rotating the problem and was frustrated by her inability to figure it out. "It's not a phone number or a docket number for any court system."

She glanced at the legal pad and reconsidered the numbers, splitting them in her head without decimal points, rearranging them in pairs and in two groups of six. A faint tingle of recognition pulled at her.

Agent Lee was looking at the pad as well. Shaking his head, he derided, "Your Navy boyfriend didn't tell you?"

At the jeer, Avery winced. The jibe struck its mark, and she groaned aloud in embarrassment. "It's longitude and latitude, isn't it?"

"Looks like it could be."

She nodded. "As I said, I should have put more time into it."

Agent Gehl moved to her computer. "Well, let's type it in as directional coordinates and see what we have." Soon, an aerial view came into focus. As she zoomed closer, the image on the screen caused all three to fall silent. They were looking at rural map coordinates in the United States.

"A nuclear power plant," Avery whispered. "In the middle of South Dakota."

"Looks like we've got another pin in your conspiracy," Agent Gehl said.

Avery tentatively suggested, "I should contact Vance to see what else he can tell us."

Lee's jaw tightened as he bit out, "You are not law enforcement, Avery. You might be a genius with an incredible memory, but you have neither the tools nor, apparently, the wisdom to discern proper behavior."

"Agent Lee—"

"And you don't have the right to gloss over what Vance has done. I will never forget what I saw on those videos or who authorized genocide. I don't know how anyone could."

Bristling, Avery retorted, "Forget? Like you said, I don't forget anything. Not an image. Not a word. Nothing. Conversations crowd in my head, images seared in my mind without any way to make them stop. I can tell you what I had for lunch the day my dad died. What I had for dinner the first time Rita passed out without feeding me all day. I can describe the faces of every person who died in the room on that video, Agent Lee."

She stalked over to the window, where cars streamed down the street below. Her eyes burned with tears she would never release, instead choosing indignation. "Did you know I can cite the holdings of every case I have ever read for Justice Wynn? I recall with perfect clarity every plea for help we've turned down. Every man wrongfully incarcerated. Every woman denied justice by a poorly crafted statute."

Pressing her hands against the sill, she reached for calm and steadied her voice. "I am well aware that I should have told you about Major Vance. But on that day, I was being accused of slander, extortion, and manufacturing evidence in a scheme to topple the president. So I kept it to myself. I apologize."

"And the second time?"

"I screwed up."

"That's not good enough, Avery."

Slowly, she faced him, entreaty and intention etched into her brow. "It will have to be. If he can help us identify who might be planning to destroy the nation's power grid and possibly disrupt medical, financial, and industrial systems, I will accept his help. Will you?"

Agent Lee responded gently, "No, Avery. I won't. As you and Agent Gehl seem aligned on this matter, I will leave you both to it. The FBI detail will escort you to Mr. Wynn's home at your direction." He nodded to Sarah Beth. "I wish you both luck."

Shocked by his response, Avery watched in disbelief as he spun on his heel and exited the office. "He's quitting?"

Sarah Beth took her by the elbow and led her to a chair. "Robert has a very strict moral code. It's what has made him so effective as an agent and as the head of OLEC. He doesn't play favorites. Doesn't shade the truth. He'll bend the rules to get the job done, but he never breaks them."

"Major Vance reached out to me," Avery protested. "I didn't go looking for him."

"Robert also values loyalty. And you hurt him."

Avery flinched. "That wasn't my intention."

"Be that as it may, you put him in a very difficult position for a man of his integrity. Accepting help from an enemy is a spy's game. He's on that side of the wall for a reason."

Avery pushed the agent. "As opposed to doing your job?"

"I color between the lines a bit more than he likes, and I have no problems if a rule snaps on occasion." Agent Gehl shrugged. "He clearly dotes on you, and it troubles him that you'd keep such an important secret from him."

With a snort, Avery replied, "Agent Lee tolerates me. There's no doting involved."

"He drove you nine hours round-trip yesterday on a hunch that you had. I've seen him ream out field agents with stacks of evidence—much more than you've got."

She sighed. "So what do I do?"

"Reach out to your contact and get us a name. I'll coax Robert back to the fold. We'll need his support."

"And if he refuses?"

"Groveling has always been an effective tactic." Agent Gehl gave her a sly wink. "What do you need to reach Major Vance?"

"He uses the app Chimera." Avery retrieved her phone, but hesitated. "I haven't used my phone outside a RFID-shielded location since Preston was shot."

"Right." Agent Gehl rose and motioned for Avery to join her. "We've got a SCIF you can use that will scramble your signal. Come on."

Trailing behind her, Avery and Agent Gehl made their way to a separate area of the NCIJTF offices. The sensitive compartmented information facility, or SCIF, typically blocked all communications in and out, guaranteeing absolute privacy to the occupants. For their purposes, the task force had created a stepped-down version that distorted rather than jammed signals. Avery powered up her device and sent a message via the application.

Danger Will Robinson.

Without knowing his time zone or whereabouts, Avery warned Agent Gehl that a response could take a while. "Luckily, I have nothing else on my dance card today."

"I, unfortunately, do have other obligations." Agent Gehl glanced at her watch. "Looks like I'm going to have to take formal responsibility for you. I've got some paperwork for you to fill out to make you official, and then you're in business. Once I get you squared away, I'll leave word with the duty agent to return you to my offices when you have completed your reconnaissance."

"Thank you, ma'am." Avery gave a weak smile. "I appreciate everything. You have no reason to believe me."

"Like Agent Lee said, I don't want to be the one who dismisses the warning signs. If he has faith in you, I do." She reached for the door handle. "Go find us some answers, Ms. Keene."

By late afternoon, Avery was heading toward stir-crazy. Guilt, doubt, and irritation cycloned in an endless loop, spinning her thoughts into useless trails. Over and over again, she replayed Agent Lee walking away. Giving up on her.

Unfortunately, she couldn't blame him. Like Agent Gehl said, he was a man of integrity. One who bent the rules for her again and again. Shame washed over her in waves. He'd stuck up for her, saved her mother's life. Risked his own.

As soon as she made contact with Vance, she would track down Agent Lee. Show real contrition and try to atone. Flipping through scenarios, Avery played out the ways she could demonstrate remorse. Deep in thought, she nearly missed the buzz of her device.

Snatching up the phone, she unlocked the screen and saw the new text.

Hello Giant Killer.

She quickly typed, Need help.

Shoot.

Avery had thought about how to pose her questions in a sufficiently vague manner that an interloper might be confused. Any chatter about power plays or electric shocks?

Vance's response took a beat. Usual bluster out of Beijing and Moscow. Bravado from Tehran and Karachi.

Just like Agent Lee warned, the major suspects would be the

governments of American adversaries like China, Russia, Iran, or Pakistan. Taking another tack, she thought about the software Jared investigated. Any rumors?

Hacktivist collective making big plays. Hired guns. No word on target. Any information.

Wilder rumors of Tel Aviv, Seoul, or Joburg. Ask boyfriend about Pegasus. Has competition. Might be supplier of services.

Timing?

No. Whispers only.

Anything else?

Neg. Will keep lines open.

The message box disappeared, and so did the lines of text. The safety protocol meant nothing to her. She launched the notes application and re-created the discussion. She'd show Agent Gehl and, with any luck, Agent Lee. Her spycraft left a great deal to be desired, but she had another data point.

Jared's initial research into the tech on Preston's phone pointed to two likely tech hubs that had created similar spyware. One, a rival to NSO based in Tel Aviv. The second was a lesser-known outfit based in Seoul, Korea, where the tech scene was heating up. Eager to join the race to dethrone Silicon Valley, the prime minister had poured billions into funding venture capital for budding geniuses. Lastly, his contacts listed a company in Johannesburg, South Africa. Jared mentioned that the CEO was an expat from the United States, but neither of them had pursued the idea. If a state actor was in league with a tech firm, looking at Israel, South Korea, or South Africa seemed absurd.

And yet, how better to hide in plain sight. As soon as she got home, she'd ping Jared to learn more about the tech companies he had flagged. She'd do more research on nuclear power. And figure out what else she was missing. First, though, she had to find and reconcile with Agent Lee.

TWENTY-NINE

Friday, October 18

Assistant Secretary for Electricity Peter Kellner listened intently to the report from a midlevel bureaucrat assigned to the NCIJTF, a project of the FBI that he had not paid much attention to until fifteen minutes earlier. Darnell Strom, the employee obliged to represent the Department of Energy in the multiagency pursuit of cyberthreats, seemed quite agitated by his meeting the day before and had begged for facetime this morning.

Peter granted the audience because very few people begged for a meeting with the assistant secretary of electricity. A longtime hand at civil service clusterfucks, Peter typically wouldn't have paid much attention to the meeting Strom breathlessly described. In fact, at any other time, he would have ignored the briefing and promptly dismissed the flunky from his mind.

Yet this was no ordinary report, and today was no ordinary day. The reinstallation of President Stokes—who had the luck of the Irish and the multiple political lives of a cat—was the talk of D.C. Peter's boss, the secretary of energy, had been one of the signatories who neutered Stokes's powers. Worse, the secretary had not relented. Which meant that his cabinet seat was up for grabs by anyone with the hutzpah to try to shove him out.

Someone like Peter.

He gathered all the details he could, scarce though they were. As soon as the Strom chap left his office, he dialed up his friend in the White House who had been on a CODEL with him to Singapore a decade ago. They'd stayed in touch and cycled back through at the same time. She had a badge ready for him and his name on the gate list in less than an hour.

When he arrived at the West Wing, he made his way to the office of the chief of staff. A hack or a novice would have demanded to see the president and been laughed out of the Oval. Instead, he knew the better route was the true second in command. A brand-new face in the White House as of that morning. A face he had been nice to when the whippersnapper had interned for him years ago.

"Acting Chief of Staff Boylen will see you now," the chipper young woman told him as she pointed to the door.

"Peter!" Luke Boylen, who had abruptly resigned his Congressional seat earlier that week, greeted him warmly. "Where are my manners? Mr. Assistant Secretary."

"Mr. Chief," Peter responded jovially, in kind. "Quite the move. Thought the first time we'd see each other in the White House would be after your inauguration."

"I am honored to serve at the pleasure of the president." Luke concealed the smirk that threatened to reveal his agreement with Peter's statement. Gesturing to one of the heavy brown leather chairs he'd inherited from his now-demoted predecessor, Luke positioned himself behind the desk that overflowed with reports and files. "To what do I owe this visit? Bianca told me it was urgent."

"Just had a disturbing meeting with a fellow in the agency. He was at a closed-door briefing yesterday convened by the FBI and some task force. The main guest was none other than Avery Keene."

Luke stilled. "What was she doing at a meeting with the FBI and Energy?"

"Apparently, she's not satisfied with manufacturing lies about the president. She now claims to have proof of a conspiracy to take down the electric grid. Which is utter bullshit. Pardon my French."

Luke demanded, "Who else was in the meeting?"

"He didn't say exactly. Mainly wanted to assure me that there was no truth to the rumors of an imminent attack, and he was perturbed by the serious audience she received. Basically, she went dumpster diving into some court cases and came up with dead fish that she's trying to sell like they're roses."

"The president does not have time to bat down fringe theories, Peter. But we can't have her starting a public panic." He ground his back teeth, speculating about how much damage control would be required. With Election Day looming, a credible rumor about the power going out would doom the GOP's chances to hold the White House or seize control of the Senate. Out loud, he questioned, "Who thought this ridiculous speculation was worth listening to?"

"Hardly anyone, from my understanding. FERC and the task force run threat scenarios whenever a researcher, reporter, or local yahoo suddenly realizes we have a power grid in this country." Peter tilted his head quizzically. "Unless you think she has something?"

"Shit, no," Luke replied. "But I have learned not to underestimate the little bitch. She's feeling the heat from her corrupt testimony, and this is probably an attempt to get some shine back on her. Creating a public panic just as President Stokes comes back into office would be a great way to divert attention. I'm betting the Democrats are behind this."

"Exactly what I was thinking," Peter said, having had no thoughts of the kind. His best outcome was that as the town snitch, he moved up a notch in the pecking order of a restored Stokes administration. But Luke had always been a faster political mind than he. "How would you like me to proceed?"

"Who headed up the meeting?" Luke would have that person in his office by lunch.

That name he did have. "Special Agent in Charge Sarah Beth Gehl. National Cyber Investigative Joint Task Force."

"Have you taken this to the secretary yet?" The pointed question had only one correct answer.

"I thought I would bring it to you. Get your opinion on next steps. The secretary has a lot on his plate right now, and because this is an interagency matter, I thought it best to come to you."

"Good call." He stood, and Peter Kellner hurriedly joined him. "I'll make some inquiries. Would appreciate it if you kept this between us for now, Mr. Secretary." Luke extended his hand with a sly smile. "I meant, Mr. Assistant Secretary."

The intentional slip of the tongue had the desired effect. Peter Kellner beamed and promised, "I'll keep this close hold until I hear directly from you."

"Good to see you. Don't be a stranger." Luke passed him off to the Gen Z'er who fluttered outside his office. His faithful assistant from the attic of the Cannon House Office Building would join him as soon as he figured out how to keep her pension safe. Until then, he'd deal with the aid of his generation's best and brightest. "Kellen!"

She popped up like a wraith. "Yes, sir?"

"Have Special Agent in Charge Sarah Beth Gehl in my office as soon as I get back from my meeting with the president."

"What if she has a conflict?"

"I'm the president's right hand, and she'll be in my office or find herself posted in Kotzebue, Alaska, by Monday."

Kellen didn't know if he had that kind of authority, and she had no interest in finding out. When her new boss returned from the Oval Office, Agent Gehl was waiting for him.

She rose from her seat and followed him into his office. He reached past her to shut the door firmly. He did not invite her to sit.

Unfazed, she recognized the intimidation ploy. If he wanted to establish dominance, she'd let him. "You asked to see me, sir?"

After a beat, he said, "I'm troubled to learn a key intelligence group is including Avery Keene in confidential briefings."

Agent Gehl held his look steadily. "Ms. Keene is consulting with the FBI related to an ongoing project."

"What can you tell me about the project?"

Absolutely nothing, she thought. His VerityVictory stunt with Avery might not be legally actionable, but it was foul. The only material he would get from her was name, rank, and serial number. With a suitably deferential tone, she replied, "With all due respect, sir, I would have to defer to the FBI director. She briefs the White House on task force operations."

Make me, she silently dared him.

At an impasse, finally, the chief of staff gave a curt nod. "I will be in touch with Director Alford to discuss the protocols that your team is using to gain information. In my new capacity, I have grave concerns about the source of your intel."

"We all have to be wary about where we get our facts," she warned. "Anything else I can do for you, sir?"

"No. Good day, Agent Gehl."

"How the hell did you manage to get rid of Luke Boylen?" DuBose Porter, the Speaker of the House, chortled as he and Minority Leader Kingston entered his office. "I could use the pointers. Upstarts who think they own the world because they can take a selfie."

"I recommend strychnine," Leader Kingston replied with a low laugh. "Or, in my case, I heartily agreed that he couldn't miss the deal of a lifetime by refusing the job of chief of staff."

"I can't tell if that administration is the *Titanic* or the *Hindenburg*." Familiar with his colleague's druthers, the Speaker poured two cups of coffee and added a splash of bourbon for his guest. "It's five o'clock somewhere," he quipped.

"The boy is in a hurry to be in charge of the world. I guess the pace of promotion was too slow in the House." Kingston sipped gratefully at the spiked brew. "This impeachment bullshit belongs to the Senate now. Other than making us hang around to watch your managers try to hang my president, is there a reason you haven't called the recess yet?"

One aspect of Leader Kingston that DuBose Porter appreciated was his candor. No wasted words, no beating around the proverbial bush. "I'd hoped we could force a vote on the Senate reconciliation bill," Porter said, "but that's not going to happen. I can't send my people home with earmarks, and you can't beat them up for it."

"Sounds like a fair trade." Kingston offered a toast with his cup and added, "But that deal was dead two weeks ago. Why are you monkeying around with the calendar? My conference is getting restless. Elections are already under way for a bunch of the members—on both sides of the aisle. I'm booked on Scott Curlee and his new primetime show Monday. Don't make me pick a fight."

"Threats are unnecessary, Paul. I called you over to agree to a truce until after Election Day. But I need you to shut down this crap about Avery Keene and the bogus tapes." When Kingston started to respond, the Speaker continued. "They've threatened to kill the girl's mother, Paul. Her best friend is a medical resident whose hospital got bomb threats, and her boyfriend is a Navy veteran. Anything happens to them, and I will be Speaker until your grandchildren are old enough to run for Congress. Bethany is four, right?"

The minority leader took a careful draught before responding. "With Congressman Boylen no longer in the caucus, I feel certain that the invective will subside. I got the same call from the FBI director. And a handwritten note from the chief justice. I was surprised a vengeful hawk didn't deliver it."

"She saves those for when she's really angry," DuBose replied. "This Tigris debacle is in the upper chamber. You send your folks home to get their butts whipped, and I'll see you back here in November. Deal?"

The clink of china sealed their agreement.

Judge Oliver wiped at his brow and checked the phone for the umpteenth time. Last night, he had received instructions on how to connect its Bluetooth to the system without detection. Over the past week, he had violated his oath more times than he could stomach. He fumbled in his briefcase for the bottle of antacids that had become his constant companion. One favor for a friend, and he became hostage to murderers and traitors.

At sixty-two, he had no idea what his machinations were doing to the computers that managed the operations of the court. Part of him longed to ask for advice, but how would he explain his curiosity? Instead, he allowed himself to be used to infiltrate the very system designed to spot and punish intruders into America's safety.

The knock at his door made him gasp. He hurriedly covered the device with a folder. "Come in," he barked.

A staffer whose name he'd forgotten opened the door. "Judge?"

"Yes, what is it?"

"Sorry to bother you, but IT needs to take a look at your computer." She looked over her shoulder. "Is now a good time for them to come in? Won't take more than a few minutes."

Waves of heat and cold washed over Michael as the threat of discovery hovered in his doorway. The incriminating phone sent signals or pulses or whatever to the system, and his fingerprints were literally all over the device. "I'm in the middle of something. Can't they come by later?"

"The network is acting up, and they have been trying to isolate the source," she explained. "Your computer and a few others on this floor are the last ones to be reviewed."

Brusquely, he shook his head. "I'm working on a matter of national security. It will have to wait."

"But, sir—"

"Go. Now!"

The unexpectedly harsh rebuff caught the staffer off guard. Judge Oliver was always unfailingly courteous, quaintly so. She stepped back and closed the door, turning to the two technicians. "He's not usually so abrupt, but they deal with high-value targets and dangerous cases. Tell your boss that he can send you back up in a few hours. I'll get you in."

Alone in his office with his secrets, Michael checked the device again. The program that had been running showed a status bar with 5 percent remaining. His panic turned to speculation. What if he terminated the link now? Told his tormentors that they'd been discovered and he couldn't risk another run?

He reached for the phone, ready to cut power, when the screen changed. "Tut-tut, Judge," the voice of his nightmares emanated from the tinny phone speaker. "We're almost finished, and your work is done."

"How did you—"

"In eleven minutes, you will take this device and exit the building. Someone will bump into you at the corner of Third and Constitution. Have it in your right jacket pocket. Then go home to your family. Take a nice long early weekend."

"What have I done?" he asked, imploring. "Will anyone be hurt?"

"Remember—your safety and that of your family depend on your silence. Take care, Judge."

THIRTY

By midafternoon, Avery was running on fumes and irritation. She jabbed the buttons once again, hoping this time her call would connect. But the ringing tone ended abruptly, to be replaced by a voicemail message she despised. "This is Special Agent Robert Lee. I apologize that I cannot take your call at this time. If this is an emergency, please disconnect your call and dial 911. If I can be of service, please leave your name and number as well as the reason for your call, and I will respond as quickly as possible."

"Unless the caller is Avery Keene," Jared said as Avery disconnected the line.

She glared at him, and his hands flew up in apology. "Just trying to lighten the mood. You've been stalking him since yesterday. He's upset, but he'll get over it."

"I hope so. It's just not like him." She sighed as she put the burner on the desk. "Agent Gehl has been out of reach today too. Maybe they've made progress on the Davies case." She'd been trying to reach Agent Lee since he stormed off on Thursday, to no avail. The sting of his disappointment bit at her conscience, and her inability to apologize rankled.

Instead of dialing again, she gave her full attention to what she could control. Research. Unraveling the puzzle in front of her. Sending a quick text, she summoned Ling and Noah, who joined them in the basement. "Now that we've added a South Dakota nuclear power plant to the mix, what else do we know? Ling?"

"Very little about Pacifica Protection is on the internet." Ling handed her a single page. "Nothing on social media. No presence on the web, except this from the local blotter. Mentions Dawson Hawthorne and Pacifica Protection during an interview with Vic Parker."

Avery read the page. "Tracks with what he told me."

"With Noah's help, I also searched for corporate records. The closest analog I can find is Pacific Protection, an environmental group out of Oregon. But when I called, they had no record of any projects in West Virginia."

"Strike one," Avery muttered. "Noah?"

"Ah, Quint Goodwin of the West Virginia Goodwins. Like Vic told you, the family owns a lot of land in the state and a company for every need you have. If the South still had company towns, he'd be the mayor."

Presenting his slightly thicker sheaf, Noah explained, "Here's a compendium of media hits on him. Second tab is a list of corporations he or his family owns. Quint, as his name suggests, is the fifth of his name. Full name is Bartholomew David Goodwin the Fifth. Family settled on 'Quint' rather than 'Barty' for obvious reasons. He has two younger siblings, Alexandra and Harris, a sister and brother. Quint has been married twice, with two kids by his first wife and none by his second—who, by the way, finished high school with his daughter a decade ago."

"Must make for an awkward family dinner," Ling suggested. "Hope she never beat her out for a spot on the JV soccer team."

"According to local gossip, he's estranged from his kids. The first Mrs. Goodwin got a hefty settlement, but she had no claim on any Goodwin holdings. Both kids received access to a trust set up by their grandfather at the age of twenty-five. One item of interest, though. His son, David, who is actually Bartholomew the Sixth, technically owns that tract of land you went to visit. He attended his father's alma mater, and he sits on the board of the family conglomerate. Guess what his major was?"

Avery arched a brow. "Computer science?"

"Bingo. With a minor in finance." Reaching for the file, he flipped to the last tab. "Junior has also been hanging out with some experts in crypto. These are from his Instagram and Facebook accounts. Courtesy of Jared's remarkable invasion of what's left of privacy."

"So the server farm belonged to him and not his dad."

Noah tapped the page in question. "David has diversified his portfolio in other ways. I did a national search, and he also owns property outside Danville, Kentucky. Twice the footprint of Lewiston."

"He could be mining bitcoin," Jared proposed. "The process is expensive for an individual, but if he has access to a cheap power source, he could dedicate the resources. One bitcoin transaction requires approximately 1,544 kilowatt-hours of power to complete. Basically a month and a half of power used in the average American household. Set up your own server farm, and he's got instant economies of scale."

Ling chided, "Pretend the rest of us don't speak geek."

"In a nutshell, cryptocurrency is virtual treasure. The value of crypto, like any treasure, is scarcity. So to create new supply, miners basically have to dig for new coins. They have to solve very complicated equations and ward off claim jumpers. The whole process uses immense computing power and—as you discovered—electricity. Miners compete with one another like the gold rush. The winning miner has to crack the code, and they win the right to add the block to the ledger and receive the reward for striking it rich."

"Amazingly cogent," Noah said. "Maybe our complex scheme isn't about taking down the grid. It's about creating more bitcoin."

Avery squinted at the whiteboard, an idea forming. The array of companies targeted by Jason Johnson didn't make sense if the only target was the power grid. "Guys, what if we have one culprit but more than one goal?"

When all eyes turned to her, Avery moved the images back to the industry overlay they'd created the first night. "Based on what Vance told me, if the mission is to attack the U.S. economy, the power grid is one way to do it. But it's only one possible attack point. I think they are going after the financial system too."

"But why focus on cryptocurrency?" Noah pushed back. "I understand it is more vulnerable than a head-on attack of the stock market, but why not go after the commodities market or something more venerable?"

"Because they are better protected," Avery explained. "Enemies of the state have been going after America's financial systems forever. But cryptocurrency is new, and it doesn't have the layers of regulatory protection that every other financial system enjoys."

Ling offered, "Your theory might explain why the server farm disappeared, but not why they were trying to hide it from Dawson Hawthorne's lawyer. Or why a phantom organization got involved."

"I might have an explanation. Let's leave West Virginia for a quick trip to Texas," Jared suggested. He nudged Avery aside and pulled up his research on the board. "Foster Energy is a small outfit in South Texas, but its footprint is impressive. I looked back through the eleven energy companies you had on the original list from Jason Johnson. Foster is connected to eight of them. As a subcontractor, a junior partner, a co-venture. You name the configuration, they've done it."

He enlarged the map and shifted it. "Right here is their sweet spot—the Southwest electric region. They've got versions of themselves in Arizona, New Mexico, and Nevada. Foster's predecessor owned a bunch of coal mines across the region, which has lower fuel costs and early adoption. At some point between rural electrification and the deregulation of the market, the mine owners got into the energy-generation business. Foster and its sibling companies not only serve Texas, they stretch down into Mexico and close to California."

"What exactly do they do?" Avery asked, growing excited by the new revelations.

"You name it. They operate coal plants, run wind and solar installations, service turbines, the works. They also own transmission lines in places where public utilities don't. With so many connections, they have been first movers in using digital technology to manage their operations. Interconnected solar arrays here, smart thermostats there."

"Making them more vulnerable to hacking," Avery surmised. "If someone can see everything that Foster Energy and its compatriots are up to, they have an inside track to ERCOT and the Western Connection."

Jared drew his finger in a circle around the area. "If I'm a hacker, I'd love to have a window into operations, schematics, employee rosters. The best intrusions anticipate the equipment and the on-site security. When the target is online and networked to others, my job gets easier."

"The FISC warrants gave Johnson the ability to gather records on their customers, to track their financial movements, and even to listen in on certain conversations."

Avery chewed on this. "Okay, Jared, suppose I'm Johnson. I've placed forty-eight different warrants, and I'm monitoring as they each gather data from across the country in multiple formats. I'm transmitting information on a regular basis. Suddenly, I'm caught and I'm sitting in a federal holding cell as the FBI figures out how I became a traitor. I start to crack, and they assassinate me. But what does the person who hired me do next to keep getting the information I was providing? They aren't going to simply quit because Johnson got arrested. They had to have a backup plan."

"If I'm your criminal mastermind, I would get a mirror inside the FISC system to show the results in real time—then there would be no reliance on Johnson. Vance told you to ask me about Pegasus." Jared rubbed at his chin, thinking aloud. "A cybersecurity firm called NSO Group created a spyware called Pegasus that could hack any cell phone—iOS or Android."

"Translation, please," Noah begged.

"Remember the issue with WhatsApp being used to deploy tracking tools on phones for journalists, diplomats, and human rights activists?" Both Noah's and Ling's heads bobbed in recognition. "The application is called Pegasus, and the company that makes it is the NSO Group."

"Why would Vance reference them in particular?" Avery wondered.

"What used to be called wiretapping is now simply monitoring the data and calls on a phone. Pegasus read text messages, snooped through your apps to see who you were DM'ing, and tracked your calls. Apple and the other providers finally figured out how to block their hack, which didn't require that the user actually do anything. It's called a zero-click exploit. No action needed.

"For a paranoid place like the FISC, I would assume their data is air-gapped—running on a system that is isolated, with no connection points to the internet. Separate servers, device protocols. Random users can't accidentally download a virus from an email."

"Then how do you get inside?" Ling asked.

The answer was clear, Avery realized. "You'd need a mule. Someone else who can get you the information you're depending on." She explored her list of judges. In the days since Jason Johnson's arrest, only two had been on duty. One had nothing odd in her background or her court actions. But the other one was Judge Michael Oliver. The judge who had hidden the server farm from discovery, and who had long-standing ties to the Goodwins. Sharing her theory with the team, they readily agreed.

"Okay, so we have a corrupt judge helping attack not only the power grid but also the financial system. What about Wisconsin and

Idaho?" Noah stood and arched his back from too long in the task chair. "How are they connected?"

"Idaho is the simplest one," Avery explained. "If I can get someone to look, I'd bet anything that Thad Colgate downloaded malware onto the system that day. He was an electrical engineer, and clearly deeply disturbed. The kind of guy someone either paid or radicalized. I doubt the massacre was part of the plan, but the sabotage that likely occurred was—while he was sitting at his desk for two hours before he started shooting."

She pointed to Wisconsin. "Redhorse is the key to the Eastern Interconnection. The company had a series of security contracts with several energy companies across the region. Our saboteur surveilled them and then got Judge Lake to paralyze them when they fought back."

"Why not just compete for the contracts the old-fashioned way? Buy them out," Ling posited, unconvinced. "Seems easier than this whole thing."

"Because they were about to go public," Avery explained. "An IPO changes everything. More scrutiny. More oversight. Plus, a greater likelihood that the FISA warrant issued for them would be exposed. Instead, undercut them and goad them into a flame war. Buy the judge instead of the company. Then Starhorse swoops in and takes their contracts, and their software is downloaded onto dozens of systems in the grid. Like Foster Energy, by taking out Redhorse, you get quick economies of scale."

She stepped back and observed the board. "Enter West Virginia. Jared said that running a hack of this size would be a massive undertaking. You need to run exploits or whatever across the country—massive and multiple attacks in dozens of systems, most of which aren't connected."

Jared picked up the thread. "You hire hackers who penetrate an array of systems, and you map their networks. Some of your targets notice you, but the malware looks like an anomaly, not a coordinated assault. The average security tech will report it if there's actionable damage. Most, though, remove the bug and never tell anyone. Where you can, you put boots on the ground."

"Thad Colgate."

"Precisely."

The dots on the map had increased in number as Avery noted each connection between and among the various entities. "Now you have more than a hundred locations with diverse roles in the power grid waiting to be launched. But you need to mirror a federal system to monitor activities."

"To do that, you'd need a hell of a setup that is impervious to reverse engineering if anyone is savvy enough to identify your intrusion and follow the trail back. If you're a criminal mastermind, you set up a server farm in the middle of nowhere, protect it from prying eyes, and dismantle it if anyone gets too close. You focus on taking down the financial system and the power grid because you want maximum chaos and to probably enrich yourself in the process."

All four had the same question. Avery did the honors. "Now the question is—who exactly are you?"

THIRTY-ONE

Are you done sulking?" Sarah Beth leaned against the door-jamb in Robert's office. "Mind your own business," Agent Lee retorted mildly. "Please."

"After the temper tantrum you threw in my office, this is my business. So is finding out who has the resources and the willingness to hire an Israeli assassin, push a federal judge to suicide, weaponize a disturbed electrical engineer, and vanish a server farm overnight." She entered the office and planted herself in front of his desk, leaning forward to prop her elbows on the absurdly clear surface. "Cut the girl a break, Robert. She's not a wayward recruit or a rogue agent. Avery didn't deserve to be dressed down like that."

"I know." He rubbed at his forehead and sighed. "I overreacted."

Gehl's eyes softened, as did her sharp tone. "Why? That wasn't like you at all. Even if you disagree with a junior agent, you never let it affect you personally."

Agent Lee held his tongue, a stony expression warning her to back off.

Agent Gehl had other ideas. "Your diatribe seemed rather personal. A grudge against Vance?"

The silence lengthened, and she jibed, "Yesterday, I get the toddler's temper tantrum, and today is the teenager's version of the silent treatment? Are we going through all stages of human development here?"

"I was on the ground in the Middle East in 1988, near Halabja," he explained tersely. "Hussein's chemical weapons attack on that Kurdish village."

"What were you doing there two years before Desert Storm? The Marines didn't have boots on the ground during the Iraq-Iran war. You'd have been, what, twenty-five, twenty-six?"

Ignoring her question, he resumed. "Hussein massacred nearly five thousand civilians with mustard gas and nerve agents. You've never seen anything like it. Mothers and babies. The elderly. Nearly ten thousand more were affected by the aftermath. I saw it. Firsthand. Bodies melting from the inside out. Mutilation. Annihilation."

Chilled, Agent Gehl shivered at the imagery. "It's unforgivable. But that doesn't explain why you took it out on Avery."

He shifted heavily in his chair. "I know we don't have an opinion on political matters, but I joined the Bureau because I believe in justice. But the president is on the verge of being exonerated for his part in Tigris. Vance fled before he could be held accountable, and he thinks that he can make up for his sins by feeding us scraps of information." Forestalling her response, he admitted, "I let my frustrations get the best of me and used Avery as a scapegoat."

"A scapegoat I doubt you've spoken to since."

He shook his head remorsefully. "The detail has kept me posted, but—"

"Before you head over to apologize, I should tell you about the meeting I just left." She shifted back, dropping her hands into her lap. "Former congressman Boylen, now chief of staff to Stokes, called me to his office to get a debrief on any potential threats we're reviewing. He specifically mentioned Avery."

Agent Lee demanded, "Is she in danger?"

She waved him back. "No, she's fine. He knows some of what

we're working on, and he's worried that she's aware of it too. He's already made an enemy of her, and it could get worse."

"Did you debrief him?"

"No. Told him to call the director."

"Smart. Who ratted you out?"

"Given his questions, I have to assume it was Darnell Strom from Energy who told his boss, Peter Kellner. But he doesn't have the juice to get to the Oval Office, so he went to his former intern, Luke Boylen."

"D.C. is an incestuous place," Agent Lee declared. "But you're okay? Is Boylen gunning for you now?"

Sarah Beth waved off his concern. "He's got another month or two in that office, and if Stokes survives the election, they'll have bigger vendettas to pursue. And as far as the FBI, Director Alford has outlasted better men than Boylen, and she is pleased with my leadership."

"So you came here to brag about longevity?"

"No." She laughed shortly. "I came because Boylen was worried. I can't quite tell exactly what he's hiding, but the possibility of an attack on the power grid has him spooked."

"Stokes can't be so reckless that he'd sanction a stunt like that. Millions would lose power. Hospitals would lose patients. Did you see worry or fear?"

"A bit of both."

"So the girl was correct. Again." Robert stood and reached for his jacket on the back of his chair. "Want to watch me beg for forgiveness?"

"I'll drive."

Agent Lee entered Jared's foyer with Agent Gehl in tow. After a quick round of introductions, he asked, "May I have a word, Ms. Keene?"

Bracing herself for another dressing down, Avery led him into the study Jared kept on the main floor. She could feel the stares following them into the office. She closed the door and turned. "Before you lecture me again—"

"I'm not going to lecture you, Avery. I owe you an apology."

Her eyes widened slightly, then narrowed. "For what?"

"Conduct unbecoming a grown man, let alone a federal agent who has benefited from your trust and counsel."

Avery grinned. "I pissed you off. Believe me, it happens."

"I appreciate the generosity, but there was no excuse for my behavior."

She gave him a pointed look of skepticism. "I am almost certain you have an excuse. One day, I hope you'll share it."

"Perhaps."

"Then we're good." She turned toward the door, ready to rejoin the others.

"You have no more questions?" Perplexed, he folded his arms across his chest. Avery Keene was one of the most inquisitive people he'd had the misfortune of encountering. Her lack of curiosity, frankly, stung. "That's it?"

With a soft exhale, she faced him again. "You had a bad day, Agent Lee. For once, you led with your emotions, and you told me off. I'm shocked it hasn't happened before."

"As am I," he said below his breath.

"But you came back. Not everyone does." She reached for the knob again. "Thanks."

Agent Lee trailed her into the living room, where the troops had assembled. Agent Gehl chatted with Jared, an animated discussion about advances in cybersecurity. Ling and Noah pretended to listen. Upon their return, conversation ceased.

"Agent Gehl, Agent Lee," Avery announced. "If you'll follow us, we think we've connected most of the dots."

"More than four?" Agent Lee asked.

"Ninety-six, at last count," Avery corrected. "We've added states, locations, and how the attack is likely to happen. I also believe that the financial system is a secondary target, hence the server farm." She started moving toward the basement and yanked at the door, gesturing for the team to go down ahead of her. "All we're missing is who and when."

"And why," Agent Gehl tacked on.

Moving to the whiteboard, Avery ran the FBI through what they'd pieced together. With everything laid out, she fielded Gehl's most recent comment. "'Why' seems to be directly tied to 'who.' We discern who our culprit is, the motive should reveal itself, I'd imagine."

"Did Vance have any insights?" Agent Lee posed the question without inflection.

"He suggested we look at companies in Seoul, Tel Aviv, and Johannesburg. Jared was about to walk us through what he found."

He took over the computer keyboard. "I found seven possible companies across the locales we were given with the capacity to write the type of code I saw on Preston Davies's phone. Did some dark web hunting and asked experts in the business, and three are very credible targets.

"There's a company based in Busan, not Seoul, but otherwise the profile fits. They got their start creating apps for phones. Mostly silly gamer stuff, until about four years ago. They go dark for about six months, and when they reemerge, they're focusing on encryption technology and monitoring. My contact found some cached information about them, but not much. Rumor has it that a billionaire bought them out and is looking to get in on the 'spyware to despots' racket."

Jared clicked on the next screen. "The Israeli company is competing with the hometown heroes who gave us Pegasus. Essentially, their mission is to one-up NSO and create zero-click exploits that can get around the firewalls that Apple and Android have thrown up. I've been at conferences with their team. Their hackers are exceptional, and their payloads can destroy systems in a matter of minutes. The company prides itself on mass destruction—they don't hurt you, they obliterate you."

Agent Lee queried, "Should we focus on them then? If they can do what you've described, that's basically what we're theorizing will happen to the grid. If I'm understanding this correctly. Taking out the power grid for much of North America is quite the calling card."

"I agree," Agent Gehl said. "I'd say they've jumped to the head of the class."

Avery prompted, "Last but not least?"

"The newest player is a company called Mamiwata out of Johannesburg. Joburg has a growing community of expats and cybersecurity wannabes. They are the most secretive of the trio. Mamiwata doesn't have a website, and the contact I had there says they are housed in a nondescript office just outside a residential neighborhood. The only way I know they exist is that I had a client use them for a project in Senegal last year. And when I put out the query to my more questionable contacts about exploits and cybersurveillance, Mamiwata was fourth or fifth in the pecking order, but it made every single list."

"Anything else grab your attention?" Agent Gehl asked.

"Their CEO. Former Navy lieutenant Hayden Burgess. She lectured at the Academy once while I was there. Formidable woman. One of the first class of women commissioned for submarines."

Hearing Jared's report for the first time, Avery stood abruptly. "Hayden Burgess—I know that name." She moved past the group to where her laptop quietly hummed. The others were too used to Avery's mental tangents to comment, so they talked quietly while she dove into her files.

The name had been on a petition for cert assigned to Justice Bringman's clerks. But Justice Wynn's edict that his clerks review the names of every case rejected for consideration meant that she'd seen it. The scant details of the case had caused a pang of regret, but their system of evaluation put it outside her jurisdiction.

Hayden Burgess v. United States. Her attorneys had filed a demand that the plaintiff be allowed to file suit against the U.S. Navy in civilian court. Justice Bringman had served in the U.S. Army, and he had no sympathy for those who sought to circumvent the military code of justice or the protections afforded by sovereign immunity. Typically, Justice Wynn would have argued for the sake of expanded access to the courts, but his attention had been divided, and he hadn't pushed for consideration. The women of the Court had been compelled by the argument but stymied by the law. So Hayden Burgess had been denied her day in court, and her military tribunal had acquitted those she accused.

Because it wasn't her case, she had no records on her system. Avery opened a web browser using Jared's VPN, and she typed in a search for the story of Hayden Burgess.

Zero.

Every reference, mention, or likeness had been expunged from the net.

She reported her findings to the team. Dubious, Jared said, "No one can erase their entire footprint."

Agent Gehl concurred worriedly, but as Jared hunted, every thread vanished, every foothold receded.

"It's a bot," Jared announced, amazed. "Somehow, she's deployed a bot that scrubs mentions and redirects traffic whenever her name or Mamiwata is input. I didn't notice it yesterday because I simply assumed there wasn't much to see."

"Then why mention it?" Agent Lee probed.

Jared frowned, unsure. "Instinct. Like I said, Mamiwata comes up as a ghost in the machine. The other two companies I mentioned want to be seen. Stealth is part of the mystique, but no one can buy a product they've never heard of."

Her instincts blaring, Avery announced, "I need to go to the Court."

"Why?" asked Agent Lee.

"Motive." Avery pointed to the empty computer screen. "I didn't read Burgess's file the way I would have had I been the one assigned to review her case. But I agree with Jared. There's something we're not seeing, and it's not just her vanishing footprint on the web."

Agent Lee got to his feet. "Let's go. Agent Gehl is driving. And she can brief you on her visit to the White House on the way."

THIRTY-TWO

Agent Gehl arrived at the U.S. Supreme Court close to 6:00 p.m., Avery and Agent Lee in the sedan with her. Rush hour had just merged with weekend traffic. En route, they determined the most efficient course of action to confirm Avery's hypothesis without causing an international panic.

"I'll take a look at the filings for Burgess and update the Chief. Otherwise, I intend to keep my head down until you come and get me," Avery assured the agents.

"Good," replied Agent Gehl. "Be careful what you tell your boss, but give her as much as she needs. I may have to ask for her assistance getting access to the FISC servers. You lawyers get a bit prickly."

"As opposed to the easygoing nature of the Federal Bureau of Investigation?" Before either responded, Avery changed the subject. "Any updates on finding the assassin who killed Preston Davies? I assume she had a hand in Jason Johnson's murder as well."

"No, and the Federal Bureau of Prisons is under extreme scrutiny right now. We don't know how she got inside."

"Which means you don't know if she can get to my mom."

"That's why I've redoubled our presence at her location and Jared's house. I don't want to risk moving your mom, but I will if you'd prefer she join you in Anacostia."

Avery considered this. "The townhouse is already too crowded.

She's got a support system at Haven, and I don't want her to be anxious about our investigations."

Agent Lee concurred. "To be completely honest, we also have no idea who we're looking for." He gave a sidelong look to Agent Gehl. "No known images of Nyx exist. Nothing from Interpol, the CIA, or the NSA, right?"

When Agent Gehl nodded, Avery asked, "What about asking the Mossad?"

Agent Gehl barely muffled her snort. "The hypersecret agency that rarely acknowledges its own existence? No, they haven't been particularly helpful. However, the murder of a federal prisoner might incentivize some back-channel cooperation."

"Preston Davies deserves justice," Avery insisted wearily. "He was just trying to do the right thing."

"We'll get him justice," Agent Gehl assured her. "We'll get them all justice."

Silently, Avery exited the sedan, and Agent Lee joined her and escorted her to the security entrance. An FBI detail waited for her at the Court to assist the Court's police and escort Avery once she finished her search for more on Hayden Burgess.

"I need your promise," he demanded as Avery entered the Court via the employee entrance.

She stopped in front of the magnetometer for the rest of the lecture. Most of the employees had already headed home for the weekend, so the area was empty except for the security guard.

"I swear I won't ditch my detail, and I will keep you apprised of any findings," Avery dutifully recited. Then she held up her hands, flipping them back and forth. "No fingers crossed either."

"This isn't a joke." Taking a step closer, he laid a hand on her shoulder. "I apologize again—"

"Nope," Avery said, backing away. "None of that. Go prove I'm right, and Western civilization is about to collapse."

"As usual, Ms. Keene, I am desperately praying you are wrong." He gave a mock salute, and once she'd cleared security, one of his agents took over. Satisfied, he returned to Agent Gehl's waiting vehicle.

They headed to the Hoover Building, using the drive time to divvy up tasks.

"I'll lean on the director and get permission to engage the FBI's Cyber Division," Agent Lee volunteered. "I want to see what they can find about the companies on Jared's target list. Hopefully, the full force of the American government can rival a consultant and some blacklist hackers."

"If only," Agent Gehl commiserated. "Meanwhile, I will take great pleasure in defying the president and his henchman. I'm going to reach out to the ones I trust most on JTF to come back in. We need an immediate scan of the FISC intranet to see if anyone has gotten inside like Jared theorized."

"Do you doubt them?"

"Unfortunately, I don't. I'll have our team start a sweep of the names Avery identified. With nearly a hundred targets, I'm not hopeful that we'll get responses from everyone before they clock out for the weekend."

One of the chief vulnerabilities of the technology age hindered their search. Businesses not only leveraged cybersecurity to protect themselves, they relied on their proprietary knowledge to keep competitors out. Getting nearly one hundred utility and energy-related businesses to admit they were being hacked would require the skills of both a diplomat and a CEO. Director Alford would need to be directly on tap for several of these awkward conversations.

Agent Lee agreed. "We have to move swiftly but cautiously. Whoever this is could be watching. We don't want to precipitate the attack by stumbling into her crosshairs."

"So we agree that Lieutenant Burgess is the most likely suspect?"

Agent Gehl inquired. "In all my years doing this, I've never seen anyone be able to erase their presence from the net so completely."

"But everyone leaves a trail. The one at the Court. Her personnel file. Still, I think you should call in your friend from the NSA. Start with Burgess and Mamiwata, but also check out the other two companies Jared mentioned and their boards of directors. Cyberwarfare is a lucrative business, and any of our enemies would love to be the ones who finally breached American soil with a national attack on our infrastructure."

She pulled into the parking garage, shadows lengthening in the late autumn afternoon. Cutting the engine, she turned to Agent Lee. "I'd better come with you to see Director Alford."

"You doubt my charm and capacity for persuasion?" he chided.

Agent Gehl managed a brief smile. "I owe her a report on my meeting with Congressman Boylen, and she will need to brief the president. He's not going to take this very well."

Agent Lee levered open his door. "Frankly, my dear, I don't give a damn."

Avery quickly pulled up the Burgess petition from the online database. Fully compiled, Burgess's application included a list of all the legal proceedings, namely the court of record, the docket number and case caption for the proceeding, and the date of entry of the judgment.

She printed out the documents and removed the files she'd brought with her. Before they left the house, Agent Lee had secured Lieutenant Burgess's personnel file, the only records not erased by her ingenuity.

Over the next few hours, Avery burrowed into the tragic ballad of Hayden Burgess. Hayden was born the daughter of Dr. Madeline Covey, a South African surgeon, and Elias Burgess, a journeyman electrician who met Madeline at the office building where she entered patient data into a clinic's electronic medical records system. Married in St. Louis, Madeline and Elias raised their three children in the shadows of the working class. Hayden, like her brothers, excelled academically. Unlike her brothers, who'd chosen basketball and baseball, Hayden became a champion swimmer with dozens of medals to her credit and an invitation to compete on college teams known for sending their protégés to the Olympics. Instead, Hayden received and accepted a coveted slot in the U.S. Naval Academy.

A star student, she found herself accepted into elite academic areas of study, courtesy of her parents' tutelage in science and math. On the fast track to leadership, her personnel file was filled with commendations and notations. Acts of bravery and plaudits to her brilliance. Placement on a nuclear submarine as a leader among her peers. A dazzling career cut short when she reported that she'd been drugged and raped by a commanding officer, Captain Donovan Casey, during a reconnaissance mission.

Seven years earlier, Burgess had reported the sexual assault, and NCIS investigators brought charges against the perpetrator, complete with DNA evidence and corroborating testimony from an ensign who saw him enter her quarters and a mess hall worker who witnessed the captain doctor her food.

Yet the jury convened by the Uniform Court of Military Justice exonerated Captain Casey, and his superiors rewarded him with a promotion. After the adjudication, the files grew thinner and less laudatory. Summaries of the proceedings exonerated her attacker and shifted the blame to a sexually aggressive commissioned officer eager to skip the hardships of promotion. The grotesque picture painted by a defense attorney was blithely accepted by the military panel that rejected her pleas for justice.

Lieutenant Burgess found herself removed from her post after she reported the captain, and her pregnancy from the assault ended in a miscarriage. Surgery following the miscarriage rendered her unable to bear children in the future. Medically discharged and denied remedy by the UCMJ, she took her suit to civilian court, but found her case rejected in hearing after hearing.

Eighteen months ago, her pleas for justice reached the U.S. Supreme Court. Petition denied.

Half a world away, Hayden sliced through the pale blue water with precise, rhythmic strokes. Strong, lean legs propelled her forward, barely disturbing the pool. She sank beneath its surface for the turn and, with an explosion of contained power, reversed her direction. For an hour each day, she traveled the stretch of the Olympic-length pool. In its cool, silken embrace, she had no cares other than the next moment.

The buzzer cut through the quiet and summoned her up. She had performed the routine so frequently that she ended her laps only steps from the ladder. Grabbing the bars, she hoisted herself out and onto the lip. A bank of towels, all precisely folded and pristinely white, waited in a bronze basket. She wrapped herself up and headed into the house.

Like Mamiwata's offices, panes of glass comprised an entire wall, overlooking the pool and, beyond it, the verdant lawn her staff carefully tended. Lamplight guided her path back to the house as the moon peeked through darkened clouds. At midnight, she would summon her troops and begin the final phase of her endeavor. The Myrina Assault.

In her bedroom, Hayden stripped out of the navy one-piece and padded into the bathroom. Beneath the stinging spray of the water, she washed away the acrid scent of chlorine, a smell jarringly different than the open water. Though South Africa was six hours ahead, she would not sleep again in the twenty-four-hour cycle. Training and nature meant she needed only three hours of sleep, which allowed her to keep watch on markets and employees distributed across the globe.

Her closet yielded her traditional uniform of a colored tunic—tangerine—and slacks in tan. The tunic skimmed her body, including the faint stretch marks that refused to fade and the surgical scars that overlapped low and tight. She traced the lines, sensory memory in the permanent ridges. Her eyes closed tight, and she allowed the shirt to fall to her hips. The abbreviated map of the battle nudged her to the dressing table, where she prepared for the second half of her day.

Yet the memories flooded in, refusing to be kept at bay. How he'd forced his way into her berth, her reflexes slowed by the drug slipped into her food. How her muffled screams had been no match for the hand over her mouth, the body forcing its way inside her. How he calmly dressed after the attack, reminding her of her position of subordinance and duty to the crew. Of her powerlessness in the face of military might wielded by even one man. And then by a system so drunk on its superiority, it thought itself invulnerable.

Hayden understood better than most that the military's strength came not from its weapons but from the faith of those they protected. Because people craved protection and stability, they permitted all manner of actions performed in their name's sake. In officer training school, part of the regimen was learning to divide her mind—to divorce the actions she must command others to take from the human toll of those actions. She learned then that she could never forget the mission, and she couldn't allow death and mayhem to distract her.

In the years since she'd been drummed out of the Navy and chosen exile in her mother's homeland, she'd assiduously applied her skills and training to the task of vengeance. To dividing her mind and focusing her rage. Her combination of expertise and street smarts joined to deliver a juggernaut dedicated to cyberwarfare for the highest bidder. Her staff included ex-soldiers who discovered the lucrative side of battle—shedding their automatic weapons for exfil-tration. She also added computer savants who would never launch Google but could strip a system's defenses in a matter of minutes.

The proliferation of private armies like Academi né Blackwater and the Wagner Group had been new to the West's consciousness, but they had a long and disturbing history abroad. With the frac-turing of nation-states into fiefdoms and the rise of unaccountable power brokers, international conglomerates had taken to hiring mil-itary contractors to protect their oil fields, diamond mines, and land incursions. Despots eager to hold on to territory without alienating constituents shoveled millions into elite sniper teams in Syria and intelligence gathering in Eastern Europe.

When the fighting moved online, a different tactical approach became necessary. Russia learned early to undermine its enemies by not only cutting off natural gas supplies but also launching DDoS attacks on key operational systems. A Dutch intelligence agency deployed the Stuxnet virus that foiled Iranian nuclear development. Spyware that doxxed diplomats had become part of the twenty-first-century arsenal of warfare. Yet few had mastered the scale and depth of attack required to permanently cripple key players. North Korea could send out its botnets, but South Korea had the capacity to repel.

Mamiwata understood the limits of warcraft online, and Hayden Burgess had been trained by the planet's finest army to anticipate and counter the brightest military minds. Mamiwata had earned its keep and her hundreds of millions of dollars by staying far below the radar. Detection was nearly impossible. Were they ever to prove her existence, dictators a bit north of South Africa would sing her praises. Middle Eastern royalty deposed by changing regimes had tasked her with siphoning funds from international accounts and leaving no trace of the funds' existence.

Her tech erased footprints like water receding from a beach. Damp impressions but no proof. Five years of concentrated rage and unbridled genius gave her an empire that spanned the globe. Hackers vied for her attention, never knowing her name. Presidents pleaded for release from ransomware threats, cursing her expertise. She and her team excelled in the quartet of assaults: sabotage, espionage, system disruption, and propaganda.

In forty-eight hours, she would climb the Mount Everest of cyberwarfare operations. The U.S. electrical grid would quake before her. And so would the nation's leaders.

THIRTY-THREE

FBI Director LaTiesa Alford started her career as a beat cop in Albany, Georgia. Prostitution, vagrancy, shootings with no witnesses in crowded neighborhoods. Her application to Quantico had been seen as a lark by the captain who grudgingly supplied her recommendation. His look of sheer surprise at her acceptance, tinged with unmistakable envy, buoyed her through the rigorous months of training. The next phase of her career required muscling through lowered expectations and petty obstacles. Serendipity, though, had been the proximate cause of her rise to the role of director. A case gone sideways led to her and a partner saving one of President Cadres's closest allies. One of a dying breed of statesmen, Cadres decided to heed his colleague's advice and buck public sentiment by putting her up for confirmation. Like the captain who had laughingly approved her bid for the Bureau, U.S. senators smugly granted her audience. To a person, save six, she convinced them to advance her on the merits and the history-making turn.

Since her ascendancy, she'd carefully avoided any appearance of political opinion. No votes cast during primaries. No social media presence at all. Her studied agnosticism resulted in a renewal of her tenure under President Stokes, who had granted her audience only once. She didn't mind. Though voting was a confidential act, she confidently never gave him a boost with her ballot. Something about his brand of patriotism had always rubbed her the wrong way. Patriots who also had a mild case of messianic fervor usually came to an end, holed up in a remote cabin with adherents and jugs of kerosene or crates of automatic weapons.

Brandon Stokes had a slick and polish that fooled the most discerning, but she had never been deceived. However, he was her boss, and her formula for longevity included never pissing off the one who signed the checks. Her rule had worked for decades, and she was loath to violate her prime directive.

Yet the duo of Lee and Gehl seemed determined to torpedo her career over the coming weekend.

"You expect me to override the White House chief of staff and the secretary of energy to authorize a nationwide sweep of computer protocols for companies that we don't own, control, or have a say about." Her restatement of their request did not include a question mark. Throughout their chilling presentation, she felt the knot in her stomach swell to the size of a boulder. Before either could respond, she held up a finger to indicate silence.

The reality of a cataclysmic attack like the one they postulated would ripple for years. Millions of lives at risk and billions of dollars lost for each day such an attack succeeded. Just last week, she'd gotten an intelligence briefing on how hackers were targeting GPS systems. If the power grid went out, an enterprising sociopath could disrupt everything from airplanes in the sky to ballistic missiles no one should know about.

Stopping this attack required extreme stealth and unparalleled coordination across a variety of agencies, an impossibility right now. The fulcrum for action should not be the FBI director. This was a job for the president, and based on the source of the theory, he wouldn't buy it. Worse, anyone who defied him was writing their ticket to oblivion, and Agents Gehl and Lee must have wanted her to be the first one on the way out.

This newly reinstated White House had already launched a purge of infidels, and new acting chief of staff Luke Boylen had already made it known that he had a list. Cabinet secretaries who had signed off on the unprecedented use of the Twenty-Fifth Amendment came first. Technically, that included her superior at the DOJ, the attorney general. He had been the one to draft the language and recruit his fellow secretaries, at the behest of the vice president. The AG had seen the videos from Tigris, and he'd carefully reviewed Agent Lee's after-action report on the events that followed. AG Dobson played by the book, and if it missed any pages, he lived by the rules of strict construction. He remained a holdout, refusing to rescind his condemnation.

The secretary of energy had cowed under the weight of history, and his capitulation had helped restore the president's power. Secretary Carlisle would not be the one to take her call willingly. He still harbored the vain belief that he could grovel back into Stokes's good graces. But POTUS had no reputation for forgiveness, which meant the secretary was among the walking dead. Convincing him, though, would likely take the entirety of the weekend, as well as hand puppets.

"The AG will have to be the one to bring this to the White House. I can't go over his head, and frankly, I don't want to. His job is to handle the politics." She narrowed her eyes thoughtfully. "Gehl, I want you to convene the JTF, but only the ones you trust implicitly. Take them to the SCIF and read them in. Hand out assignments and insist they hunker down for the weekend. Bring in cots if you have to, but no one who comes onto your division is leaving this weekend. Warn them before you get started—they'll need to be offline completely for forty-eight hours. Do not explain why. If anyone that you see as essential hesitates, call me immediately and we'll decide how to handle."

Mind revving, she rose from her desk. "Take a handful of cyber jockeys that you trust too. While we are notifying and dismantling, I want them hunting across the dark web for any trace of who's behind this. Bring in Jared Wynn if you think he'd be useful. With his security clearance, we can justify adding him as a consultant."

"On it."

The director turned to Agent Lee. "Keep Ms. Keene's other friends under lockdown. Smooth over whatever you need to, but keep them safe. Anyone who possesses the sophistication to design this might have located them."

"I'll add more agents," he agreed. "What about Ms. Keene?"

"Does anyone in this room believe she'll stay put if you try to corral her with the other two?"

"No," they replied in unison without irony.

"Then she's your responsibility, Robert. Fetch her from the Court, find out what she knows, and get her in here."

"I'd like to move her mother to a safe house." As long as Nyx was unaccounted for, he couldn't trust anyone but his team. "I'd like to pick the agents."

"Agreed." The director continued. "Also, have Ms. Keene's detail take her to the FISC and meet her there. Read her in on what y'all found out about Judge Whitner, unless she already knows."

This time, the duo's expressions mirrored the exact same degree of impassivity. Which no one believed. "After this crisis, we will have a refresher course on how we treat civilians who are not cleared for high-level intelligence."

"Yes, ma'am."

"Robert, I'd also like to have her contact Major Vance again. We'll need to read in anyone who can help us find the attackers quickly."

"With all due respect, ma'am, he didn't provide much in the way of help with his last interaction," Agent Lee argued. "I don't see a reason—"

"The apocalypse is the reason, Agent Lee. I don't know what he knows, and I don't care. But if he has any way to get us to a clear target quickly, then we use him. That's an order."

.   .   .

Her research completed, Avery had no doubt as to the identity of the mastermind behind this. She would wait to hear back from the FBI about their deep dives into Geonchug and Sinai, but the cartoon flashing lights of "Look Here" pointed directly at Hayden Burgess. The "how" had revealed itself over the past few days, and now the "why" was also obvious.

Rage. Grief. Betrayal. Vengeance. Any of these had been known to drive good people to extremes, yet the combination of this tragic quartet manifested in a plot that boggled the mind. Destroy the national power grid, using the collapse to steal money and secrets. Avery had not proven the collateral intention yet, though the proof lay in the computers at FISC. Agent Lee had given orders for her FBI detail to take her there immediately, as soon as she finished collecting materials and printing out her manifesto on Hayden and what she had dubbed the Grid Gridlock. The name would never stick, but the shorthand helped with her typing.

According to the Chief, who called before she left her office a half hour earlier, Avery was the only person left in the building except for some support staff and security. A timid knock at her door likely meant the janitorial team was doing its rounds early in order to escape for the weekend. She called out, "Come in," as she continued to organize her notes.

"Sorry for the mess. Most of it will be shredded Monday," she apologized.

"Gracias."

She heard the waste bin tap against a larger container, the rustle of a plastic bag. Instinct trilled a warning shiver down her spine. The next second, a forearm vised around her throat and a strong hand wrenched her right arm behind her.

Avery dipped her chin to block the arm from crushing her windpipe, and she used her free hand to claw at her attacker, finding nothing but air. Behind her, Nyx cranked her arm higher, and Avery screamed.

Nyx ignored the muffled shriek. The floor was empty. Supreme Court Police stood in the lobby with the FBI detail, and another two were responsible for rounds. Likely courtesy of hers truly. During her surveillance, she had anticipated a time when infiltrating the Court might become necessary. To that end, she'd commissioned a uniform like the one worn by Ms. Isobel Nogales. Isobel currently lay unconscious in her apartment, where the building super would discover a gas leak that had miraculously shut itself off. Nyx had regulated the dosage so as not to kill her, only incapacitate. Wearing Isobel's uniform, she had timed her arrival between shift changes at the guard station.

The guard and his watchdog FBI agent scanned her badge and searched her bag. The magnetometer permitted her entrance, sans the convenience of a firearm. Nyx preferred heavy weaponry; however, her tradecraft did not require more than her hands and office supplies, if necessary.

In the lobby, her fellow workers saw that her badge read *Luciana,* and they found their attempts at camaraderie rebuffed. She mutely accepted her list of offices and broke off to begin her rounds. Nyx had dutifully cleaned office after office. Finding Avery's had been trial and error. The light beneath the door and the whirring of the printer gave her away.

Sneaking up behind her had been child's play. A quick choke hold that cuts off the air supply, a jiujitsu maneuver to snap the neck. One of her stock moves to eliminate a target. But Avery had sensed her approach and blocked her choke hold. She further ratcheted up the captive arm to trick her body into arching in search of relief.

Instead, Avery dropped the hand that clawed at her face and instead punched her in the groin. The blow, described in countless YouTube videos aiming to aid women in danger, stung—but she lacked the testicular vulnerabilities the instructional videos assumed an attacker would possess. Irritated by the discomfort, she read-justed her hold to gain tighter leverage around Avery's throat, taking care not to expose herself to a vicious bite.

Unable to scream with her chin tucked in, Avery shifted tactics. Nyx was correct in assuming Avery had learned about choke-hold escapes, but she was incorrect in assuming it was all she knew. The groin hit ineffective, Avery suddenly stepped out and hooked a leg behind the woman attacking her. For the first time in Avery's life, she tried to perform a judo lock and knock the other woman to the ground.

It worked. The pair crashed to the floor, but Nyx had trained in judo, jiujitsu, and muay thai. Her body succumbed to gravity, and her hold on her prey tightened. She began to aim blows at the girl's kidneys with one hand while she retrieved a plastic bag from her pocket. With a scissor kick, she straddled Avery, pinning her by the elbows. Hands free, she pressed the waste basket liner over her nose and mouth. Slightly smaller than her target, Nyx kept her center of gravity heavy on Avery's chest as she smothered the life out of her.

Gasping, choking, dying, Avery forced herself to hold her breath. To stop the autonomic response of inhalation and exhalation. Of panic and despair. Black spots danced before her eyes, as did one last video. Her thrashing legs went limp, and her eyes fluttered closed. Her heart continued to pound in her ears, thud in her chest.

Unconvinced, Nyx leaned forward to apply additional force. Avery felt the shifting weight and had her cue. Like a Cirque du Soleil gymnast, she tucked her legs and arched her body in a sud-den, tight arc that caught Nyx off guard. The delay was less than a second. In that blink of time, Avery brought her knees up to anchor the tight, strong form pinning her to the carpet. Like a human cata-pult, she flipped the body over and began to rain down punches on the prone form.

Nyx tried to regain control, but Avery headbutted her viciously in the chin and landed a solid blow to her kidneys. Neither strike was crippling, so Nyx twisted against the surprisingly combat-ready attorney in an attempt to finish her off.

The night she thought she'd been followed, Avery accepted that it might have been a figment of her imagination. Still, her experiences with Rita over the years meant that she never let her guard down or allowed herself to be unprotected. Her tenure at the Court meant that she rarely had to go through the metal detectors and never had to open her bag.

Because she outmatched the woman beneath her by a good three to four inches and at least thirty pounds, she used her reach and weight to land harsher blows with her right hand. The attacker countered effectively with several hits that had her fighting back whimpers of pain. With her left, she fumbled in her pocket for the knife bequeathed by her dad. *AOK,* read the inscription. In a practiced move, she released the blade and jabbed it into the woman's side. The screech sounded as much of outrage as pain. Her second swipe grazed the woman's shoulder, drawing blood. Avery pierced her upper thigh with the third strike and used the injury to squirm free. A strike from her victim's elbow dazed her, but she managed to stay alert. She stumbled to her feet and streaked out of the office, bounding down the stairs. She didn't stop until she reached the lobby and burst into the vestibule.

"Upstairs," she choked out, holding up the bloody knife and her equally soiled hands. "She tried to kill me. My office."

Court Police rushed to the stairwell. The lead agent on her detail gingerly removed the knife from her hand and calmly instructed, "We're going to get you out of here now. Follow me."

Avery followed blindly, sweat and tears and possibly blood dripping indiscriminately down her face. She heard the call for a lockdown and the blare of an alarm as they exited the building. She wiped vainly at the wetness, only to recoil from the blood. The agent bundled her into a waiting SUV, and they peeled away from the curb. She listened dazedly as they radioed in a description of what had occurred. The squawks continued until the last one caught her breath. "No sign of the intruder. Repeat. No sign of the intruder."

"Well, do another goddamned sweep," the agent riding post demanded. "This isn't Keene's blood on the knife. We locked down the building. Find her."

In an alleyway, six blocks down, Nyx sank against a dumpster and reached for her phone. She bled from three wounds, two of which would need stitches. Once she made it back to her perch, she would sew them up herself. But Hayden would be livid at the report, and Nyx did not believe in delaying the inevitable. She called in and delivered her report, and she accepted her dressing down. New orders were given, a new timetable of accelerated urgency.

In sixty minutes, she would regroup and redouble her efforts. However, her prey would be harder to capture this time. Avery Keene was most likely headed to FBI headquarters, and according to the papers Nyx had grabbed before fleeing her office, the Myrina Assault was officially compromised.

THIRTY-FOUR

G o away," Avery begged and shook her throbbing head, an action she quickly regretted. Though the attack from Nyx had been hours ago, the repeated blows to her head and the near strangulation had left their marks. "I'm not dying," she croaked out.

"This time," Ling corrected. "And no thanks to your FBI detail." She continued her ministrations despite Avery's grousing. She flashed a pen light into her eyes in a repeat of a test she'd administered several times already.

"I don't have a concussion," Avery complained as she rubbed at her sore, tight throat. "You've checked and double-checked." Struggling to sit up against the headboard in Jared's bedroom, she demanded hoarsely, "I need to know what's going on."

Once Nyx attacked her, the FBI detail had been dispatched to return her home. Unconcerned about her protests, Ling bundled her into bed and plied her with a concoction that seemed equal parts homeopathy and voodoo. She'd woken every hour or so, only to be poked at and prodded back into sleep.

"At least let me talk to Jared," she whined. The instant she heard herself, she winced. Petulance annoyed her, especially from her. She sat up straighter. "Ling, I appreciate you taking care of me, but we are in a crisis. I've rested or slept for hours. It's time to get back to work."

"It's three in the morning, Avery." Ling put down her light and reached for the slender wrist with its bracelet of bruises. The slight flinch told her what her eyes confirmed. "Everyone is asleep. Jared is still with Agent Gehl. No one in or out for forty-eight hours. He only stopped harassing them to return because I'm watching you tonight." She probed the darkening marks with a stern look. "You were nearly suffocated, she damn near broke your wrist, and you've got marks all over."

"You should see the other guy," Avery quipped. Ling didn't laugh. "Come on, that was funny."

Ling shifted her attention to Avery's rotator cuff and relented. "If you'll agree to sit still and let me finish my examination—"

"Yes!"

"And go to bed without arguing, I will bring you up to speed."

"Deal."

"Good." Ling removed her stethoscope and placed it against Avery's ribs. Her breathing was stronger, and she didn't squirm as much when Ling pressed gently against the tender areas. "Jared and Agent Gehl confirmed your theory. Mamiwata is the most likely company behind the software and any possible attack. None of the other companies appear to have the capacity to pull this off."

"Anything from Agent Lee?"

"Not yet. He checked in on you a few times, and I told him you could talk to him in the morning." Ling got up from the bed and looped her stethoscope around her neck. "A deal is a deal. Lie down and close your eyes."

Suddenly, Avery felt violently drowsy. Her lids started to close as she slid beneath the covers. Before she succumbed, she popped up. "Shit! My research! Did anyone find my files?"

"You didn't have your bag with you, honey. Agent Matthews, the one who brought you home, said they had to take your stiletto into evidence. Get DNA evidence from the blade."

Avery rubbed at her temples as a vicious headache formed. "Hayden Burgess knows we're on to her. If she didn't figure it out when I went onto the West Virginia property, she absolutely knows now. I wrote a damn memo outlining how and why she was doing this."

"And the woman who attacked you got it?"

"Once I stabbed her, I ran. I forgot—" She gave a mirthless laugh. "For once, I forgot something. She also has my phone and the videos from Preston. All my contacts."

Anticipating her next worry, Ling assured her, "Agent Lee went out to Laurel and personally moved your mother to a safe house. She's got round-the-clock security." She pressed lightly at her shoulders, urging her to lie back. "Give me another four hours of sleep, Avery, then I'll let you take on the world."

Exhausted and anxious, Avery let her head fall back on the pillows. "She knows we're coming, Ling. We must stop her."

The first plane landed in Kenosha on a private airstrip at dawn. Its two passengers, strangers to each other until they met at the departure point, quickly gathered their gear. The taller hit man, recognizable only by his bald pate and childlike features, took the lead. He directed his compatriot out to the parking lot, where a 2004 Ford Ranger with dull green paint and a stolen license plate awaited their arrival.

"Seat belt," he instructed the wingman, who pouted but complied. He shifted the truck into gear and pulled out onto the blacktop state road that led to their destination. Seat belts topped his checklist for a successful mission. Cops out in the boondocks looked for minor reasons to stop cars and make their monthly quotas. Broken taillights, tinted windows, and missing seat belts were easy tickets to write and stupid reasons to kill.

The trip out to the cabin occurred without the distraction of errant chatter or the cacophony of popular music. He disliked the tinny sound of car radios, preferring the pure tones of an expensive stereo setup, and he reviled any music produced after 1969. His companion had reached for the dial, but his grunt of disapproval had been understood. In the quiet of the car, he mapped out their moves and cycled through contingencies. There should be none. The target was in his sixties, a pudgy middle-aged man who had ransomed his future. The bill was due.

They parked a quarter of a mile down the road and walked from there down the dirt road to the stream that bisected the property. Early morning sunlight dappled tall grass and gilded the dew that clung to the sharp green blades. The simple A-frame wooden cabin had seen better days. A sagging porch boasted a couple of hand-carved rocking chairs. A woven hammock waited patiently for a guest. On the opposite side of the stream, a ranch was taking shape. Property records indicated the presence of a corral filled with Thoroughbred horses, a three-story house complete with a verandah and a cellar. The fishing cabin had been on the property for decades, and that's what had attracted the new owner. His wife had always imagined a retreat for their family that rivaled the Waltons' after they'd won the lottery.

Baldy motioned to his partner to hang back. Their target approached the steps of the cabin, a mess of fish dangling from a string. Like a true fisherman, he rose with the sun for the morning catch. The bald man appreciated the skill of a good hunter, regardless of prey. Like music, there was a purity he admired. Out of respect, he would take the freshly caught fish with them. The plane had a cooler on board, and there was probably one in the cabin he could purloin.

His approach was muffled by his care and the jaunty whistle from the judge. A little pitchy but pretty strong. And quickly ended by the silent eruption of his HK45 with suppressor. As Judge Lake crumpled to the ground, Baldy signaled to his partner. The thinner, younger man took the stairs with a quiet speed that he respected. Seconds lapsed, then two shots in rapid succession.

One more minute passed before his partner returned. "The wife was inside. No signs of any other occupants."

Baldy nodded. One down, two more trips to go.

"Good morning, Ms. Keene."

"Did they find it?" she asked without preamble.

"No, I'm sorry. Your bag, the materials you described, and your phone were not recovered."

Avery caught her breath. Sometime in the early hours, she realized that with the disappearance of her satchel, one more piece of her father's legacy was gone. The pang of loss mingled with remnants of fear. She'd nearly died yesterday, would have had it not been for another bequest. "Will I get my knife back?"

"Legally, no, but I'll figure something out." Agent Lee cupped Avery's elbow and guided her to the living room sofa. He nudged her to sit and took a chair nearby. "After she escaped, the Supreme Court Police secured your office, and my agents tailed her. She moved too quickly, and they lost her a few blocks from the Court."

"How did she get inside?" Noah demanded angrily. "Avery could have died."

"She was disguised as a janitor," Avery said dully. "It's not anyone's fault."

"To the contrary," Agent Lee replied stiffly, "we failed. No one should have made it inside without proper authorization."

"She and her boss managed to infiltrate the most secure court system in the world. Sneaking in as a custodial worker is child's play."

"That's beside the point," Agent Lee replied. "But let's focus on the matter at hand. Based on your theory, we spent the past twelve hours combing through the FISC. One of our searches identified another judge who served on the FISC until a year ago. Judge Webber died in a home invasion in upstate New York."

"I missed it?"

"You could not have seen it. The FISC warrant system shows the judge approved a business records search against the leading manufacturer of replacement parts for a digital monitor of a popular type of turbine generator. As well as two of its competitors."

"So Hayden has a list of every company that uses that hardware and software. Which she could then use to target her hackers and her malware."

"My team and the Cyber Division agents have been waking up CEOs across the country. Agent Gehl and her team have been doing the same. We've got folks at that South Dakota nuclear plant, and every other nuclear facility, lighting up the country. We're trying to get all of these important people to actually protect the grid."

"Are they complying?"

"Sarah Beth likened it to herding cats with syphilis."

"Oh." Avery felt a smile curve her mouth. "Colorful."

"Accurate." He shrugged. "The AG and Director Alford are en route to the White House. A few of the more well-connected behemoths began ringing his phone this morning. We'll keep pushing until we get another directive."

"I know the focus is on the energy companies, but y'all are reaching out to the tech and finance companies on her list too?"

"Yes, we are, Agent Keene. Any other orders?"

She shot him a hopeful look. "Can you spare an agent for another project?"

"What, exactly, do you need?"

"Hayden Burgess's assailant was a naval officer named Donovan Casey."

He gave her a look of confusion. "The former secretary of the Navy?"

"One and the same. Now, he's a retired rear admiral who lives in Charlottesville, where his wife is a professor at UVA. I'd like more background on him—and possibly to speak with him. And maybe figure out how he got confirmed with that type of accusation on his record."

Agent Lee responded tightly, "Closing ranks isn't simply a military term of art."

"If the accusations are true, if he raped Hayden Burgess . . ."

"We're not investigating Lieutenant Burgess or her complaints, regardless of how valid. Our obligation is to stop her," Agent Lee said flatly. "Don't get distracted, Avery."

Avery saw the image of the complaint in her mind's eye, the description of Burgess's injuries as reported by the ship's doctor. She needed to understand more about Casey if she wanted a full picture of Lieutenant Burgess. They learned in criminal law about the trifects: motive, means, and opportunity. If Donovan Casey was the motive, she'd better understand how and why Burgess planned to take action. "All I'm asking for are some files, Agent Lee. On him and on two others. Petty Officer Carolyn Hugley and crewman Tyler Boozer. They were court-martialed shortly after Burgess received her general discharge. They're both serving time in naval prisons."

"Exoneration is not the priority, Avery."

"Comprehension is. I'm missing part of the picture here, and I think this information can fill in the blanks. Will you help me?"

"Help yourself. We're expected back at the Hoover Building in thirty minutes."

AG Dobson and Director Alford sat stiffly across the Resolute desk from a baleful President Stokes. A few paces away, Acting Chief of Staff Luke Boylen was ruddy-faced and outraged.

The president allowed the tension to build. The asshole he had boosted from obscurity into the most powerful legal job in the world was once again trying to screw him. At 5:00 a.m., he received the first of an angry fusillade of calls from titans of energy, finance, and technology, all demanding to know why the FBI wanted to create a public panic.

He had dolefully ignored the urgent request he'd received for an audience from the bastard Dobson yesterday evening. On his orders, Dobson's phone call went unreturned, and his unannounced visit to the residence had been turned away like the plague. But when the head of a Fortune 10 company demands your attention on your first week back in office, it is mortifying to be completely ill informed and unaware of the oncoming calamity.

None of that mattered now. He'd harangued his new chief of staff for withholding vital information that he had refused to hear. Duly chastened, Luke waited like a leashed pit bull to rip the AG a new one. On his command.

But first, he steepled his long, elegant fingers and tapped the indexes against one another. Dobson shifted his weight almost imperceptibly and cut a glance at the FBI director. The president had never been entirely comfortable with his head of law enforcement. She had been a darling of his predecessor and a ready talking point on the election year diversity circuit. Unlike her direct supervisor, the AG, she'd had nothing to do with his temporary ouster. Thus, he turned toward her for his first volley of questions.

"What the hell is going on, LaTiesa? Is it true that we have a terrorist attack planned on U.S. soil and I'm just now hearing about this?"

Director Alford started to answer, but AG Dobson spoke over her. "You're just now hearing about it, Mr. President, because you've been acting like a petulant teenager for the past forty-eight hours. You're pissed at me, and that's your right. But as long as you're in that chair, your goddamned duty is to this country. And that means taking my calls and answering your freaking door."

Mouth still agape, both the director and Luke Boylen waited for the eruption from POTUS. When he started to chortle, everyone froze.

"I don't think anyone has dared insult me that directly in years."

"The threat to our nation is real, sir." The AG dropped a file on his desk. "This is a list of companies that may be compromised. Our teams have been calling their leadership, with mixed results. Until I can marshal the entire cabinet to help, we're going to get nowhere."

"What is going on?"

The AG explained the events of the past few weeks and the findings of the investigations Director Alford initiated. As he spoke, President Stokes quickly read the hastily assembled memo about the imminent threat. When Dobson concluded, Luke stepped forward belligerently. "You failed to mention a key part of this, Mr. Attorney General."

Dobson thinned his lips, and his nostrils flared. He'd been grilled by this pissant during his short tenure on the Judiciary Committee. Tamping down his annoyance, he dutifully explained, "Avery Keene is involved in this, Mr. President. This is based on her theory, which multiple teams have now verified as actionable."

"She's been busy, hasn't she?" While the president continued skimming the brief, Luke stepped forward aggressively. The president's engagement meant his chance to prove management skills. "What's the ask?"

"To start, I need the secretaries of energy, commerce, and defense to help me make some calls. We'll save the heavies for the president, but I need people to take this seriously without creating a national panic."

The president reached for an official gold pen embossed with his seal and began circling names. "Luke, have Eliza come in immediately. We'll ring through these names first. If I don't get the answer I want, we'll start hauling in board members." He turned the page, continuing to highlight contacts. "I also want the head of the NYSE and NASDAQ and the commodities exchange on the phone at eleven a.m. We'll need to be prepared to halt trading on Monday."

"Reach out to the Joint Chiefs. I need to see the chair and vice chair, plus chief of naval operations and the secretary of the Navy in my office at noon."

"The chair is in Oslo, sir."

"Then put his ass on a plane. Norway doesn't need him. We do."

THIRTY-FIVE

Sunday, October 20

Avery sat upstairs in the West Wing in a conference room with Jared, Agent Lee, and Agent Gehl. She idly rubbed at her throat, which was covered up by the black turtleneck she wore. Her side still ached where Nyx had pummeled her, and it hurt to turn her head. Ling's tending had relieved most of the pain, but she'd be feeling the effects of the fight for another day or so.

Reports had rolled in of the deaths of two federal judges in separate unrelated incidents. News feeds had only learned of the death of a judge and his wife in Kenosha in a case of murder-suicide, but Agents Lee and Gehl had been fully briefed. The FBI had reports of a car accident in Texas that Austin's field office was investigating. Avery understood that Hayden Burgess was behind the murders and had begun purging her information network, and that more mayhem was likely in the offing. When the FBI took her theory up the chain, they had been ordered to the White House and confined to a small holding room, where they had been sitting now for nearly an hour.

Meanwhile, the White House and its operatives were on high alert and had been contacting potentially infected entities. FBI agents, FERC senior managers, and cyber jockeys from across the U.S. government were hunting through computer systems in search of snipe. A creature of ridicule, the snipe hunt, by its nature, was destined to fail. So thought the operators of energy companies—who were being contacted and told to bare their systems to bureaucrats in search of the time bombs that Hayden Burgess and Mamiwata had planted in the networks across the power grid.

One of the threats of the modern age was incredulity. Even at the highest levels of power, leaders habitually, instinctively, rejected the improbable as wholly impossible, and they grounded their doubt in a phony pessimism that cloaked blind hope. Again and again, the energy CEOs and vendors refused to comply with the White House's requests because they refused to believe the claim. When logic and cajoling failed, the call went up the chain of command to an undersecretary pulled from a weekend's rest to staff harried cabinet secretaries trying to stop catastrophe. That led to a summons to the White House for a majority of department heads. Scattered across offices and conference rooms, manned with phone lists and talking points, they'd been dialing for attention.

However, on orders from President Stokes, no one was allowed to utter the word *terrorism,* lest all hell break out. Robbed of this galvanizing tool, the assembled leaders had to talk in circles to convince their targets to take action.

"Emily," the secretary of commerce had begged, "this isn't a scheme to distract America from the impeachment trial tomorrow. President Stokes is truly concerned about the rumor that a massive ransomware attack is planned against your company. We've got it on good authority—"

"Whose authority?" demanded the CEO of one of the nation's premier hedge funds, whose client list and bank accounts had been painstakingly recorded via a FISA warrant over the past nine months, unbeknownst to her.

"I can't tell you that," the secretary insisted. "But trust me, you do not want to wake up tomorrow regretting that you wouldn't listen to me."

Emily Ellison planned to do exactly that. Her board would replace her in an instant if she gave the Stokes administration access to their servers and system. She had personally maxed out to the U.S. senator vying to replace him in next month's elections. But just in case the election tipped in the other direction, she pledged, "I'll have my team run a system-wide diagnostic in the morning. First thing."

"I urge you to have your team start on this tonight, Emily."

"Sure, Drew. I'll get right on it."

The secretary of commerce had cursed in frustration. "I don't want to hear you bitching about a bailout if they clean you out!"

Across the room, the defense secretary was becoming even more voluble. "Hank, goddamn it, take your thumb out of your ass and listen to me! Your security is compromised, and if your power plants take a hit, we lose Texas and northern Mexico."

The slow drawl that replied carried the veneer of a Rhodes Scholar. "I appreciate the heads-up, Jimmie. ERCOT makes us run system tests nearly every day, and I trust our engineers. I'll alert them to your concerns, but unless you can tell us what to look for . . . well, I'm not sure what you want."

"Let our boys take a look under the hood," he urged. "We promise not to tell anyone what we see."

"I'm not explaining to anyone down here why I invited the government to go thrashing about. Especially this one, when your boy is about to be taken to the woodshed. I hear your warning, and we'll pay attention. Give Karen a kiss for me."

The brush-off happened again and again. At midday, the president convened the cabinet in the Situation Room for an update. "How many are listening to us?"

AG Dobson made the report. "Right now, we have about forty-five percent compliance from the electric companies and thirty percent from financial firms. Tech companies have basically told us to fuck off."

President Stokes looked to the trio closest to him: the energy secretary, the chairman of FERC, and the chair of NERC, the weightily named North American Electric Reliability Corporation. NERC controlled the power regulation for the Eastern Seaboard—the ancestral home of money and political power. The chair had been read in on the crisis. POTUS suggested the same for ERCOT and the other regional leaders, but to a person, he was cautioned against their inclusion.

"What the hell do we do now?" He posed the question with an even tone, almost conversational. Though disaster loomed, he was in his element. A decorated war veteran, Brandon Stokes never panicked during a crisis. "To stave off absolute disaster, what's the threshold?"

Chairman Peterson of FERC answered first. "To knock out the grid, they'd need different levels of success in each region. This issue, Mr. President, isn't threshold."

"It's a multivector attack on the power grid," inserted the head of the NSA. "Based on the scenarios we've been running, they've had time to get into critical safety equipment. They can rewrite code to transmit fake data. For all we know, they've gained access to the computers controlling the circuit breakers."

"Which will reduce the amount of electricity flowing across the three interconnections—basically crippling the whole country," Peterson explained. "Mr. President, I don't think we can repel an attack unless the operators actually believe one is coming."

Stokes heard the unspoken plea. "Can't do it. I declare the nation is facing a terrorist attack that can take out power across the entire goddamned continent, and it'll set off a national stampede. Runs on grocery stores and banks, mass looting, not to mention the economic collapse that will follow. No, that's off the table." He pinned the defense secretary with a sharp look. "What did DARPA learn from its doomsday planning? The RADICS project?"

The head of DoD responded, "The Rapid Attack Detection, Isolation, and Characterization Systems project gamed out several of the scenarios at play here. But—"

"But?"

"But we never expected resistance from the grid operators." He swiveled in his seat to look at the energy secretary. As the head of the Defense Department, he had refused to participate in the soft coup attempt, and he regarded his fellow cabinet officers who did so with scorn. Though a civilian himself, his father and grandfather had served in the Army, and his daughter was first-generation Air Force. "Why won't the utilities listen to reason?"

"Because of the politics of the moment," Vice President Slosberg inserted flatly. "The timing seems too convenient."

"Perhaps if you hadn't tried to overthrow the government," challenged the education secretary, who had known Brandon Stokes for nearly thirty years. "If you hadn't undermined confidence in our national integrity—" he blustered.

"Bullshit," she retorted sharply. "The minute the Supreme Court ruled in July, we were already suspect. However, this is not the time." She focused on the president. "Short of creating a national panic, we can only try to control the chaos, sir. Force the grid operators to take this seriously." She stopped, unsure of her reception.

Stokes said tersely, "Go on."

"Order a series of rolling blackouts by the governors who have state-run utilities. Announce to the public that this is a precaution brought on by concerns of a virus that's infecting power systems."

"How is that not going to create panic?" argued the defense secretary.

The VP replied acerbically, "Americans will freak out at the thought of a terrorist attack. But warn them of rolling blackouts created by a virus, and they'll understand having to turn the power off and on to flush out the system."

"And how do we get the governors to agree?" The tentative query came from Secretary Espinoza of HUD.

President Stokes gave the room a steady look. "I'll issue an executive order. Dare them to disagree."

"We should bring in congressional leadership," the VP urged. "They can help with the locals who balk. Threaten earmarks or something."

"Do it." He squared his shoulders, summoning the grit of Eisenhower and swagger of Reagan. "We're weeks out from Election Day, and nearly everyone is on the ballot or trying to stay off the radar. No one wants to do it in the dark. AG Dobson, get to work on the language. In one hour, I want everyone back here to start making calls."

"Initiate the Myrina Assault. Phase Two."

The directive rolled across the communications hub to Hayden's most trusted lieutenants. Years of planning, months of plotting, narrowed to a few precious hours of action. A timetable accelerated due to her newest annoyance, Avery Keene.

Lucky for Avery, Phase I had been completed, the targeted theft of $4.2 billion in cryptocurrency. The server farm she forced out of hiding in West Virginia had to bypass its Kentucky safe house and squat in an abandoned textile factory in southern Indiana. From there, the pilfering had proceeded apace. One more set of targets remained, and the farm's use would reach a natural end.

Despite the interference, Hayden couldn't rightly bemoan her fate too deeply. Their FISA-enabled surveillance had been a stroke of genius. She'd first infiltrated the court system as a value-add to her more committed clients, a selective feature that allowed her to piggyback on the efforts of others to gain market share and insight.

As the Myrina Assault came together, though, she saw the broader possibilities. Lawyers and judges who could deliver insights on command rather than having to shop like a peasant. Jason Johnson had opened Pandora's box, she thought. Then she corrected herself. She now had the Oracle of Delphi. She could see the future and, if she proceeded properly, control it. Judge Oliver's last mission had embedded her deep into the federal system, and they'd never root her out.

Access allowed her to monitor the hasty attempts of the Stokes administration to warn their targets of the coming storm. Hayden kept close watch on the nearly one hundred hosts they'd procured for the attack. For each of the three interconnections, the threshold for maximum damage was roughly 10 percent of the generating capacity in each of the regions to cause a cascade. But she wanted more than outages. She'd planned for carnage. Thus, her operatives had established redundancies and explored abandoned avenues of mayhem.

Due to Keene's warnings, their malware had been flagged. But chaos could still reign. Even a partial collapse of the grid would wreak havoc. Havoc she would revel in and capitalize on.

"Where are we?" she demanded of the lieutenant on the main screen.

"A cascade will begin shortly. If Bonsai did its part, the latent malware will spread exponentially."

"Good. Inflict as much damage as you can. I want everyone scrambling for cover. I want to weaken their trust in the systems. In the electrical system. In the financial system. I want Americans to doubt what they think they know about stability. Go!" She terminated the call and rocked in her chair, both pleased and perturbed.

Years as a competitive swimmer, a naval officer, and the youngest of three had taught her the value of multivector attacks. Her new adversary, Ms. Keene, had dented the impact of her plan, but there was still much chaos and damage to sow. Hayden would exploit it all.

The night was still young.

THIRTY-SIX

Agent Gehl paced the small White House meeting room with increasing irritation. On the television screen behind her, a reporter mentioned power disruptions. The story was a brief mention, the journalist unaware of the scope of the calamity that could befall the nation.

She caught the chryon as it scrolled. "This is my case, damn it! I should be in on whatever is happening."

"The director asked us to be here on standby. Think of this as the cushiest stakeout we've ever done," Agent Lee offered mildly.

"The JTF brought this in, Robert. I don't like being on the sidelines." Then she held up her hands in surrender. "But this isn't about me or the team. I know. I'm just wired."

"Maybe one of you can ask the chief of staff for an update," Avery ventured. "Although I'm not sure which one of us he hates the least."

"I've never met the guy," Jared chimed in. "I volunteer as tribute."

When the others chuckled, he felt his phone vibrate. He checked the number, which showed up as restricted. Ordinarily, he would have sent it to voicemail, but times were not normal. "Jared Wynn."

"I need to speak to your girlfriend," Major Vance said in gruff greeting. "Now. I've been trying to reach her for hours."

Biting off an insult, Jared stiffly handed the phone to Avery. "It's your friend from overseas."

Avery accepted the device, and both FBI agents lasered in on the speakerphone she activated. "Hello?"

In his humid, ramshackle hotel room, Major Vance swatted at a mosquito. The sat phone he used had layers of encryption, and his contacts had heightened degrees of paranoia. "You haven't responded to my hails."

"My phone was stolen on Friday. As well as a stack of proof that our concerns were justified."

"So you know Mamiwata is behind the attack on the grid."

"Yes."

"Do you know about the heist?"

"Heist?" Avery became rigid, unsure of what Vance knew and what he was sharing. Despite his outreach, he remained a threat. Gingerly, she offered, "We know she's targeting a number of financial institutions and tech companies." Unless he mentioned it, she wouldn't reveal the servers and the connection to cryptocurrency.

"I know about the servers in West Virginia, Nancy Drew. Do you know what they've been up to?"

"Why don't you just tell me?"

"Blockchain hacking. Somehow, your foes have been able to watch various cryptocurrency exchanges. They got behind the security systems and into the passwords for several of them. Basically, they've stolen the keys to billions and redirected them to unhackable wallets."

"How much have they stolen?"

"More than four billion dollars and counting. They are looting accounts around the globe."

"How do you know it's the same team?"

"I can't prove it, but my informants and I have no doubt. That's why I'm telling you. Have Agent Lee or whomever he's playing lackey to—have them check my facts. If I'm right, you'll find a signature that might lead you back to Burgess and her merry band of thieves."

"Anything else?"

"Don't underestimate her. She's pissed, paranoid, and looking for payback. This is her grand debut, and you've upstaged her by uncovering her scheme."

"Maybe she'll back down," Avery said, realizing how naïve she sounded the moment the words left her lips. "She has to know the best play is to cut her losses."

Vance grunted. "Patriotism and vengeance are powerful forces, Keene. Like loyalty. What wouldn't you do for those you love?"

Although she refused to answer him, Avery understood the question. Extraordinary lengths, she thought wanly. She'd go—had gone—to extraordinary lengths. "What do we do?"

"Pass the phone to Agent Lee. I assume he's not letting you out of his sight. In a matter of days, if she doesn't get what she wants, Hayden Burgess will disappear. The U.S. government has to scoop her up right now, or they'll never get another shot."

Avery extended the phone to Agent Lee. He brusquely accepted the device and planted it against his ear. "What?"

The seconds stretched on as Vance relayed his intel to Agent Lee. Finally, Lee handed the phone back. "Here."

Though no one could hear him, his volume suddenly dropped. "Avery, you have no reason to believe a word I say. But listen to me. You've done your part. Get out now."

"I can't."

"Why not? You found the bad guys and told the good ones. But what you've uncovered is more than a plan to disrupt the grid or steal some money. You're playing in international waters now, and the sharks have much bigger teeth. If you're smart, you'll get out now, take Rita and the rest of the money Cooper gave you, and disappear."

"I appreciate the advice," she responded blandly.

"Fine. Take Wynn with you. But go. Run and keep running. Don't let Hayden Burgess find you. You won't like the consequences."

The call ended abruptly before Avery could form a question.

Warnings were irrelevant, she knew. It was too late to run anywhere but into the fire. Or, she corrected herself, to dive into the waters. Sharks and all.

The door to the room opened without a knock. Luke Boylen stood in the doorway with his arms akimbo. Behind him stood a young man of indeterminate purpose. Agent Gehl rose, and the rest joined her in standing.

"The president wants to thank you for your service," he said with obvious insincerity.

Agent Gehl took him at face value. "What's the status?"

"If you'll follow me," he instructed. Turning, he headed toward the Oval Office. Avery and the others followed in silence. They entered through the outer vestibule, passing a clutch of worried faces hovering over cell phones. Boylen gave a quick rap on the door.

"Enter."

The president stood by the windows, hands clasped behind him. Because he was standing, the other occupants were as well. Avery recognized the attorney general, the FBI director, and DHS secretary clustered in conversation beside one blue sofa. The secretary of energy paced nervously across the blue eagle rug, and the FERC chair followed close and murmured. The Treasury secretary stood in deep discussion with the head of the NSA. The only new face belonged to someone Avery recognized from her research.

Rear Admiral Donovan Casey stood at parade rest beside the president's desk. His air of calm command felt almost palpable, accented by a Brioni suit and crimson tie. A square jawline, piercing green eyes, and a hawkish nose fairly screamed "put me in charge." The Navy had obliged.

"Ms. Keene," the president greeted serenely. "Welcome to the Oval Office. I don't believe you visited me here before."

Given that you'd kidnapped my mother, no, she thought angrily. "No, sir. I have not had the pleasure."

Clearly reading her mind, he smiled smugly. "I understand that America has you to thank for the current fire drill we're running."

"I filled in some missing pieces," she demurred, studiously avoiding eye contact with Admiral Casey. "Agents Gehl and Lee deserve all the credit. Hopefully, whatever is planned can be averted before anyone else gets hurt."

"Depends on which crisis you are referring to, exactly." The president gestured toward the admiral. "I understand that our likely terrorist is harboring a grudge against a decorated war hero."

She responded carefully, "My research suggests that Lieutenant Burgess is seeking revenge against Admiral Casey and others, yes."

"Revenge for an imagined slight," Admiral Casey bit out.

"Meritless complaints notwithstanding," President Stokes interjected, "she poses a threat to national security. I invited Admiral Casey to join us because he best understands her skill set. You, Ms. Keene, apparently have relevant insight about her intentions."

"I'm not sure—"

"Director Alford assured me that you were the source of this panic we're currently in, and as such, that you can reassure me the use of significant governmental resources is warranted. As the target of one of your witch hunts, I am loath to allow anyone else to be a victim of your zeal."

"With all due respect," Agent Gehl said before Avery could respond, "Ms. Keene followed up on leads that she'd identified on her own that jibed with intelligence the Joint Task Force secured. So far, her theories have led to actionable items."

"Ah, yes, the missing server farm in West Virginia, where the Bureau allowed her to trespass on private property," the president sneered. "And the mysterious attack in her office at the Supreme Court. Yet another culprit no one saw."

Jared, who had hung back by the door, stepped forward. "I saw the bruises on her ribs and around her throat."

"Mr. Wynn, skulking in the shadows as usual, I see. How's your father?"

"Stubbornly alive, despite your best efforts, sir."

The attorney general moved to flank Avery and conveniently block Jared's advance. "Mr. President, I recommended we speak with Ms. Keene because I am fearful that we only have part of the puzzle with Lieutenant Burgess. According to what we've discerned, her intention is to collapse the grid, and we have scant information about how and where she will carry out her attack other than the targets Ms. Keene has identified. We know Burgess has already orchestrated a cryptocurrency heist, which accounts for the missing server farm. And we are on high alert that she may try to cripple some social media giant or a bank if she is able to execute her plan. My question is, what else are we behind the eight ball on?"

All eyes turned to Avery. She straightened her shoulders and exhaled. "She wants revenge."

"That's your insight?" Admiral Casey scoffed.

Without looking at him, she continued, "I honestly believe her other major target is the admiral. She blames him for the loss of her dignity, her job, and, most tragically, her child."

"There was no child," the admiral barked. "Goddamn it, I will not stand here and be insulted by a smarmy upstart who thinks she's smarter than everyone else."

"Is that what you thought about Lieutenant Burgess?" Avery queried frostily. "That she was just another smarmy upstart?"

The admiral grunted and muttered, "I apologize for my outburst. There's no excuse." He tried to look chagrined, but the remorse never reached his eyes. He straightened his absurdly stiff posture. "Imagine my position. My record has been tarnished. My name dragged through the gutter. When she made those false accusations, I nearly lost my family."

"When she was attacked, she lost her career and nearly lost her life. The miscarriage almost killed her, and she will never be able to bear children," Avery reminded him sharply. "No one in charge believed her. She got demoted and drummed out of the service. Lieutenant Burgess simply asked for justice, and at every turn, she was denied."

"It didn't happen!" Admiral Casey insisted. "If someone did attack that woman, I had nothing to do with it. I refused to be held responsible for another man's poor judgment."

"She believes it was you. That you and the U.S. military denied her the reckoning to which she was entitled. And the U.S. Supreme Court abdicated its responsibility by denying her a day in court. She swore to protect America, and it turned its back on her."

"Which justifies attacking our nation?" The DHS secretary closed ranks with the president and admiral. "I'm surprised at you, Ms. Keene."

Refusing the bait, Avery replied, "I didn't say she was justified. The attorney general wanted to know what he was missing. It's that—the failure of every system that should have protected her. Collapsing the power grid is an obvious metaphor but an effective one. She was denied agency and retribution. Now she's seizing control. If she can't have justice, she'll take revenge by crippling the strongest nation on the planet." She stopped and turned to Agent Gehl, a new idea tugging at her conclusions. "But that's so melodramatic," she murmured to herself. "And predictable."

Agent Gehl cocked her head. "What do you mean?"

"Most people are driven by base instincts. Anger. Sadness. Lust. The usual. Hayden Burgess is no different." Avery cocked her head. "Still, when I say it out loud, it sounds so pedestrian. No, there's got to be more to this. Her plan has been meticulous. Elegant. Multifaceted. And, if this shutting down the electric grid is her big play, it's just . . . hackneyed."

The president gave a reluctant nod of agreement. "We took her power, so she takes our power. I hear it too. A kindergartner has higher-level plans."

Secretary Carlisle ceased fidgeting. "Do you think the attack on the power grid is a hoax?" he asked hopefully. "Maybe the outages we're seeing are just a test."

Musing, Avery shook her head. "No, it's real. She's pissed and intends to do as much damage as she can. But it's not the whole plan. The cryptoheist is about her bottom line. Money you can't trace and can't take back. The grid attack is what it looks like. Breaking the other kid's toys. I'm still missing a piece."

"Then what is, young lady?" demanded the admiral. "If I am the supposed source of her outrage, what does she have planned for me?"

"I honestly don't know, Admiral. And quite frankly, whatever she has in mind, you probably deserve."

"Avery—" Agent Lee spoke up for the first time.

"But," she continued evenly, "she has no right to pursue rogue justice. Yes, the systems failed her, but innocent people have died because of Hayden Burgess. She has blood on her hands, and no one is above the law." The pointed look she shot the president was met by a cold blue steel, their moment of agreement now in the past.

"I recommend we put the admiral into protective custody," Agent Lee suggested to the director. "The assassin Nyx remains at large, and she has proven very effective. In addition to the suspicious death of Jason Johnson, we suspect she orchestrated the murders of three judges and their families today."

Admiral Casey shook his head. "No. I will not hide. If Hayden Burgess wants me, she can come at me head-on." He spared a dismissive glance for Avery. "If the young lady can survive this so-called assassin, I and my arsenal can do the same."

"Don't be a jackass, Donnie," President Stokes warned. "This woman murdered two people in broad daylight, got to someone in a federal prison, and breached the Supreme Court."

"Thank you for acknowledging that I was actually attacked,

Mr. President," Avery chimed in. When Agent Lee arched his brow, she fell quiet.

The admiral relented slightly as he recalled the briefings earlier on the deaths of the judges. "Fine. Post a detail at my house in Charlottesville. Livvie is visiting friends in Colorado, so she's out of harm's way."

"Attacking Admiral Casey isn't the endgame," Avery warned. "He's her motive but not her only means of exacting revenge."

President Stokes took a seat behind his desk. "We appreciate your warning, and now the finest minds in Washington are on this matter, Ms. Keene. We can take it from here. Good day."

THIRTY-SEVEN

Monday, October 21

Myrina Assault Phase II commenced in earnest at 2:29 a.m. PST.

In Bozeman, Montana, an operator sat before a massive bank of computers. On each screen, he monitored the amount of power traveling through the system and checked that it equaled the needs of the neighbors, businesses, and hospitals that relied on the flow of electricity. The first phone call came in at 5:11 a.m. from a police station. They were being flooded with calls about power outages across multiple blocks. The operator, tagged by his boss, checked his screens. Nothing. No outages, no spikes. Nothing but the steady stream of current being rebalanced by the second.

Soon, engineers, managers, and techs crowded around the bank of screens, perplexed. Reports of outages were streaming in from across the state, where other operators sat behind other screens. None of the data matched. The computers they relied on to tell them what to do could tell them nothing.

In Texas, a turbine ground to a halt without warning.

New Hampshire reported generator failures, a dire warning echoed by Missouri, Rhode Island, Louisiana, and North Dakota.

System operators, grizzled veterans of hurricanes, earthquakes, and snipers, cursed at the equipment that refused to respond to age-old commands. Techs who'd trained for the apocalypse chased malware through the downed systems trying to find a way out.

Governors who'd heeded the president's warning took to emergency broadcast systems and simulcasts to warn residents of rolling blackouts and a freak virus infecting power systems. Those state executives who chafed at the directive scrambled to explain why hospitals were suddenly running on emergency power and prayer.

Power stations went offline across the three interconnections—West, East, and ERCOT. Rushing to contain the damage, regional managers urged shutting off power to avoid a full-scale system collapse. Bickering and accusations flew across hardened phone lines, and energy purveyors fretted over the worst-case scenario: a black start. If they lost power too extensively, the grid would have to be reinitialized from beyond the blackout zone.

Frazzled administrators tried to explain to suit-wearing overlords just how dangerous the next few hours might be. If they couldn't stop a cascade failure, the hackers in the system owned the power grid. The assholes responsible for shutting down the electrical generators, the control stations, and the transmission lines could control everything. Translation: once hackers shut the grid down, they'd basically chew through the wires and smash everything until it was impossible to turn the lights back on without their permission.

The feckless masters of the universe who'd blithely ignored the warnings all weekend jammed the lines to Washington, D.C., as system after system malfunctioned. The energy secretary huddled with the leadership of FERC and NERC to assess the damage. The NSA and FBI popped into the Situation Room to deliver new reports and collaborate on suggestions. At 1:38 p.m., Secretary Carlisle waited to be admitted to the Oval, the others on his heels. "Mr. President," he offered in genuflection.

"Chris, what have we got?"

"Kansas is in free fall, and so is Mississippi. Good news is Wyoming, Utah, and Delaware barely had blips."

"And what's the word on the street?"

"News channels and social media are buzzing. But at the moment, the conspiracy nuts are losing the information war. As we planned, the outages are being explained as selective brownouts—preventive measures to recalibrate the system based on a fluke virus. Sort of like Facebook going dark. Annoying but not panic-inducing. Overall, we think the worst damage is contained, but we're getting reports of outages and other troubles that will stir up public anxiety, sir."

"How do you know she hasn't got something more sinister planned?"

"Frankly, we don't know, Mr. President. But the contingency plans are holding steady. The rolling blackouts stopped full-scale grid collapse. Other than Mississippi and Kansas, whose governors refused to heed our warnings, no one else will likely need to go to a black start to get up and running. If we'd been caught flat-footed, the whole continent would be melting. Because we got a head start, even in the states that ignored our warnings, the damage was contained. In fact, we'll have teams dispatched to purge the malware and inspect the equipment."

The NSA director coughed into her hand, and the secretary amended, "We'll be able to purge the malware we can identify."

"You can't find it all."

"No, sir. We don't have a clue what got into these systems or how long it will hide there." He shook his head in defeat. "We're sitting ducks, Mr. President. The operators will scrub what they can find, but no one has ever seen code like this. This bitch can hold us hostage for years, and we'll never see it coming."

The president pointed to Peterson, the FERC chair. "How the devil did she get buried so deep?"

"I concur with the secretary's assessment, sir." She pulled out the report she'd compiled minutes before. "This threat actor is highly skilled, and apparently she infiltrated an extraordinary number of systems. Malware has to be configured specifically to exploit the vulnerabilities of its hosts. We're getting reports of almost every style of exploit."

"In other words, Burgess and her team are damn good, and we're going to be spending years trying to flush the systems," translated the NSA director. "Every scenario we've modeled over the past twenty years assumes a pretty standard assault on the grid—go after the generators or go after the computerized monitoring systems. The assumption has always been that the hackers would need to focus in order to achieve maximum damage."

"What happened instead?"

Director Alford explained ruefully, "They did everything. All of the above. They attacked hardware, software, and, according to our reports, extorted or bribed personnel to deploy their riskiest attacks."

The NSA director finished, "If Keene hadn't spotted this, sir, we'd have been fucked back to the Dark Ages. Sir."

While a litany of curses shouted in his head, President Stokes maintained his mask of solid equanimity. "What's the triage plan? How are we helping Mississippi and Kansas and the others deal with humanitarian issues?"

Luke Boylen, who had been on a short leash since his earlier bungling of the matter, took a tentative step forward. "I've tasked FEMA to coordinate with the National Guard and the states' governors on response plans. Like the secretary said, the damage has been fairly limited."

Feeling bolder, Boylen slyly changed tone. "I must ask, though," he said, "if we're giving our adversaries too much credit here? Did we get lucky in stopping them, or did they simply fail to live up to the hype? It looks to me as though a rogue set of hackers tried to attack the power grid and were thwarted by the protocols and resilience of this administration."

President Stokes smothered a chortle. Damn, he liked how the man operated. Digging diamonds out of shit.

Secretary Carlisle jumped first. "Mr. President, your strong leadership this weekend was the perfect response to this fire drill. We will need to evaluate the after-action reports, but I would concur with Mr. Boylen's analysis."

Chairwoman Peterson barely stopped her eyes from rolling in mockery. Aloud, she simply said, "The dispersal pattern for the attacks is broader than anything I've ever seen, sir. Even in our scenario planning about Russia or North Korea, we don't profile a continent-wide breach. Had this played out as it could have, this nation would be in chaos right now."

"That is speculation, is it not?" Boylen pushed back.

"Forty-three states reported some degree of penetration. Over the weekend, we contacted and secured prophylactics against more than seventy-five percent of the potentially affected systems. Those are hard numbers, not guesses."

Luke squared his shoulders. "Meaning?"

"Meaning," the NSA director elucidated as though speaking to a child, "that we nearly got our asses handed to us. Out there, we can play down the threat for the politics. But in here, we'd do better to admit the truth. Someone, either working for herself or—more likely—a foreign actor—managed to squirrel inside the fucking national goddamned grid and nearly take it down. Spin it however you want, but don't forget what actually happened."

"No one is downplaying anything," President Stokes said. "However, until all the reports are in, we'll keep all theories to a minimum. I would like to know exactly how we found ourselves here. I am especially looking forward to your analysis of how the NSA failed to identify that a disgruntled expat with elite training in computer science and nuclear technology was running a clandestine security firm out of South Africa." He met his aggressive stance with a look of mild derision. "That will be all."

One by one, everyone filed out except for Boylen. "Well done, sir."

"Oh, cut the shit, Luke. We nearly got screwed on this whole debacle, and the entire cabinet knows it. If not for Avery Keene, we'd have been fucked beyond precedent. They know. I know. And goddamn it, that pious brat knows it."

Luke frowned and offered, "But her credibility is weakened. VerityVictory.org is having an effect, like we thought. I have your latest polling top lines. She's losing favor with your base."

"Why am I fighting with her to keep my most loyal voters? Because she told a better story, and the people I handpicked to serve me chose to believe her and not me." He waved his hand imperiously. "I want a memo by the end of the week naming an entirely new cabinet. I won't pull the trigger until after the election, but by God, I want every one of these motherfuckers out of my White House."

"Including the defense secretary? He's been loyal, sir."

"Especially him." The look the president sent Luke was sly and pleased. "I intend to make him my new vice president. I think it's vital that America understands that this shit show developed on Vice President Slosberg's brief watch, and she is to blame for what nearly transpired."

Catching on quickly, Luke filled in the blanks. "Faced with public disfavor, she'll be forced to resign in disgrace."

"Leaving two openings—SecDef and VP."

Luke's expression mirrored his new boss's. "On it."

An hour later, President Stokes commandeered television stations and radio broadcasts to caution against the nightmare scenarios being speculated about by unnerved anchors. "My fellow Americans," he intoned from behind the massive desk, flanked by reassuring flags and a well-lit room that reminded the nation of his model-good looks and brilliant blue eyes. "This weekend, we became aware of a virus that has infected several of the nation's power systems. Unfortunately, during the temporary lapse of leadership, oversight of our systems faltered. But since my return, and at my direction, an investigation of our national infrastructure brought this danger to the attention of my administration."

He offered the viewing public a reassuring half-smile. "I am proud that our reinvigorated team came together to tackle this crisis. I have worked closely with the secretaries of energy, defense, and commerce among others to coordinate a response. Our finest minds have already been dispatched to purge the virus and patch the damaged systems.

"Our country has endured a great deal of turmoil recently. Tempers flare, nerves are tight, and patience is limited. One thing I do know, however, is that in times of trial, America comes together. We check on our neighbors and reach out a hand to those in need. As we work to restore our remarkable electrical grid to full capacity, I ask each of you to dig deep for the patriotism that allows us to remain the greatest country in the world."

Across the city, in the vice president's residence, a ceramic cup shattered a television screen.

Avery, Jared, Ling, and Noah watched the broadcast from the living room in Anacostia. After the frantic activity of the weekend, the actual blackout felt anticlimactic. D.C. and the Eastern Seaboard had been the most responsive to the president's entreaties. As a result, while some substations reported glitches, hardly a resident of the DMV felt the effects. Ling flipped through the channels for more local color. The newscaster, on air hours earlier than normal, read his script with crisp inflection.

"According to the White House, the virus in the power grid will continue to cause challenges across the country. The DMV largely escaped any harm. However, the greater Virginia area has borne the brunt of the malware's impact. Across the region, communities are reporting lights out. Even the Naval Station in Norfolk has been struggling to keep the electricity flowing despite military-grade generators."

"Norfolk?" Avery's head whipped around toward the television. She thought about what Vance said to her. *Loyalty. What wouldn't you do for the ones you love?* "This isn't just about chaos. It's about revenge and saving her family," she said quietly. "Her family is gone."

Seated next to her, Noah shifted to watch her instead of the television. "You mean her siblings? Parents? They're still in Missouri."

"Her Navy family—the ones who stuck up for her. Tried to protect her." Avery jumped off the couch and rushed to the front door, pulling it open. "Where's Agent Lee? I need to speak with him immediately. It's urgent."

"Agent Lee has been called in to meet with the director," the agent on duty explained. "Can I help you?"

"Yes," she said gravely. "Interrupt him. Now."

Having watched their interactions for the past few days, rather than argue, the duty agent nodded briskly. "Yes, ma'am. But please wait inside."

Avery hurried back into the house and started hunting for her shoes. Aware her friends were staring at her with varying degrees of concern and confusion, she impatiently explained, "Hayden Burgess had two friends whose lives were destroyed by Admiral Casey. According to the reports, Petty Officer Carolyn Hugley realized that Casey had spiked Hayden's food in the mess hall. When they heard her struggles in the cabin, she and Crewman Tyler Boozer tried to intervene."

"She had witnesses?" Noah asked incredulously.

"Yes. They got her to the infirmary after the attack, and both testified against Casey. But no one believed the testimony of a petty officer and a crewman against a captain. It was in my memo, but I never read it to the agents because I was so focused on the grid attack and the heist." She whirled around, one white canvas sneaker in hand. "Anyone see my other one?"

"Keep talking," Jared prodded as he joined her by the sofa. Pushing her to sit on the arm, he knelt and reached beneath the couch. He quickly handed her the missing shoe. "Why does Norfolk matter?"

"Because Hugley and Boozer were court-martialed. After Casey was exonerated, they were accused of running a drug-smuggling ring, using the galley and the med bay to hide and distribute narcotics."

"It's been known to happen," Jared cautioned. "Drug addicts and drug dealers find one another."

"Both claimed their innocence. They swore it was payback due to their testimony against Casey. Neither of them had ever been in trouble before, but they both were convicted. Hugley got three years, and Boozer got four and a half."

"Let me guess," Jared said. "Boozer is serving his time in the brig at Naval Station Norfolk."

Avery's head bobbed in assent. "Bingo. A brig on a base where the power has gone out, and the generators aren't working," Avery announced. "Where the devil is my bag?"

"The assassin took it," Ling answered helpfully as she shoved a black satchel into Avery's outstretched hands. "You're using this one instead. It's got the phone Jared cloned for you in the front pocket." As Avery slung the strap over her shoulder, Ling asked, "If Boozer is in Virginia, where is Hugley?"

Jared retrieved a jacket for Avery and motioned for Noah to grab her laptop. He explained, "Women get sent to California. The Naval Consolidated Brig in Miramar." Anticipating Avery's next question, he waved her off. "I'm on it. I'll see if they've had a similar blackout."

A firm rap on the door preceded Agent Lee's entry as Avery reached for the knob. She took a quick step back to let him enter. Using the pause, Noah slid the computer into her bag.

"Agent Lee! How'd you get here so quickly? I thought you were at the Hoover Building?"

"Meeting was pushed back an hour because the director is at the

White House, so I was on my way here to check in first. What new mischief are you making?"

Avery didn't smile. "You need to send teams to Norfolk and Miramar, California. Hayden Burgess is breaking her friends out of prison, and there's no telling how much collateral damage she's willing to accept in order to get them out."

"Are you sure?"

"It's her family. The family that knows what happened to her when Casey stole her life. She's desperate to save them and to make him pay. These blackouts are serving multiple purposes. Not just money and revenge. Camouflage."

"Is her actual family in danger?"

"No—she's indebted to those who protected her. The ones who got punished for her. This is all about what happened on that submarine. And after."

Convinced, Agent Lee turned to Jared. "May I use your bunker?"

"Follow me." Jared jogged down the steps with Agent Lee close on his heels. Avery followed them down.

Security protocols engaged, Agent Lee began making phone calls. As his expression grew darker, Avery knew her fears had been realized. "Was I too late?"

"This isn't on you," he corrected. "But yes, she has broken them out already." He expounded, "Both Petty Officer Hugley and Crewman Boozer escaped during the coordinated blackouts. Hugley was reported missing less than an hour ago. Boozer has been gone for around the same length of time."

"And?" Avery knew Agent Lee, and his expression suggested nothing—which meant more was going on. "What else?"

"No known casualties. They were both medium-security prisoners with impeccable records," he started. "Separately, the commanders at each facility had given them more freedom than normal. Nothing outrageous. Hugley was studying for her nursing license online, and the guards often allowed her extra computer time. Boozer helped other inmates with projects and earned additional access."

Avery knotted her brow, recalling the petty officer's jacket. "Carolyn Hugley has an associate's degree in computer science. Why would she switch to nursing?"

"Based on the forensic review they are doing of their systems, she never did. Agent Gehl is working with them, and what she's found already is terrifyingly familiar. Hugley was working with Mamiwata to set up the Western Interconnection cascade failure."

"How many escapes have ever happened from a military prison?"

Jared shook his head. "None that I know of. To orchestrate a dual escape would take—"

"A national crisis and a collapse of the power grid," Agent Lee finished. "That's a hell of a lot of work for a prison break."

"It's not simply about the break, guys. It's proof. She manipulated and broke the power system. Rescued her friends. Stole billions of dollars. And if this ever goes public, she has humiliated the man who stole her dignity and the president who let him get away with it." She thought again about the scope of Hayden's ambitions. What she'd accomplished was tremendous, but a niggling suspicion prompted Avery to ask, "Has NCIS found anything else?"

Agent Lee shot a suspicious glance at Jared. "How'd you know?"

"Educated guess. What happened?"

"Apparently, she also managed to access classified naval research. Which I am only sharing because I believe you may have some thoughts about her next play. Care to share?"

"Every strategy has layers," Avery explained. "The metaphor, the practical, and the innovative. She's a futures thinker. *What's next?* Which begs the question—what did she take?"

"Some stealth technology that a third-party consultant has also been advising the Navy about. Trident Security."

At the mention of his firm, Jared looked stunned. "She got into Cyrano?"

Agent Lee nodded. "The JTF is coordinating with NCIS, but initial signs show a hack hours before her escape. What exactly is *Cyrano*?"

"This is a technology that we've—they've—been working on for years," Jared hedged. "I'm not at liberty to say more. But it won't impact what's going on today, I swear."

Agent Lee gave Jared a disapproving look, then relented. "Agent Gehl said the same, but she's working to get a more thorough briefing. We may bring you in since you're already read in on the situation."

Avery nudged, "And Crewman Boozer?"

"He's been in communication with Hugley sporadically over the past eighteen months. No connection so far to Cyrano. No word at all on what his part in all this was."

"Where is Admiral Casey?" Avery asked. "Is he still being protected?"

"As far as I know. We've had the detail you recommended on him since yesterday."

"They're looking out for Nyx. Boozer might be on his way there too. Charlottesville isn't that far away from Norfolk."

"I'll call it in. Tell them to be on the lookout for Boozer too. I doubt they think he's headed their way." He logged out of Jared's system and sighed heavily. "Come on."

The trio returned upstairs, and Avery quickly updated Noah and Ling. "Jared and I will be back as soon as possible."

Agent Lee exited first and pulled Agent Osa to accompany them. Bringing civilians made little sense, but Avery had been one step ahead of all of them. Perhaps there was one more piece missing. He waved her forward, then dropped a heavy hand on her shoulder. "This time, you two must absolutely stay in the damn car. Or I'll shoot you myself."

"Yes, sir," they replied in chorus. Everyone knew they lied.

THIRTY-EIGHT

On the drive to Charlottesville, Avery peppered Agent Lee for more details. He patched Agent Gehl into his system to speed the process.

"What's the relationship between the president and Admiral Casey?" Avery asked. She glanced at Jared. "You saw their familiarity yesterday, right?"

Jared cocked a brow. "Are you referring to the fact that he promoted a mediocre, scandal-tainted captain to rear admiral, or that he called him 'Donnie'? Yeah, I noticed."

"Your point?" asked Agent Gehl.

Avery replied, "Hayden has planned overlapping contingencies. We figure out the server farm; it vanishes with billions in crypto. We partially block the grid collapse; she breaks her friends out of prison. She's given herself multiple options to outsmart us. Assuming she intends to go after Admiral Casey, what's her backup plan if she fails?"

"Do you believe she'll target the president of the United States?" Agent Gehl couldn't mask her skepticism. "I have a hard time believing that Stokes is part of her master plan."

Avery disagreed. "He has everything to do with what she believes happened to her. POTUS is the commander in chief. It was his job to protect her, and he failed.

"Worse," she added, "he promoted his buddy and may have helped him out at her expense. I read the transcripts from his trial. The DNA evidence was contaminated and inconclusive, and the eyewitnesses were deemed not credible due to their drug charges. And Casey's attorney was one of the best in the nation."

Next to her on the backseat, Jared had powered up his computer. "Attorney's name?"

Avery told him and continued. "The jury barely deliberated before they acquitted him. Then a should-be-court-martialed Captain Casey goes back to work and skyrockets up the ladder, and her career starts to crumble."

"Casey served briefly as secretary of the Navy, but he stepped down after only a year," Agent Gehl acknowledged.

"Doesn't matter. Casey rapes her, gets promoted, and eventually becomes secretary of the Navy because Brandon Stokes appointed him. He was secretary when she sued, and Stokes gave him power over her. Again. To her, Casey is guilty, and Stokes is complicit." Avery watched as cars jockeyed for position on the highway. Road rage around D.C. turned the normally docile into vigilantes willing to use their two-ton vehicles to exact retribution. "President Stokes had the power to hold Casey accountable, and he refused to do so. Even worse, his administration fought her in the circuit court and the Supreme Court."

"And, as you suspected, Casey and Stokes are old friends," Jared confirmed. "The attorney who represented him was one of Stokes's groomsmen, according to an article about the guy. Top in his class at Columbia Law, and a specialist in military court-martials."

"Lieutenant Burgess knows this, and she knows both the president and Admiral Casey will be heavily guarded." Agent Lee caught Avery's eye in the rearview mirror. "She's enraged. Thwarted. Out of moves. What's next?"

.   .   .

The runway on the recently acquired Seychelles island had one vehicle. The bespoke AW169 helicopter had been outfitted in Mamiwata's signature cerulean blue inside and out. Tan leather accents complemented the color scheme, and its luxurious interior accommodated twelve passengers. Nine people boarded, an air of nervous excitement running wild through the group. All were among the most proficient hackers on the planet. All had worked for the last two years for the hacktivist collective known as Bonsai. And all were now comfortably wealthy beyond normal imagination.

For their loyalty and service, they would be transported from this private island to Madagascar, receive their newly keyed cryptowallets and matching identities. Madagascar had no extradition treaty with the U.S. For a wealthy Westerner, slipping America's reach and into a new life would be child's play. But one wrong word, one misplaced keystroke about Hayden Burgess, whom they knew only as the uberhacker who lorded over the entire Bonsai operation, and mutually assured destruction couldn't begin to describe the hell that awaited them.

The chopper lifted into the air and streaked toward its destination.

Minutes later, a private jet appeared low on the horizon and touched down on the airstrip. The Gulfstream G650 had taken off from Los Angeles days before with necessary stops. Eleven passengers were on board. As the plane taxied and came to a halt, an open-air coach approached. Motorized steps slowly lowered from the jet to the tarmac, and all eleven passengers carefully descended to the viciously hot ground. A well-groomed porter who had driven the coach approached them.

"Dr. and Mr. Burgess?" he asked.

A handsome older couple stepped forth from the group and responded briskly, "Yes."

"David and Eliza Burgess?"

"Here," David answered.

"Malcolm, Maxwell, and Reena Burgess?"

"Accounted for."

"Isaiah and Aloysius Hugley?"

"Right here."

"Naima and Sebastian Boozer?"

"Yes." The young siblings each raised a timid hand. In the intervening years after their father's imprisonment, their mother had died of cancer, and their only living grandparent had recently been moved to hospice.

"Thank you, and welcome to you all. Please take a seat. We'll be departing shortly."

Sebastian, the elder child at nine, raised his hand. The porter nodded for him to continue, and he asked, "Where are we going?"

He smiled kindly. "To meet your father's best friend."

Nyx broke the first agent's neck with a brutal snap. She had clocked their rounds since her arrival in Charlottesville the day before. One section of the house proved vulnerable, where the pool jutted out into a whimsical but illogical curlicue. The odd shape required a guard to skirt around the edge in order to avoid falling in during nighttime rounds. None of their cameras picked up the blind spot, despite the rush job demanded yesterday by the FBI director. She'd taken advantage of her ability to stand for hours in absolute stillness. Her outfit consisted of black tactical pants and parkour shoes, a black fitted tee, and her natural dark brown hair pulled into a tight braid. When the agent slowed to pick his way past an errant chair, she struck.

With one man down, she bounded onto the wrought-iron chair and landed lightly on the roof. Her slight weight would barely register in late autumn with the wind picking up. Charlottesville was a college town, and its residents were not staring up at the shingles of the houses next door. Especially not a house with Tudor ambitions that had a series of ersatz turrets strategically placed to disguise an interloper. The FBI detail had attempted a cursory inspection upon arrival, but Admiral Casey had grown impatient and interrupted their close inspection.

The failure was poor tradecraft, but an understandable oversight. The drone they'd sent up to take photos could not distinguish a camouflaged body from a pileup of autumn leaves. With a series of strategic jumps that she'd mapped out in her mind the night before, she crossed to the area of the roof where the second guard held post. The configuration made sense. A guard posted at every point of ingress—the front door, kitchen, side patio, and upstairs balcony. A fifth agent patrolled the grounds, and a car sat down the street, pretending to be empty.

She fitted the silencer to the barrel of her trusty Jericho. Levering her body to dangle over the eaves at the kitchen door, she planted two shots into his brain. With an agile roll, she gained her feet and sprang across to the side patio. The angle this time provided a gentler slope, requiring only one bullet to eliminate her target. As she inched closer to the balcony, she saw the woman stationed below tap her earbud. Nyx crouched low, then belly-crawled the remainder of the distance.

"Holloman, respond." The agent tentatively emerged from beneath the protective shading of the balcony. "Holloman, respond."

"I can't raise him either," she reported. "Checking now. You try Adelstein again." The agent checked the perimeter and carefully advanced, her body poised for ambush.

Nyx waited until the agent cleared the balcony overhang. The trio of shots hit her in the back of the head and the back of the knees. The crippling technique had been necessitated by the radio chatter. If the head shot wasn't fatal, the brutal kneecapping would keep her out of the skirmish.

Her surveillance told her that the only way she would be able to make a frontal assault was head-on. The turrets that disguised her presence also impeded her visibility. She could not get a clean shot without revealing herself to the observation car and any nosy neighbor out for an evening stroll. To take him out, she would need to drop down and use the element of surprise. Nothing she hadn't done before, but she could not entirely trust her right leg. A dead drop tested every muscle, every fiber, and some had been punctured by Avery Keene's knife.

Her homemade stitches had started the healing process, but the pain was a steady reminder of her final piece of business on American soil before her retirement. Three targets to go.

She waited until he chimed his partners again and got nothing in return. Complaining about interference, he moved around near the side of the house. Nyx timed her attack precisely. As he cleared the first corner, she dropped. Her heel clocked the side of his face, and he stumbled. One hand reached for his weapon, and he called out for reinforcement. The choked cry ended with a bullet through his throat and a second into the base of his skull.

Limping, she made her way to the side door, avoiding the security cameras that should have alerted the occupant to her carnage. She slipped inside the admiral's home with its cavernous rooms and sterile decor. Their intel had mapped the interior as thoroughly as the outside. The sound of a sporting event came from the middle of the house, where re-created blueprints placed the entertainment room. He would be in there alone, as seemed appropriate.

Nyx debated how to enter. A fast roll keeping her low to the ground? A high kick to distract and discombobulate? Before she could decide, the mahogany double doors opened. He wore a silk robe, loosely knotted. Matching silk pajama pants in a dark crimson had been paired with a white T-shirt emblazoned with naval insignia. Glasses rode low on his nose, and his feet were encased in brown leather slippers.

"Admiral Casey."

He spun toward her, sputtering, "Who gave you permission to enter my home? I gave strict instructions that the detail was to remain on the grounds."

Nyx lifted her weapon and gestured to the room. "Inside. Now."

"I will not," he huffed. "Do you know who I am?"

"Yes, I do." She motioned toward the open double doors. "Inside."

"Fuck you."

Her first shot pierced his right hand. He shrieked in agony but cut off his cry as she advanced. With forced bravado, he gritted out, "Is this supposed to scare me?"

"No. It is supposed to remind you. I understand you put your hand over her mouth that night. Your right hand." Closing the distance between them, she aimed at his left knee. "I would prefer to do this with you sitting down, but it's up to you."

He cradled his hand to his chest and turned toward the entertainment room. "She's lying. That bitch is lying about everything."

"I don't believe so." Scanning the area, she located the seat she'd imagined for this showdown. She aimed the Jericho at a plaid recliner designed to look homey despite its outrageous price tag. "There."

As he dropped into the seat, she activated a tiny device on her lapel. A nearly microscopic light started. "From this point on, she can see and hear everything, Admiral. Do not lie to me again."

"I haven't lied once," he blustered.

A second bullet exploded from the short barrel of her Jericho and lodged in the top of his foot. He squealed and began to weep. "Stop this!"

"Then do not lie. You are now under oath and your testimony has begun." Nyx had a full clip and clear instructions. "Question one, did you or did you not proposition Lieutenant Hayden Burgess while on board the USS *Janeway*?"

"I did not."

The next shot shattered a bone in his ankle, and excruciating pain radiated up his leg. He writhed in the seat and screamed in agony. "Try again."

"No."

His kneecap jerked once as the bullet ripped through soft tissue and semihard plate. Tears flooded his eyes, and his shrieking cries echoed throughout the house. "Goddamn it, stop! I'll tell you. I'll tell the truth."

"Did you proposition her?"

"Yes." Crying, blubbering, he fumbled with the tie on his robe and tried to wrap it around his knee. Blood poured down his leg in a steady stream, the identical crimson hue as the lustrous fabric. He whimpered and panted, his face red with pain.

"Did she refuse you?"

Donovan Casey had never been held accountable in his lifetime and had never seen a day of real combat, already chosen for leadership by the time he left the Academy. The details of war were theoretical, and the anguish of physical harm a matter of cosplay. Suddenly, though, he couldn't run, could barely focus. His legs had been set on fire by bullets. By a sadist and her henchman. He whined meekly, "Yes."

"Did you tamper with her food?"

"Yes."

"Did you enter her room without her consent?"

"Yes."

"Did you rape Hayden Burgess?"

"No!"

Nyx dropped the gun by her side, stunned. "Why would you lie to me now?"

"I am not lying," he sniveled, wiping at his face, smearing blood across his cheek. "She wanted me. For months, she'd told me. I helped her get comfortable that night. That's all." His teeth gnashed against the burning waves of pain.

"That's all," he repeated weakly.

"You made her comfortable by drugging her? By forcing yourself inside her? By ruining her reputation?"

"She wanted me!" The sniveling became a cry of outrage. "The bitch wanted it. Why else do you think a woman would join a submariner crew? She wanted it," he sobbed over and over.

Appalled, Nyx abandoned her plan for a fuller confession, extracted one question at a time. He wasn't human. Not really. A confession would solve nothing. Only justice would. Aiming the Jericho again, she shot in a quick burst that did nothing to cover the outrageous, indescribably brutal pain. The bullet lodged in his genitalia, and he would bleed out fairly soon. Unable to walk. Unable to run. Unable to lie again.

Satisfied, she watched until he passed out from the pain. Hayden had specifically described the contours of her final revenge against Casey. Strip him of his manhood and his ability to harm another. Because surely, she had not been the first. But no one else would follow. Nyx knew that for certain.

The creak of the door was nearly imperceptible, and her ears had been tuned to his moans and cries. Still, she evinced no surprise when the FBI agent who'd escorted Avery Keene appeared in her line of sight.

"Drop it," Agent Lee demanded. He leveled his Glock at her chest. "You've survived this long. Don't be stupid, Nyx."

In her espionage training, capture was to be avoided at all costs. Her compatriots often whiled away hours of boredom by discussing how they would evade capture or die trying. But the allure of death by cop stupefied her. Why let them kill you because you might be imprisoned? Incarceration was temporary. Death was forever.

She dropped the Jericho and laced her fingers behind her head. Surrendering immediately also guaranteed her a protection from their bloodlust when they discovered how many of their compatriots she'd killed. The body count was irrelevant to her. She had accomplished her mission, and Hayden's tormentor lay in a pool of his own soiled blood.

Agent Lee swiftly cuffed her and was reading her rights when the first report of her handiwork rolled in.

The light on her device winked out.

THIRTY-NINE

Avery watched from the car window as Nyx was led outside in handcuffs, several weapons trained on her every move. Ambulances and more law enforcement vehicles arrived, and stretchers moved inside and around the house. Agent Gehl arrived on scene and disappeared into the admiral's home with Agent Lee.

Neither she nor Jared attempted to fill the heavy silence in the car. He had seen the queasy expressions from the other agents as they circled the perimeter. One fresh-faced newbie vomited into a bed of ornamental grass. By the time the body bags appeared, he'd counted five.

Admiral Casey emerged on a stretcher, a white sheet stained with blood that refused to stop seeping out. The red created a halo around his crotch and along his legs, and Jared felt his stomach churn. IVs pumped fluids, but he did not look long for this world.

Avery's eyes remained on Nyx. She desperately wanted to spring from the vehicle and demand confirmation of her suspicions about Hayden's motives. That the entire enterprise had been designed to both humiliate and obfuscate her more personal revenge. But the death toll and horrible torture were their own proof. As were the billions in missing funds. Avery may have stopped her destruction of the power grid, but Hayden Burgess had come out on top.

As streetlights began to wink on, the FBI set up strobe lights and a tent to further cordon off the crime scene. No one had come to check on either of them during the time they secured the premises. On the backseat, Avery lay her head on Jared's shoulder, and her eyes drifted shut.

"Hayden won," she whispered into the gathering dark. "Preston Davies came to me hoping I could stop whatever was happening, but she still won."

Jared stroked the silken mass of hair that had come undone. "Bullshit."

Her head popped up. "Excuse me?"

"I said that's bullshit, and you know it." He shifted to catch her chin in his hand, drawing her eyes to his. "A notorious assassin has been apprehended. This country still has electricity, and Hayden Burgess has been exposed as a terrorist. If you're keeping score, you won."

She retorted stubbornly, "She stole four billion dollars. Her best friends escaped from inescapable military prisons, possibly with stealth technology. Judges, clerks, FBI agents, and others are *dead* because of her. That isn't justice."

"And you're not Maat, Avery—regardless of what my father or Preston Davies or even Agent Lee thinks. You were not sent here as a goddess of justice. You're simply one of us mere mortals."

A quick rap on the car window warned of Agent Lee's return. "I'm sorry," he began. "I can't leave the scene or spare a vehicle to take you home. We've set up a perimeter, so no one can get in either." He gestured helplessly at the house. "It's bad."

"We understand," Avery assured him. "Take your time."

"Okay. Good." He returned to a knot of agents and barked out new instructions.

Jared leaned forward to softly kiss her forehead and lingered. "I worry that you're getting lost in this, Avery."

Though she could have pretended not to understand, she knew

exactly what he meant. In the past ninety-six hours, she'd solved an international mystery and nearly died in the process. Again. All the years of law school and clerkships had been to help her escape uncertainty. To plot a way to a nice, normal, steady, boring, predictable life. Enough money to take care of Rita and enough distance to not have to worry about her.

Her life plan had included August in Martha's Vineyard with other bougie girls from Spelman and Yale who'd made good or had never had to look for their path to success. They'd been born privileged. She'd envisioned a gorgeous husband with an impressive résumé, and not a boyfriend with a comatose father who could topple the judiciary.

The Avery she imagined should have read about Hayden Burgess in a news feed on her phone or a thought-provoking article on military rape culture in *The Atlantic*.

Avery closed her eyes again and tucked her head beneath Jared's chin.

She had no idea where that Avery had gone. Or if she really, truly wanted to find her.

FORTY

F reedom!" Former crewman Tyler Boozer leaped down the stairs of the plane. Years in prison had hardened him even more than basic training. Once he descended, he spun around to help Carolyn Hugley to the tarmac.

In their time together aboard the submarine, Hayden had never condescended to Tyler or Carolyn. She'd seen them as comrades and colleagues, and she'd always treated them with respect. When they witnessed what Captain Casey had done to her, they helped her because it was the right thing to do. And she had done right by them.

Carolyn lowered her oversize sunglasses to search the Seychelles airstrip with a tight throat and painfully dry eyes. "Where are they?"

It had been months since she'd kissed her husband. Hugged her baby boy. No longer a baby, though. He'd turned thirteen during her time in prison. Her breath caught on a sob, but she refused it voice. She was free now, and according to the news, the man who'd stolen her time with her child lay near death.

The pilot and crew deplaned and herded them toward a Range Rover. "Your host will greet you at the villa."

A cheery woman of indeterminate age and ethnic origin reached for her bag. Carolyn clutched it tighter, as she had the entire ride. "I'll keep it with me, thank you."

The ride to the compound was brief and smooth. Tyler chattered the entire ride, a low hum of meaningless conversation with the driver that felt achingly familiar. She knew the chatter covered a darkness that had grown with the death of his wife and his parents, leaving his two children alone while he was confined in prison. When the storm broke, the thunder would be epic.

"Follow me, please," said the woman as she alighted from the vehicle. "The others are out by the pool."

Tyler helped Carolyn out of the truck and tried not to run ahead. Terror warred with impending joy and a keening sorrow that threatened to break him. No contact had been allowed since he escaped from Norfolk.

Bright, vivid sunshine, gilded white chairs, and ivory cobblestones. They moved swiftly through the house, scarcely taking in the luxurious setting. The patio stretched on forever, playing host to a full swimming pool and an infinity pool. Giggles and laughter floated from the broader one. Kids playing and splashing around without a care to be found. Tyler stopped in the doorway, one hand lifted to shade his suddenly damp eyes. He marveled at them, his children. They'd learned to swim almost before they could walk. "Naima? Sebastian?"

Like magic, they turned toward him, and the twin expressions of joy broke his heart. He knelt on the ground and motioned them forward. Sebastian lifted his sister out of the water and hoisted himself out with arms already beginning to muscle. "Daddy?" They raced to him.

Carolyn heard the greetings vaguely as she made her way forward. Her husband enveloped her in a hard, forever hug, carrying her to the poolside. Ali, her little fish, came onto the land—eyes wide with astonishment. "Momma?"

"I'm home, baby."

From the shadows of the portico, Hayden watched the reunions unfold. Only Nyx had been left behind, caught by the machinations of Agent Robert Lee and Avery Keene. She would find a way to free herself, and she'd let Hayden know how best to help. As her final act of loyalty, she'd secured Casey's pitiful statement. Over and over again, she'd replayed his confession, but it was incomplete. Nyx had done her best, but until every part of her story had been told, the wrongdoers would feel safe. Comfortable. At least one more would be brought low by his words, and she would revel in his fall.

Displeasure and impetuosity urged her to strike out again now at all of them, while her foes were vulnerable. Though she'd had to scrap her Myrina system, the data it had collected would feed her clients for years. Surveillance, business records, falsified documents, labyrinthine financial mechanisms, and energy infrastructure, all at her fingertips. Agent Sarah Beth Gehl, like her counterpart, Agent Lee, had proven more formidable than she expected. As had Avery Keene. But their zeal to catch her had exposed the depth of the National Cyber Investigative Joint Task Force, and for that, she was grateful. Knowing her enemies kept her ahead of their wrath.

Hayden shed the swim robe that revealed a sleek bikini. The juvenile trills of laughter floated in the air, and she rubbed absently at her taut belly, the scars easily seen. Beyond the villa, the ocean waves lapped at white sand. Mamiwata had relocated to a nonextradition island that it wholly owned and controlled.

Her mother had laughed at the name she'd chosen for her company, though she'd been critical of Hayden's actions. Mami Wata, a water spirit of African myth, exhorted her followers to manifest their own realities by imagining themselves as inhabitants of Mami Wata's worlds. To create their wealth and power as proof of devotion. As she had.

As she would.

Wednesday, October 23

The Senate majority leader organized himself in his office, preparing for the momentous day ahead. He had delayed the impeachment trial by a day due to the attack on the power grid. Though instinct told his side to leak the information, a rush to blame Stokes could have backfired and turned into a pox on all their houses. Led by surprisingly competent impeachment managers from the House, the case against President Stokes had been made to the satisfaction of all Democrats and a number of Republicans who would staunchly refuse to admit it. And he knew they would lose.

No president had ever actually been convicted by impeachment due to the high bar set by the constitution: two-thirds agreement by the U.S. Senate. He couldn't fathom how anyone got sixty-seven of the tightest asses he'd ever met to agree to anything so important or consequential. Today's closing arguments had a very different audience. The Senate jury had already rendered its verdict, but the public would be issuing its ruling in a matter of weeks on Election Day.

Leader Neighbors gathered his materials for the day, which his chief of staff had carefully prepared according to his preference. On top of the stack was a manila envelope. Assuming it was also from his chief, he tipped over the envelope to retrieve its contents. A black thumb drive clattered to the desk. With a shrug, he pushed it into his USB port.

The autoplay feature opened a window on his laptop, and sound poured out. After his third or fourth viewing, he dialed up the Speaker and urged him to come over posthaste. An hour later, the impeachment hearing proceeded on Capitol Hill while a phalanx of attorneys and techs validated the contents. Though cutting it close, Fate had indeed delivered an October surprise.

. . .

Avery and Jared took one end of the sofa. Noah and Ling took the pair of chairs. Like most of America, they'd been summoned to a special evening edition of Scott Curlee's new show, *Prime Politics.* Avery's invitation had come directly from the Speaker's office, and she was eager to comply. In a matter of hours, her role in the fall of the House of Stokes would be behind her—one way or another.

"Welcome to tonight's edition of *Prime Politics.* As the president of the United States fights to stave off impeachment, another storm is barreling toward him before Election Day. I have exclusive information that threatens to upend next month's elections. Stay with me for this shocking revelation."

Before the doorbell rang, Jared gently disentangled from Avery and moved to the front door. The extra surveillance he'd added showed Agent Lee and Agent Gehl approaching. He pulled open the door and waved them inside.

"I didn't expect y'all for dinner," he chided.

Agent Gehl smiled in greeting, but Agent Lee was completely serious. "I take it you're watching Scott Curlee's show."

"The Speaker of the House commanded it thusly," Avery intoned. "Why?"

"Because Agent Gehl and I have had a chance to review the information in question, and we thought it fitting that we join you. If you don't mind?"

"The more, the merrier," Jared offered graciously. "Seriously, we've got plenty of food in the dining room. Help yourself. He's on a commercial break."

The agents took seats as the show came back on the air. After quick introductions by Curlee of his evening's guests, he built up his great reveal.

"Mr. Leader, I understand that both you and the Speaker of the House received a copy of a video this morning?"

"That is correct."

"I also understand that you have asked independent sources to verify its authenticity."

"Indeed we have. Two outside labs have both authenticated the material." The leader gave a grave look to the camera. "The contents are deeply concerning to all, and neither the Speaker nor I felt we could keep this to ourselves given all that's at stake."

Curlee stared directly into a single camera shot and frowned meaningfully. "I will warn our viewers that we did seek comment from the White House about what you are going to see. There was no official response, other than a suggestion that the video is some type of deepfake, but no independent source has been able to confirm this allegation. According to our sources, experts tell us that the angle suggests that this recording was made from a device on the president's desk in the Oval Office. A suggestion that will no doubt lead to more questions. It is unknown at this time if the participants were aware."

The screen then shifted to a surprisingly sharp image of the Oval Office, courtesy of the type of camera clarity now standard in smartphones. Only the president could be seen at first, in front of the familiar bank of windows. Then a man stepped into view, one Avery easily recognized as Admiral Casey. She'd been in the room with them at some point that day. She recognized the suit. The blood-red tie.

And the upright Casey had to have been recorded before the attack by Nyx that would keep him bedridden and impotent for the rest of his life.

"What the hell are you going to do about this? I've been accused of attacking that skank on the sub. I will not have my reputation damaged again."

"Cut the shit, Donnie. You raped that sailor because you couldn't keep it in your pants for a few weeks at sea. Lucky for you, no one believed her."

"I was secretary of the Navy, Brandon—"

"Yes, for less than a year. I called in favors on Capitol Hill to put you there and had to remove you before another accusation surfaced. And now I'm cleaning up your shit again. I could get royally screwed on this power grid debacle, and the entire cabinet knows it. We are hours away from having the whole damn shooting match collapse. The NSA thinks she might have done more than infiltrate FISA. And none of these goddamned agencies are listening to me because Slosberg tried to neuter me in front of America."

"That bitch is clearly insane. It strikes me that she might be in collusion with Avery Keene, who has already been a toxic boil on your ass. Can't your lapdog Boylen use his Verity site to discredit her?"

Stokes grimaced. *"We've already tried that. Didn't work. I never should have listened to the party about needing a woman to balance the ticket."*

"Imagine what we could have done together." Casey sounded wistful. *"We have to stop that Keene woman from spreading her theory. I'm not responsible."*

The recording shifted abruptly. The angle had changed, and President Stokes sat behind his desk, his eyes sunken and dark. Luke Boylen stood at his elbow.

"How the hell did two convicts escape different military prisons? Not to mention an assassin taking out federal agents and a former cabinet secretary. I want this entire episode classified."

"It's too late, sir." The brash chief of staff looked uncharacteristically timid.

"It just happened. Tell Alford and the AG that I don't want a word of the attack to leak. Classify it as foreign counterintelligence, but keep it quiet."

"It's already on the news, sir. No one has the body count, but a neighbor's drone filmed the ambulances and the law enforcement swarm. Cable and Twitter have the paramedics removing Casey on the stretcher running on a loop. The bloodstains are very telling."

"Can't we confiscate the footage?"

"From the internet?" Boylen asked incredulously. *"The best we can do is try to spin this as the fault of Admiral Casey. Without a full grid collapse, most Americans will assume this was just an act of revenge. We can keep the names of the dead agents out of the public domain."*

"Do it. And make sure the Joint Chiefs are in my office in an hour. We have to put a lid on this Burgess debacle. Otherwise, the world will learn that the Navy allowed classified military technology to fall into the wrong hands. And I'll be crucified for letting it happen on my watch."

"Keene said Burgess wasn't through. How did she know?"

"Who cares? I hate that woman. Goddamn it. We've got to get through the election, and I'll clean house. Starting with finding out how they managed to—"

Scott Curlee once again filled the screen. "On the advice of legal counsel, we have decided to not play the remainder of the recording in the interest of national security. But the video raises serious questions about what has happened in the past few days in our nation and under the watch of President Brandon Stokes."

"Holy shit." Noah spoke first and scanned the room.

Ling pressed pause on the remote. "You okay?"

Avery couldn't look away from the frozen screen. All this had started with a doctored video and a threat to a district court judge in Idaho. By morning, Washington, D.C., would be in the throes of a presidential spin cycle, and voters already casting ballots would start to regret or rejoice in their choices.

"Avery?" Jared lightly clasped her hand where it lay on her lap. "You called it."

"Can they impeach him again?" Ling asked. "Seems like they should."

Agent Lee kept his gaze locked on Avery. "Ms. Keene? You're being awfully quiet."

"It's like watching a car wreck," she said slowly. "I can't celebrate what happened, but I'm so glad the world has seen it with their own eyes. Even now, he keeps lying."

"Apparently, Hayden Burgess agrees. Our techs assume that she hijacked his phone or one of the devices in the Oval," Agent Gehl offered. "They are exploring how to air gap the White House without crippling communications."

Jared shook his head. "With what Hugley and Boozer stole, that's not nearly enough."

A sharp look from Gehl lapsed him into silence, but he shared a glance with Avery, confirming her fears. "Boylen was right. It's still not over. She's not done."

"No, she's not," Agent Lee agreed. "But you've done all you can. However, we have another development to share with you. It can go no farther than this room." He extended a single sheet of paper to Avery.

She skimmed it and her eyes widened. "For real?"

"Yes. And despite the Treasury Department's concerns, we have no legal recourse or reason to reverse the transactions."

Avery felt her eyes go a bit glassy, and she blinked several times.

"What is it?" Ling demanded. "Share with the class."

Avery skimmed the page again and composed herself. "Nearly a hundred organizations received simultaneous wire transfers early this morning. The average transfer was ten million dollars. Rape crisis centers. Domestic abuse shelters. Homeless shelters. Legal aid funds. Military sexual assault trauma centers and advocacy organizations. Just over a billion dollars in total."

Noah exhaled. Jared whistled in amazement.

"Extraordinary," Ling said, sitting next to Avery and peering over her shoulder. "But why are you smiling like you personally won the lottery? Did you personally win the lottery?"

"Not quite. Haven Recovery and Restoration Center in Laurel, Maryland, is on this list . . . and they received *seventy-five million dollars* for rehab and indigent treatment."

The room fell silent.

"Hayden did this for your mom?" Noah asked, puzzled. "I thought she wanted to kill you."

"Stokes has first dibs," Ling corrected. "Hayden might have decided Avery is no longer a threat."

Jared rolled his eyes at the wishful thinking. "Just give it a few days."

Avery shrugged impassively. "She'll have to get in line."

ACKNOWLEDGMENTS

Avery Keene is back. This time, she has to navigate political land mines, national crises, and a cunning nemesis. This time, recounting her derring-do required that I dive into energy policy, cybersecurity, federal law, and military protocol. I am grateful to my siblings Andrea, Leslie, Richard, Walter, and Jeanine—especially Leslie, Richard, and Jeanine—for their eyes, expertise, ideas, and third-act advice. Gratitude also goes to my parents, Carolyn and Robert, for listening to my worries, and to my niece Faith for supplying me with Skittles and support. I am indebted to Dara Lindenbaum for her careful reading, Mandis Supris for her precise note-taking, Lauren Groh-Wargo and Carmen Mohan for their encouragement, and the incomparable Samantha Slosberg for charting a path to make this book happen in the midst of another major endeavor.

Rogue Justice leaped from random thought to hundreds of pages with the aid of an exceptional duo. First, my agent and friend, Linda Loewenthal, who continues to see around corners to opportunities and possibilities. And most particularly, Jason Kaufman of Doubleday, who possesses the patience of Job—trusting that, despite delays, the words would come. I thank him for his care in reading, editing, and cheerleading as Avery Keene adds layers and dimensions to her story.

My appreciation to the backbone of binding these pages into a novel: the careful copyeditors, inventive graphic designers, creative art editors, indefatigable marketing team, and all others who help shape this process, including Michael Goldsmith, Lily Dondoshansky, and Nora Reichard.

Gratitude too to all the readers who ask where Avery has been and what she'll be up to next. Onward!

ABOUT THE AUTHOR

Stacey Abrams is a *New York Times* bestselling author, entrepreneur, and political leader. She served as minority leader in the Georgia House of Representatives, and she was the first Black woman in U.S. history to become the gubernatorial nominee for a major party. Abrams has launched multiple nonprofit organizations devoted to democracy protection, voting rights, and effective public policy. She has also co-founded several successful companies, including a financial services firm, an energy and infrastructure consulting firm, and the media company Sage Works Productions, Inc.